THE
CHANGELING
MURDERS

C.S. QUINN

THE
CHANGELING
MURDERS

 THOMAS & MERCER

Published by Thomas & Mercer, Seattle

www.apub.com

Amazon, the Amazon logo, and Thomas & Mercer are trademarks of Amazon.com, Inc., or its affiliates.

ISBN-13: 9781477805114
ISBN-10: 1477805117

Cover design by Lisa Horton

Printed in the United States of America

THE
CHANGELING
MURDERS

Prologue

It was an inauspicious day for a wedding. Dark clouds had gathered as Maria tightened the ribbons on her blue dress. She'd begged and borrowed pieces of lace and silk, tucked flowers into her long blonde hair and curled the front into fashionable ringlets. But she still didn't feel ready.

Maria could hear the church bells ringing the hour across London. She was late for her own wedding, she realised with a sliding sense of panic. She couldn't remember the last time she'd been late for anything.

Be honest, whispered a snake voice in her head. *Your heart is still with Charlie Tuesday.*

A hackney carriage drew up outside, large metal wheels striking loudly on the cobbles. Maria watched from the window of her rented room. She frowned in confusion as the driver emerged and knocked on her door.

The man was dressed strangely. Courtly clothes, old-fashioned and moth-eaten. Unease swirled in Maria's stomach. 'I didn't send for a carriage,' she said as she opened the door.

'It looks to rain,' he said in a clipped voice. 'Your betrothed thought it best you were driven to church.'

Maria eyed the carriage behind him. It was small, black and slightly scruffy. The kind of modest vehicle that ferried middling sorts about the city. It had large wheels, one horse and space for two people. A considerate yet frugal expense from a lawyer to his wife-to-be on her wedding morning. Exactly like Percy. So why did she feel so apprehensive?

The driver smiled in a way that didn't reach his unusual blue-green eyes. 'I have no other passengers inside,' he said. 'You have it to yourself.'

For some reason, this filled Maria with fear. She swallowed, trying to pull herself together. *Every bride feels anxious on her wedding day*, she told herself.

She glanced up at the sky. She'd been looking forward to the walk, to collect her thoughts in the green of Lincoln's Inn Fields on the way to St Dunstan's Church. But she couldn't very well refuse the gesture. It was so thoughtful of Percy.

Maria stepped towards the carriage, ignoring the sense that something wasn't right. The driver opened the small door to the black space beyond. *You mustn't keep Percy waiting*, Maria thought.

She ducked through the opening. The dark interior smelled of damp wood and horses. Maria settled herself on the padded leather seat, arranging her skirts as the driver shut the door.

The windows were covered with thick canvas curtains. When she moved to push them aside she found they'd been nailed down on all sides. A spurt of alarm jolted through her. *It's a London cab*, she reminded herself. *They seal the windows to keep out bad air*. But it had been over three years since the plague that had claimed Maria's family. A long time not to open the curtains again.

There was a narrow opening at the back, just wide enough to pass coins for the fare, and through it she saw the driver sit on the narrow plank seat. He flicked his long whip and the horse jolted forward.

As the large wheels were set in motion, Maria forced her anxiety to subside. Percy must have been listening after all when she'd told him how hard she'd worked on her dress, that rainfall would ruin the watered-silk panels. Such thoughtfulness boded well.

The carriage rolled through Fetter Lane, loud with tin kettles and pans being beaten into shape. The smell of frying pancakes and fritters drifted from a huddle of food stalls; hot butter and woodsmoke.

Maria leaned back, closed her eyes and tried not to let the nerves overwhelm her. She regretted deciding to travel to the church alone. But she had no one to give her away, and she hadn't wanted her friends to witness her uncertainty.

Maria could hear the colourful sleaze of Covent Garden now and guessed they'd passed the huge maypole marking the beginning of the party district. She imagined the bright dandies and beautiful hopefuls weaving drunkenly along the dirt streets and past the brothels. Tallow candles would be burning in every rickety wooden window, despite the spring sunshine.

Then she felt the carriage wheels strike spongy ash, the sodden beginning of the Great Fire's devastation. The vast black desert of blackened nubs of burned buildings.

Maria sat up. 'Why do we come this way?' she demanded. 'It's dangerous in the ruins.'

The carriage shuddered to a halt. Maria glanced through the narrow opening at the back. She could see the driver's knees and a glimpse of a sooty backstreet amongst a jumble of charred walls. She could hear a chicken clucking and scratching around in the dirt.

'Why do you stop?' she asked, her nerves making her speak more sharply than she'd intended.

'Someone wants to see you,' said the driver's disembodied voice. 'Before you are wed.'

Maria digested this. Something in her heart fluttered. 'Who?' she demanded.

'Charlie Tuesday. The Thief Taker.'

A bubble of joy rose up. *He wants to see you. Beg you not to marry.*

Of course, she would never betray Percy, who was likely already waiting at the aisle. Honest, sensible Percy, whose courtship had been faultlessly mannered, who had offered her the life she'd always wanted – before Charlie came along. A comfortable wife in a comfortable home.

Maria opened her mouth to say 'drive on'. But temptation pricked at her. Surely there was no harm in talking to Charlie one last time? Afterwards she would be married and never see him more.

'Take me to him,' she said, attempting to sound indifferent.

The carriage lurched down one narrow street and along another. Maria found herself trying not to smile at the thought of seeing Charlie. It wouldn't do to give him hope. She would be measured, sorry and sympathetic.

Maria peered from the window. The streets were getting darker, the buildings closer.

A deep unease prickled back through her. She'd heard of girls being driven out of London and robbed in the hackney carriages. *The driver knew you were to be married*, she reminded herself. *He knew Charlie's name and his thief taker work, chasing down criminals.*

'Wait,' she said. 'I've changed my mind. We'll to the church straight.'

But the carriage kept moving.

Maria knocked on the roof. 'If you please,' she said loudly, 'I want to go to the church.'

The driver was silent. Trepidation took hold. Maria put out a hand and tried the door handle. It turned, but something was preventing it from opening.

A feeling of panic rose up, tightening her throat. She pushed at the tightly nailed canvas window covering. It didn't move. She turned to look out of the back. The alley they were travelling along was completely deserted. Not a soul in sight.

Maria took a full few seconds to think about what this might mean. No innocent explanation was forthcoming.

'Let me out!' she demanded in a louder voice. 'Now!'

The driver's knees bent. He lowered his head level with hers.

Maria's blue eyes silently took in the mad smile playing on his face, the twitching fingers. She was absorbing everything about him now. His hair was jet black and his skin was clean-shaven and youthful. But the eyes were old, and he was deathly pale.

'Who are you?' she whispered.

'You know me very well,' he said. 'You have always known me. I am Jack in the Green. I am Robin Goodfellow. I am all the dark things that stalk the night.'

She suddenly realised what was wrong with his clothes. They were inside out. A charm to deter fairies.

'What do you want?' she said, forcing herself to speak calmly.

'You know very well what I want,' he said. 'The Lord and Lady.'

Maria's stomach turned to ice. He somehow knew of the mystery she'd stumbled across whilst transcribing Percy's legal documents. She'd been so careful to conceal her findings. Maria closed her eyes as the magnitude of her situation drew in. The Lord and Lady, vanished from the Tower of London during Cromwell's reign.

'You won't find the Lord and Lady,' she said. 'There's only one man who can. And he'll never help you.'

'Charlie Tuesday?' The man smiled. 'The man you jilted?'

'He isn't . . .' Maria stopped herself.

How could he know that?

It didn't matter. Not now.

'You think Charlie Tuesday worth dying for?' he asked.

'No,' she said quietly, 'I wouldn't die for Charlie Tuesday. But I'd die to protect the Lord and Lady.'

A sudden rush of calm filled her. He would kill her, Maria knew. Nothing she could do about that. But she could choose how she died.

'I won't help you,' she said steadily. It felt unreal, as though she were reading lines in a play.

'You will,' he said, straightening out of view. She heard the whip crack and felt the horse pick up speed.

Maria began kicking at the door with all her strength. It held firm. She threw herself against the window. 'Help!' Maria shouted, pressing her mouth to the curtains. 'Help me, please!'

'No one can hear you,' came the driver's voice as the carriage raced on. 'Didn't your mother warn you about fairies? We make people disappear.'

Chapter 1

Charlie Tuesday was running. He'd easily kept pace with the carriage as it left Temple Bar and moved along the half-burned remains of Fleet Street. But as it passed Lud Gate into the sooty devastation of Paternoster Row the vehicle gathered speed.

Charlie sprinted past the scorched stationers' shops, his bare feet stirring up a pale-grey confetti of burned books. Street children were playing on the road ahead. Charlie shouted a warning and they scattered as the carriage barrelled towards them and out of sight.

He made a quick calculation. Only busy Cheapside was broad enough for horse-drawn traffic. This hackney carriage would be lost amongst the multitude of identical vehicles.

Charlie swung right, cutting across the great black void where St Paul's Cathedral had once stood. Ash-streaked labourers were erecting the beginnings of a mighty scaffold and filling sacks of dark rubble.

Charlie's gaze landed on a parked stonemason's wagon, wheels thickly grimed with red clay from Brick Lane. He raced towards it, freed a handful of rosy earth from the wheel-spokes and bolted for the scaffold. A few men shouted a protest as Charlie climbed the timber frame with a speed born of his street-urchin childhood. He made the top and ran easily along the narrow beam of a large crane, eyes scouring the black streets below. The scaffold beneath his feet shook and he glanced down to see a stonemason's apprentice moving determinedly towards him brandishing a hammer.

Charlie looked north. The wake of the recent Great Fire spread out before him, like a monstrous black bite out of the chaotic city streets. Then he spotted the carriage, cornering at speed towards Cheapside. Behind him, the apprentice was closing in.

Keeping the carriage in his sights, Charlie jumped onto the arm of another large wooden crane, this one stretching high over the building works. Taking aim, he threw the clod of red earth. It arced towards the departing carriage, then burst in a bright scatter on the hackney's dark wood roof.

He heard a creaking beneath him. The hammer-wielding apprentice had made it onto the highest part of the scaffold.

Charlie held his hands up. 'Easy, friend,' he said, keeping his bare feet balanced on the crane. 'I'm a thief taker. Following that carriage.' He inclined his head to the red-spattered coach now easing into the Cheapside traffic.

The apprentice lowered his hammer slightly. 'Thieves don't ride in carriages,' he said.

'True,' agreed Charlie. 'But lawyers do. And I need to see where that man goes.'

Charlie was keeping half an eye on the carriage. Yesterday, he'd received an anonymous request from an address in the legal district, to meet in a backstreet theatre. Charlie wasn't naïve enough to trust mysterious invitations. So tailing the carriage of the suspected author prior to their meeting seemed a sensible precaution.

Charlie assessed his aggressor. 'You're an apprentice?' he said. 'It's Lent. Why don't you go pull down brothels with your fellows?'

The boy narrowed his eyes. 'How did you know I'm a 'prentice?'

'Young men not permitted wives have a certain look about them.'

'Who do you think you are?' challenged the apprentice.

'I'm Charlie Tuesday.'

The apprentice laughed contemptuously. 'Charlie Tuesday is tall as King Charles and broad as an ox.'

Charlie smiled. 'Quick thinking and middling height serve me well enough.'

'If you're so clever,' said the apprentice, 'you would never have let yourself be cornered.' He hefted his hammer. 'Up here there's no way out.'

'Only if you lack a certain perspective for distances,' said Charlie. He stooped and cut the rope at his feet. The crane went swinging wide, the beam on which Charlie stood heading fast towards Paternoster Row. He spread his bare toes, then braced as the beam jolted to a halt and leapt towards the blackened roof timbers of a burned-out shop.

Charlie landed on a charred rafter, then ran across the rooftops. As he took in Cheapside below he saw the carriage, now clearly distinguished by its red dusting.

He watched as it headed towards Covent Garden.

'Just as I thought,' muttered Charlie under his breath as he slipped down to the spongy burned earth of Newgate Street. 'Headed to the theatre.'

Now he knew for certain the identity of the man inside the carriage. But Charlie could think of no good reason why this individual would want to meet.

Chapter 2

Charlie slipped into the theatre and was greeted by the familiar smell of spilled beer and trodden orange peels. The benches in the pit were dotted with ragged boys holding seats for wealthier folk. At the edges, women were laying out baskets of stewed apples and greasy pig knuckles.

The Birdcage was London's most dangerous illegal theatre. It attracted an explosive mix of drunks, prostitutes, prize fighters and the odd pack of thrill-seeking aristocrats.

Charlie stepped down behind the stage, where a bulky man with a bad skin condition lounged on a wooden stool. A well-worn truncheon rested near his feet.

'It's a penny to watch the actresses dress,' said the man, scratching a patch of flaking scalp and examining his fingernails.

'Not if you've a friend inside,' said Charlie. 'Is that infectious?' he added.

The man gave him a hard stare. 'The only friends our girls have are noble,' he said, nodding pointedly to Charlie's bare feet and patched breeches. 'That coat of yours might once have belonged to a rich sea captain, but you've given it a Cheapside polish.'

Charlie fingered the empty threads in the row of tiny buttons along his brown leather coat. 'This coat is a favourite of mine,' he said. 'As was your best actress before she dropped me for someone richer.'

The man rubbed at a scaly elbow, causing more skin to fall. 'You're Lynette's old husband?' he said in obvious disbelief. 'Charlie Tuesday? I thought you'd be taller.' He peered closer. ''S dangerous work, is it? Chasin' down thieves and villains? Or do you find lost people and property?'

'A little of both,' said Charlie.

There was a rustle of skirts and a flame-haired woman with shockingly rouged cheeks appeared at the door, fanning herself mercilessly.

'God's fish it's hot!' she began. 'Can we get some fan-beaters inside . . .' She hesitated, then beamed in greeting. 'Charlie! What are you doing here?'

She threw her arms around him and Charlie found himself enveloped in the familiar smell of his one-time wife. Orange-blossom water, cheap hair pomade and marzipan. Lynette wore the bouncingly short dress of a stage actress, ending at mid-calf, and her red hair had been elaborately coiffed with plaits, curls and flowers.

Charlie smiled back. 'Come to watch you perform, of course.' He nodded to backstage where skirts and petticoats were flying.

Lynette batted him with her dog-eared fan. 'You never! You seen it all before anyways.' She clasped both his hands. 'You alright?' she said. 'I heard your brother died.'

Charlie swallowed. The unexpected sympathy took him by surprise.

'You're not alright,' said Lynette, nodding, ''course you're not. Fool question. Rowan was your only family.' She leaned forward, gripping his hands tight. 'You can't protect everyone, Charlie, remember it, wontcha? Don't let this drag you down.'

She was staring into his eyes. He nodded automatically, and Lynette released his hands.

'You wanna come in?' She inclined her decorated hair towards the actresses beyond.

He shook his head with a wistful glance at the scantily clad women. 'I've not time. I'm looking for a man whose carriage arrived recently. We're due to meet, but I want to take the measure of him first.'

'Charlie Tuesday,' she said, shaking her head, 'always working.' She nodded to the missing buttons on his coat. 'Isn't it time you got yourself a wife?'

'I had one, remember?' replied Charlie. 'She left me for richer pickings.'

'Oh, Charlie, that was a long time ago. You weren't never there. Always out rescuing some poor soul or other. I had to take care of business, din' I? Like me mother always said, love don't—'

'Love don't pay the bills,' said Charlie. 'I remember. And I did pay them. I just didn't realise the kind of bills you had in mind.'

'I heard you got yourself a very proper sort of girl after me,' said Lynette, toying with a lace cuff. 'Maria, was it? You played a little house. But things didn't last. Shall I guess it? Were you away too much? Solving mysteries for those who couldn't pay?'

'When I wasn't drinking,' admitted Charlie. 'That was our downfall, wasn't it? Too much wine.'

'P'rhaps.' Lynette reached out her pale fingers and lightly touched the key hung around his neck. 'The orphan boy with his murdered mama's mysterious legacy. Did you solve your own past yet? Discover what this key opens?'

Charlie didn't reply. Lynette glanced at the doorman, who was watching them both with interest, scratching determinedly at his groin.

'You're happy here?' Charlie asked. 'No ambitions to the Duke's or the King's Theatre on Drury Lane?'

'Nah. Smell that?' Lynette's eyes glittered. 'That's a true theatre smell. Sweat, spilled beer and trodden oranges.'

'To me it smells of broken promises.'

'Don't be bitter, Charlie.' She smiled disarmingly. 'I've changed since then. Older. Wiser. Don't drink like I did. I moved on to bigger and better things than being a thief taker's forgotten wife, is all.'

Charlie raised his eyebrows. 'Bigger?'

She laughed. 'Better then. Although you've heard the rumours about King Charles and his sceptre,' she added with a conspirator's wink.

'You've caught the eye of the King?' asked Charlie, torn between disbelief and admiration.

'Hadn't you heard?' Lynette raised the fan coyly. 'I've even been inside the palace, Charlie. You should see it,' she whispered, eyes flashing with childlike glee. 'Rugs as thick as your arm, and wine served in gold cups.'

Charlie smiled.

'The King loves the theatre,' continued Lynette. 'And actresses. But the others are terrified of the mistress. Lady Castlemaine. Her Ladyship doesn't scare me.'

She set her jaw and Charlie had a glimpse of the girl he remembered from Coal Yard Alley. Tough, clever and funny. Lynette had honed her acting skills by begging to support her drunk mother and fighting anyone who got in her way.

A horn blast sounded and Lynette glanced backstage. 'Almost time for curtain up,' she said, rearranging her skirts. 'How can I help you?'

'I had a request to meet here,' said Charlie. 'In the theatre. I don't trust it.'

'So . . . ?'

'I want to be sure of who I'm meeting. See if he's armed. I don't need much' – he nodded to her fan – 'just a plan of who's sitting where.'

It took her a moment to understand and then she unfurled her fan, revealing an entire seat plan of the theatre drawn carefully on the back.

'Be careful,' she said as he took it from her, 'that's my whole business on there.'

Charlie nodded, examining the various symbols. Lynette couldn't read and learned scripts by dogged repetition. The seat plan of the theatre was annotated with crests, sketches and a scattering of little hearts indicating potential suitors.

'Lawyers always sit here?' he confirmed, tapping an outline of a judicial wig.

She nodded contemptuously. 'Lawyers and legal men. They don't often visit and aren't free with their coins when they do.'

He folded the fan and passed it back. 'Thank you.'

'You'll come watch the play?' asked Lynette.

He looked at the stage. 'I don't know if I can stay to see it. I . . .'

'I know,' she interrupted with a slight smile. 'You've a mystery to solve. It could be our last till the end of Lent. The apprentices are already out in force. You know how they hate us actresses.'

He touched her arm. 'You should be careful. Lady Castlemaine is a dangerous enemy. I've heard rumours she's had actresses imprisoned and worse.'

'That's in the licensed theatres,' scoffed Lynette. 'The Duke's and The King's. She can't do nothing to us illegals. We're too slippery.'

She grinned, and Charlie had a sudden fond memory of life in the illegal theatre, the tricks they played to stay one step ahead of the authorities.

Lynette took his arm and steered him past the half-dressed women. 'What would you wish for me, Charlie? To grow old and steal leftovers at parties like the other ageing whores? There are two ways out of the theatre, and I've no relatives to bury me in linen.'

'Have a care is all I ask,' pressed Charlie.

Lynette rolled her eyes. 'Oh, Charlie,' she said, 'I don't flatter myself I would ever be in enough danger to warrant your help.'

Chapter 3

In the manicured grounds of Whitehall Palace, the Ice House loomed large.

Lady Castlemaine was walking as quickly as her little-heeled shoes and heavy silk dress would allow. At her side, the Duke of Amesbury kept an easy pace, with the long marching strides of a man who'd spent his life in combat.

'It's hot,' muttered Lady Castlemaine, wiping her face with a lace handkerchief. 'Why is it so hot in spring?'

She'd not lost all the pregnancy weight from her fifth child, Amesbury noted, and her beautiful face was finally beginning to show a few faint lines of age. Her shining auburn hair was limp in the heat.

They'd reached the Ice House door.

'You're sure you want to interrupt His Majesty?' said Amesbury.

Lady Castlemaine laughed unconvincingly. 'Nothing he does could shock me now.' Though she hesitated. 'Let's just get out of the sun,' she muttered, flicking her lovely eyes up to the blue sky.

A blast of blissfully cold air enveloped them as they stepped inside the Ice House. The shaded interior was walled with vast blocks of ice and divided by snow-filled pits. A few hanging tapers decorated the domed roof, giving the appearance of a starry night.

For a moment, Lady Castlemaine's shining face relaxed in relief. Then her large violet eyes took in the scene and hardened in fury.

A bevy of naked actresses ran in front of her screaming with delight, hurling snowballs. The King and the Duke of York were shovelling snow and heaving ice bricks to make forts and ramparts.

The King made a snowball and let fly. 'Look out, James!' he roared. 'This next one's for you!'

The Duke of York sprinted across the slippery floor of the Ice House and dived behind a defensive wall of ice bricks. The snowball smashed at his escaping feet, splattering a nearby actress. She gave a wild, play-acted shriek.

'I'm hit!' she shouted, affecting a deep voice. 'Help me!'

The King caught sight of Lady Castlemaine and paused in the act of rolling a second snowball. His face broke into an easy smile. 'Lady Castlemaine.' He bounded towards her and summoned someone to serve her wine.

'Why do you send money to protect brothels?' demanded Lady Castlemaine, her hand closing around the chalice from a proffered tray. 'Apprentices pull down whorehouses every Lent. It's nothing. Part of London life.'

Charles's smile faltered. 'This is politics. It doesn't concern you.'

Her face darkened. The servant moved forward to pour wine, thought better of it and retreated.

'You told me your allowance from Parliament was spent,' accused Lady Castlemaine.

The King turned helplessly to Amesbury.

Lady Castlemaine directed the full force of her rage towards the old general. 'Forgive me,' she said tightly, a brittle smile on her face. 'His Majesty and I were in France for many years. Before you Republicans' – she glared at Amesbury – 'realised England needed a king.'

Amesbury nodded patiently.

'My understanding,' she continued, 'was that the apprentices start up every Lent. They attack brothels, burn a few dresses, smash some windows. A necessary bloodletting,' she concluded. 'Allowed, overlooked, even condoned.'

Amesbury nodded.

'You've already given money to build the new theatre on Drury Lane,' said Lady Castlemaine, addressing the King bitterly.

'The people need some joy,' said the King, 'after the plague and fire. They had years of Cromwell; no playhouses, no gaming, no maypoles . . .'

'So why would you send more funds,' hissed Lady Castlemaine, 'to protect whores and *actresses*? They already have their fine playhouse.'

'We have reason to fear the apprentice attacks could escalate this year,' supplied Amesbury. 'A reserve was found.'

The King glared. The old general raised his thick shoulders in a 'can't-help-you' shrug.

Lady Castlemaine's pretty mouth settled into a tight, hard line. 'Your rightful daughter—'

'Don't begin it again,' interrupted Charles angrily. 'There is no possibility—'

'By God you will own her!' shrieked Lady Castlemaine. 'She is yours – just like the others I have borne you, to whom you awarded titles!'

There was a hard glimmer in Charles's eye. 'Even if I believed you, there is nothing left. Parliament delight in keeping me on a small allowance. All my ready funds have gone to pay off your gambling debts.' He took her shoulder and attempted to draw her away. She shook him off crossly.

'Barbara, be reasonable.' Charles had lowered his voice. 'It's hot. You're tired.' He moved closer and slipped an arm around her waist. He let his hand play with the ribbons of her dress. 'Take off some clothes and enjoy the fine new Ice House,' he said. 'Have a drink with me. Cool your brain.'

She smiled, just a little. The servant, feeling braver, moved forward to fill her chalice.

'White,' she added with a frown as a servant poured from a decanter of red. 'I take white wine. Charles,' she demanded, her voice rising dangerously as she took the drink. 'Why is he serving me what *she* drinks?'

There was a dreadful pause. Actresses began surreptitiously slipping on clothing. The Duke of York eyed them sadly and began putting on his stockings.

'Has she been here?' demanded Lady Castlemaine. 'In Whitehall?'

'Barbara . . .' began the King.

Lady Castlemaine erupted, hurling the wine the length of the Ice House. The metal goblet clanged against the brick floor, spraying a bloody spurt of red wine against a snowy battlement.

'IS THIS WHAT LOYALTY MEANS?' screeched Lady Castlemaine, her face black with rage. 'Eight years I've been at your side! Before you were king! Before you were *anyone*.' She pointed a shaking finger at the actresses. 'Whilst these bawdy-baskets were fucking Roundheads!' She took in the actresses again, who were holding their clothes, mute with terror. 'Get out!' she said. 'GET OUT!'

The half-dressed women fled.

'You were *nothing* when I met you,' raged Lady Castlemaine. '*Nobody*.'

'Be a little careful, Barbara,' said the King.

'If you do not own little Betsy for your daughter I shall dash her brains out against the floor!'

Charles's resolve faltered. 'Barbara,' he said, 'please.'

Lady Castlemaine sent out a vicious kick with her fashionably heeled foot, levelling a wall of ice bricks. The Duke of York sighed.

'I gave up everything for you,' said Lady Castlemaine. 'My marriage. *Everything*. You swore you'd love me forever. Remember that when you next go to the theatre.'

She turned and stalked out in a swish of silks.

There was a moment of embarrassed hush. Then there was an unceremonious gurgle as melted water exited the Ice House down the central drain.

The Duke of York was the first to break the silence. 'Charles,' he complained, staring at his devastated ramparts, 'you must manage her better. I spent *all morning* building that wall.'

The King turned to Amesbury. He took a long sip of wine. 'What think you, Amesbury?'

'I think for a man who claims to love the theatre,' said Amesbury, 'you dally with bad actresses.'

Chapter 4

Repent slipped into the locksmith's workshop, his eyes casting about. A sad-looking bundle was on the floor, covered in a threadbare blanket. Repent nudged it with his foot. The bundle moved. Repent ducked low.

'Psst!' he whispered. 'Bolly! Hey, Bolly! Wake up!'

Repent was a gangly man-boy, stranded between puberty and adulthood by too much work and not enough food. He was tall, with round, prominent joints and dark, greasy hair flecked with premature grey.

A face emerged from under the worn-out coverlet, looking confused and sleepy.

'Your blanket stinks,' said Repent.

'Keeps the fleas off,' mumbled Bolly, sitting upright. Repent took in the hard wooden floor, the smouldering little fire.

'This where my father makes you sleep?' he asked Bolly.

'Yeah.' Bolly sat up. 'You never seen your own father's workshop?'

'No,' said Repent. 'He doesn't trust me. Too many pretty servant girls come to buy his famous locks and keys.' Repent was looking about at the metalwork. Half-finished pieces were strewn around.

'Shame not to be apprenticed to your own father,' said Bolly guilelessly. ''Spose your brickmaker's apprenticeship is a good future. Half the city needs rebuilding after the fire.'

'Yeah,' said Repent, unconvincingly. His eyes had lighted on one nearly finished lock. He picked it up and hefted it. 'This yours?' Repent couldn't keep the awe from his voice.

Bolly stood, revealing strong tanned legs. He was an attractive boy with a cherub face, sandy-blond hair and golden skin. Even in the single ragged suit of clothes allowed to apprentices, he looked handsome.

He crossed to where Repent was standing. '"S my masterpiece,' he said. 'If you break it, I'll kill you.'

'It isn't finished yet?' Repent traced the swirling metalwork fronds with his finger. They were mesmerising in their intricacy.

'Your father says a few more days,' said Bolly, removing the lock from Repent's hand. 'Then I'll be an apprentice no more. Master locksmith. Free.' He was looking at the elaborate lock. 'I meant it for her,' he added after a moment. 'She was who I thought of, when I made it.' He sighed. 'Seven years apprenticed was too long to wait.' Bolly slipped the lock into his hanging pocket. 'I never let it out of my sight,' he concluded. 'Imagine if it went missing. I'd be here another five years, listening to your father rant about God.' He laughed.

Repent didn't even smile. Instead, he rubbed his chin, where a beard was conspicuously absent. Childhood smallpox had scarred his lower face, destroying all but a few downy hair follicles. 'We might go find your girl,' said Repent. 'The one you made the lock for. Today's the day, Bolly. Time to riot. Yearly tradition.'

But Bolly only shook his head. 'She's not like the other whores,' he said. 'She didn't go by choice.'

'Don't be soft, Bolly,' said Repent. 'They'd all be whores, the women, if we let 'em. Big black holes that can never be filled, ain't they?'

'Maybe,' said Bolly agreeably.

'Don't forget your apron,' said Repent, nodding to where the blue apprentice uniform hung. '"S your ticket to the best butter-box in the city.' He mimed a circle over his groin.

Bolly shook his head. 'We don't actually get to do the whores. We just tear the brothels up.'

Repent handed Bolly his apron and sniffed. 'Smell that? There's somethin' different in the air. Whores 'ave bin getting above themselves, on account of the King flaunting his mistresses. The boys are all talking about a proper protest. Once we're inside the brothels, who's to say what happened and what didn't?'

'What's your father got to say about it?' Bolly asked, taking in Repent's expression uneasily. 'I thought old Praise-God-locksmith had a mission for us.'

Repent nodded enthusiastically. 'We're to be soldiers,' he said, voice ringing with pride. 'Someone's let something slip, Bolly,' he added conspiratorially. 'There was a document, lost in legal paperwork for all these years. One of the Royalists who smuggled free the Lord and Lady confessed on his way to the noose. Left a clue. There's a dress, left in a brothel, that would summon the Lord and Lady.'

'Which brothel?'

'That's the great joke of it,' said Repent. 'The old Royalist spies would have known which whorehouse.' He paused. 'But those men died. My father hunted and executed 'em all.'

'There's a thousand brothels in London,' said Bolly. 'More.'

'Then we'll have to knock over all of 'em,' grinned Repent.

'The Lord and Lady,' said Bolly thoughtfully. 'You really think they can be found?'

'My father says so,' opined Repent. 'They've been lying low, but their sinful stench rises like a devil from hell. 'S why the King's court is full 'a whores.'

'You sound like him,' said Bolly. 'Old Praise-God.'

'He's been telling me things,' said Repent. 'About how Cromwell captured the Lord and Lady, had them imprisoned in an iron cell. Queen Mab and the Elf King.'

'Royalists smuggled them free,' supplied Bolly, 'and the country fell. You told me already.' He rubbed sleep from his eyes and threw on his apron. 'Let's go to Saffron Hill,' he said. 'Brothels there got wine. I need to wake up.'

'Nah,' said Repent. His eyes slid to Bolly's purse, where the masterpiece lock was stored. 'My father says we start in Wapping Docks. The sailor's place. Ratcliffe Highway.'

Chapter 5

Charlie stood back as a pack of market traders from nearby Covent Garden rolled a barrel of beer across the stained floorboards. They were pointing enthusiastically at the badly painted scenery and perilous stage of loose-nailed planks. Several deeply rouged girls sat on the edge, legs dangling.

'It were worth bringing a king back to the throne,' opined one man happily as a skirt raised and dropped, 'if just to see the playhouses reopen.'

Charlie slid into the shadows and watched. He called to mind Lynette's fan and its crabbed seating plan. Something about how his mind worked allowed him to hold on to pictures easily and he scanned the rows of the theatre methodically, matching professions.

Charlie began systematically discounting faces. A pair of gaudy women, a gingerbread seller attempting to get his large cart inside.

Not you, not you.

Charlie hesitated. Behind a heavily armed wine seller he'd seen a figure moving with a little too much purpose.

Could be . . .

The man was smaller than Charlie had expected, and neatly dressed in a buff-coloured coat and matching trousers, with a powdered wig. He cast a quick glance over his shoulder, as though aware of being watched. He looked to be heading to the part of the theatre where the lawyers sat.

The light above shifted suddenly, and Charlie took an instinctive step back. Two chandeliers were swaying, their heavy load of candles fluttering as staff conducted a final wick-trimming. When Charlie looked back the figure had vanished. He sucked his scarred lip in annoyance. His eyes ranged the theatre, panning this way and that.

He saw him again near the vizard sellers and painted fans.

Found you.

Charlie watched his mark slide free from the crush of theatregoers and moved quickly to head him off.

The man removed a pistol from his belt and continued towards the lawyers' seating. He'd not taken two steps when Charlie appeared at his side.

'Easy, friend,' said Charlie pleasantly. 'What need for the gun?'

The man started in alarm. Charlie's hand clamped on his.

'It's not as though,' added Charlie, freeing the pistol from its owner with an expert flick of his wrist, 'you could discharge a weapon in a theatre and escape unharmed. During Lent you're liable to start a riot.'

The man watched helplessly as Charlie examined his weapon.

'A pistol is loud,' concluded Charlie, 'for such a purpose. Even in the noise of a theatre.'

'I . . .' The man was frowning furiously. 'I only bear arms for my own protection,' he returned huffily. 'You have a reputation. Although,' he added, appraising Charlie's wiry frame, skinny legs and bare feet, 'I thought you'd be bigger. London's famous thief taker.'

'I'm fast,' said Charlie.

'But with no head for business,' said the man. 'I might have been a paying client. Do you treat all meetings with such discourtesy?'

'You're a special case,' replied Charlie. 'Percy Berry. City lawyer at Temple Bar. Of good family. A very proper gentleman by all accounts. And your new wife once meant a lot to me. Maria,' he concluded, surprised to find his voice stuck a little at her name. 'Is she why you came here armed with a pistol?'

Percy coloured. Then he swallowed and, to Charlie's discomfort, his reserve melted away. 'Where is Maria? Have you seen her? How is she?'

There was a pause. 'What do you mean?' asked Charlie. 'How should I know? She's your wife now, isn't she?'

Percy seemed to slump a little. 'Maria never arrived at the church on our wedding day,' he said. 'And I thought you must know where she was.'

Chapter 6

In Wapping, sailors thronged in packs, weaving drunkenly, arms draped around one another's shoulders. Ratcliffe Highway was lined with brick houses, narrow and high, with groups of scantily clad girls whooping and beckoning from the windows.

Every other building bore a makeshift sign advertising sex. There were broom handles draped with underskirts, clusters of hanging dildos and inventive icons to suggest the speciality of the house.

Clancy and Viola sat in the first-floor window of an old town house, bare legs dangling from under their bright skirts. Hanging next to them was a swinging sign – a large gilded lock with a suggestively spurting key.

'Her,' Clancy pointed to a sad-eyed girl selling lucky charms. 'She's got it.'

'No!' Viola was horrified. She moved closer to look. 'She's . . . How old?'

''Leven, maybe twelve,' said Clancy, bouncing her legs against the window. 'Saw 'er buyin' pox-salve.' Clancy was an ex-pickpocket with a weasel face. Sometimes she whored, sometimes she stole. Mostly, she drank. She eyed Viola's lovely face: Italian with dark eyes, creamy skin and a straight Roman nose.

'Dontcha have little whores in Italy?' asked Clancy.

'Maybe,' said Viola. 'It makes me sad to think it.' She watched the small girl vanish into a jumble of stalls selling smutty trinkets, bootleg rum and contraceptives of dubious merit.

'Thas right,' said Clancy airily. 'I was forgettin'. You came to be an actress, dincha? Betcha never expected to end up in a dockside whorehouse.' She cast a careless glance into the room behind her. Partly clothed women sat on the stained floorboards, drinking pottage from bowls. Two children were squabbling over a broken wooden sword.

'I won't be here long,' said Viola, watching the street.

Clancy picked at a scabbed fleabite and adjusted her plunging neckline. ''S what we all say when we start,' she said philosophically. 'Always make 'em wear the pig gut, don't let 'em drop anchor in Bum Bay.' She waved a hand to the street to illustrate the inevitable shedding of such precious affectations.

'You think it's true, what they say about our mistress?' asked Viola. 'You think she press-gangs men?'

'I know she does,' said Clancy. 'She's a hard woman, Damaris. Sold for a slave, weren't she? She got no pity for men. 'S what makes her such a good madam.'

Clancy's eyes settled on two drunk men, recently docked from a long voyage, judging by their ragged clothes.

'You boys sin the world?' she bellowed. 'Where yers bin?'

They turned to look, taking in Clancy and Viola; their identically dressed hair, curled in fashionable ringlets, the thick rouge on their pretty young faces and the expensive skirts hitched around their knees.

'Everywhere!' shouted one.

''S that so?' Clancy grinned, preparing for her favourite line. 'I betcha ain't never sin the famous bearded oyster!' And she lifted her skirts high and spread her legs.

The sailors whistled appreciatively.

'It don't bite!' said Clancy. 'Come find out for yerselfs. I'll have you, blondie, and my friend will sit on your friend's face. She's *Italian*. Exotic. Half a guinea each.'

They laughed, turning away.

'A shilling each then,' bartered Clancy. 'Mouth fuck. Hands where you like.'

She began pulling down her low-cut dress. But the men were already walking away. A pair of bare-breasted women walking arm in arm accosted them, pulling them enticingly towards a doorway. Viola watched in fascination as one of the men peeled off with the cheaply dressed street girls, but the other crossed the street and approached an old hag who was raising and lowering her tattered skirts over withered legs.

'Mamma *mia*,' breathed Viola, as the sailor pushed money into the liver-spotted hand and began unbuttoning his breeches. 'Who knew?'

'Nothin' surprises me anymore,' said Clancy. 'Dirty bastards the lot of 'em.' She took out a leather flask of rum and offered it. Viola shook her head and Clancy upended it, coughed, then drank some more.

'Not too much,' winced Viola, as Clancy drained the flask. 'They'll try for all sorts if you stink of rum.'

'My head hurts from last night,' said Clancy, wiping her mouth. 'I need to take the edge off.'

A small girl appeared behind them and climbed into Viola's lap.

'Hello, darling,' said Viola, wrapping her arms around the little body and kissing her. 'Is your mama in the bedroom again?'

'Get out the window!' hissed Clancy, shooing the little girl away. 'You want these men to think you're for business?'

'No.' The girl was reluctantly moving back.

'No,' said Clancy fiercely. 'And you never will. A princess you'll be. Eatin' sugar . . .' She stopped, staring up the road. At the far end of Ratcliffe Highway was a faint sheen of rising dust. As though a great body of people were moving towards them.

There was a roar from the street below.

Clancy's mouth dropped open. 'Apprentices,' she said, eyes wide with fear.

'I thought they came every Lent?' Viola craned her head to see. 'Don't we just bolt the door?' She took in the shapes emerging from the dust cloud, then drew back aghast.

'Ring the bell,' said Clancy, scooping up the little girl.

The door was flung open. The tall figure of Damaris Page strode through the doorway. She wore a neat pink taffeta dress and her tightly curled dark hair was divided in a razor-sharp parting. The edge of an old slave brand could be seen at her shoulder, pink and raised against her shining ebony skin.

'Apprentices!' gabbled Clancy, holding the child tight to her chest. 'Outside. More than I've ever seen.'

Damaris nodded, taking in Viola's terrified face. She glanced towards the window and her brown eyes grew round. Damaris moved to a strongbox in the corner of the room. She flung open the lid and lifted free a blunderbuss, her tall frame holding it easily.

A chant had struck up. An ugly chorus about whores and His Majesty's pleasure.

'I've never seen them like this,' said Clancy. 'Those men mean murder.'

Chapter 7

Charlie and Percy sat in the raised seating of the Birdcage Theatre. Several food and ale sellers had already passed. Charlie had bought them both a beer and a pig knuckle.

Percy was eyeing Charlie's crooked nose and scarred lip. 'Maria told me you usually attract reprobate aristocrats or poor Londoners hoping for a favour.' Percy's gaze drifted to the empty stage and back to the thickening crowd.

'And yet here you are.' Charlie worked to keep his tone neutral.

Now Charlie had the opportunity to observe Percy better he understood even less what Maria saw in him. Everything about him seemed determinedly average. His height, his thin build. His washed-out eyes, caught between brown and green, the neutral colour of his buff suit. He had no charisma to speak of and seemed unfamiliar with London crowds, habitually checking his purse and starting at unfamiliar noises.

Percy eyed his pig knuckle suspiciously and ventured a tentative bite.

'You've never been to a theatre before?' guessed Charlie, watching him negotiate his food.

Percy swallowed a chunk of sinew with effort. 'I was to be married. I've no interest in such entertainments.' He toyed uncomfortably with a crucifix at his neck.

'But you've ventured south of the river,' Charlie supplied, watching Percy's face. 'Once would have been enough. The illegal playhouses shocked you.'

Percy was silent.

'The shin has less gristle,' said Charlie helpfully. 'People mainly buy them so they might have a bone left to throw at the actors. Same with the orange peel.'

'The Watch won't believe me,' said Percy, looking ahead to the stage. 'They think Maria decided not to marry me. But she would never have left me standing at the altar . . .'

'You're certain?' said Charlie.

Percy reddened.

'I'm a thief taker,' continued Charlie, unable to help himself. 'So I notice things. Your stockings have been cheaply laundered. And all that powder does not quite disguise your periwig is not horse hair. Does Maria know she marries a lawyer in straitened circumstances?'

'I am of well enough fortunes,' snapped Percy. 'She will not want for anything.'

But you haven't told her everything, decided Charlie, assessing his reaction.

Percy huffed, seeing Charlie's expression. 'We quarrelled,' he admitted. 'The last time I saw her.' He seemed annoyed rather than concerned.

The orchestra struck up a tune and their conversation was momentarily halted. A few people began to applaud. Lynette sashayed onto the stage to approving hoots and cheers.

Percy shook his head, watching the painted women stalking the crowd, rubbing up against wealthy men, laughing a little too loudly. 'Actresses.' He shook his head again. 'I would *never*,' he concluded haughtily, 'let *my* wife act.' He took in the tumbledown playhouse with a shudder.

Charlie got up to leave. He was a little drunk, he realised. Playhouse ale was stronger than he remembered. 'If Maria doesn't want to marry you, it's her business,' he added. Though as he said the words he knew Maria wasn't the kind of woman to run. She would have faced Percy and told him the truth. It was just how she was.

'Wait.' Percy spoke in a sudden rush. 'I think Maria may have found out something she shouldn't. Something that has put her life at risk.'

Charlie stayed silent, waiting for Percy to continue.

'She transcribed my documents for a time,' continued Percy. 'Legal things. She only has a woman's understanding, of course, but she has a good hand.'

Charlie bit back a retort. The Maria he knew was easily clever enough to understand legal documents.

'There was an old confession,' continued Percy. 'A Royalist condemned to death at the end of the war had told his crimes to the judge. I saw nothing unusual in it, but Maria thought it contained some lost clue of great importance. She believed it would lead to some people who went missing during the war. A lord and lady.' He coughed hastily. 'I didn't think it fitting for a woman to be interested in such things and I told her so.'

'This was your quarrel?' guessed Charlie.

'In part. But now Maria is missing,' he concluded guiltily. 'As I say, I think she might have . . . pursued an interest. Then you asked to meet with me,' Percy concluded. 'And I assumed she'd come to you for help.'

'I?' Charlie was momentarily thrown. 'It was you who requested we meet in the Birdcage.'

'No,' said Percy. 'A boy came to Temple Bar with a message.'

Fear flashed through Charlie. He grabbed Percy's surprisingly bony arm. 'We need to leave,' he said.

'Unhand me!' demanded Percy, his body rigid. 'How dare you . . .'

Charlie swung to face him, gripping the thin arm tight. 'Maria is the only link between us,' he said. 'She is missing. And someone has summoned us both to the most dangerous theatre in London. Half the audience would cut your throat for a shilling. Do you really want to wait around and discover why we've both been tricked here?'

A sudden mechanical thud echoed around the theatre. They turned to see a shadowy figure had dropped above the stage and swung suspended there.

'Something is wrong,' said Charlie. 'The swing of the figure is wrong. A person wouldn't drop like that, unless . . .'

A high-pitched wail confirmed his worst fear. Lynette was clutching both hands over her mouth. And now screams began shooting up from those nearest to the stage.

'It's a body,' said Charlie. 'That's a real dead woman hanging there.'

'What?' Percy's voice was thick with scorn.

'Lynette is not that good at acting,' said Charlie.

'But you can barely see in the candlelight,' scoffed Percy. 'It's only theatre trickery. All I can make out is the dress . . .' His words petered out and all colour drained from his face. 'Oh, Lord preserve us,' said Percy. 'Sweet Jesus and all the saints above.' He took a shuddering step backwards, treading on the foot of a seated lawyer who swore loudly. 'It isn't,' whispered Percy. 'It cannot be her. It isn't.'

Percy had begun shaking uncontrollably. Charlie took him by the shoulders. The lawyer's pale eyes were unfocused.

'It's her,' murmured Percy.

Candles were being brought to the stage now. The figure was illuminated.

A blue dress, painstakingly panelled in watered-silk and lace.

Percy's thin lips parted. 'Maria,' he managed. 'It's Maria who hangs there.' He turned to Charlie, eyes wide with speechless horror.

But Charlie was already running for the stage.

Chapter 8

In the gloomy theatre, Tom Black was watching the thief taker. His thoughts drifted to Maria. How brave she'd been. He'd loved watching her face, the expressions. How she'd kicked and clawed at the carriage door as he'd vanished her.

Charlie Tuesday was racing towards the hanging corpse. The shouting and disorder were making Tom uncomfortable. He tapped his fingers together nervously.

To his surprise a woman wearing a black mask slipped herself in beside him. *Stay calm,* he reminded himself. *It's only a theatre-prostitute in her vizard.* He could smell the herbs she'd scented her washcloth with, a woody blend of rosemary and camomile. His stomach tightened.

'The play is over,' she said with difficulty, after a moment. She was holding the mask to her face by means of a button secured between her teeth. It made her speech come out strangely. 'Want to go outside?' she tried.

'No.'

She followed the line of his gaze. 'Stage tricks,' she observed, looking at the swinging body. ''S just an effect. You like theatre?'

'It was an awakening for me,' said Tom. 'Before I discovered theatre, I had to watch people secretly.'

She laughed uncomfortably. 'You like to watch people? To act?' She was trying for seductive, but the button-secured mask was hampering her efforts.

Tom saw himself as a boy, watching children play. He'd always been on the other side of the glass, looking in. Then he'd discovered theatre, acting. It had been a revelation, seeing the rehearsals and plays. Tom had gorged himself on this exaggerated human emotion. It made him feel alive. Then he'd transferred his growing obsession to the real world. He began watching the dying animals in the butcher's killing stalls, fascinated. Soon after, Tom had discovered executions. He'd devoured the tortures and hangings like a starving man, waiting every week with an eagerness that disturbed even his butcher father. Fear and pain were so rare they had to be savoured and rationed. Too much summoned the fairy folk.

'No,' Tom replied. 'Acting is a great sin. But I made my weakness a strength.'

She took off the mask now, tiring of the button speech impediment. Her features were rounded and pleasant, free from cosmetics. Wisps of badly curled hair framed her chubby face.

He smiled at her, watching her response. 'Watching theatre performances, rehearsals, I slowly pieced it all together,' he said. 'What the faces meant, the tilt of the mouth, the twitch of an eye. The subtlety fascinated me. I worked until I became a master of it.'

'Oh?' She tapped the mask coquettishly on her chin. 'Can you tell me what I'm thinking now?'

He turned to her, absorbing her expression. Her smile faltered slightly. It was as though he were staring into her soul. 'You're hoping our transaction will be swift,' he said. 'You're calculating how many men you might bed before dusk.'

Her face fell, but she rallied, moving closer, and he felt a spike of unease. Tom could feel the chaos churning beneath the surface, like something heavy waiting to fall.

'Don't . . .' he began.

She took hold of his trousers roughly. 'I'll give you the time of your life,' she promised, eyeing the crowds below. 'No one's watching. They're all in a panic.'

He flinched at the contact, sending a hand flying up. It cracked across her face and she fell back. All hope of self-control slipped away.

'You don't know what I am,' he said, grabbing her. 'I am one of the fairy folk. I come from the dark city, through the lake of fire.'

He was losing speech now, thoughts flying randomly. Tom heard himself saying the words from far away. Underneath, another, weaker, voice was screaming in his mind.

Don't. Kill. Her.

It was like shouting through treacle. His hands were shaking, jolting the girl in their grip.

'I hunt creatures like you,' he hissed, his eyes wide. 'Drury Lane teems with prospects. The trick is to go early. Too late and all the fresh ones are gone. Only toothless hags left.'

The girl's face was racked with horror. Tom drank it in.

'The brothel whores are tempting but too dangerous,' he continued. 'They are under the protection of the whorehouses and would be noticed. I look for the ones like me.' He brought his face closer. 'The nothings. The nobodies. The ones who won't be missed. Tell me, who knows you are here?'

She was about to scream: Tom could see it in her face. The realisation brought a flash of shock and with it a sudden measure of control. He felt as though he were walking atop a thin wall, inches from an abyss on either side. He screwed his eyes tight shut.

'Don't fall,' he muttered. 'Don't fall.' Teeth gritted, he forced his fists to open. He felt the girl spring free.

Tom opened his eyes. To his relief the girl was backing away, terrified. She wasn't going to scream and shout. He could tell. He straightened his clothing and returned a pleasant expression to his face. For some reason he couldn't fathom, this seemed to make her even more frightened.

'Too much wine,' he said, passing an apologetic hand across his head.

The girl ran. His eye followed her, assessing the threat. There was no need for another girl now. The fairies already had their changeling.

Tom returned his attention to the matter at hand. *The Lord and Lady want to be found*, he reminded himself. *Now is the time.* He had to be sure the thief taker took the bait.

Chapter 9

Amesbury was sat in the King's bedchamber drinking, rolling the wine goblet around his large hands. In front of him was a paper.

'The Lord and Lady,' muttered Amesbury. 'Who could have possibly imagined they would survive?'

His bull-like bulk fitted awkwardly on the ornate chair, thick legs pointed back in the attitude of a man who was more used to sitting on stools and floors. Amesbury had retained his thick leather military jerkin and boots, a purple sash his only concession to his recent earldom.

He sat back, considered, then picked up a quill and scratched some numbers on the paper. Amesbury glanced towards the sumptuous four-poster bed in the centre of the room. As if on cue, a seductive muttering drifted from behind the thick curtains, then laughter. He shook his head and returned to writing.

There was a prescribed knock and he stood to greet his one-time friend.

It was the first time Praise-God Barebones had seen inside the King's bedchamber and Amesbury could feel the scorn pouring off him. The imposing royal bed, festooned with thick red silk with closed curtains, the sumptuous tapestries and glass chandeliers.

His eyes said, '*Is this what we fought for, my old brother in arms?*'

'Master Barebones.' Amesbury bowed.

Barebones returned the leanest of bows, flashing Amesbury a glare. Amesbury thought it took all his old friend's restraint not to hiss '*turncoat*'. Amesbury had a sudden memory of them fighting side by side. The King's court was distinctly lacking in men like Barebones, with his dense muscle and steely air of danger.

'How might I address you now?' asked Barebones, his voice thick with scorn. 'Your Earlship? My liege?'

Amesbury smiled slightly. 'You may call me what you like.'

'Stories of your brave escape from Cromwell are legend,' said Barebones. 'They say you were pulled out of the Thames half dead.'

'Almost all dead,' corrected Amesbury. 'The nuns who found me didn't even try to dress my wounds.'

'A heroic tale. And history is written by the winners,' observed Barebones. 'His Majesty will arrive soon?'

A flash of anxiety flared in his even features. Amesbury understood immediately. Barebones was a common man, with no experience of royalty. But he'd fought for the Republic and was ashamed of his nervousness.

'His Majesty is here,' said Amesbury. 'But currently engaged.' He nodded towards the bed.

'I thought . . .' Barebones was racked with confusion.

'You thought the King's bedchamber was name only,' supplied Amesbury. 'A place to conduct official business. It is usually so.'

Barebones began to speak and then stopped himself. A dainty white hand had slipped out from between the curtains, grasped the silken cord used to tie them and drew it inside. A giggling shriek followed.

Barebones's face reddened with fury. 'I represent the common people,' he said. 'God-fearing people.' His eyes flicked to the bed again. 'We made this country good, clean . . .'

Amesbury held up a quick hand. 'Don't lose your head,' he cautioned quietly.

Barebones breathed hard, calming himself. There was an awkward pause. Barebones spoke first, clearing his throat. 'You summoned me,' he said. 'You think I know of plots against the King. If you hope to recruit me as one of your tattling rats, you never knew me at all.'

Amesbury missed this kind of straight-talking. No good came of wallowing, he reminded himself. He gave the slightest incline of his head. 'You were one of Cromwell's best soldiers,' he said. 'You returned to your lock-making business when the war was over. A humble man, to live in the working district of London. Not much of that part left, now the fire has come and gone.' Amesbury's eyes were trained on Barebones.

'If you think I am part of the unrest,' growled Barebones, 'come out and say it. Are you a courtier now, mincing words? That isn't the man I knew.'

From behind the curtains came a throaty groan of pleasure.

Barebones glared. 'I will tell you this, Amesbury,' he said, his voice growing louder. 'The common people talk much of Lady Castlemaine. Particularly those made homeless by the fire. The King gave her a house, did he not?'

'She stripped the roof of lead and sold it for cash,' supplied Amesbury, calmly. 'To pay off her gambling debts. The King knows.'

'Does he know last night she lost fifty thousand on the turn of a card?' demanded Barebones.

The bed was silent. For a moment Amesbury thought the King might be astute enough to be listening. But then a sound of heavy breathing began, along with some disturbingly loud lip-smacking noises.

'I need a drink,' said Amesbury, as Barebones stared at the bed. 'Wine?'

'I don't break Lent,' said Barebones.

Amesbury poured two goblets of wine. 'People claim the Lord and Lady survived the war,' he said. 'You imagine the consequences of what that might mean for the King.' He proffered the second goblet impatiently.

Barebones hesitated, then took the wine and drank. 'A fairy tale,' he said uncomfortably. 'An immortal brother and sister, with ancient blood. Fallen angels . . .'

'The mob likes fairy tales,' said Amesbury. 'The apprentices seem to be running wilder than usual.'

The sound of heavy breathing started up again from behind the curtain.

Barebones gestured to the bed. 'I knew a little Shambles girl,' he said. 'Due to wed. Honest, sober, hard-working. One day she sees Lady Castlemaine's carriage. She thinks it must be the Queen, so fine she is, in her silk and pearls.' Barebones's lip was curled in contempt. 'When the girl discovers it to be the King's whore, she leaves the Shambles the very next day. Takes up in a whorehouse in Covent Garden. Her father died of the shame of it, and she was dead of the pox within a year.' He drew himself up taller for effect, his eyes flashing with preacher's zeal. 'That girl's brothers and cousins were apprentices,' he concluded. 'How might those young men behave, when given licence to sack brothels at Lent?'

'I heard the same story,' said Amesbury. 'Only it was a Wapping girl, and the mother who died of shame. I suggest you save your fables for preaching.' Amesbury drank his wine. 'Some of the attacks have a military feel to them.' He looked pointedly at Barebones. 'As though someone is searching the brothels systematically.'

'You think I hunt the Lord and Lady?' demanded Barebones. He was looking carefully at Amesbury now.

'I hope you don't,' said Amesbury. 'I hope you are not so foolish as to plot. I've seen too many good men on the scaffold.'

Barebones took a step closer. 'You know me as a truthful man,' he said, his blue eyes blazing. 'So you'll believe me when I tell you, I make no plots.'

Amesbury nodded.

'I am a man of action,' concluded Barebones. 'Not a conspirer or intriguer.'

'The Lord and Lady were in the Tower when Cromwell took power,' said Amesbury, his tone beseeching his old friend. 'It's not possible they were smuggled out. They were burned as heretic in one of the secret bonfires.'

'More wine!' the King's disembodied voice sailed out.

'Butter!' called Lady Castlemaine.

Their voices dropped to laughing whispers.

Barebones touched the plain wooden cross at his neck and muttered something.

'Pay it no mind,' said Amesbury. 'She loves an audience.'

The door was pulled ceremonially open and the Duke of York entered, walking quickly. He gave Barebones the disinterested bow of a king's brother to a commoner and Amesbury felt his old comrade bristle.

'They're back in love then?' said the Duke of York, shooting a weary tilt of his head towards the bed.

Amesbury nodded.

A theatrical female groaning had begun.

'My brother's only fault is loyalty to that woman,' said the Duke of York sadly.

'Loyalty is overrated,' said Barebones, 'as Amesbury will tell you.'

The Duke of York looked back and forth between the two men.

'If those apprentices spark a riot they may turn on Whitehall,' said Amesbury. 'We have not the army to defend it.' He seemed to be the only person wholly unconcerned by the sounds filtering from behind the curtain.

'It's royal sin they object to,' said Barebones. 'The public adultery, the parties. His Majesty might think to spend more time with his wife.'

The moaning grew suddenly louder.

Barebones glanced at the bed, then tipped wine into his mouth.

'It's too late for that,' said Amesbury. 'We need to put it down before it escalates.'

'You're a politician, now, Amesbury,' said Barebones. 'I'm sure you have planned for this.'

'I've made arrangements,' agreed Amesbury, 'with one of the theatres.'

The Duke of York shook his head. 'The actress? You won't distract him for long,' he said bitterly, nodding towards the bed. 'She's got her claws in too tightly. And he loves the children. My brave brother has weathered fire, plague and a Dutch attack,' he continued, raising his voice slightly, 'but I fear Lady Castlemaine may have finally lost him the crown.'

Chapter 10

The Birdcage Theatre was chaos as Charlie slipped towards the stage, weaving expertly through the panicked crowd.

Lynette had a high flush on her cheeks, breathing hard beneath her tightly laced costume. 'Cut her down,' she whispered, unable to take her eyes from the swinging body. Her voice grew to a shout. 'God's blood won't someone *cut her down*?'

The cry was taken up by the crowd. A ragged sailor in naval calico began climbing the side of the stage. Realising the opportunity to win approval from London's favourite actress, several other men began elbowing their way towards Lynette.

'Wait!' shouted Charlie. If the suspended body smashed to the floor, vital information would be lost. He broke into a run, shouldering through the tightly packed crowd.

A sailor was halfway up the scenery now, knees gripping the large canvas frame, knife between his teeth. The scene, a painted forest, swung at a wild tilt.

'Lynette!' shouted Charlie. 'Don't let her be cut down!'

But his one-time wife was still transfixed by the hanging body, hands gripped into fists.

A few of the crowd turned angrily on Charlie. Hands grabbed at his leather coat, trying to stop him getting to the stage.

The sailor began slicing at the rope to cheers. The cut caused the thick hemp to unravel sharply down, flicking the dead girl's head at an obscene angle and starting the body on a slow rotation. Several drunks applauded.

Charlie broke free of the crowd and swung up easily onto the stage, now thick with men trying to get to Lynette.

'Leave her alone!' shouted Charlie, pushing through. He jostled a pack of blind-drunk aristocrats and one of them turned on him angrily.

'Ho ho, fellows,' boomed a slurred, plummy voice, 'this street rat wants to keep the poor girl hanging.'

Charlie dodged one man's drunken sword blow, relieved a pistol from the belt of another, ducked low and slid across the polished boards.

'Stop!' he commanded, forcing his eyes towards the swinging corpse and pointing the gun at the sailor. The unravelling rope had rotated the dead face towards the back of the stage, a long curling wig covering her features. Her arms and head slumped down, bare legs and feet turning slowly. The toes and fingertips were black with pooled blood.

The dead face was swinging back into view.

Charlie saw the eyes first. The whites were stained a shocking yellow. The dark wig concealed most of the face, but he'd seen enough.

It wasn't Maria.

The relief was so intense it seemed to knock him sideways. But he'd paused long enough for the aristocrats to collect themselves. They closed in, staggering, murderous, swords drawn. Charlie made a quick assessment. Five armed men, all young and inexperienced enough to have something to prove, wealthy, privileged and drunk. He reckoned them the most dangerous kind of men to offend in London.

'Look at this barefoot rogue,' said one, advancing. 'Thinks to command his betters.'

There was a creak of rope above.

For a moment the hanging corpse twirled on a single strand, then it broke, and she plummeted to the stage in a heap of lifeless limbs. Groans and cheers came from the crowd.

Charlie and the drunk lords stood stupidly, the body between them. Then one of them spoke. 'Thief,' he slurred, pointing his sword at Charlie. 'He holds my pistol!'

Charlie swallowed, realising the gun wouldn't be enough to deter them. He made a quick assessment of the stage and judged his chances of escape poor.

Suddenly Percy was at his side. Charlie saw him take in the face of the dead girl, then turn to the aristocrats.

'This man broke no law,' he said. Charlie blinked. Percy spoke with deep authority. 'He is a thief taker. I saw you all attack him as he attempted to bring order.' Percy's mouth was puckered in contempt. 'I am a lawyer of Temple Bar and would swear to it,' he added. 'He only took the pistol in self-defence.' Percy nodded that Charlie should return the gun. He slid it across the floor.

One of the men picked it up. There was a pause as they stood, undecided.

Charlie nodded towards the crowd. 'People are helping themselves to your barrel of wine,' he said. It was enough to galvanise their thoughts. The aristocrats left the stage, jostling to reclaim their drink.

Percy took a step closer to the dead girl. 'It's not her,' he said.

'No,' agreed Charlie.

They looked at one another and, just for a moment, Charlie liked Percy better than he had before.

Now the body was no longer displayed above the stage, the atmosphere in the theatre had calmed a little.

'Get 'em out of here!' Lynette had recovered herself and was shouting. 'The show's over!' Playhouse employees began herding people away from the macabre spectacle.

'He stays,' she added, pointing to Charlie. 'Seems like someone's playin' dirty tricks to shut us down. Charlie might be the only person who can keep us open.'

Chapter 11

Maria's mouth was dry. It was dark. The floor beneath her felt cold and damp. She began to sit up, wincing at the throbbing in her head. A bolt of panic sliced through her. Heavy iron manacles had been locked around her wrists. They dragged loudly on the floor as she tried to move her arms. A dreadful surge of nausea threatened to overwhelm her. She closed her eyes and took a breath.

Keep calm. What would Charlie do?

The sudden, safe memory of him brought a welling sob to her throat.

No self-pity, she told herself sternly. *That won't help you. Only think.*

She began testing for the restrictions of her manacles. They gave her about two feet, she thought, feeling on the floor. At the very widest edge of her range her damp fingertips touched on something grainy. Like sand or dirt. She raised the substance to her face and found it had melted away. Maria put her fingers tentatively to her mouth.

Salt.

She reached back into the gloom, making sense of it.

Her captor had placed her in a salt circle.

Memories of her countryside childhood bloomed. Salt circles were to ward away evil, banish the devil, repel pixies and sprites and . . . *fairies.*

She remembered something her mother had told her, as a little girl.

The Green Man puts his green thumb in the earth and the harvest comes. He is the sun, the earth, all things. When the first kings came, the Green Man split in two. He became a man and a woman. A fairy lord and lady to ordain the King.

The realisation brought a rush of memories.

The Lord and Lady.

As the thought swirled in her mind, her fingertips touched something else in the dark. A basket. The rough-wicker kind that women took to market. She could feel a handkerchief laid over the contents.

Maria started to draw it away, then hesitated. What if something terrible was inside? But she thought she could smell food. Bread or cake, or something fresh baked. Her stomach growled, and she realised she couldn't remember when she'd last eaten.

Steeling herself, Maria dug her hands under the handkerchief. Nestled inside the basket she made out three perfectly round little cakes, still warm from the oven. Laid alongside them was a corked bottle.

Maria hesitated, wondering if it was some kind of trick. What if the food was poisoned or drugged? If the alternative was starving to death, she reasoned, it hardly mattered.

She sat back, considering. If the food wasn't adulterated, then it meant her captor wanted her to eat. Not cheap food either. What did it mean?

Maria toyed with the idea of refusing the food, but her hunger got the better of her. She reached out again and this time the moment her fingers touched the warm cakes an animal instinct took over. She stuffed her mouth full, chewing.

They were honey cakes, she realised, swallowing her final mouthful. And as far as she could tell there was nothing bitter or unusual about them. She lifted the bottle from the basket. Maria eased out the cork and sniffed the contents. It was sickly sweet. A smell she recognised from the countryside. Mead. She'd not drunk it in years. Not since coming to London, where wine and beer were the common drinks.

Maria weighed the bottle in her hand. 'Mead,' she said. 'Honey cakes and a honey drink.' She tried to consider what significance that might have but none came to mind. 'Charlie Tuesday,' she whispered to herself. 'If only you were here.'

The memory of him brought a rush of emotion and, in a bid to quell it, Maria lifted the bottle to take a sip. For some reason she stopped. She suddenly saw Charlie in front of her, his bent nose and scarred lip.

'Why would he give you mead?' pressed Charlie. 'Why honey cakes?'

Maria hesitated. 'You're not here,' she reminded Charlie. 'You didn't come.'

She raised the bottle and sipped. It was good, and the sparkle of alcohol and sugar brought an immediate rush of warmth.

'Not too much,' she warned herself. 'Keep your wits.'

Maria took a deeper swig. *Drugged? Poisoned?* But she felt no ill effects.

Then suddenly a story bloomed in her mind. A tale from her childhood about salt circles and honey cakes. What had the fairy king said?

My little changeling. If you drink or eat in the fairy kingdom you must stay forever.

As she set the wine down, Maria noticed she wasn't wearing her own clothes. Her hands followed the line of an unfamiliar dress, stiff and strange. It was heavy. She could smell the musty fabric and guessed it to be old. There was fraying lace at the collar in the style of the royal court, from before the war.

Where were her own clothes?

She was slowly putting things together. There had been a corpse. A yellow-eyed dead girl who Tom had described as her changeling. Then she remembered the mystery she'd been trying to solve, the clue in the old confession.

A dress in a brothel to summon the Lord and Lady. Maria shook her head at her own foolishness. What better person to discover the hidden dress than a thief taker raised in a brothel?

Not only was she trapped, but Charlie Tuesday was in danger too.

Chapter 12

The playhouse had been cleared. Lynette had persuaded the manager to let Charlie and Percy remain.

'It's a trick, s'what it is,' Lynette was raging. 'Them high-ups in the Duke's Theatre. They can't stand us illegal playhouses. They've done this to ruin us!'

Charlie was silent, examining the body of the girl. He stooped closer and Lynette drew her handkerchief to her mouth.

'Don't get so close, Charlie,' she begged. 'There's vapours in dead folk.'

'It's a pity the noose was cut,' said Charlie thoughtfully. 'Makes it more difficult to tell how she died.' He was looking at a small puddle of dark blood, where the body had hit.

He glanced at the rope. Something about the knot had been unusual, he thought. But now it lay unravelled.

'Not an executioner's rope,' said Charlie, picking up the two ends. 'This is double-twisted hemp. Hangings use triple.' He held the rope in his hands, studying it. 'Might tell us something,' Charlie decided, cutting away a small blood-stained piece and putting it in his pocket.

He switched his attention to the corpse, taking a wooden sword that had been discarded on the stage and carefully moving the body. The girl flopped onto her back, staring upwards. She was smiling.

'Her eyes, Charlie!' Lynette was covering her mouth. The whites of the dead girl's eyes had been stained a livid yellow.

'Iodine would give that colour.' The suggestion came from Percy, who'd been standing silently.

Charlie shook his head. 'It's not a dye,' he said. 'A dye would have pooled at the edges of her eyes. The shade is the same all across.' He pointed to the ghoulish pigment. 'I think this came from within,' he decided.

'You think she was poisoned?' asked Lynette.

'Perhaps.' Charlie frowned at the corpse. 'She wasn't hanged,' he added. 'No rope burn on the neck. And look at her expression. Hanged men and women don't die like that.'

They all stared at the girl's placid face.

'Do you recognise her?' he asked Lynette.

She shook her head. 'Should I?'

'Perhaps,' said Charlie. 'I think she was an actress. Not a good one,' he added.

'I've never seen her on stage,' said Lynette. 'What makes you think she acted?'

'Look at the suntan on her calves.' Charlie nodded to where the dishevelled skirts exposed the bottom of the girl's legs. 'She wore dresses too short to be a decent kind of woman. But' – Charlie pointed at her lips – 'there's a residue of dark lip paint. You can't get that depth of red without cochineal. Expensive for your average whore.'

'She might 'a been high class,' said Lynette. 'I wore cochineal in my day,' she added with a saucy wink at Percy. He blinked in alarm and straightened his smart coat.

'But she's too thin to have been earning a good living,' said Charlie. 'Expensive whores are well fed. And she has candle wax blisters and rope calluses on her hands. I think she was given the occasional background role, but was mostly delegated to more menial theatre tasks. Raising the curtains, trimming the candles.' He thought. 'She wears Maria's clothes,' he said. 'Someone means to leave a message in that, surely. It's like a changeling, isn't it? From the fairy tales. Someone vanishes into the fairy realm. Another takes their place.'

'Fairies crave Christian children,' agreed Lynette. 'They steal them and replace babies with a weak member of their own kind.'

'Could someone mean us to know Maria is alive?'

'Changelings are usually alive,' Percy pointed out. 'Someone might mean us to know Maria is dead.' He was twisting his hands together, the knuckles white.

Charlie noticed something in the hand of the dead girl. A paper was clutched in her fingers. He tugged it free. It was old, inked in careful writing. Charlie started to decipher the letters, his poor reading making the process painstaking. Percy began reading in a loud clear voice:

> Deep and dark the old ones sleep,
> Crowned Lord and girdled Lady of the Keep,
> They at first and last will come,
> And false earthly Kings will be undone.

It was written in a sloping script. And underneath, in a newer hand, was scrawled:

> I've taken your Maria. Find the Lord and Lady before the
> end of Lent and she will live. The Lady will tell you where
> to find me. Come for me without them and she will die.

It was signed: 'Tom Black'.

Chapter 13

On Ratcliffe Highway, the sound of alarm bells rang out up and down the street. Women scattered, screaming as an army of blue-aproned boys rampaged. Drunk sailors were making for the docks. Parrots and monkeys fled in all directions.

In the Gilded Lock, Damaris Page was loading her blunderbuss as the door of her whorehouse splintered and cracked. Behind her, terrified women and children were escaping down a rope ladder slung from the window. Viola was halfway down, cursing in Italian. Clancy was handing children to her, a determined expression on her pointed features.

There was a loud shriek of splitting wood and an axe blade appeared through the door. Then a torrent of blue-aproned boys and men broke through.

Damaris arranged her large body in front of the women, gun held easily.

A stocky man moved to the front. His hair was cropped in the Roundhead style and he moved with the easy authority of a military leader.

'You're not an apprentice,' she said.

The man was dressed like a soldier, with a thick brown coat, canvas breeches and square-cut tan shoes.

'No. My name is Praise-God Barebones.' He gave the short bow of a soldier. 'And you need no introduction,' he continued. 'Tall as a man and black as the devil. Slave brand on your pretty shoulder. You're the talk of London. Damaris Page, the sailor's bawd. I hear you've been press-ganging your customers.'

'I was sold as a slave,' said Damaris, her voice lilting with its African accent. 'You think I do wrong? Sending them to sea for a shilling? You'd better believe they did worse to me.'

Barebones eyed the inside of the house, its threadbare fixtures and cheap décor.

'You're not here to riot,' said Damaris. 'You're looking for something.'

'The Lord and Lady rise, Mrs Page,' said Barebones. 'We feel their evil influence. I think you whores have been hiding them all these years.'

Damaris's jaw tightened. She levelled the gun at him. 'There's nothing here for you,' she said. Her eyes flicked to the rope ladder.

Clancy was passing the last little boy to Viola, who lowered him to the ground.

'I fought for the Republic,' said Barebones. 'All men equal. Women dressed cleanly. Not for whores to frig themselves on the street.'

Damaris's eyes fell on a boy with beard-shaped smallpox scars and flecks of premature grey in his greasy hair. He was transfixed by Viola, escaping down the ladder, her dark hair swinging. Damaris tightened her trigger finger.

Barebones followed her gaze and his brow knitted. 'Repent,' he said sharply. 'Remember what we spoke of. Temptation.'

'They're only whores,' said Repent, licking his lower lip. He hadn't taken his eyes from Viola. 'That one's foreign, I reckon,' he added hungrily. 'Not even English.'

'We do not gratify desires of the flesh,' said Barebones.

Repent turned away from the Italian girl petulantly.

Damaris looked from the apprentice to Barebones. 'Your son?' she guessed, marking the resemblance. 'I see him afore, 'round Wapping. Takin' things he's not paid for.' She nodded meaningfully at the escaping women.

Rage flared deep in Barebones's lined features. 'You women,' he said in a soft, dangerous voice. 'You get above yourselves under this new king. Forget your proper place.'

He looked at the women, still trying to escape through the window by the swinging rope ladder. Clancy was at the rear, moving slowly.

'Search the women and children,' he decided, raising his voice. 'Lay hands on them.'

Damaris took a quick step forward, positioning herself in front of the escaping women, aiming the blunderbuss.

Barebones moved suddenly, grabbing the muzzle of the large gun. There was a deafening explosion. A cloud of gunpowder smoke filled the room and horsehair plaster and shattered roof timbers rained down. Barebones punched Damaris in the stomach. She doubled over in pain, dropping the gun. He pushed her to the ground and put a heavy foot on her chest.

'Stay down,' he warned, 'and you won't get hurt.'

Barebones looked at the assembled trunks and chests, then at the ceiling. Dusty daylight now beamed through a ragged hole in the roof. A concealed attic floor had been revealed in the wreckage. Barebones's gaze rested on his son, deliberating.

'Bolly,' said Barebones eventually, shifting his attention to a golden-haired boy with a handsome face, 'look in the attic. Repent, take your boys and search the chests.'

Repent's sour expression grew furious.

Damaris watched as Repent beckoned a little pack of boys to fall on her scant possessions, ransacking, tearing open chests, upending trunks and smashing apart desks and wardrobes. Her dark skin was shining with sweat.

Barebones was watching Damaris, who lay prone on the ground.

'It doesn't concern you?' he asked. 'The destruction of your property?'

'I came to England with nothing,' said Damaris. 'I can make it all again. Men who cheat and steal, it is you who will always be poor.'

'Nothing here,' called Repent. 'Only trinkets. Whores' things.' He dropped a string of glass beads on the floor and shattered them underfoot.

'Tear it up,' commanded Barebones. 'Rip the dresses, throw everything from the window.'

'Master Barebones.' He was interrupted by Bolly, who had emerged from the smoking wreckage of the attic and was pointing. 'There's two hidden beds up here.'

'Well, well,' said Barebones, looking down at Damaris. 'It seems you weren't being quite truthful, Mrs Page.'

'They are long gone,' said Damaris. 'You will never find them. Not if you hunt your whole life.'

'Repent, come question the black whore,' commanded Barebones. 'I think there's more she can tell us.'

Chapter 14

The thin walls of the Birdcage Theatre seemed to close in around Charlie. He tore the note from Percy's hand, the threat resounding in his mind. *Bring me the Lord and Lady.* Charlie's eyes glided to the dead girl, with her yellow eyes and strange smile.

'Tom Black,' he said quietly. 'I've never heard that name.'

He glanced up at Percy and Lynette. They both looked as blank as he did.

'But I have heard of the Lord and Lady,' Charlie continued slowly. 'It's a legend, is it not? I remember it from boyhood. A lord and lady with the power to make kings.'

'We act it here, around Lent,' agreed Lynette. 'It's an old story. England's last magic. The Lord and Lady were England's fairy king and queen.'

'What happened to them?' asked Charlie.

Lynette waved a chubby hand. 'They sleep for one 'undred years. They're leading children like a pied-piper. Take your pick. It's a folk tale.'

Charlie turned to Percy. 'You told me Maria was transcribing a confession,' he said. 'It mentioned the Lord and Lady.'

Percy nodded. 'It was a criminal's last words before he was executed. The judge condemned him as a Royalist traitor against Cromwell's

Republic.' He frowned, remembering. 'It said something about a dress in a brothel. A dress to summon the Lord and Lady.'

Charlie turned to Lynette. 'You ever heard of that in your plays? A dress to summon them?'

Lynette shook her head.

Percy breathed out through his nose. 'It is God's curse on women to make them so curious,' he opined. 'She . . .' Percy was clearly struggling with the admission. 'Maria wanted to ask you about it.'

'Me?'

Percy's mouth had set into a thin tight line. 'She didn't go into detail. As I told you, we quarrelled. The confession she found spoke of a very unusual dress. Green and gold, stitched with leaves. Maria was convinced that if she found the dress, it could be used to find the Lord and Lady.'

Charlie sucked at his scarred lip.

'Why would she think that?' asked Percy, watching him carefully.

'I'm a thief taker,' said Charlie. 'I can use property to track people.'

'Maria was behaving strangely,' said Percy slowly, 'before she disappeared. Secretively. I asked her if she was thinking of calling the wedding off, but she denied it. So I . . .' He hesitated. 'I followed her one day.'

Charlie said nothing.

'We were about to be married,' said Percy hotly, catching his expression. 'I thought she might be . . . I thought she might be secretly meeting with you.'

'Why would you think that?'

'Even a country dolt hears things. I saw her go inside a bawdy house on Clarges Street.'

'Mother Mitchell's house,' Charlie filled in. He knew the high-end brothel well. Mother Mitchell had partially raised him, and Maria was known to the elderly madam.

Percy nodded. 'At first, I assumed she was meeting you there,' he said, his voice tight with confusion, 'then I concluded she was searching for this lost dress.'

'Looking for the Lord and Lady,' said Charlie thoughtfully. He was calling to mind the Maria he knew. 'She would never have believed in a lost fairy lord and lady.'

'She's from the country,' Percy pointed out. 'Many have seen fairies in those parts.'

'Maria has faith only in God above and things she can see with her own eyes,' said Charlie.

Percy made a tight nod of agreement. 'She was always very sensible,' he said with pride. 'Feet on the ground, yet . . .' Percy coughed. 'It seems she put herself in great danger.' His pale eyes were on Charlie again, hoping the thief taker would correct him.

'We'll find her,' said Charlie. He tapped his fingers together, feeling there was a connection he was missing. 'The bawdy house riots,' he said. 'Maria was looking for something in a brothel. Theatre and brothels . . . those professions often overlap.' Charlie thought for a moment. 'Better you lie low for a while,' he said to Lynette. 'It might be no coincidence that someone chose your theatre.'

Lynette laughed a loud unladylike guffaw. 'God's bones, Charlie! Do you think we'd shut down for this? There's another performance tonight and the devil 'imself wouldn't stop us.'

Charlie had forgotten how stubborn she was. He turned to Lynette. 'Promise me you'll be careful,' he said, squeezing her hand. 'If you're in the King's favour, you're a target.'

'Oh, Charlie,' said Lynette, 'you know full well I'll do no such thing.'

Chapter 15

The ship was magnificent, its bow a curving tower of twinkling glass windows and carved wood. The sound of music trickled from the deck. A party was taking place aboard.

A half-naked girl was hanging from the rigging. She was dressed as a mermaid, with seaweed plaited in her long hair and a necklace of shells wound around her bare torso. Her tail was a length of transparent silk tulle wound loosely around her legs.

'Permission to board!' called Charlie.

'You can board all of us together for the right price!' she shouted, making an impressively gymnastic manoeuvre on the rigging to give them a fuller view of her scanty costume.

Beside him in the rowing boat, Charlie heard Percy make a strange grunt of disapproval. A ladder was thrown down the side of the ship. They began to climb up.

Another girl appeared, giggling drunkenly. Her hair was held up by an expensively jewelled ivory comb and the rest of her perfect figure was painted in blue woad. Three more decorated mermaids joined her in quick succession, whooping and flashing an array of uncovered body parts.

'Hello, Charlie!' shouted one. 'We're havin' a party. Come join us. Best wine on the seven seas.' She burped and covered her mouth.

'Who's the cheap-wig?' demanded a blonde girl with her mermaid tail raised carelessly. She was examining Percy's pale demeanour, his tight-lipped absorption of the scene. 'We only fuck titles on this boat!' she shouted at him. 'Go back to Temple Bar with your legal pennies!'

'This is Maria's husband-to-be,' said Charlie, trying to dampen any high feeling.

'Is that so?' The blonde girl leaned to take a better look. 'Are hers as good as mine?' She staggered drunkenly, grabbing hold of the rail to steady herself with a shriek of laughter.

Charlie jumped easily aboard, then turned to help Percy, who was holding his wig awkwardly.

A larger figure appeared amongst the girls. Mother Mitchell.

Charlie smiled. As a boy, growing up under the madam's protection, she'd always reminded him of a great gaudy butterfly. Now she was more like an armada, the broad sails of her thickly embroidered dress buttressing her from male advances. Iron-grey curls were waxed like a helmet above her ageing good looks, and she was armoured in jewels; a battalion of expensive gold-mounted gems arrayed her neck, wrists and fingers.

'Hello, Charlie,' she said, moving towards him and holding his face in her hands. 'I hear you're light of purse,' she added, 'yet you've been working hard.' Mother Mitchell was looking at him keenly.

'Why should you be interested in such things?' Charlie smiled at her.

Mother Mitchell released his face from her perfumed fingers and adjusted the top of her thickly boned dress. 'You needn't think I check on you,' she said, fiddling in her pocket for her silver pipe. 'I only hear things. About where your money goes.'

'Then I daresay you know the answer.'

Mother Mitchell's mouth drew into a line. She tamped tobacco into the ornate pipe and glanced around for a candle. 'How can you even be sure it is your brother's child you pay for?' she asked. 'The mother is a Covent Garden strumpet.'

Percy was looking back and forth between Mother Mitchell and Charlie, fascinated. 'You pay for your brother's love child?' he deduced.

'My brother is dead,' said Charlie, shortly. 'You really need to be on a boat?' he added, turning to Mother Mitchell and pointedly changing the subject.

Mother Mitchell hesitated, then decided not to pursue her line of enquiry. 'Something dangerous in the air,' she said. 'I can smell it. These brothel attacks will turn nasty, you mark my words. Wanted my girls out of danger.'

With no candle close at hand, she returned the pipe to her hanging pocket.

'Can't you band together with the other wealthy brothels?' asked Charlie. 'Defend yourselves?'

'We don't get along,' said Mother Mitchell. She hitched her bosom and sniffed. 'There was a business with a black pudding,' she added obscurely. 'I shall never forgive.' She put her hands on his shoulders and drew back, assessing. 'What's wrong?'

'It's Maria,' said Charlie.

As he explained, Mother Mitchell looked increasingly concerned. When he'd finished, her small eyes turned to Percy. 'So this is the husband-to-be?' she said. 'I've heard about you.' Her tone suggested the meeting wasn't a pleasure.

Percy stood a little more upright. '*My* betrothed,' he said with an air of possessiveness, 'was known to you?' He drew himself tall. 'I *demand* to know the meaning of it.'

'She used to work for me,' said Mother Mitchell, amused. 'Acting parts.'

'*Acting?*' Percy's face was mask of horror.

65

'She didn't tell you?' asked Mother Mitchell innocently. 'She was good. So good I tried to arrange for the King to see her,' she added. 'Maria could have turned his interest. But you know her.' She directed this remark solely at Charlie. 'Always proper. After she was betrothed to be married she gave up acting.' Mother Mitchell shook her head with a frown, unable to comprehend such idiocy. She turned pointedly back to Charlie.

'Percy says she paid a visit to your house. When did you last see Maria?' asked Charlie.

Mother Mitchell frowned in concentration. 'Maria did come a few days ago. She seemed uneasy. Out of sorts. I assumed about her wedding,' she added, her eyes sliding again to Percy.

'Why do you say Maria wasn't herself?' asked Charlie.

Mother Mitchell's brows drew together. 'Everything and nothing,' she said. 'She wanted to try one of my dresses for her wedding. But the ones she considered' – her brow wrinkled again – 'they weren't in her style,' she concluded. 'Old. Out of fashion.'

'Did Maria ask about a dress with green-and-gold stitched leaves?' asked Charlie.

Mother Mitchell blinked. 'Why, yes she did. She talked of a design that sounded ancient. The kind that fairy-tale maidens wore. It's why I assumed she had cold feet. Maria is always so well dressed.'

'Maria *did not* have cold feet, as you vulgarly term it—' began Percy hotly.

'What about the Lord and Lady?' interrupted Charlie. He passed Mother Mitchell the strange poem they'd found. 'Did she say anything of the dress leading to them?'

Her eyes followed the writing, lips muttering words. Percy watched, quietly fuming.

'The Lord and Lady?' she said finally. 'That old story. Why should that concern Maria?'

'Maria found an old confession,' said Charlie. 'It suggested that a green-gold dress hidden in a brothel would lead to the Lord and Lady. We think Maria was looking for the dress.'

'Unusual for Maria to be investigating some ancient mystery,' observed Mother Mitchell, her eyes drifting again to Percy.

'What do you mean?' demanded Percy rudely.

'I only know rumours, same as other old Londoners,' shrugged Mother Mitchell. 'It was some dreadful war crime of Cromwell's. A lord and lady were sent to the Tower to be secretly burned alive, or that's how it was told. There were whispers someone smuggled them out, but no one believed it. Something about a butcher's son, I think. Or a baker's.'

'Were this lord and lady relations of the King?' asked Charlie.

Mother Mitchell shrugged again. 'I always assumed so. It was best not to talk of birthright and nobility during the Republic. People disappeared, didn't they? Whole families.'

'Yet if someone important survived,' said Charlie, 'surely they'd reveal themselves on the King's return?' He considered for a moment, then turned to Mother Mitchell. 'The dresses she was interested in; might we see them?'

Chapter 16

Amesbury looked up from his tankard to see the spy approach. The old general sat back on his stool and pulled another closer to him. This half-timbered little tavern was the safest place to conduct business without being overheard. Amesbury gestured towards a broad barrel as the other man sat.

'I'm tired of wine,' Amesbury said. 'I miss the fireside with the other soldiers. Real English beer.' He opened the tap and held a tankard underneath. It filled and frothed. He stood to fill a second for the spy then settled his great bulk back onto his stool. 'So?'

Amesbury was slightly drunk, the spy realised. Something was greatly troubling the old general.

'Your old soldier friends are safe,' said the spy. 'Arrived in New England. All Republicans there. No one will sell them out.'

Amesbury nodded.

The spy lifted his eyes to the old general. 'You play a dangerous game. Working for the King and yet rescuing his enemies.'

Amesbury's thick fists balled. 'His Majesty promised mercy,' he said. 'On his glorious return. It's the old nobles who clamour for blood.'

'Even so . . .'

'I fought with those men.' Amesbury's fist crashed on the table. 'You think I want to watch their balls cut off? They are men of courage and conviction who bought us a fairer country and they deserve a safe old age.'

The spy said nothing. He'd also seen the traitor executions of men promised clemency.

Amesbury drank more beer. 'What of the other matter?' he said.

'We found one of the suspects,' said the spy. 'Made him talk.'

Amesbury's eyebrows lifted slightly. 'And?'

'Mostly the same things. The King's rule is nothing from God. It was the fairies who gave the first monarchs the power of their earthly magic.'

Amesbury nodded, rolling his hand to suggest a story oft-told. 'Then good Puritans came and we killed the King and we burned his furs and jewels and melted his crown. His fairy lord and lady were flung into an iron prison, then we burned them in the hottest forge in the land. It's a good story.' He smiled faintly. 'Perhaps even one of my best stories. Better people believe the Lord and Lady fairies than guess at the truth. Anything else?'

The spy hesitated. 'There's another plot,' he said. 'You were right. Someone is using the brothel riots for an attempt on the Crown. They're organised.'

Amesbury frowned. 'What's the idea? Rile up a load of skinny boys and march on Whitehall? Sounds like a Royalist plan,' he added. 'Run in wearing a colourful coat with your long hair swinging. Hope for the best.'

'They were mad bastards,' agreed the spy. 'That's what comes of marrying your cousin ten times over.'

They both laughed. Then Amesbury picked up his tankard, turning it in his large hands. 'What else then?' he said, his smile dropping away.

'There's someone at the head of it.' The spy swallowed. 'We think Tom Black has returned.'

Amesbury's mouth set tight. 'Cromwell's assassin? You're sure?'

'Sure as we can be. He's a master of disguise, he's . . .'

Amesbury raised a thick hand. 'Spare me. I'm aware of his talents.' He rubbed his forehead. 'What I don't know,' he added meaningfully, 'is what he wants. Money and jewels mean nothing to Tom Black. He is incorruptible. Why do you think he was chosen to guard the Lord and Lady?'

The spy swallowed. 'One of the men from the Mint talked. The Lord and Lady weren't burned with the others.'

There was a long pause. Amesbury was sitting very still. 'Who else knows?'

'Only the man who carried the message. He's one of the King's guard.'

'You're sure? No one else?'

The spy nodded.

'Does he have history with the Republic?'

'He fought for Cromwell.'

'Kill him,' said Amesbury shortly.

'Sir, he has family . . .'

'Pay them off,' snapped Amesbury. 'If the Lord and Lady return, they could depose the King,' he said. 'The monarchy would collapse. I receive daily intelligence that the Dutch will invade at the slightest show of weakness and we have *nothing*.' He slammed his fist on the table again. 'No army, no navy. The money has all gone on the King's whores.' He eyed the spy. 'Come closer,' he said. 'Let me tell you a story.' Amesbury poured him another beer. 'Tom Black is cleverer than you could ever imagine,' he said. 'If he hunts the Lord and Lady he may well find them. And in the midst of these riots he could cause great mischief.' Amesbury stared into his tankard. 'If the King falls, it's all of us,' he said. 'Your head, mine. Every man who stood for the monarchy will spill their guts on the scaffold.' He tipped back his cup and drank deeply. 'Drink,' he instructed, nodding to his colleague's beer. 'These riots are no accident. You'll need it when I tell you what Tom Black is capable of.'

Chapter 17

Mother Mitchell led Charlie and Percy across the neat boards of the deck, where thick swags of ribbon and expensive rugs had been draped.

'Disgusting state these sailors sail in,' she opined. 'Took my girls near a week to scrub clean this deck and bail out the slop. The bilge in the bottom would turn your stomach.'

They passed an elaborate table of cold cuts and a huge silver bowl of punch.

'We're to have a bust of Venus fitted to the prow,' continued Mother Mitchell, 'and all these old interiors replaced. White pine from Sweden. Chantilly lace. I've a liking for boats,' she added. 'I'm thinking to turn this unrest to my advantage. Branch out.'

She led them into the captain's cabin, which was filled with untidily arranged trunks.

'There,' she said proudly. 'All the dresses of my house. Maria looked in there,' she added, moving to a trunk near the back. 'Plain things inherited from Mrs Jenks's house,' she said dismissively. 'Quite out of fashion.'

'Inherited?' Charlie raised an eyebrow.

'In fair compensation for business of mine she took,' said Mother Mitchell.

'You mean to stay you stole dresses from a rival?' Percy was shaking his head in disapproval.

'Mrs Jenks is more than a rival,' said Charlie. 'She's the doxy queen. Laid claim to Covent Garden and runs half the brothels there.'

'I think I've seen her parading in her carriage,' said Percy. 'An elderly woman with a lot of false hair and make-up.'

'I'll never hire south of the river again,' opined Mother Mitchell bitterly. 'Those stupid boys took the wrong trunk,' she added, throwing back the lid. 'As I say, they're all worthless old things.'

Charlie held up a few dresses. They were cheaply made and badly stitched. He took them out and examined them. But to his disappointment he found nothing unusual.

'Only old dresses,' he said.

Percy was frowning deeply, fists clenched. 'It's not like her,' he said. 'Why should Maria have been interested in a fairy tale? Some ancient mystery?'

'Isn't it obvious?' replied Mother Mitchell, looking at Charlie.

'Enlighten us,' he said.

Mother Mitchell laughed throatily. 'Perhaps Maria was searching for something about you, Charlie. Your past. What if she thinks this lost lord and lady are relations of yours?'

Charlie was surprised at the ricochet of emotions this suggestion awakened.

'You?' Percy was staring at Charlie, eyes roaming his bare feet and shabby leather coat. 'Why should you have noble relations?'

'I never knew my father,' said Charlie. 'He died at sea. My mother was murdered, leaving me this key.' He lifted the unusual key he carried around his neck. 'It led to some documents relating to the King.'

'Seems your family was born under a dark star,' said Percy with a sniff. 'And all kinds of people handle royal documents, myself included. It doesn't make me noble. Although my family has gentry claims,' he added hastily.

'It drove you apart, did it not?' asked Mother Mitchell, adjusting her bosom under its thick whalebone. 'Your mysterious lost family. Do you ever wonder why you feel compelled to help anyone who asks you? The little orphan boy who watched his mother die,' she added poetically, 'grows up to save all the poor victims of London's crime. Only you can never save them all, can you?'

Charlie felt a wave of terrible guilt. What if Maria had put herself in danger trying to discover the truth of his lost past?

'I don't think Maria was looking for something involving me,' he said, trying to sound more convincing than he felt. 'She knows how much I can deduce from clothing, even old clothing. Most likely she wanted to find the dress and have me track this lord and lady.'

'I don't think Maria found the dress she was searching for,' said Mother Mitchell grandly. 'She left to go looking elsewhere. Maria asked about one of your old flames, Charlie. A little gypsy thief named Lily Boswell.'

Chapter 18

Maria thought she might have been asleep. The world felt strange, slow-moving and thick. She'd been in the dark so long it was difficult to know.

Was there something in that mead?

Maria was seized with a sudden wild need to be free. She yanked at her restraints, heaving at the manacles. When the chains held firm, a guttural scream burst from her lungs and she kicked furiously. The scream turned to shaking sobs. And then she was suddenly, eerily calm. Her brain seemed to bob gently in her head, like a ship on a quiet sea.

Keep calm, Maria urged herself. *Be logical.*

She spread her bound hands, feeling for clues, trying to act methodically. There were floorboards beneath her, she was sure of it. Maria closed her eyes, listening. Charlie always said that the strangest thing to hear in London would be silence. He could identify any district by sound. The rag sellers along Cheapside, the paper-presses at St Pauls, the animal herds of Smithfield. But Maria could hear nothing but a faint ringing in her ears.

She shook her head in annoyance and the ringing grew louder.

There was a familiar dry smell on the air. She let images drift through her mind, trying to seize on where she'd encountered it before.

Thoughts seemed to come and go like feathers on the wind, soft and rolling away.

The answer flowered slowly. It was hemp she could smell. Maria remembered it from a trip to Bridewell Prison, where convicted prostitutes were forced to beat hemp. She'd been bringing food to the women prisoners. Percy hadn't approved.

For a moment, Maria thought she might be incarcerated in an isolated cell. Then she remembered. Bridewell had burned down during the Great Fire.

Now she heard approaching footsteps. Her stomach lurched.

Maria drew to mind what she knew of her captor. The pale skin and strange eyes. If he meant to kill her, she reasoned, why leave food?

The footsteps grew louder. Tramping over floorboards. Then a hatch opened, and she heard someone ascend a ladder.

I'm up high, she decided. *In some kind of attic.*

A blaze of light flared in the dark and she caught a sudden flash of her prison. Had she imagined it? The floor appeared to have been completely covered in snakes. Like some terrible portal of hell. She blinked, trying to call back the image of where she was, but her mind wasn't assisting. Thoughts kept sliding free.

A flame grew closer, bobbing at the end of a thin wax taper. It revealed him by degrees. The jet-black hair and strangely old eyes. She'd remembered him as passably attractive, but the thought was shocking to her now. Up close his skin was thin and waxen, as though the muscles beneath it had wasted away. The blue-green eyes were pale-rimmed, with clumps of the dark eyelashes missing. Up close he looked shocking.

'You are very interesting to watch,' he said eventually. There was a silence as he peered at her. 'I forget myself,' he said. 'You must be introduced. I am Tom Black.'

Maria said nothing.

'You don't want me to know you are afraid,' he decided. 'You give yourself away, of course. Fear and pain are two of the easiest.'

'Why do you keep me here?' she demanded.

'I need Charlie Tuesday's services,' said Tom. 'You are a means to keep him engaged.'

'You think he'll find you the Lord and Lady?' asked Maria. 'He won't. Charlie would never help you bring down England . . .' She stopped.

Tom was blinking at her in confusion. 'You think I mean to use the Lord and Lady to dispossess the King?'

'What other motive could a man like you have?'

He shook his head. 'My plans are far . . . humbler.'

'Then what?'

'I am a changeling,' said Tom. 'A fairy. My own kind swapped me for a human child. I was raised as a cuckoo in the nest. Only my mother knew the truth.' His face darkened. 'The Lord and Lady can send me back,' said Tom. 'They have the power to let me go home.' The idea of this seemed beautiful to him.

'Old magic,' said Maria, suddenly understanding. 'They can open the door to the fairy place.'

He nodded. 'It would only take a touch of the Lady's magic girdle,' he said, 'a nod of the Lord's sacred head. Think of their powers.' He closed his eyes. 'I've dreamed of it. The fairy kingdom. I have no place here. I've tried so hard to become one of you, but it does not stick. I've learned every nuance of your strange emotions and still they make no sense to me. You are so . . . confusing.' He closed his eyes and shook his head. 'Such an unpredictable species. One moment rational, the next letting your feelings run you into unspeakable foolishness.' His eyes opened. 'Consider our situation,' he added. 'If Charlie Tuesday does not bring me the Lord and Lady before Good Friday, my chance to return will have passed.' He blinked. 'I would take no pleasure in killing you. But it would be a necessity.'

Chapter 19

On the luxurious ship, Mother Mitchell was eyeing Percy triumphantly. The deck beneath them rolled slightly on the swell.

'I wondered why might Maria have been asking after one of Charlie's women,' she said archly, 'if she didn't have wedding fears?'

Percy had turned deep red.

'Lily Boswell is not an old flame,' corrected Charlie. 'She's a spy for the King and I found her services valuable. We worked together once upon a time. And she's long gone. I last saw her aboard a ship set for the high seas.'

'Yet *I* hear she's back in London,' said Mother Mitchell. 'Sunk her ship, came back with her tail between her legs,' she added with obvious satisfaction. Lily had once worked at Mother Mitchell's house and had run away with a valuable suitor – a crime for which the old madam held a lifelong animosity. 'She's working in Ozinda's, in St James's,' concluded Mother Mitchell. 'How the mighty have fallen.'

'The chocolate house?' asked Charlie. 'A brothel by any other name?'

Mother Mitchell nodded. 'Think themselves exotic,' she said. 'They imagine Lily a dark-skinned beauty. They'll soon find out when she steals their best silks.' She smiled smugly. 'Once a gypsy, always a gypsy.'

'So Lily's working in a bawdy house, of sorts,' said Charlie. He called to mind the ludicrously priced Ozinda's, with its decorated tables full of actresses and beautiful women.

'Girls for talking to only,' snorted Mother Mitchell. 'As if an actress would not lift her skirts for a farthing.'

Percy was blinking hard, trying to follow the conversation. 'Who is Lily Boswell?' he demanded.

'An old friend,' said Charlie, keeping his tone neutral.

Mother Mitchell made a noise that could have been 'bollocks'.

Percy's eyes bulged. 'You've . . . fornicated with this woman? And she's the only person who can help us?'

'She doesn't hold grudges,' said Charlie untruthfully.

Percy was shaking his head in disgust. 'Is there any woman in London you don't have carnal knowledge of?'

'A disappointingly large number.' Charlie's scarred lip twisted in concentration. 'Maria reads about a lost dress in an old confession she's transcribing,' he said, sifting what he knew methodically. 'First she comes to Mother Mitchell. Then she asks for Lily. Both high-end whorehouses.'

Percy curled his lip, disgusted any distinction had been made. 'A whorehouse is a whorehouse,' he said.

'Maybe in Bumpkinville,' said Mother Mitchell, running a disdainful eye over Percy's provincial suit. 'In London we divide it up.' She listed on her ringed fingers. 'Damaris Page takes the sailors and dockers in the east. Mrs Jenks has the theatregoers in Covent Garden. And I have the west,' she concluded proudly. 'The nobs and the royalty.'

'Ozinda's doesn't open until nightfall,' said Charlie. 'That's hours away.' He took out the paper again and stared at it, willing an answer to present itself.

'You said,' said Charlie, turning to Mother Mitchell, 'that the story of the Lord and Lady might involve a butcher or a baker's son?'

She nodded.

He thought for a moment. Facts were sliding together but as yet nothing was making sense.

A lord and lady.

The double-twist noose.

'The noose,' said Charlie with sudden certainty. 'I remember where I've seen it before. It's a butcher's truss. A rope for hanging carcasses.' He thought a moment more. 'You only find rope like that in the Shambles.'

'The slaughtering district?' supplied Percy.

Charlie nodded. 'Behind Cow Lane. Where Cromwell got his best soldiers. Almost all fought against the King.' He extracted the bloodied piece of rope from his pocket. 'I'll go to the Shambles first,' he decided. 'Ask some questions. Maybe someone knows something.'

Percy was bristling. 'You *can't* think of visiting the Shambles. It's a hotbed of men who want to overthrow the King.'

'Can you blame them?' said Charlie. 'They work twelve hours a day to stop their children starving. They never wanted the King back. Now they pay hearth tax so Lady Castlemaine might buy more jewels.'

'You want to question blood-soaked Republicans with meat cleavers? I will not step one foot—' began Percy.

Charlie held up his hands. 'I wouldn't suggest you do,' he said. 'A lawyer would hardly live to tell the tale. Go back to Temple Bar. I'll come find you when I have something worth telling.'

Percy snorted derisively. 'If you come out of the Shambles at all,' he replied. 'It's a fool's errand.'

'I must take action,' said Charlie. 'Whoever took Maria demanded the Lord and Lady by Good Friday. That's three days away. I have three days to find two people who are probably long dead if they ever existed at all.'

Mother Mitchell put a ringed hand on his shoulder. 'If anyone can do it, it's you.'

Chapter 20

Women streamed from the building screaming, sobbing, clutching at ripped clothing. A great pyre of broken possessions was amassing from items hurled from windows.

'No!' a woman's voice was shouting. 'Not the basin! It doesn't belong to me!'

Two apprentices were holding the brothel-keeper as she struggled. Her hair was dishevelled and the thick circles of rouge on her cheeks were sliced with tears. She blinked in disbelief as a blue-aproned boy brought a flaming torch and set light to the broken things. A savage cheer went up from the apprentices. The brothel-keeper gave a wail of despair.

Repent was watching the women, lips slightly parted, his breathing a little too hard. One of the apprentices was dragging a prostitute from the house by her hair. Her dress was open at the front, bare breasts swaying loose. Repent tilted his head, the ghost of a smile playing on his thin lips. He walked towards the house.

At the window, a group of wild-eyed youths were hurling beautiful furnishings. An ornately carved chair exploded into pieces on the hard cobbles. A decorated porcelain wash-basin smashed beside it, and then a matching hand-painted jug.

'Do you regret it now?' grinned a boy. 'This life of sin?'

The brothel-keeper said nothing, staring blankly at what had once been her property.

From the top floor two men were hurling dress after heavy silken dress. They flopped like ghostly suicides onto the muddy street below.

Barebones watched the dresses. Then his eyes roamed the apprentices and stilled.

Repent had a woman pinned to the wall, a knife at her throat. One of his thin hands was under her skirts.

'Repent!' Barebones was next to him in a few short strides.

'I was teaching this harlot the price of her sin,' he said, but his hands fell back all the same and the girl fled, crying.

Barebones put his hands on Repent's shoulders. The boy looked up at him, his young frame tall and thin to his father's soldier's muscle.

'I did no wrong,' muttered Repent, toying with the cross at his neck.

Barebones looked carefully into his son's face. 'Good,' he said after a moment. 'Good. We will uproot the evil at the heart of it.' He fingered the iron sword at his hip. 'We will kill the Lord and Lady. Together.'

Barebones strolled to the front of the mounting pile and turned to the brothel-keeper. 'Perhaps you have something to tell us?' he said. 'We know you hid the Lord and Lady during the civil war. We know they came through your house.'

The brothel-keeper shook her head. 'Cromwell's men came already,' she said. 'Years ago, many times. I told them then. We never hid them here. We're no Royalists.'

'You are every inch a Royalist,' said Barebones with thick contempt. 'Cromwell's rule was a time of safety and sobriety. No acting. No parties. No gaudy clothing. It was . . .' He closed his eyes and breathed deeply. 'A good time. We made laws for the good of the people, not to feather a mad king's army, or dress a selfish queen in pearls and gold.'

Barebones held up a silk dress and dropped it onto the pyre, eyes blazing. 'Women like you,' he said, 'broke the Republic.'

'No!' she shouted. 'That's my business you burn!'

'You send your girls in their finery, flaunting themselves,' said Barebones. 'You condemn men to hell.' He looked around at the destruction. 'But you may keep a few things. I could persuade the boys. If you tell me what I want to know.'

She watched as a box shattered open on the ground, spilling marzipan sweets. Apprentices fell on it, stuffing their mouths hungrily.

'I don't know nothing!' gabbled the brothel-keeper. 'I swear it . . . I . . .'

Barebones nodded at the boys. More dresses were hurled onto the pyre. There was a strange hissing shriek as the silk caught light.

The brothel-keeper sagged. 'There was a dress,' she admitted. 'An old one. Like you said.'

Barebones gripped her tightly.

'It looked like a fairy thing,' continued the brothel-keeper. 'All green stitched leaves, hanging ribbons and gossamer-fine.'

'What else?' growled Barebones.

'I don't well remember,' stuttered the brothel-keeper. 'Only it was old. Very old. It was supposed to lead to the Lord and Lady. Or summon them. That's all I know, I swear. I thought it nothing but a story.'

Barebones frowned. 'Where?'

'In one of the high-ups,' said the brothel-keeper. 'Mrs Jenks's on Chiswell Street. But it was years ago. It will be long gone . . .'

Barebones moved closer. 'Chiswell Street. You're certain?'

She nodded.

'Interesting,' said Barebones. He turned to the apprentices.

'Burn everything here,' he said. 'Pull the house to tinder sticks. We must pay a visit to Mrs Jenks at the Golden Apple.'

Chapter 21

The Shambles was a broad blood-soaked dirt road stretching behind Cow Lane and Smithfield Market. To the south, the ramshackle shops of Milk Street and Bread Street were only just beginning to be rebuilt after the fire. But the Shambles' thick-armed butchers had quickly re-erected their pole-and-awning abattoirs and resumed slaughtering and gutting.

Two butchers were dragging a squealing pig by its hind legs. Amongst the covered stalls were ragged flags of the New Model Army. The Shambles was a Puritan stronghold, long after Cromwell's death.

Women still wore black and covered over their hair with modest white caps. The single workmanlike tavern bore the sign of a crown, roughly painted over with the leafy head of a Green Man.

Charlie's eyes lighted on a butcher's stall where the carcasses of wild pigs hung, and he drew to a halt. The butcher didn't look up.

'You supply the palace with meat?' said Charlie.

'They got their own butcher,' he said, 'at the palace. No call for the likes of us.' He wiped his brow on the bloody sleeve of his shirt, put his knee in the centre of the carcass and snapped the spine with an audible crunch of cartilage.

Charlie winced. 'Those wild pigs are from Hyde Park,' he countered, nodding to the rack of pigs hung behind him. 'Commoners don't have licence to hunt on the King's land in summer.'

The butcher raised his heavy knife, took aim and drove the blade through bone. 'If you can prove I broke a law, then come back with a watchman,' he said.

'I'm trying to find out more about a lord and lady,' tried Charlie, 'who went missing during the war.'

The butcher shook his head. 'We're common folk here,' he said. 'Don't know nothing 'bout no nobles.'

'What about fairies?' asked Charlie. 'A fairy lord and lady?'

The butcher looked up fiercely. 'Who's asking?' he demanded.

'I'm Charlie Tuesday,' replied Charlie. 'I've helped some folk from hereabouts with stolen property . . .'

'Any lord or lady from before the war are long dead. We don't like questions here in the Shambles. Best you be on your way.' The butcher drove the blade into the notched chopping board and glared.

'My friend has gone missing,' said Charlie, choosing his words carefully. 'Someone very dear to me. I think—'

'Best you be on your way.' The butcher resumed his chopping with a final, heavy-handed air.

Charlie hesitated. 'I can pay,' he said.

The butcher's deep-set eyes flicked up. 'I've never been practised at keeping my temper,' he said. 'And I don't much care if you are Mr Tuesday or Wednesday or Thursday. I've turned this blade to harder uses during the civil war. Begone before I take up my old soldiering.'

Charlie turned reluctantly to leave, but as his bare feet hit the bloody dirt of the main thoroughfare he heard a woman's voice.

'Shame on you, Samuel Cleaver! We are good Christians here.'

Charlie turned back to see a chubby woman had emerged from the little shack.

'Mr Tuesday! Wait.' She turned her round face towards Charlie.

He returned to the stall, expression hopeful. The woman was a wet-nurse, judging from the overlapping circular stains on her woollen dress and her faintly cheesy aroma.

'I know who you are, and my husband forgets your kind services,' she said. 'But we repay our debts here. We are not Dutch.' She glowered at her husband, who seemed to have shrunk in size since the emergence of his wife.

'Tom Black's father was his cousin,' she added apologetically. 'One of the old King's generals stuck a pike through him at the Battle of Naseby. He's never got over it.'

'Tom Black?' asked Charlie.

'The butcher's son they talk of,' said the woman patiently. 'Kin to the lost lord and lady. That's who you speak of, is it not? You're not the first to come looking,' she added. 'Though I'm not sure we can help you a great deal.'

'A man named Tom Black was related to the lost lord and lady?' asked Charlie, his heart racing a little faster.

'You'll never find Tom Black,' grunted the butcher. 'Not if you search a thousand years. He went to work for Cromwell. Dark things. There's a price on his head.'

The wet-nurse cast an affectionate look at her husband and Charlie tried unsuccessfully to imagine a sentimental heart beneath the butcher's bloody apron.

'He's right,' she said. 'Tom Black vanished without a trace after the war. Same time as the Lord and Lady.'

Chapter 22

In the butchers' district a haze of flies was winding lazily from the blood-soaked ground. The sudden screech of a pig being slaughtered rang through the air.

'You think the Lord and Lady were relations of Tom Black?' pressed Charlie, trying to ignore the sounds of butchering.

'We-ell,' considered the wet-nurse, 'it was talked of, wasn't it, Sam? But we never believed it. Tom wasn't related to no fine gentleman. You could tell just by looking.' The wet-nurse nodded, pleased with the revelation.

'Did he have any friends?' asked Charlie. 'Any connections or relatives in the city besides the Shambles?'

'He was a strange boy. I think he did a little carpentry for the theatre or something of that nature. I heard one of the playwrights took pity on him. Tom was never going to become a butcher like his father.' She gave her husband a meaningful glance. 'Tom was a born villain and liar. Same as his mother.'

'His mother wasn't from hereabouts?' asked Charlie.

'No. Daughter of beekeepers on Honey Lane. Married one of ours.' She lowered her voice. 'But we knew, didn't we, Sam? We all knew.

There was always talk about Bridey. That was how the rumours about Tom started, wasn't it, Sam?'

The butcher grunted non-committally.

'Bridey did *acting*,' said the wet-nurse with a knowing wink. 'Took part in the mystery plays, all kinds of men looking.' Her mouth was set in tight disapproval. 'Sam knew her,' added the wet-nurse, 'when she were a young maid on Honey Lane.'

'All the young men had a turn on Bridey,' said Sam, a slow blush creeping up his thick neck.

'She made him do playacting, during the business,' guffawed the wet-nurse. 'Him, fifteen and mad with green-lust.'

'Bridey always seemed too young for a woman's body,' said Sam, with more sensitivity than Charlie might have credited him.

'What was it she had you do?' crowed his wife. 'A fairy lord, wasn't it?'

Sam was silent, chopping his meat with more force than necessary. Charlie noticed the blush had reached his cheeks.

'She was set up higher than she should have been, on account of her good looks,' continued the wet-nurse. 'The family was devastated when she fell pregnant by a butcher.' The wet-nurse leaned forward. 'Bridey certainly thought herself fine. I remember thinking, she'll never last here. She'll never make blood puddings like the rest of us. I was right about that. Wasn't I, Sam?'

'Aye.' The butcher didn't take his eyes from the block.

'What happened to her?' asked Charlie.

'Oh, she turned lunatic after Tom was born.' The wet-nurse paused, remembering. 'We all heard a terrible commotion. Just after dawn. Bridey, that's Tom's mother, runs out screaming. Hysterical. Shouting fairies have stolen her baby. I went in. And I think she's turned mad. The babe is right there in the crib, crying its little red head off. I say, "Your babe is here. Can't you hear him? Why don't you go to him?"

'She says, "No. That's not my baby." I'll never forget the look in her eyes. "*That's not my baby*," Bridey says. "Can you not see? The fairies have taken him. That's a changeling child."

'I peer into the crib. I'm a simple God-fearing woman. Tom's a pretty babe to be sure. But I do think there's something not right with the child. His eyes seem too old for a baby. Now I'm uneasy. And I think perhaps there *is* something pixie-like about that little pointed nose.

'"No," I say, "it's your babe." But I cross myself all the same, because it seems the devil is in him, he screams so. Bridey sees the gesture, though, and starts up worse than before.

'"You see it," she says. "They've taken him. The fairies have taken my baby and left me that."' The wet-nurse shifted her large bosom around. 'We don't hear much of them after that,' she concluded. 'All us Shambles women know the truth. It's guilt, isn't it? On account of how she got with the baby.

'Whenever mother and babe are out the child's eyes are pinned open, roving around with that peculiar way he always had. Not quite looking at you. The child doesn't smile. Doesn't laugh. Only watches. The talk is, Bridey's been told changeling tricks. To make the fairies take back their own.' She nodded with satisfaction.

'What kind of tricks?'

'I don't know,' said the woman, 'but there were always strange marks on the boy.' She squinted at him. 'Are you quite well, Mr Tuesday?'

Charlie realised the corners of his mouth were pulled hard down. 'You say the whole family was killed?' he asked.

She nodded. 'I believe so. The father and brother in the civil war. They fought for Cromwell. Like all of us in the Shambles.' She glanced proudly at her husband.

'What of the mother?'

The wet-nurse blinked slowly. 'Bridey disappeared,' she said. 'Fell back to whoring herself, so they say. She'll be dead of the pox. Aye,' said the wet-nurse pleasantly. 'She'll be burning now for her crimes against that poor babe.'

And with the sun setting, Charlie realised that his next move needed to be the one he'd been dreading. Ozinda's would now be open and with it he would have his chance to go and see the last person Maria had spoken to before she disappeared. It was time to pay a visit to Lily Boswell. Charlie had last seen Lily setting sail, without the treasure they'd hoped to find. He had a bad feeling she wouldn't be pleased to see him.

Chapter 23

Tom Black was staring keenly at Maria's face. She looked back, fighting the instinct to drop her gaze. He lowered the flame, and Maria quickly tried to absorb everything she could of the room again. It was a cheap taper, giving off a smoky glow, barely illuminating beyond her circle of confinement. The light danced tantalisingly.

At first, she saw the snakes again. Hundreds of them, coiled everywhere. Then her mind seemed to clear, and she made the connection. Ropes. It was ropes she could see. The floor was covered in them. The smell made sense now. Bridewell prostitutes beat hemp for rope.

'I enjoyed it hugely, seeing you act,' said Tom. 'You have a subtlety of expression that is fascinating. But we must not forget what the theatre is. It is a doorway. For the fairy folk.'

Maria said nothing. Her tongue felt thick in her mouth, her heartbeat strangely slow. She tried to think. A rope-makers? It was the only place she could imagine with so many lengths of rope all in one place. But a rope-makers had a long trough to turn the hemp in and neatly stacked coils for sale. She'd only caught a brief glimpse of the floor, but it had seemed chaotic. Ropes heaped in piles all over. And stretching up to hang on the walls as well.

'You're trying to work out where you are,' said Tom. 'I can see that, but it won't help you.' He hesitated. 'You don't like the dark?' he asked.

Maria swallowed and shook her head.

'I am sorry for it. I'm not accustomed to . . . mortal visitors. I myself have no great need for food and light. But I shall be sure you have a candle.'

Tom raised the taper with a pallid hand. His fingernails were flaking away, Maria noticed, greenish in colour in the half-light. She'd seen the same thing happen to malnourished street children and wondered if her captor existed on the same diet of honey cakes he'd left her.

'Might I have a pail of water?' asked Maria. 'For washing?'

'No water.' His voice was high and strange. 'It is a way they can get in.' His fingers began tapping on themselves. 'I watched you,' he said. 'I saw you go to Mother Mitchell's house. You wouldn't have noticed me,' he added. 'I have a way of making myself' – he looked up at the ceiling – '*invisible*.' His blue-green eyes settled back on her face with a sudden intensity. 'I was watching, waiting, when the old papers were sent to lawyers to be transcribed,' he said. 'You understood the Royalist confession was a coded message. How?'

Maria frowned, trying to keep track of the conversation. Then she realised what Tom meant. The old confession she'd transcribed for Percy.

'I . . . Something about how it was written,' she said. 'It didn't read like other confessions.'

'You realised the condemned man was trying to get a message to his fellow Royalists?' pressed Tom.

'Not at first. And then . . . some of the meaning became clear.'

'You understood it?'

Maria nodded. 'My family is minor gentry,' she said. 'Was,' she corrected herself. 'Our fortunes changed, after the war. But I was raised to know of kings and their sons. In the country we call the Lord and Lady "The Old Ones", out of respect to their being related to kings. I realised a condemned man was trying to leave a clue.'

'You knew what they were? The Lord and Lady?'

Maria nodded.

'And you decided to investigate without telling your lawyer husband?'

'Husband-to-be,' Maria corrected. 'It started as a game.' Her eyes lifted to his. 'Then I discovered things. And somehow I couldn't stop.' She toyed with the hem of her dress. 'I suppose they had me in their thrall.' She smiled. Tom didn't smile back.

'I always suspected the needless confession was some kind of code,' he said. 'What I didn't count on was how long it would take to make public record.'

'Cromwell's death and the King's return brought legal work to a standstill,' said Maria, realising. 'Court documents take months to be made official record, but with a regime change . . .'

'Eight years,' said Tom.

'But you didn't search for them,' said Maria. 'Did something happen to you? After you failed Cromwell?'

Tom nodded tightly. He was running his thumbs along his knuckles. Maria noticed they were covered in thin scars. They were the kind of lacerations that came from shattered glass, she thought, but there were perhaps too many of them for that to be likely.

'You are very strange for a woman,' Tom decided. 'Too clever.'

Maria found herself smiling. There was an innocence about her captor. 'That's what Percy says,' she admitted.

'Your betrothed doesn't enjoy your intelligence?'

'No. Maybe that's why I was trying to find the dress,' she admitted. 'Investigating the old spy networks was a last little bit of excitement before married life.'

'Or perhaps you were trying to win Charlie Tuesday's admiration?'

'I try no such thing.'

'You made a detour on your wedding day,' Tom pointed out. 'Reckless, which from my observations is unlike you. You're the kind of person who tells the grocer when they've given you a half-pence-worth of extra soap.'

'Charlie is my friend,' said Maria defensively.

'You're a liar!' The shout came suddenly. Tom covered his mouth with his peeling fingernails and closed his eyes. 'You mustn't lie,' he said, his voice calmer. 'It is how they get in.' He scanned the room. 'They love tricks and games. You mustn't lure them.' His eyes settled back on her. His fingers played a little dance on his palms. 'But now is the time. They want to be found. The King's gaudy lies and depraved court, they call to the Lord and Lady. They will dance all night to fairy bells and drink only wine and dine on sweet cakes.'

Maria had a sudden awful memory of the dead girl. Her changeling. 'The girl,' she whispered, swallowing hard. 'The hanging girl. Was she dead?'

Tom seemed mildly surprised. 'I sent her to the other place,' he explained. 'The fairy place. She'll be dancing, even now, as we speak.'

Maria felt her throat constrict. 'Why?' she managed.

'You cannot take people, not without an exchange. That would make them . . . unhappy. He wouldn't like it. He can be' – Tom frowned – 'very cruel.'

'Who is he?'

'The boy,' said Tom patiently. 'The boy who was taken.'

'What boy?'

'The changeling,' said Tom. 'The one whose place I took.'

'You . . . You see this boy?' ventured Maria. 'He visits you?'

'He is behind the mirror,' said Tom. 'The first time he came, she was hurting me. I remember fire. Burning. Pain.' He rubbed at his forearm. 'I saw him in the copper kettle. The boy.' Tom paused, remembering. 'Then he took me inside, with him. There was no pain there, in the fairy place,' said Tom. 'Then the boy whispered to me. He said he wanted to come out. There was a ringing of bells and it was cold again. I was lying on the floor. My arm hurt.'

Maria felt a rush of sympathy for him. 'Your mother did changeling tricks?' she asked. 'Hurt you, to try to make the fairies take you back?'

Tom frowned. 'It never worked. The boy stayed in the world of the fairies.' He glanced up at Maria. 'It's changed him,' he admitted. 'He's become cruel, over the years, like them.' Tom pursed his lips. 'He used to protect me. Now he torments me. Makes me do his bidding.'

'You're frightened,' said Maria, understanding. 'You have to do what he says.'

'I have no fears he will harm me,' said Tom. 'But he might make me do something . . . disorderly. The smell of blood and death disturb me greatly.'

'What do you think he could make you do?' asked Maria.

'I think he's taken against you,' said Tom matter-of-factly. 'I think he wants you hanged and gutted.'

Chapter 24

Ozinda's signature blend of cocoa, cinnamon, vanilla and jasmine wafted along the wide-paved streets of St James's. There were crystal street lamps outside handsome brick mansions and a neat green. On the grass, a boy in a suspiciously clean shepherd's outfit was spritzing a cluster of dozing sheep with oily perfume from a hand-operated pump.

As always, the broad pavements of the gentrified district made Charlie uneasy. He preferred an alley or lane to duck down.

The heavy chocolate smell grew more intense as Charlie passed by into the luxurious entrance hall, brightly painted with murals of exotic jungle and cocoa trees. Ozinda's was a mansion house, with high windows and stylish fittings. Sitting at the back was a crowd of women dressed in various exotic costumes. There was a Turk in an open-fronted dress and turban and an African queen in a gaudy gold headdress and see-through white chiffon dress.

An immaculately dressed man stepped forward. 'Welcome to Ozinda's,' he said without warmth. 'I presume you have an account with us?'

'Since I'm certain you memorise every visitor,' said Charlie, 'you'll know I don't. I'm here to see Lily Boswell. She's . . . a friend of mine,' he finished lamely.

'We're not a tavern,' said the man. 'If you want to speak with her you must buy her drink. That's the rules of the house. The gypsy's price is a flagon of burgundy. One guinea.' He took in Charlie's patched breeches and well-worn coat. 'And you, friend,' he said, 'look not to have that kind of coin about you.'

They were interrupted by the entrance of two peacock aristocrats, resplendent in plumes of frothy lace, bright ribbons and shining buckles.

The manager was suddenly all smiles, pushing Charlie to one side. 'Gentlemen,' he beamed, clicking his fingers impatiently at a servant loitering in the background. 'You come to us early. Will it be the usual table? Burgundy?'

'The apprentices are out in force,' grumbled one, adjusting his powdered wig and causing a drift to dislodge like falling snow. 'Half the bawdy places in the east have been pulled apart.'

'No fear of apprentices here,' said the manager, his false smile never shifting. 'Who shall it be? Elizabeth again?'

'Only have her a little more lively this time,' said the first, taking a snuff box from his coat and inhaling deeply.

'She was acting at the Duke's all last week,' apologised the manager. 'I'll be sure she is all smiles for you.'

He glared in the direction of the assembled women and a familiar actress rose in an eddy of perfumed skirts, painted mouth drawn tightly upwards, a loose approximation of a dress falling off her bare shoulders. Both men instantly brightened. Once they were seated, the manager returned his attention to Charlie, all pretence of civility gone.

'Don't look to the girls,' he snapped haughtily, as Charlie tried to spot Lily. 'Unless you can afford some accord with one.'

Charlie saw her, sitting alone throwing cards. Lily had been dressed as a native American, in a thin red cotton dress that tied at her waist and crossed to cover her bust. She was as strikingly beautiful as he remembered, her long dark hair falling haphazardly amongst a thick collection of charms and trinkets strung around her neck. Her ring-decked fingers shuffled cards rapidly with a restless energy that reminded Charlie of an animal trapped in a cage.

There was a clear space between her table and the others.

A passing drunk man shot a leering glance down her low-cut red dress and she glared at him until he looked away.

'She knows me,' said Charlie, pointing to Lily.

'That's your hard luck,' opined the manager. 'If it was up to me, I'd have sent her away long ago. But she's popular in her way. Some men love danger.'

'Only ask her. She'll spare me a moment.'

The manager shook his head. 'No exceptions.'

'How about I give you a shilling just to pass a message?' tried Charlie.

The manager considered, then held out his hand for the coin. 'You're lucky it's Lent,' he said, pocketing it. 'No one looking for much in the way of sin. I'll ask.'

Charlie let out a sigh of relief. The manager clicked his fingers and nodded meaningfully to an over-worked boy racing around the tables.

'The gypsy,' said the manager. 'This man claims to be her friend.'

The boy looked alarmed at this possibility, but ventured nervously towards Lily nevertheless. She looked up from her cards, then glanced across at Charlie. Her expression soured, and she shook her head.

'Hard luck,' said the manager. 'She doesn't want to talk to you.'

'Might I not just take a drink with her?' asked Charlie. 'A full barrel of burgundy can be got for a shilling.'

'Not in Ozinda's,' replied the manager. 'Take your leave.'

He tilted his head towards the door. As if by magic a heavy-set guard lumbered over, his white silk waistcoat and jaunty yellow silk cravat straining at his thick middle and bullish neck.

'Wait!' protested Charlie. But the guard took this as a sign to begin manhandling him out.

Charlie was fruitlessly trying to resist the wall of muscle. 'A moment, please,' said Charlie, addressing the manager. 'You collect Royalist things, do you not? War mementos?'

The manager frowned.

'I'm a dealer in such things,' lied Charlie. 'So I notice your buttons are from the coat of a cavalier soldier and your snuff jars were once owned by a Royalist household.' He paused for effect. 'And it's just your good fortune I came across a sacred royal relic,' Charlie concluded, hoping he sounded persuasive. 'Only yesterday.'

The manager raised a hand and the guard halted, still holding Charlie by the collar.

Charlie delved into his pocket and pulled free the bloodied strand of rope in his coat, pocketed from the theatre corpse.

'I took this from a Cheapside thief,' said Charlie. 'Before she met her end on the gallows, she admitted to stealing it. A strand of rope,' he concluded grandly, 'that once bound the hands of the late King Charles, before he lost his head.'

The manager leaned towards the bloodied rope. He took it reverently. 'This is his blood?' he asked. 'His Majesty's?' His hand quivered slightly.

Charlie nodded. 'Worth a bit, a trinket like that, to the right person,' he added pointedly.

'Blood looks fresh,' observed the guard suspiciously.

'Which proves it's royal blood,' supplied Charlie quickly. 'Keeps its colour. Not like the common sort.'

The manager made a rapid benediction and kissed the rope. 'Very well,' he said. 'I'll give you one glass of wine with the gypsy.'

'A true Royalist would pay a guinea for a memento like this,' replied Charlie smoothly. 'That's a full barrel.'

The manager's eyes shifted to Lily, who was now watching them with interest.

'The lady don't seem to like you,' he said. 'Two glasses is all I'll give.'

Charlie looked over to Lily. 'A bottle,' he said, closing the manager's hands over the bloody rope. 'She's likely to throw at least two glasses in my face.'

Chapter 25

Lynette was lying on thick linen sheets, tracing her fingers across the King's broad chest.

'This one?' She touched on a raised mark.

'I fell from a horse escaping Roundheads.'

Her fingers danced down to the next scar. 'This?'

'Yachting with James. The prow caught me.'

'You're quite the adventurer.'

'I was.'

'And what about your feet?' she added. 'I've never seen such a mess.'

He drew up his mangled feet, the undersides criss-crossed with thick raised scars.

'I was escaping from Cromwell,' he said. 'I lost my boots and had to run five miles through scrub forest barefoot.'

Lynette winced. 'Must 'a hurt,' she said sympathetically.

'They'd just killed my father,' said Charles. 'I didn't really feel it until afterwards.'

'I'm sorry,' she said.

'Be sorry for my brother,' he said. 'Poor young James had to escape England dressed as a girl. I'd take scarred feet over that indignity any day.'

She tilted her head, not quite believing his casual tone. 'So tell me the truth,' she said. 'Why did your thick-skinned old soldier send for me?'

'Amesbury?' Charles laughed. 'He thought you would lift my mood. He's good like that.'

'I'm sure he is.' She narrowed her eyes, assessing. 'Did you know,' she said carefully, 'the apprentices are running hotter than usual? Lot of the girls are afraid, really afraid. They need protectin'.'

Charles sat up in the large bed, reached for their wine goblets, poured two and handed her one.

'I thought we were talking about war stories,' he said. 'My brave escape from Cromwell's soldiers.'

'And what about your other stories?' she said.

'Oh, everyone knows everything about me,' he said easily. 'I don't even shit without a man to attend me.'

Lynette took the smallest of sips and lowered the goblet.

'You don't drink?' he said, watching her hands.

'Not anymore,' she admitted. 'Led me to bad places. Me old mum died of it.'

Her eyes rested on his face. She let her fingers drift up to his chin. 'Who'd ever believe it,' she said. 'Me, in bed with a king. Tell me true, was it my acting, or the parts where I wore less clothes?'

He rested back, a smile on his face. 'There was a particularly good play with you and Sissy Leech.'

'She's a friend of mine,' said Lynette. 'More like a sister. It would be incest.'

'You've not spent enough time with royalty,' said Charles, 'if you think a king would be against incest.'

Lynette laughed. 'You're funny,' she said. 'I didn't think you would be so funny.'

'What did you think?'

She breathed out, making her mouth a little 'o', resting her fingers on her perfectly shaped lips. 'Well,' she said, tilting her head to one side and clasping her hands under her chin, 'we've all heard things about your sceptre.'

He laughed, pleased.

She rested the glass and stood, moving towards her clothes.

'You're leaving?' His voice was filled with disappointment.

'I've never missed a performance,' she said, kissing him on the nose. 'Not even for royalty.'

He leaned back and took a gulp of wine. 'Most women would stay,' he said, leaving the bed to stand opposite her. There was an edge to his voice. Hurt mingled with annoyance.

She smiled, turned to a large mirror and began plaiting her hair. 'When I was eleven,' she said, 'my mother sold me, to a merchant. Not a nice man. I worked my way out. Got into acting. Never let a man tell me what to do since.'

'England sold me to a Portuguese wife,' he said. 'In return for Bombay. Women tell me what to do all the time.'

'I wondered why you had so much Indian calico.'

She began pulling on her dress, throwing him a smile over her naked shoulder.

'Have you any idea how much I want to run away with you, right now?' he asked. 'Disappear into Covent Garden and never come back? I'm due a conjugal visit this evening. The Queen eats whole garlic bulbs, you know.' He feigned an expression of terror.

Lynette laughed loudly. She pulled up the dress, pretended to let it drop and gave a faux gasp as it slipped to her hips.

The King stood and moved to her, dancing his fingers across her shoulders and down her back. 'There's a story,' he said, 'of a man who fell in love with a fairy. He stole her dress whilst she was bathing in a river and trapped her in the mortal world.'

'Oh?' She watched his face.

'What if I were to keep your dress?' he suggested, holding it at the waist. 'Trap you here, with me?'

She pretended to consider. 'Did she have any children, this poor fairy prisoner?'

'Seven,' said Charles. 'They became England's first kings and queens.'

'Temptin',' said Lynette. 'But I'm hopin' to raise me children to better. Seems you royals have a lot of cares and responsibilities.'

'And you are a free spirit.' He smiled at her.

'Money never did bid me keep my mouth shut,' she agreed.

'I'd be sad if it did.' He gave her a roguish grin. 'And there are other ways to keep you quiet.'

'You know,' she said, 'it was you who set me free. 'Long with a lot of other girls. You brought back theatre. You let women act. You allowed us to believe we could be more than wives and mothers.' She nodded to the street outside. 'You should defend those girls,' said Lynette. 'They love you. When the apprentices attack them, they attack you.'

'I thought you weren't interested in politics.'

'This isn't politics,' said Lynette. 'It's . . . people. I'm good at people. You are too, I think.'

'What if I shut the theatre?' he suggested, drawing her close. 'I could, you know.'

'You wouldn't, I know you wouldn't,' she said, inching the dress back up. 'In any case it's you I act for.'

'Oh? Then why not act in the King's Company?'

Her expression twisted. 'Nah,' she said. 'Actin' in your fancy new theatre on Drury Lane? For a *licensed* theatre troupe?' She rolled the word in exaggerated aristocratic tones. 'Me friends would all reckon I got above meself.'

He looked hard into her eyes. 'My brother and I made the licensed theatre companies for a reason,' he said. 'We wanted to show our respect for the art. The illegal playhouses, some of them are little more than brothels with stages. You're good.'

Lynette swallowed. 'Brothels with stages 's what I was raised to,' she said. 'Besides, someone should show those apprentices,' she concluded, drawing her ribbons tight, 'us sinners have no fear of them.'

Chapter 26

A violinist had started up in Ozinda's.

'So you want my help?' Lily didn't hide her incredulity.

When Charlie didn't answer she leaned forward, resting her weight on her elbows. The bracelets on her toffee-skinned wrists slid down her forearms with a tinkling jangle.

'What could you possibly have to offer me, that would make me want to help you?'

'Would it make a difference if I said I was sorry for throwing your share of the treasure in the ocean?'

Her face flashed suddenly with anger. 'I didn't care about the money. We were partners. And you let me go without a backwards glance.'

Charlie hadn't expected this. 'You left!'

'Did I? Like Maria left?'

'I . . .' Charlie hesitated, sensing a trap. 'You wanted me to come with you?' he tried. 'Out to sea?'

'No. London is your place. For all the good it does you. Are you still sleeping in a dusty truckle-bed above a butcher's shop?'

Charlie was speechless. Never, not even in three lifetimes, would he understand women. He tried a change of subject. 'I heard you'd stopped spying for the King. You were making your fortune at sea as one of his privateers. I would imagine legal pirating suits you now there's less call for spies.'

'There's more need for spies than you might imagine, but I'm not currently engaged.' Lily drained her glass meaningfully. Charlie refilled it. 'I'm trying to get back to sea,' she continued, drinking more wine. 'Merry Monarch or no, there are too many Puritans in London for me. A woman is either a good wife or a whore.'

Charlie's eyes caught a quick movement from under the opposite table. An actress had flicked the contents of her glass onto the rug at her feet, then brought the empty vessel back to her lips and pretended to take a sip. None of her companions had noticed. Charlie watched her gesture her cup and smile demurely as more was ordered by her resigned gentlemen.

'You cannot talk to a girl with an empty glass,' said Lily, following his gaze. 'When the wine is gone, they'll throw you out.' She drained her glass with relish. A servant moved forward and quickly refilled it. 'I don't make a habit of spilling mine,' she added, taking a long swig, 'but there's a first time for everything.'

Charlie sipped slowly. The bottle had already diminished by a third.

'So you need another ship,' he tried, flashing her a smile.

'And you're the man to get me it?' she suggested coldly. 'The problem with you, Charlie Tuesday, is you think your charm will get you through life. It won't.'

'You think I'm charming?'

Lily hid her smile with another deep swig of wine.

'We worked well together,' said Charlie. 'Tell me you missed me.'

'I don't like lying to people.'

'You're pleased to see me though. I can see it in your eyes.'

Lily leaned forward and knocked over her glass. Dark wine spilled across the lacquered table and dripped onto the floor.

'I am all thumbs today.' She gave him a dazzling smile.

The servant stepped forward and dispensed another long measure of wine. Lily lifted it, downed the contents and held the glass high for more.

'Maria's gone missing,' said Charlie, speaking quickly. 'Mother Mitchell said she was asking about you before she disappeared.'

He saw something in Lily's face then. A glimmer. The servant refilled her wine and withdrew. She sat back, rolling the glass back and forth in her ringed fingers.

Charlie glanced at the bottle. It had only half a glass of wine left.

'She came here, didn't she?' said Charlie, reading something behind her inscrutable eyes. 'Maria came to see you.'

Lily leaned forward, putting both elbows on the table and letting her necklaces swing free of her scanty dress. She rested her fingers on his and looked deep into his eyes as if trying to work something out. Charlie realised he was holding his breath. Then Lily eased free the wine from his hand, upended the drink into her mouth and put his glass back on the table a little too hard.

'Please,' said Charlie, dispensing with his pride. 'I need your help.'

Lily sat back, drinking, considering. 'Maria did come to me,' she said, after a moment. 'I liked her.'

'She was looking for a dress?' asked Charlie.

'An old one,' agreed Lily, her forehead wrinkling in memory. 'Said it would be decorated with green-gold leaves and ribbons. Made of fine silk. The way she described it . . .' Lily hesitated, looking down at the table.

Charlie sat a little forward.

'It made me think of fairy tales,' she said, raising her eyes to his with a half laugh. 'Enchantresses or sorceresses. Fair maidens and dragons.'

'Old as in old-fashioned?' Charlie was trying to match his scant knowledge of female fashion.

'More than that,' said Lily, toying with her glass. 'But . . . We didn't have the dress she wanted. Ozinda's turns over a lot of dresses.

Old theatre stock, trader-auctions, anything that looks foreign. If we ever had that dress, it was likely sold and passed around the city.' She shrugged. 'A dress like that could be anywhere.'

Charlie was thinking rapidly. 'What happened then?' he asked. 'When you didn't have the dress?'

Lily's dark brow furrowed again. 'She wanted me to get her into Damaris Page's brothel. Black-Damaris,' she added. 'Used to be a slave.'

'I know of her,' said Charlie. 'She hates Mother Mitchell. They fell out, years ago, over a man.'

'I've had some trade dealings with Damaris,' said Lily. 'A few smuggled barrels here and there. Maria hoped I could gain her a favourable audience. Damaris isn't a woman for cosy chit-chat.'

'No.' Charlie was picturing the dark-skinned Wapping brothel-keeper. 'It takes a hard woman to run a sailors' whorehouse. Did you take Maria there?'

'No,' said Lily. 'I told her it was too dangerous to visit a Wapping brothel at Lent. Said I'd take her in a few weeks for the right price. She never came back.'

Lily picked up the bottle and drained the remaining wine in one large mouthful. 'By your leave,' she said, making to stand.

'Wait,' said Charlie. 'What if I told you I could make you enough money to buy another ship?'

'Remember the last time you promised me great wealth?' answered Lily. She leaned forward angrily. 'Treasure?' she continued. 'I ran half-way around London with you, near got myself killed. And when we found your great treasure, you threw it in the ocean. I made not a penny.'

'You left with a boat!'

'A boat now sunk.' Lily stood. Her eyes flicked to the servant and she nodded to the empty bottle. He hastened forward to eject Charlie.

'Maria was looking for a lost lord and lady,' said Charlie, glancing towards the impending servant. 'You spied for the King. You must have heard of them.'

Lily hesitated. 'The Lord and Lady are a fairy story,' she said. 'How can two people be the magic behind the throne? And if they ever did exist they are long murdered, died during the war.'

There was a sudden commotion near the door. Charlie turned, expecting to see another man being ejected. But instead the large manager and several other men were shouting. The skinny boy raised a large bell and clanged it with all his might.

Lily jerked in her chair. 'That's the alarm,' she said. 'Apprentices.'

Chapter 27

Ozinda's was wild with panic. Actresses ran in all directions. Several were cowering under tables. One was stuffing boxes of snuff into her pockets. The security men were clustered by the door, grim faced and armed with blunt cudgels.

'We're not prepared for Lent riots.' Lily was pale. 'They never come here. We're' – she searched for the word – 'reputable.'

'You mean you have male staff to protect you,' said Charlie. 'And skinny apprentices only like to attack defenceless women.' He looked at the door. Shouts could be heard from the other side. 'But you're right,' he said. 'Apprentices have never attacked coffee or chocolate shops at Lent.' He grasped her arm. 'Maria thought you could get into Damaris Page's house. Can you?'

'Maybe.'

'Whoever the Lord and Lady are, they're worth a fortune,' said Charlie. 'The dress Maria was looking for, it leads to them. It's hidden in a brothel.'

Lily considered this. 'That's a bad coincidence,' she opined. 'With the apprentices tearing up brothels.'

'Perhaps not,' said Charlie. 'What if these riots are just a cover for something? And perhaps someone's already found some clue to the Lord and Lady, hidden all these years.'

'What else?' Lily leaned forward. 'I'm a card sharp, remember, just like you. I can tell when you're hiding something. You're not looking for money, Charlie Tuesday, or some long-lost treasure neither. So what is it that would make you want to run through the city's brothels during Lent?'

Charlie hesitated. 'It's Maria,' he admitted. 'She's gone missing, and then a body turned up wearing her wedding clothes with a demand to find the Lord and Lady.'

Lily was silent.

'Help me,' said Charlie. 'Get me into Damaris's brothel. We could buy you a new ship.'

She considered for a moment. 'No,' she said. 'Not for any price. Besides,' she added, casting an assessing glance at the door, 'it's not just a ship I need.'

'Then what?'

'A privateer's licence.'

'Permission to be a legal pirate? I thought you had one?'

'Mine was . . . retracted.'

'Why?'

Her face darkened. 'Mistakes were made,' she said.

There was a roar of splintering wood and the men at the door raised their weapons.

'They're in,' said Charlie. 'I can help you. Only say you'll help me.'

'I don't need your help,' said Lily. She was removing a knife from under her skirts. 'The first apprentice who lays a hand on me loses an eye.'

'And what of the third and fourth?' asked Charlie. 'You've never seen an apprentice riot. They're ugly. Women get torn apart.'

'I thought they only broke up property?' Lily's voice had risen an octave.

'Half the old whores in London have scars from apprentice riots. I can help you.' He held out a hand. 'This building is an old mansion house,' he said. 'During the war, London nobles built escape tunnels and I've a good idea where one might be.'

Lily hesitated. Apprentices had begun pouring in. Young men began overturning tables, smashing bottles.

'Very well,' said Lily, staring at the apprentices. 'Only get me out.'

'Say you'll help me.'

'I'll help.' Lily waved her knife in annoyance.

'Swear it,' insisted Charlie.

Lily breathed out through her nostrils. 'I swear it,' she said. 'Now will you please get us out before those men tear us to pieces?'

'There's a trapdoor,' said Charlie, 'beneath your feet. I noticed it when I sat at your table. Most likely it leads to the tavern across the street.'

He knelt and heaved it open. A set of old wooden steps yawned below.

'After you.' He gave her a little push. She stumbled through the hatch, giving him an angry look. Charlie stepped down after her.

Chapter 28

Tom's hand shook slightly as he approached the cell.

She was inside.

The stone corridor reminded him strongly of the Tower of London. He had a sudden memory. The shock of realising the Lord and Lady had gone. Tom had raced down the stone staircase to the deepest darkest depths of the Tower. He'd seen the iron prison blasted apart by gunpowder. Felt the sinking horror of his failure.

Tom gathered his courage and pushed open the thick door. As usual when he arrived, his mother was deep in prayer, lips muttering, Bible gripped in her hands.

She turned and stood as he entered. Bridey Black's dark greying hair was neatly tucked under a white cap. Her face retained its striking contours around the eyes and cheekbones, but the jowls and mouth had fallen slightly. She was thin, save for a protruding pot belly; a side effect of frequent purges.

'Hello, Mother,' said Tom.

Bridey put the Bible down and crossed the well-swept stone floor. Her room was large and scrupulously clean, as Puritan living dictated. There was a hard chair and a small functional table on which a plain loaf of bread had been half sliced, but no bed. Bridey Black slept on the floor. It was one of many mortifications she visited on herself for the purification of her soul and better attainment of her visions.

'They won't let you stay here unless you start prophesising again,' said Tom. 'This cell is expensive. Others of this size house seven lunatics.'

'You told them about Lent?' she said. 'My powers are low.'

'They are saying other things,' said Tom. 'About men who visit you.'

Bridey twitched in annoyance. 'I thought you had money enough?' she demanded, shaking her head. 'Your blood money. Your father would have been so ashamed at what you turn your powers to. Remember how disappointed he was when you began working in that theatre? Tricks and illusions.'

Tom nodded. She loved to remind him of this.

'It doesn't matter what they think,' said Bridey. 'We will spin straw to gold. The Lord and Lady can bring endless wealth, if managed correctly.' She looked at him. 'Don't you want to go home? Back to your own kind?'

Tom nodded.

'I knew the thief taker was a gift from God,' she said. 'A man raised in brothels, thrown straight into your path by that girl.'

Her eyes flicked to his face. 'The problem haunted you,' she said. 'How do you fool a clever man into going against what he believes in? The fairies gave you the answer,' continued Bridey. 'You don't persuade him. You force him. You take away something dear to him.' Her lips trembled dramatically. 'How did it please God to take your father and brother and let you live?' she said, shaking her head. 'God knows how I have suffered. The sights of the Shambles brought daily horrors to my delicate constitution. Yet I was a devoted wife. The best of mothers.'

It was a sentence he'd heard her say many times.

'Royal court are the fairy folk,' she said. 'Selfish. Interested only in trinkets and gold, power and tyranny.' Bridey nodded to herself. 'You are one of that cursed kind.' She thought for a moment. 'Lent will be over in two days,' she said. 'On Good Friday your chance to return home will have passed. Your thief taker isn't moving fast enough.'

'Maria thinks he will succeed,' said Tom, 'though she doesn't want me to know her thoughts.'

'Maria?' Bridey pronounced the name pointedly, raising her eyebrows.

'It is the name of the girl,' said Tom. 'The thief taker's jilt.'

Bridey had gone very quiet.

'What's the matter?' asked Tom. 'You're having a vision?'

She shook her head. 'I'm only wondering what the fairy folk would make of it all,' she said. 'I'm wondering if there's any need for this . . . *Maria* – she eyed him as she said the name – 'to be kept alive.'

Chapter 29

Scattered broken things littered Wapping's dirt tracks as Charlie and Lily approached Ratcliffe Highway.

'It's an old spy trick to leave a coded confession,' Lily was explaining as they approached. 'If you're condemned to death with vital information, you confess a clue only your allies can understand. The court is legally bound to keep an accurate record of your words,' she added, 'so it's much safer than a verbal message, or a letter that could be intercepted. But it's a desperate trick,' she concluded. 'By confessing you seal your fate.'

'Then someone thought this lord and lady were worth being half-hanged, castrated and gutted for,' said Charlie. 'But his friends never got the message. Perhaps they would have known which brothel he meant.'

Shattered wine bottles and chamber-pot shards ringed the dirt. Burned scraps of dresses and bright parrot feathers drifted on the breeze.

Lily's eyes widened as they took in the destruction that had befallen the famous pleasure district. Windows were smashed in, signs hung askew and the smoking remains of large bonfires punctuated the dirt track.

'Look at it,' she breathed. 'They've broken up the whole street.'

'This was no disordered mob,' said Charlie, taking in the dusty air as he and Lily moved through the streets. 'Look at the path they took.' He pointed towards Blue Anchor Yard and Cartwright Street. 'Apprentices usually charge down Smithfield. Gives the old houses time to close their doors. Those people came from the side streets in a pincer movement.'

Charlie eyed the usually packed-out taverns. They were almost empty save for a few bruised-looking drinkers. A drunk old woman with a faded anchor tattoo raised her skirts hopefully as they passed.

'So, this missing lord and lady,' Lily was saying. 'You think they're related to a butcher's son named Tom Black? And this man has taken Maria?'

'The local Shambles folk seem to think them relations of his,' said Charlie. 'They believe his mother an adulterer, and her son to have noble blood. But Bridey Black thought her son a fairy changeling.'

'And the legend of the Lord and Lady speaks of them as a fairy king and queen,' Lily filled in.

They walked in silence for a time. Street children were picking through the half-burned remnants, searching for anything of value. On the road up ahead, strange dust hung in the air.

'Whole aristocratic families fled England during the civil war,' said Charlie. 'Anyone with a claim to the crown had a price on their head.'

'But why would people like that stay in hiding after the King's return?'

'Because they still pose some threat to the Crown?' suggested Charlie. 'Perhaps our Merry Monarch isn't as nice as you think. What if the riots are somehow linked to the Lord and Lady?' continued Charlie. 'Bawdy houses were known Royalist sympathisers. They often hid noble-born fugitives. Perhaps one hid the Lord and Lady.'

'You think the apprentice riots are an effort to flush out two long-lost fugitives?'

'Well, they would give someone the perfect cover to search brothels. The Gilded Lock got the worst of it,' observed Charlie as they approached. He remembered it as having a tumbledown grandness, with wrought-iron balconies and full-length windows clustered with bare skin and colourful skirts. 'There's hardly anything left.'

The Gilded Lock's familiar wrought-iron sign hung at a dangerous angle. The first two floors had been completely destroyed. Pulled down into the street and smashed into tinder sticks.

'They burned their nice things,' said Lily, looking at the scraps of silk in the fire. 'For no reason. Just to hurt them. Who would do that?'

'Angry young boys with nothing to lose,' said Charlie.

The door bore an ugly rent where a large boot had smashed it open. A pathetic barricade of an old cotton scarf was looped across the threshold.

Charlie stepped forward and knocked loudly on the broken doorframe. When there was no answer he shouted into the gloom. 'Damaris Page?'

A movement came from the dark of the devastated house. Then Lily jumped back with a gasp. They were both staring into the barrel of a gun.

Chapter 30

Lady Castlemaine looked left and right. No one had seen her. Carefully she slipped into the bedroom. There was a familiar perfume on the air. *She* was here, sleeping in this room. Did the King love her? Everything hinged on it. Holding her breath, Lady Castlemaine tiptoed further inside, trying not to make a sound.

There was a sleepy female murmur in the dark and she froze. But then a rhythmic breathing resumed and she moved further forward. Lady Castlemaine's face softened. Her baby was sleeping peacefully in her expensive crib. She reached out and stroked the soft cheek with her ringed finger.

'My little darling,' she whispered. 'My treasure.' She leaned deeper into the crib, cupping the little head in her hand. 'They want to take your fortune, my darling,' she said. 'I know all of what happens to girls with no dowry. I've lived it. But you mustn't fret.' She arranged the bedclothes. 'Your mama wouldn't let that happen,' she said. 'You will never have to do the things I've had to. Never.' She smiled at the sleeping child. 'Best beloved,' she whispered, stroking the curled fingers. 'He will protect you. I will make him. There is a darkness behind his throne,' she said. 'It has always been there. From the very beginning of kings.

The magic ones who shadowed King Arthur and Queen Guinevere. The sorceress and the wild man. I know it, my precious. I have seen.'

Lady Castlemaine looked at her baby sleeping on white linen, a lacy cap tied under her chubby chin. The room was vast, the crib enormous, of dark beautifully carved mahogany, high at the top, like an arc. A marble fireplace gave gentle heat from a cleansing sandalwood fire.

'People talk of the Lord and Lady as fairies,' she smiled. 'But I know the truth. Without them, a king cannot be legally crowned. That is why they are so important.'

The door opened and the royal wet-nurse bustled in. She saw Lady Castlemaine, curtsied, and approached the crib.

'God has brought you an angel,' she clucked, fussing about the linen covers. 'Such beauty.' The wet-nurse looked about the room. 'I didn't sleep a wink until your wee jewel was christened,' she said. 'You know fairy folk covet pretty babes. They will have been lying in watch for this little one. But she's safe now,' added the wet-nurse, happily. 'Christened into God's church. The fey folk must have champed their teeth in envy,' she concluded.

Lady Castlemaine watched as the wet-nurse left the room. Her fingers tightened on the wooden crib. 'He'd not be five minutes cold and they'd take all this away,' she said. 'All the maids that fuss and pet you, the courtiers that bow. They'd be no friends to you.' She arranged the covers carefully. 'I will find the Lord and Lady. I will take their power. For you, my most beloved, for you.'

Betsy's little rosebud mouth opened in a soundless red yawn. Lady Castlemaine smiled, love radiating from her eyes.

'You will have a title,' she promised. 'Wealth of your own. I will get it for you. Anybody who stands in your way will regret it.'

Chapter 31

Charlie and Lily stood frozen, looking at the gun. It poked from the gloom of the deserted bawdy house.

'What you want?' demanded a female voice with a strange accent. 'Don't need no trouble here. We already have enough trouble.'

Then a woman with jet-black skin appeared. She stood a little back, hidden by shadow. Her profile was Amazonian in proportions, tall with broad shoulders and a shapely bust projected upwards by cheap willow-boned corsetry.

Damaris moved into the light. Her hair was in disarray, tightly curled dark ringlets springing haphazardly from a centre parting. The handsome features of her dark face were contrasted by the deep, jagged wound on her cheek. A rough 'W' was painted in dark blood, raised red and swollen with bruising.

'They cut you?' said Charlie, taking in her injury with horror.

Damaris nodded shortly. 'And worse.' Her face was impassive, stony. 'Don't need no gawkers and gogglers,' she said. 'You seen it now. Be off.'

'Damaris, it's me.' Lily's voice was hushed and unusually sympathetic. She was staring at the ugly wounds on the other woman's face. 'It's Lily Boswell.'

Damaris hesitated. 'I remember you,' she said. 'The gypsy-pirate. You free slaves at sea.'

'If I find them,' said Lily, avoiding Charlie's surprised expression. 'We need your help,' she added. 'We think someone is targeting brothels, looking for a dress. A dress that leads to a lord and lady.'

Damaris's face darkened. 'Don't know nothin' bout no lord and lady,' she said, moving to shut the door.

Lily stepped quickly into the gap. 'Please,' she said, holding the door with her little hands. 'We need to stop anyone else getting hurt.'

Damaris's eyes switched to Charlie. 'Not him,' she said. 'I'll have no men inside. Not after what my girls have been through.'

'I grew up in Mother Mitchell's brothel,' said Charlie. 'I know you have people here you want to protect, children.'

Her face softened slightly. 'Yes, there be children.' Damaris hesitated, taking in Charlie's expression. He felt acutely aware of the slight kink in his nose, his scarred upper lip. But something must have convinced her Charlie was genuine, because she let go of her hold on the door.

'Better come inside,' she decided, glancing quickly left and right along the street.

They followed Damaris down a dark corridor, the shape of her muscular legs showing through her dusky-pink skirts as she walked.

'You free slaves at sea?' whispered Charlie, raising his eyebrows. 'You told me you sailed for gold.'

'Gypsies are enslaved along with blacks,' hissed Lily. 'I protect my own people, is all. Mostly I'm a treasure-hunter.'

'I'll never believe you hard-hearted again,' said Charlie, enjoying her annoyance at being discovered.

Damaris led them to a bare-planked room where a huddle of terrified girls was gathered. Charlie swallowed, taking in the bruised faces and ripped dresses. A few recognised Charlie and mumbled a greeting.

Charlie eyed the devastation of the room. 'They were apprentices?' he asked, taking in the systematic destruction.

'Some of them were,' said Damaris. 'One was different.'

'Different how?'

Damaris thought for a long moment. 'Older,' she decided. 'Had an authority about him. Went by the name of Barebones.' Damaris gestured to her mutilated face. 'And him that did this. I'd think it to be his son. He was crueller. Wanted to hurt us.' She trembled slightly.

Lily reached out, took the older woman's hand and squeezed it. 'We'll see him brought to justice,' she promised.

'You mentioned a dress?' continued Damaris. 'Barebones was looking for a special dress too. When I couldn't give it to him, he had his boys throw the others from the window. Everything we owned.'

'Barebones was especially interested in a particular dress?' asked Charlie. 'Can you tell me anything about it?'

Damaris nodded. 'He wanted to know about a dress stitched with green-and-gold leaves. Hung all over with ribbons like the May festival dresses. Barebones tried to make me speak of it, but I wouldn't. I gave my word, you see, a long time ago, to protect the Royalists. When I give my word, I don't go back.'

'You think this dress belonged to a Royalist?' asked Charlie.

'In a manner of speaking,' said Damaris. 'A Royalist escaped wearing it, during the war.'

Chapter 32

Lynette gazed around the apartment. A slow smile crept onto her face. It was better than she'd ever imagined.

She took a few tentative steps inside, allowing her feet to sink into the soft rug. She grinned, bouncing on her heels. She moved to the walls, with their bright Indian calico coverings. Her fingers drifted over the red embroidered flowers and deep-green leaves.

Lynette pressed her lips together and turned to survey the rest of the apartment. A little bubble of laughter welled up. Towards the back was a beautiful French mahogany desk with a decanter of her favourite wine and two glasses on top. Then there was the bed. She'd never seen so much deep silk and linen.

There was a sound from the closet and a girl stepped out, dressed in a neat chambermaid's uniform. She curtsied low and Lynette laughed out loud.

'Sissy!' she said. 'He never got you?'

She curtsied again. ''Is Majesty thought you'd like me,' said Sissy, grinning. 'Reckon 'e saw us actin' together?'

'I know 'e did, the old skirt-grabber,' said Lynette. 'Listen, if 'e tries to get us both in bed, you tell 'im you've got the clap.'

Sissy laughed. 'He likes you,' she said, suddenly serious. 'The King.'

Lynette chewed her lip, looking around the interior happily.

They were interrupted by a sharp tap on the door. Sissy moved to open it.

'Oh, let me,' said Lynette. 'I can't 'ave you waitin' on me, Sis. You'll just expect it in return when my star wanes. Only go see if 'e's left us any marzipan fruits in the other room. We'll share 'em.'

Sissy hurried away as Lynette opened the door. It was Lady Castlemaine.

'Of course you open your own door,' said Lady Castlemaine. 'You've been raised from the gutter, but you'll never lose its manners.' Lady Castlemaine was staring intently at Lynette.

''Oo let you up?' demanded Lynette.

Lady Castlemaine looked Lynette up and down. 'Good performance?' she asked, archly. 'No hecklers or ruffians?'

Lynette smiled broadly. 'Now you mention it, I think there were a few loud fellows at the back.'

'Oh dear.' Lady Castlemaine smiled. 'I do hope they didn't hurl fruit. I heard you were pelted most viciously.'

Lynette laughed. 'Us actresses are practised at dodging missiles.' Lynette walked lightly towards the bed. 'And you know how thick-skinned commoners are.'

Lady Castlemaine's smile dropped as she watched Lynette. The lovely violet eyes narrowed in fury. 'Enjoy your short time with the King,' she whispered malevolently. 'I taught him everything he knows.'

'I was raised a whore,' said Lynette cheerfully, bouncing on the bed. 'Perhaps there are still a few things even his Majesty could learn.'

Lady Castlemaine turned and stalked away, fists clenched.

As the door shut, Lynette sagged in relief. She gritted her teeth, limped heavily to the nearest chair and collapsed onto it. Then, screwing her face in pain, she unlaced her dress and peeled away the layer of bandages wrapping her ribs.

The door opened, and Sis came through bearing a tray of marzipan fruits. She shrieked, sending the food tumbling to the floor.

'You're hurt!' She ran to Lynette's side, eyes goggling at the deep purple bruising that wound around her torso.

'Pay it no mind, Sissy.' Lynette winced. 'Only help me with this ointment, won't you?'

She took out a pot of greasy yellow salve and began unscrewing the lid with shaking fingers.

'Here,' Sissy took it. 'Let me.' She opened the pot and began dappling Lynette's bruises with light fingers.

Lynette hissed in pain, her eyes filling with tears.

'Does it hurt very much?' asked Sis.

'Not so much as poverty,' said Lynette, managing a smile.

'You walked all this way from the theatre,' admonished Sissy. 'That must have made it much worse.'

'It was worth it to see her face,' said Lynette.

'Lady Castlemaine? She did this?'

'She hired thugs to pelt me on stage,' said Lynette. 'I had a mind it might happen, so I had my own men ready to throw them from the theatre. But they got a few in.'

Sissy's mouth twisted in concern. 'You mustn't anger her anymore,' she pleaded. 'I saw Lady Castlemaine walking away. I've heard about her rages. The palace servants are terrified of her.'

'I grew up in a brothel on Coal Yard Alley,' said Lynette. 'Next to Mad Sal with the pointed teeth and Dave the Knife, she's not so bad.'

Sissy laughed. 'You're a fine actress,' she admitted begrudgingly. 'Lady Castlemaine thinks you completely unscathed.'

Lynette smiled.

'You're brave,' said Sis. 'You're not a bit scared of her, are you?'

'Maybe she should be scared of me. I know something, Sis. Something I heard at the theatre. Lady Castlemaine is trying to find a lord and lady who went missing during the war. They were thought dead, but it seems like a Royalist spy smuggled them out. She's mad to track them down. I think they know something compromising. Some dark secret about her ladyship.' Lynette's dark eyes glittered. 'Maybe if I found them first, I'd have something on her.'

Sissy's face dropped. 'Sounds political,' she said. 'Politics are dangerous, Lynette.' Sis eyed the bruising. 'Lady Castlemaine has seen off every other mistress,' she said. 'She's one of those who has to win at any cost. I honestly don't know what she'd be capable of if she were pushed.'

'Nor do I,' said Lynette, her eyes glittering. 'Shall we give her a shove and find out?'

Chapter 33

In the shattered remains of the Gilded Lock, Charlie and Lily were listening intently to Damaris Page.

'I was a young woman at the time,' she was explaining. 'Fresh off the slave ship and sold into a Wapping whorehouse. The girls were all of a flutter,' added Damaris with a smile. 'A handsome Royalist fugitive. He'd made some dramatic escape, dressed as a woman. We hid many Royalist nobles in the attic. This house was part of a secret underground, smuggling them out of the country. We dressed them as whores, servants,' she explained. 'They passed through the bawdy houses and illegal theatres. But this man was different.' She sighed deeply. 'He was the only Royalist we couldn't protect,' she concluded guiltily. 'The mistress of the house gave him up.'

'Why?' asked Charlie.

'He was too dangerous,' said Damaris. 'The mistress said it was all our necks. He'd broken some people free from the Tower. People said it was to protect the King's true power on earth.'

'A lord and lady?' asked Charlie.

Damaris nodded.

'So Cromwell's men arrested this man?'

'He was executed,' said Damaris. 'The mistress said it was all our necks, or his.' She looked sad.

'Did he leave the dress here?' asked Charlie.

Damaris shook her head. 'I never saw the dress after he was taken. Maybe it was sold, or sent away. The mistress wasn't hard-hearted enough to keep it.'

Charlie felt the dead end close around him. There were thousands of brothels in London.

'He left something else though,' said Damaris helpfully. 'A safe-passage ring. Said someone would come for it, but they never did.'

'What's a safe-passage ring?' asked Charlie.

'To get into the secret underground,' said Damaris. 'Royalists passed a ring around. It contained a riddle only the worthy could solve.'

'Worthy as in aristocratic?' suggested Lily scathingly.

'Those who solved the ring found a key,' said Damaris. 'A key to get them into a safe house and smuggled out of the country.'

Charlie's thief taker talents were ticking. 'I can tell much from a ring,' he said. 'Where it was made. Who made it. Do you still have it?'

Damaris shook her head. 'It was a mourning ring,' she said with a shudder. 'A ghoulish habit of the English,' she opined, 'to wear a ring for your dead. The mistress was afraid of it. Called it a fairy thing. Hid it away, I know not where.'

'What happened to your old mistress?' asked Charlie.

'She's dead now,' said Damaris matter-of-factly. 'Assassinated by Cromwell's men. We always suspected another bawd had reported her. Wapping is a cut-throat place for the flesh trade. The mistress had many enemies. She made all manner of little charms against them, but it didn't protect her in the end.'

'Yet perhaps they protected something else,' said Charlie thoughtfully. 'I think I've an idea where the mourning ring is after all.'

Chapter 34

Maria was sat in the dark, listening. Manacled in the attic, she thought she'd heard the distant cheers of a crowd. The kind of bloodied roar that signalled the end of a dog or bear fight. That would most likely place her in the old part of the city, which she didn't think possible, because she couldn't hear the cacophony of noisy trades, street sellers, beggars and livestock.

She tried to remember what the candle had revealed about her prison. Ropes, like ship's rigging, slung all over. And she thought she could smell canvas on the air, as well as hemp. But she couldn't be near a dockyard. She would have heard and smelled it.

She tried to think, but her thoughts were hard to get hold of. And then she saw the edge of a candle, rising up in the dark. Her heart quickened. He was coming.

The soft light grew, lighting tumbling ropes, wooden floorboards, huge wooden beams.

Maria squinted in the candlelight. A man she'd never seen before entered the rope-strewn attic. He had an arrogance to his stride and she instinctively drew back. As he passed the candle she saw a man in soldier's dress. He was older, the broken capillaries on his face suggesting him a hardened drinker.

The man pulled up a stool and gave her a leering smile. 'Pretty,' he said. 'He never said you were pretty.'

'Who are you?' said Maria, hoping the tremble in her voice was noticeable only to her.

The man adjusted his breeches, legs splayed. He smelled of alcohol, she noticed, as a waft drifted towards her.

'I'm his general, thas who,' he said. 'I gets 'em all riled up. The lads. 'Prentices.' He sniffed, reached inside his coat and drew out a battered flask. He uncorked the top and took a deep swig, sucking it back over his teeth. 'I take 'em the right way through London.' He raised his flask in a toast towards Maria, but didn't offer her a drink, only splayed his legs out further from his stool. 'Problem is,' he continued, 'we got a thief taker interfering in my business.'

Maria felt her heart miss a beat.

The man sat suddenly forward. 'Don't suppose you'd know anything about someone named Charlie Tuesday?'

'If I did, I wouldn't tell you,' said Maria.

To her surprise, the man laughed, a strange, haunting laugh that didn't belong in his body at all. A chill went through her. Because now the man's demeanour seemed to morph before her eyes. And as she watched he stood and moved closer to her.

'You're braver than most men,' he said. 'Don't you recognise me?' The voice was now horribly familiar.

Maria swallowed.

The man reached up and unhooked the knotty beard from behind his ears. The bottom of his face was pale and didn't match the top.

'It's you,' she managed, seeing Tom Black's face.

He smiled and bowed low. And now she saw him, under the stage-paint. The bristle-cut hair didn't suit him. Tom took a rag from his coat and began wiping his face in long practised strokes. Something about the way he did it sparked a realisation in Maria.

He enjoys acting.

'Cheap rouge,' he explained, wiping it away, 'mixed with lead paint and applied with a brush. Reddens the cheeks. The scar is only a little charcoal and grease.'

'You're a good actor,' said Maria, trying for an admiring tone.

'Acting is a sin,' said Tom. 'I intrigue for a noble cause.' But he looked pleased. He continued cleaning away the paint, working away the heavy dark eyebrows, red nose and scarred cheek. Underneath, his real greenish-toned skin was revealed in stages, with its pockmarks and chalky texture.

His sleeve fell as he cleaned away the last of the paint. Maria froze in shock, taking in what was left of his forearm. Her eyes followed the deep webbing of ugly raised tissue that spoke of burns made on burns. Only a few patches of shining red skin remained.

Maria knew what they were.

Changeling marks. The worst she'd ever seen.

'Tom.' Maria took his brutalised arm. 'She did this to you? Your own mother?'

Tom nodded mildly. 'They never came for me,' he said.

Maria bit her lip. 'Have you ever considered,' she said carefully, 'that you were a human child, with an inhuman mother?'

'She was a devoted wife,' said Tom mechanically. 'The best of mothers.'

He jerked suddenly. Maria thought he seemed in pain.

'What is it?' she whispered. 'What's wrong?'

'Do you hear the bells?' asked Tom. 'He calls.'

'I don't hear anything.'

'The boy.' Tom winced. 'He is angry with me. I must go.'

Tom stood so fast that Maria jerked back. But she saw something in the movement, a kind of acted grace. Suddenly the ropes and the rigging meant something. She'd been somewhere like it before.

Think Maria. Think.

Ropes tied high. Canvas. Hemp. Cheers. Applause. Chandeliers.

She remembered sweating men pulling at the ropes, lowering something . . .

Scenery. I was up where the scenery is winched and lowered. That's why there are ropes everywhere.

Maria breathed in. She knew where she was.

I'm in a theatre.

Chapter 35

In Damaris Page's brothel, Charlie was considering what he knew. 'I have an idea where the ring the Royalist left could be,' he said.

'How could you know where the mourning ring is?' asked Lily.

Charlie was looking at Damaris, hope glimmering in his eyes. 'Mrs Page,' said Charlie, 'is this the same building and do you have the same doorstep from when your old mistress ran things?'

Damaris blinked her round dark eyes. 'It is the same building, so I suppose so,' she said. 'Why?'

'Might I take a look at it?'

'No reason why not,' she said. 'It's only a doorstep.'

'Why do you want to look?' asked Lily, as Charlie made for the thick slab of stone by the entrance to the devastated building.

'It's common practice for bawds to hide a witch-bottle under the doorstep,' said Charlie.

'What's a witch-bottle?'

'A bottle to deter witches,' replied Charlie. He scanned the doorway and found a half a discarded pike.

'Obviously,' said Lily dryly.

'It's old ways,' said Charlie. He inserted the broken end of the pike under the thick slab of the step, worked it further in, then levered with his foot. 'Houses of sin need all the protection they can get. Brothel-keepers almost always keep a glass bottle under their front step,' he said. 'Filled with sharp things. Iron nails, pins. Sometimes salt and ashes. Things to deter fairies, witches, evil spirits.'

The stone step raised a few inches.

'If she thought that ring fairy,' he continued, 'there's a good chance she would have put it inside. The entrance to a house is a powerful place,' he added. 'Someone who employed spells and such would have used the chance to put a little fairy magic to good purpose.'

Lily was on her knees, charms dangling down, peering underneath the slab. 'I think I see it,' she said. 'There's something buried here.' She began loosening it from the packed dirt. Her fingers clasped a corked clay neck. 'A bottle,' she said, grasping hold. 'You were right.'

Lily worked the bottle free, bringing it up to examine it as Charlie lowered the step. It was made of brown clay. Lily gave the bottle an experimental shake. It tinkled musically. 'Nails?' She drew out the cork and a little cloud of ash floated upwards. Lily upended it and soot poured free. 'There's something else trapped inside,' said Lily, closing one eye and peering into the bottle neck. She shook it again. 'If it's a bottle for fairy protection,' she said, 'we must be careful. If we break it we could anger . . .'

Charlie eased it from her fingers, raised his arm and smashed the bottle down on the step. 'We don't have fairies in London,' he said. 'They're country things.'

Lily crossed herself as a clutch of nails and pins fell free, along with more ash. Then a ring came pinging free.

'You were right,' breathed Lily. 'A ring.'

Charlie picked it up carefully. The ring was thick gold with black enamel panelling. Towards the front was a raised crest.

'Expensive,' said Charlie. 'Owned by someone wealthy. And on the back,' he said, turning it, 'the year of the old king's death.' Charlie looked at Lily. 'This kind of ring is usually worn by mourners to commemorate dead relatives. But during the war, secret Royalist supporters wore them,' he explained. 'They were inscribed with the year the old king was beheaded. And they had secret compartments, lids or concealed parts, to hide a portrait of the king.'

He ran a finger around the edge and found what he was looking for. A tiny indentation. He flicked it up and the front of the ring opened. Underneath was a brightly coloured portrait of King Charles I, with his distinctive pointed beard.

'The kind of thing a Royalist spy would own,' said Charlie. 'Carrying this would show your allegiance to the old king. You'd risk treason for wearing it, if this secret picture was seen by the wrong person.'

'Or gain help from the right person,' said Lily.

Charlie nodded. 'There's an inscription inside,' he said, turning it. The gold inner was etched with tiny letters. He passed it to Lily to read.

Her lips moved slowly. Lily looked up at Charlie. 'No wonder the old mistress thought this ring fey,' she said. 'Read the inscription.' She passed it to him, then remembered he struggled with letters. 'Seek the gold on London's fairy ring,' she read, 'for the key to Avalon.'

Charlie took it from her, repeating the words she'd just read. 'A fairy ring?' he said. 'In the city?'

'I've seen fairy mushroom circles in the country.' Lily shrugged. 'Not in London though.'

'They sometimes come up in the greener parts,' said Charlie. 'The common land, towards the east. Braver locals put livestock to trample them.'

'Foolish,' opined Lily. 'Fairies are vengeful creatures. Neither man nor beast should step inside a fairy circle.' She thought for a moment. 'Witches make circles, do they not?' she suggested. 'Salt circles or candles, so they might keep safe from whatever fairy or demon their powers attract. Is that not a kind of fairy circle?'

Charlie nodded. 'There's likely hundreds of circles of that kind in London,' he said, 'but they'll all be well hidden. It's death to practise such things.'

They were both silent in thought.

'What's the key to Avalon?' asked Lily.

'Avalon is just a story,' said Charlie. 'The place where King Arthur was buried. It's an island. I can't see why it would have a key.'

Lily shook her head. 'King Arthur and fairy rings,' she said scathingly. 'No wonder the old monarchy fell,' she added. 'It's like children, playing at spying. Seems to me the Royalists were so in love with the idea of being brave knights, they forgot the horrors of war.'

Charlie looked back at the front of the ring. 'Ring-crests are mostly made by token houses,' he said. 'They use the same presses for stamping coins. But this' – he ran a finger over the metalwork – 'was not. See the clean edges? It was stamped with a bronze press. Cleaner lines, less wear.' He turned it thoughtfully in his hand. And then the answer came to him. 'This was made in the Mint,' he said, calling to mind London's only legal coin press, a rickety jumble of wood, built against the Tower of London. 'The Mint employs skilled workers,' said Charlie. 'People who stay for life. There's a good chance the person who made this ring still works there. We only need to get inside the Mint.' He looked hopefully at Lily.

Lily had taken his meaning and was shaking her head rapidly. 'No,' she said. 'I won't get you to the Mint. I kept my word to get you inside Damaris Page's house and you took *that* from me through trickery.'

'Lily,' said Charlie. 'Maria's life hangs in the balance. She has perhaps less than a day at best to live.'

'Ask Percy,' Lily said. 'He's Maria's betrothed and a lawyer. Surely he could get you in the Tower?'

Charlie shook his head. 'Percy is less successful than he pretends,' he said, remembering the cheap wig and spotted stockings. 'I'd likely waste time and then discover he doesn't have those kinds of privileges.'

'Really?' Lily nailed him with a look. 'Is that the real reason? Or do you fear Maria's husband-to-be would thwart your romantic rescue? It's only right that you ask Percy to help save his future wife.'

Charlie felt his blood rise. 'This isn't a game!' he said angrily. 'There's too much at stake. Do you think I would take even the smallest risk with Maria's life out of some misplaced sense of propriety?'

Lily considered this, turning the rings on her fingers with a pained expression. 'I couldn't help you even if I wanted to,' she said finally. 'They took my spy privileges with the privateer's licence. I don't have access to the Tower of London any longer.' Lily delved into the jangle of charms at her neck. 'All I have left is this.' She showed Charlie a medallion with a royal crest. 'Gives me a few privileges to ask questions, nothing more.'

'Shouldn't you have returned your medallion when you went to sea?'

'I still undertake some missions for the Crown,' said Lily evasively.

Damaris tilted her head, eyeing the medallion. 'You can go inside the Tower,' she said to Charlie. 'The ring will let you inside. It's a safe-passage ring. Will take you into any Royalist place.'

'But the ring is yours,' said Charlie, holding it out to her. 'It's gold. You should have it to help you rebuild.'

Damaris shook her head hard. 'You think I want that cursed thing?' she said. 'It's brought nothing but bad luck,' she added, touching her wounded face.

Charlie opened his mouth to insist, but Damaris pushed the ring onto his finger, her expression implacable. 'If you can find this dress before Praise-God Barebones, it's payment enough for me,' she said firmly.

'Even if the ring takes me inside,' said Charlie, looking at Lily, 'I've no right to speak with the men in the Mint. Come with me.' He held up his finger, banded with the mourning ring. 'You can have this in payment.'

'Barely enough to buy me a parrot and an eyepatch,' said Lily, looking at the gold. She paused. 'Very well,' she decided. 'If we find the Lord and Lady you are to let me take them to the King. He might grant me back my privateer's licence.'

Charlie nodded gratefully, turning to Damaris. 'If we find the Lord and Lady, I'll bring you money to rebuild, I swear it.'

Damaris's eyes filled with sudden, unexpected tears. 'It's the children I fear for,' she said. 'We're not wealthy people here. Only work not to starve. The clothes and fine things we have are part of our trade.' She gave a great sniff. 'Lent will be over soon,' she said. 'It's Maundy Thursday tomorrow. Come Good Friday we can sleep safe in our beds.'

Charlie nodded, feeling the time close around him. Maria's life seemed to be ticking away. He put a hand on Damaris's shoulder. 'If you're afraid, you might ask Mother Mitchell,' he suggested. 'She has the best guards in the city.'

Damaris shook her head proudly. 'Don't need none of Mother Mitchell's help,' she said, setting her jaw. 'Never did, never will. Mother Mitchell took you in from the orphan house. And perhaps she was kind to you, in her way. But I've known her for a long time.' She drew a breath. 'Eliza Mitchell,' concluded Damaris, 'is nothing but a selfish old dragon, guardin' her pile of golden girls, and hell would freeze over afore I asked her for anything.'

Chapter 36

At first glance, the architecture of the Mint looked impossible. The rickety wooden structures had grown up against the thick walls of the Tower of London over the years. Each decade of coin production had added ever more dangerous storeys and teetering extensions, like a dark creeping plant slowly suffocating its solid host.

Charlie held up the mourning ring. 'If Damaris is right, and it gets us inside, then we could learn something important. Someone here might remember making it.'

He was looking at the solid turreted square of the Tower, its little arched windows like black eyes.

Lily pointed. 'Like I said. You get us in the Tower and I can pass inside the coin house that way.' She held up the spy medallion strung around her neck. 'So long as we're inside the Tower it should be enough to enter the Mint with no questions. Spies go in through Traitor's Gate,' she concluded.

Charlie lowered his gaze from the thick turrets of the Tower to the ominous archway. 'Traitor's Gate?' Charlie tried to keep his voice calm. 'There's no other way?'

'Are you afraid?'

'Afraid of entering the biggest torture chamber in London by the condemned prisoner's entrance? Of course not.'

They moved towards Traitor's Gate, where dark water swirled below a low brick arch. A hooded man sat on a floating barge with a curved prow. Behind him was the latticed wood of Traitor's Gate, sealing the waterway entrance to the Tower beyond.

'The boatman is there.' Lily pointed. 'The one who sails under Traitor's Gate. Just . . . show him your ring,' she suggested. 'Spies have to say the right words,' she added, 'on His Majesty's service. Likely that will serve.'

Charlie took a step towards the ominous-looking boat, holding out the ring.

To his surprise the boatman let them aboard without question, looking slightly bored as Charlie mumbled 'on His Majesty's service'.

As they floated slowly towards the gate it opened with a grinding of cogs, then closed behind them. Charlie eyed the dark Tower as the curved prow of the boat glided towards it. A desperate shout carried on the breeze, drifting up from the Tower dungeons.

'Prisoners,' grunted the boatman in answer to their stricken faces. 'Them poor souls that were close to Cromwell and didn't get out of England fast enough.'

The barge floated to a halt and they disembarked.

'There,' said Lily. 'That's the safest way into the Mint.'

Chapter 37

Lynette was at the window of her apartment, looking out. She could hear the roar of the riot. She turned to the King. 'You should be out there, you know.'

'Do you hear that?' He opened the window. 'That's the sound of men who want to kill me. You think I am foolish enough to give them more ammunition?' He sighed. 'Why are they so angry? I did everything to be a good King. I touch the heads of scrofulous vagabonds every month, wash common feet at Lent.'

'Do you want the real answer?' asked Lynette. 'Or do you only want to pity yourself?'

He hesitated.

'I could tell you a courtesan reply,' she continued. 'You are a great king, Your Majesty, the finest we've ever known.'

'Tell me true then.'

'Those boys are little better than slaves,' she said. 'They work for nothing more than bed and board. Most are half-starved, worked to the bone and beaten. They look at girls like us and think we have it easy. And they have nothing to lose. Why wouldn't they tear the city apart?'

'How can I help that?' His shoulders drew up in an exasperated shrug. 'I can't change the apprentice system. It's been that way for centuries.'

'You can't do anything for them,' she said. 'It's the girls you should help.'

He leaned forward and took her half-plaited hair. 'Let me,' he said, starting to draw the strands together.

'Who taught you to plait hair?' she asked, amused.

'My wet-nurse,' said Charles, frowning in concentration.

'Isn't a booby-maid supposed to do her own plaiting?'

'She was no longer my nurse at that point,' said Charles. 'We'd moved to a more . . . physical relationship.'

'You never!' Lynette was scandalised. 'With your own nursemaid? How old was you?'

'Fourteen.'

'How old was she?'

'I don't well recall. The country was in turmoil. We were losing the war badly. She was perhaps . . . thirty-three. My advisors at the time hated her. Thought she revelled in her power over me. Distracted me from dull politics.'

'What did you think?'

'Me?' Charles laughed. 'I was having the time of my life.'

'Hmmm. And now?'

'What do you mean?'

Lynette turned to face him. 'Do you think you're being distracted now? From dull politics?'

'If I am, it is worth the distraction. The people don't like me much in any case.' He let his fingers drift down her back.

She took his hand crossly. 'They like you well enough,' she said. 'It's her they hate.' She tilted her chalice in the direction of Lady Castlemaine's apartments.

'You are too bold.'

143

'That's what you like about me. Why pluck me from the gutter if you didn't want a girl who spoke 'er mind? You've got your pick of laced-tight court ladies.'

The King sighed. 'I fear for Lady Castlemaine,' he admitted. 'Part of the Tower was rebuilt recently, and two little skeletons were unearthed.'

Lynette's eyes widened.

'We think they might have been the two young princes,' added Charles. 'Remember that story?'

'The princes in the Tower,' said Lynette. 'They vanished. People tell it that evil King Richard did for 'em and took the crown. Even commoners know that tale,' she added.

'It seemed to affect Lady Castlemaine very deeply,' said Charles. 'She was seen standing over the little bones, rain pouring down, and she didn't even notice she was soaked to the skin.'

'You think she fears for her own children?' asked Lynette softly.

'She needn't whilst I am alive,' said Charles. 'I will always protect them. But when I'm gone . . . We didn't think of that at the time.'

'Remind me again why anyone would want to be king?'

'When you're not in fear of your life, the wine is excellent.' He smiled, finishing the plait and letting it drop.

'Very good,' she said, feeling with it her fingers. 'The girls will never believe me when I tell 'em.'

Chapter 38

The Mint was even more chaotically constructed up close. They entered from the Tower side by means of a rotting plank ramp that rocked disconcertingly underfoot. Charlie eyed several holes where the wood had split and been hastily nailed over with fresher lengths.

A thin wooden door hung open at such an angle that Charlie doubted it had been closed in years. As they moved further inside, the ringing chink of men beating metal surrounded them. The timber room was stifling, dotted with a jumble of dilapidated coin-makers who sat on stools, tapping farthings from sheet metal at dizzying speed.

Charlie watched as they peeled up the punched bronze. A boy with a brush moved in, sweeping the tinkling money into a rapidly filling crate.

Lily cupped her hand and shouted into the mass of industry. 'On the King's business!'

Almost immediately the most incredibly shaped man emerged from the presses. He was tiny with thick grey hair tucked behind his ears. Starvation-thin and barely more than five feet tall, but with the full-sized muscular arms of a giant. He had a single tooth in his gummy old mouth and had stripped down to a ragged pair of breeches in the heat, exposing a surprisingly muscled chest for a man of his years.

'Help you?' he asked amiably, rubbing machine-greased hands on his shirt. His tone was casual, but Charlie noted his quick eyes were roving all over Lily's dress and gypsy trinkets. 'I'm the foreman hereabouts,' he added.

Lily showed her medallion and the man nodded slowly, looking her up and down.

'Takes all sorts, I suppose,' he observed, 'to keep the Merry Monarch on the throne. But I never thought I'd see a gypsy employed by the King. We're very busy,' he added. 'Proving to His Majesty his new machines are a fool's errand.'

'I don't see any machines,' said Charlie.

'Other part of the building,' said the foreman. 'We're having a race, of sorts. The King comes back here with his Frenchie ways. Not his fault, I suppose. But we'll soon show him an Englishman with a hammer can best a Frenchman with his machine, won't we boys?' The foreman raised his voice at this last part and the coin-makers mumbled a muted assent. The pace of coin tapping intensified. The foreman grinned gummily, watching the stamp and sweep of coinage. 'What do you need to know?' He addressed his question to Charlie.

'Do you know anything about this ring?' asked Charlie, holding it up.

The foreman took it, turned it, then brought it to his single tooth and gave it an exploratory bite. 'Made here,' he agreed. 'Bronze press.' His finger circled the front and he flipped open the hidden panel to reveal the face of the dead king. 'Aha,' he said. 'There was a fashion for macabre mementos of this kind. Royalists were nothing if not dramatic.'

'Do you know who might have made it?' asked Charlie. 'It was a safe-passage ring,' he added, 'for Royalists hoping to be smuggled from the country.'

'They loved their cloak-and-dagger,' said the foreman, shaking his head. 'Codes and hidden treasure. This kind of thing was treason.' He tapped the face of King Charles. 'Whoever made that ring would likely have kept it to himself.'

'There's a puzzle inside,' said Charlie. 'Seek the gold on London's fairy ring for the key to Avalon.'

The foreman laughed rudely. 'They weren't built for war, were they, those poor Royalists.' He shook his head. 'Sendin' letters whilst Cromwell was making swords.'

Something had changed on the foreman's face and Charlie was suddenly sure he was hiding something.

The foreman scratched his chin. 'I'm sorry I can't help you so well,' he concluded. 'We never made keys in the Mint.'

'You said the Royalists sent letters?' said Charlie. 'During the war.'

'Did I?' said the foreman, his casual tone not quite ringing true. 'Well that's true enough, isn't it? Letters and plots. That was how the Royalists fought.'

A possibility formed in Charlie's mind. The brass-cut shape of the ring would have required a specialist worker. 'The Mint makes seals as well as coins, doesn't it?' he said, watching the foreman's face. 'The kind you press into wax, to sign a letter.'

'Aye.' The foreman nodded uneasily. 'Best seals in the world, made in London. Cannot be forged. Grant you passage and give your word authority.'

'Might the person who made this ring have been employed making seals?' suggested Charlie. 'The brass cut is the same.'

'Possible, I suppose,' said the foreman hazily. 'But if you're looking for the old Royalist seals, they were locked away, a long time ago.' He eyed the ring.

Charlie glanced at Lily. She seemed not to have noticed the foreman's suspicious manner, and was chewing at a ragged fingernail with her white teeth and surveying the coin-making equipment.

'Might we take a look at some of the old seals?' asked Charlie.

The foreman hesitated for slightly too long. 'You have the King's permission to see what you will,' he said eventually, 'but I couldn't tell you where they are.' He gestured to the creaking wooden walls. 'The room was built over, after the King returned.'

'Built over?' Charlie was taking in the mouldering wood.

'Cromwell won the war,' explained the foreman. 'Everything to do with the old King was thrown in a cupboard. It was done in a hurry. No one knew if the Republic would last. So destroying Royalist things seemed unwise.' The foreman nodded. 'Soon after there was a great call for new coins, seals, everything. We had to build quick to meet demand. The Royal things got lost in amongst it all,' he concluded.

'You don't know if anyone kept a record of where this lost room is?'

'Those who made it are long gone. America. You didn't await the King's return if you were one of those who fought for Cromwell,' he added. 'And when you're as old as I am, you learn not to ask too many questions. Regimes change, men come and go.'

As the foreman continued speaking, Charlie was building a strong impression of a man protesting too much.

'I keep my head down and do my work,' continued the foreman. 'You don't involve yourself in politics if you work in the Mint.'

'Where do you suggest we start looking?' asked Charlie.

The man shrugged his massive shoulders. 'The pressing house at the back is most likely,' he said airily. 'Though I doubt you'll find it. Don't walk across the old Gully Walkway,' he added, pointing towards a rickety exterior walkway. 'Best to go through the coin-blank room, past the sheet-rollers.'

Charlie noticed Lily was watching the foreman keenly.

The foreman looked towards the presses. 'I must get back to my labour,' he said. 'We've two hundred pennies to press before dark and no money for more candles.'

'He's lying through his single tooth,' hissed Lily, as the foreman walked away. 'What's he hiding?'

'The old seals,' said Charlie. 'Did you see his face when I mentioned them?'

Lily nodded. 'Perhaps we should have asked him about a green-and-gold dress with leaves stitched over,' she said. 'In any case, the fore-man doesn't want us to find the old seals. What should we do?'

'Start in the furthest room to where he suggested,' said Charlie, 'by the route he told us not to go. Let's cross the old Gully Walkway.'

Chapter 39

As night fell, the party at the Golden Apple was gearing up to full swing. On the narrow stage, girls cavorted and danced to a lively tune. Outside, Covent Garden was filling with revellers.

'Claret is a penny a glass, or a shilling in the boxes,' Mrs Jenks was explaining to her newest two girls.

They'd come to her from Damaris Page's devastated brothel, frightened and desperate – exactly the combination she liked. Sadly, only one was suitable. Viola was Italian and hoped to be an actress. The other, called Clancy, was Wapping-lewd and pretty only in a youthful way, with a weasel slant to her nose and teeth. But Mrs Jenks could hawk Clancy's virginity a few times before she turned her out with the other Covent Garden street walkers.

'What do the girls drink?' asked Clancy. It had been several hours since her last slug of rum and she was beginning to feel the effects. She was eyeing the barrels hopefully.

'Nothing,' snapped Mrs Jenks. 'You'll keep your wits under my roof. I've worked hard to make us reputable,' she added. 'The Golden Apple used to be the blackest brothel in Covent Garden. Now look.' She gestured proudly to the stage. 'It's a proper theatre.'

Clancy bit her lip. Her hands had started to tremble.

Mrs Jenks steered the young girls through the drunk patrons and rouged faces in the theatre pit. Unlike most other bawds, Mrs Jenks had been bred to finery. She was an immaculately attired woman, with every lacy cuff, bright ribbon and snowy frill in place. Her blue eyes were eerily dilated by excessive belladonna and expensive lead paint set her features in a perfect white oval, giving her the appearance of a black-eyed doll.

'You'll work the pit with the other rub-and-tug girls,' she explained, adjusting the line of pearls that held her false blonde curls in place. 'If you prove popular we might try you in a box.'

Mrs Jenks pointed to the high boxes. Arranged twelve feet above them was the noble seating. Twenty theatre-style boxes held actresses in black masks, each doing whatever it took to attract the richer blood. Several had succeeded and were occupied with well-dressed patrons. Some drew curtains or called for wine and spirits to be winched up using an elaborate pulley system. Some were openly servicing gentlemen in plain view.

'What of the other theatres you supply?' asked Viola tentatively. 'We were told you send girls to the licensed theatres. The King's and the Duke's.'

The black eyes settled on her. 'I manage the whores at all the theatres,' said Mrs Jenks. 'But they must work their way up from the Golden Apple. Every girl in Covent Garden wants to work the licensed theatres. Some even end up acting privately for the King,' she added tantalisingly.

Clancy glanced at Viola, wondering if her friend was falling for the lies.

'Half of what you make is due to me,' continued Mrs Jenks. 'If you're late, you're fined. If you cheek a man, you're fined. Any complaints, it's a shilling comes from your earnings.'

Clancy was trying not to stare at Mrs Jenks's peculiar eyes. The huge black pupils gave her an ethereal quality, like a fairy. A sailor with his trousers open staggered onto the stage and the doll-like face shifted. Now the back eyes were shark-like, thought Clancy, gazing into their murky depths and remembering a terrifying sketch she'd seen in a sailor's effects.

On the stage, the man glimpsed Mrs Jenks's predatory expression and quickly produced a gold coin. The nearest actress took it, then threw her skirts over the man's head, whilst winking at the crowd. The shark-eyes faded, the red mouth flicked upwards. Mrs Jenks turned back to Clancy and Viola.

'Your dresses,' she said, her eyes lingering on Clancy's armpit stains. 'Something will have to be done.' She clicked her fingers that they should follow and led them to a row of trunks.

'You can trust us with your fine dresses,' said Clancy, manoeuvring her features into an earnest expression and trying to clip her vowels.

Mrs Jenks opened the oldest trunk. A musty smell wafted up. 'Something from in here,' she said, delving in with a veined hand.

She pulled out a red courtly dress, woefully out of fashion, and handed it to Viola. The dark-haired girl took it, her mouth turned down.

'Now,' said Mrs Jenks, eyeing Clancy. 'For you.' She extracted a faded yellow dress with a sizeable rash of orange mildew.

'I'll smell like an old docker,' complained Clancy. 'It stinks worse than boat-bilge.'

Mrs Jenks glared. Mistaking her silence for hesitation, Clancy threw both hands into the trunk.

'What about this one?' she suggested, pulling out a strange old dress. 'It looks like somethin' from one of the old masques,' said Clancy, admiring it. 'Fairies and enchantresses.'

The thin silk fluttered delicately as she drew it free. It was stitched with hundreds of tiny green-gold leaves, so they seemed to be falling. A mess of green ribbons splayed out from between the leaves, like a May Festival crown.

Mrs Jenks's ruby-coloured mouth opened and shut. 'I'd forgotten about that dress,' she said, reaching to take it. 'No, you may not wear it. It's far too valuable . . .'

'Mrs Jenks!' A scrawny girl with thick face paint skidded into the room. 'The 'prentices, Mrs Jenks! The 'prentices! They're heading up Cheapside!'

Clancy was looking at the barrels of wine again. Her gaze dropped down to the green-gold dress. Each of the fabric leaves could be sold, she thought, for a penny or so.

'Stop squawking, Millicent,' Mrs Jenks scolded, releasing Clancy from her glare in her annoyance. 'What did I tell you about speaking properly? There's always talk,' said Mrs Jenks. 'The apprentices haven't attacked the Golden Apple for fifteen years. Do you know why?'

Millicent shook her head.

'Because Covent Garden is where royalty goes for their wine and whoring. An attack on us is an attack on the throne.' Mrs Jenks took in the seedy exuberance of her stage with pride. 'And the theatres are the safest places of all.'

'They're organised,' said Millicent, enunciating carefully. 'Like an army.'

'Do you think a pack of blue-aproned boys could threaten me?' said Mrs Jenks. 'I'm three steps ahead of them.' She gave a slight smile. 'Any apprentices dare try attacking my houses, they'll soon discover the penalty for treason.'

Something seemed to turn in Mrs Jenks's mind. Her lips moved of their own accord.

The old dress. The riots. Something very important had suggested itself.

Mrs Jenks turned quickly back to where Clancy had been standing. But the young pickpocket had fled, taking the old dress with her.

Chapter 40

Charlie and Lily were staring out into the void. The Gully Walkway was an ancient rope-bridge of rickety wood, strung high between the inner and outer walls over the putrid moat. What remained of the splintering steps was roughly tacked into the loose brickwork with rusting nails. The entrance onto it had been boarded over at each end with thick planks.

'Maybe the foreman was telling the truth,' said Lily uncertainly, staring down at the green moat far below. 'Maybe he just didn't want us to die.'

'It's already boarded up,' Charlie pointed out. 'Why warn us not to come this way? Suggests excessive concern for two strangers, don't you think?'

He looked at the rickety falling-down walkway.

'Easy,' he decided. 'It's just like wooden roof-tiles in Cheapside. Step lightly and avoid the green bits.'

'It's all green,' said Lily, looking warily out.

Charlie stuck a leg over the crossed boards and put a tentative foot on the creaking platform. It shifted ominously beneath him.

'Sound as a bell,' he called back, stepping forward with the other foot. 'Only keep to the wall.'

He heard Lily step over and take a gasp of fright. 'It moves!'

'I thought you weren't afraid of heights,' said Charlie, inching along with practised dexterity.

'It's not the height,' said Lily, stepping carefully. 'It's the water.'

A gust of wind went tunnelling through the old planks, causing them to ripple disconcertingly.

'You're used to London rooftops,' said Lily, breath catching in her throat. 'I'm not.'

'Take your shoes off,' suggested Charlie. 'Easier to balance.'

Lily closed her eyes, swallowed and managed to pull one shoe off. She staggered slightly, and her bare foot split a mouldering plank along the middle.

'I can't do it!' she shouted to Charlie. 'I'm going back.'

He crossed nimbly back to where she stood. 'Hold on to me.'

She looked at him, then down to the moat. 'This isn't worth a gold ring,' she said. But she took his hands gratefully.

'No,' agreed Charlie, turning backwards to inch her further across. 'But we know the foreman is hiding something. He's obviously a Republican. Perhaps there's some secret here. You could share it with the King, earn back your privateer's licence.'

'I *knew* this would happen,' said Lily bitterly, trying not to look down. 'I *knew* I'd end up in some mortal peril with you, Charlie Tuesday. I promised myself I would never do this again.'

'You're already over halfway across,' Charlie pointed out, keeping a tight hold of her hands. 'No sense in going back now.'

Lily raised her eyes to the heavens. 'Why do I always have to be in the most dangerous of places,' she importuned a nameless deity, 'with the most persuasive man in London?'

He smiled at her. 'I knew you missed me.'

They'd made it almost the whole way across, Charlie moving slowly backwards.

'I can't see anything here the foreman might be hiding,' admitted Charlie, looking around. 'Nothing carved on the wall.'

He looked out to see London ranged before him, a thick wall winging its way from the Tower to encircle the old city. The sun was beginning to set, casting blood-red fingers across the sky. Tomorrow was Maundy Thursday, Charlie realised. Good Friday the day after. He was running out of time to save Maria, and all they'd encountered were old puzzles and dead ends.

'Just let's get off this walkway,' said Lily, fixing her eyes on the welcome interior of the far side with relief.

Charlie's bare feet touched something jagged on the smooth planks. He glanced down to see one of the planks bore a key-shaped hole, ragged where the metalwork had been pulled off.

'Some of these planks were reclaimed from an old door,' said Charlie, assessing the size and weight of the lock. A thought occurred to him.

'Why have you stopped?' demanded Lily, her voice launching high.

'I'm looking at the planks,' said Charlie. His eyes settled on one behind Lily's shoed foot. 'There!' he said. 'Look. Something's been written.'

Lily swung to glance down, then lurched back, green-faced. 'Why did you make me do that?' she muttered, holding his hands tight and closing her eyes.

Charlie stooped low.

'Don't let me go!' she shrieked.

'It's only for a moment,' he assured her. 'I won't let you fall.' He could make out the plank behind Lily's shaking foot. There was a crest carved into it. A sun with waving rays. It was enclosed in a bobbled circle of dots.

'There's a sun crest,' said Charlie. 'In some kind of circle. Lily,' he added, 'it looks like a Royalist thing. You might have seen it before.'

'No.'

'Just take a quick look.' He stood and held tight to her hands. 'The barest of glances,' he pleaded. 'I'll hold on to you.'

Lily glared at him, took a breath, then flashed her eyes briefly towards the carved crest. She stood for a moment, steadying herself. 'It's Sun in Splendour,' she said. 'I recognise it. There's an inn of the same name towards Islington,' she added. 'It's heraldry.'

'Heraldry as in knights of yore?' asked Charlie.

Lily nodded. 'King Arthur again.' She rolled her eyes, then staggered slightly. 'Just get me off the walkway,' she said. 'Please.'

He drew her carefully along and helped her over the crossed boards barring the far side. She sighed in relief.

'The size of the keyhole in that door,' Charlie was saying. 'The thickness of the planks. You don't see that in ordinary houses. The Tower used to have an old wooden lockup by the gates. An overnight gaol for felons waiting to be assigned to a prison. It was demolished years ago.'

'So that plank was carved by a prisoner?' said Lily.

'Most likely,' said Charlie. 'And the foreman thought it should mean something to us. Something he didn't want us to deduce.' He thought hard. 'The ring,' he said, 'the puzzle. The sun is a sign of gold in alchemy,' he suggested.

He called the plank to mind. The heraldic sun, surrounded by the circle of dots.

'The circle surrounding the sun,' he said. 'It was made up of different-sized circles, wasn't it? Like a fairy ring.' He was picturing the mushroom fairy rings that grew on the common land surrounding the city. Fungus sprung up in a perfect circle, made of different-sized round mushrooms.

'It did look like a fairy ring,' agreed Lily. 'A large circle made of different-sized small ones. But the Sun in Splendour isn't how alchemists represent gold. They use a simple sun. And that sun was *in* the ring,' she pointed out, 'not on it.'

'So the Sun in Splendour could represent London,' said Charlie. 'Surrounded by a fairy ring.' Charlie looked out to the walkway, feeling he was missing something.

'Only the worthy,' said Lily, her tone slightly scathing. She drummed her fingers on her lips. 'I'll bet this puzzle is something high-borns were taught as schoolboys. The fairy ring around London.'

Shapes flashed in Charlie's mind. The uneven circle around the sun, and the wide vista of London he'd seen from the Tower.

'London's fairy ring,' he said slowly. 'We weren't thinking large enough.' He turned excitedly to Lily. 'London Wall,' he said. 'A circle to repel bad things. The whole old city is a fairy ring. A circle bordered by gates and turrets.'

'One big fairy ring,' said Lily, calling to mind the London Wall, punctuated by sentinel gates with the Tower of London closing the loop. 'So what's the gold?'

'The Mint,' said Charlie. 'The Mint is the gold. This is where the city's gold is kept.'

'We've been in the right place all along,' said Lily excitedly.

'It fits,' said Charlie. 'Whoever made this ring was a Royalist. If they worked in the Mint, they could easily have kept a key here, for those who solved the riddle. But we're back to where we started,' he concluded. 'The Mint doesn't make keys.'

Lily frowned in thought. 'Charlie,' she said slowly. 'What was it the foreman didn't want us to find?' She grasped his hand. 'The seals, Charlie,' she said, 'the old Royalist seals.'

'You think a key is hidden with the seals?' he suggested.

She shook her head. 'Think of what a seal is, what it can do. The right seal can get you into select places. So a seal is a kind of a key, is it not?' she added.

'Which means the foreman knew the entire time what the puzzle meant,' said Charlie.

Lily was nodding. 'We should go back to where he is,' she said. 'First rule of spying. If someone's on edge, lying, watch what they do when they think you aren't looking. Likely it will reveal something important. He might go straight to where this secret room is.' She chewed a fingernail. 'The only problem is,' she said. 'How do we spy on him without being seen? This whole place is full of men pressing coins.'

'In all my years of thief taking,' said Charlie, 'there's something that has always held true.' He pointed to the dusty network of old beams holding the crumbling ceiling in place. They spread outwards in complicated overlapping shapes. 'No one ever looks up.'

Chapter 41

Mother Mitchell raised her jewelled fist, hesitated, then knocked. The door began to open. There was a young girl on the other side. Mother Mitchell didn't recognise her.

The girl tilted her head insolently. 'Muvva Mitchell, is it? I've seen your fine carriage.' She made a mock curtsey. 'Think you're better than us. Does noble cock taste better than sailors'?'

She was eyeing Mother Mitchell's jewels and coiffed hair. An unusual sight in Wapping.

Mother Mitchell moved slightly closer. 'Mind your manners, girl. This fancy dress don't mean I won't box your ears. I'm here to speak with your mistress . . .'

They were interrupted by a commotion in the hallway. A tall woman was shouldering her way angrily through a gaggle of morose-looking girls.

'What is she doing here?' demanded an African-accented voice. 'She may not enter this house.'

Mother Mitchell held up a pacifying hand as Damaris strode to the door, glaring. She was taller than Mother Mitchell remembered, and her black skin still had its sheen of youth. Her pink dress wasn't real silk,

Mother Mitchell noted. It was taffeta, and her cuffs were thick-stitched Cheapside imitations of Chantilly lace.

'What do you want?' demanded Damaris. Her large dark eyes were narrowed.

Mother Mitchell caught sight of the wound on Damaris's cheek and raised a hand towards it, her face drawn. 'Oh, Rissy,' she said, reverting to Damaris's old nickname, 'what did they do?'

'What's one more scar?' Damaris shrugged. 'Don't be pretending you care. You stole my best customer.'

Mother Mitchell stamped her foot. 'You used a lock of my hair for voodoo!' she accused.

'It din' work,' said Damaris. 'He never came back.' Her voice was pained. 'Mens is all the same. They think us animals. All of us with black skin.'

'And now you press-gang the poor young men who come to your house?' said Mother Mitchell. 'You must have known there would be consequences.' She was looking at the wound on Damaris's face. 'These aren't just apprentices' high jinks.'

Damaris waved her hand, with its single battered tin ring. 'I know it,' she said. 'The fire. People poor. Got nothing. Lookin' for someone to blame.' She smiled sardonically. 'Everythin' always the fault of the whores.'

'They're heading to Covent Garden. The apprentices,' said Mother Mitchell meaningfully.

Damaris's round eyes widened. 'The apprentices never go to Covent Garden,' she said. 'That's the King's place. His women.'

'*Her* women,' corrected Mother Mitchell. 'Mrs Jenks manages the whores in Covent Garden. She took the theatres for herself, didn't she? London's richest pickings. Left us common bawds the dregs.'

'That's what high breedin' gets you,' said Damaris. 'Jenks is friends with high-ups. Ain't no one going to cross her.'

''Cept now there is,' said Mother Mitchell. 'The mob is so riled up I think they might dare an attack on Covent Garden. And, after all these years, the doxy Queen's got no guard. She's sat fat on her high breeding.'

Mother Mitchell took a breath. 'If Jenks falls we should move in together,' she said. 'We could divide Covent Garden in two.'

Damaris hesitated. 'That's the difference between you and me,' she said. 'I never was a builder of dynasties. I happy enough with Wapping.'

Mother Mitchell absorbed this. 'I don't believe you,' she said. 'I think you're scared of her. Of Mrs Jenks. Mutton-dressed-as-lamb with her sugar-paste blonde curls.'

'She like a salamander,' said Damaris. 'She evil. Besides,' she added, 'I don't believe them 'prentices would dare Covent Garden. It's treason.'

Mother Mitchell opened her mouth to say something. For a moment Damaris thought she might demand her lock of hair back. Then she turned to go, her huge silken skirts making an impressive orbit around her broad hips.

'Your boy was here,' said Damaris as Mother Mitchell walked away. 'The one you raised. The thief taker. Charlie.'

Mother Mitchell turned her head back.

'He's a credit to you,' said Damaris, stepping back from the threshold.

Mother Mitchell nodded. 'Tell your girl that noble cock does taste better than sailors',' she called back as she left. 'Though I've never been partial to either.'

Chapter 42

Charlie inched forward, tensing to propel himself across the beams.

Beneath him men carried crates rattling full of coins. If the heat of the forge-heated rooms was unbearable, the rising trapped air in the rafters seemed to wrap tight around them.

'I can hardly breathe,' said Lily. 'I think I may faint.'

'You're wearing too many clothes,' said Charlie.

Lily glowered at him, sweat beading her face.

They'd tracked the foreman to the part of the Mint where the latest machines had been employed. The roar of clanking metal, slamming presses and tinkling new coins enveloped them.

Sweating men with downturned mouths manned the machinery. Several worked to turn the huge iron press, propelling a heavy stamp rhythmically downwards. One man rapidly slid blanks into the machine's ravenous maw, whilst an unfortunate boy quickly flicked the pressed coins free before the next heavy stamp of the press broke his fingers.

The foreman was talking to a worker and Charlie inclined his ear towards the conversation. But the noisy presses drowned everything out.

'We need to get closer,' he hissed, inching further along the beam. 'This way.'

'It won't take our weight,' said Lily, eyeing the ancient structure.

Charlie looked at the dowel pinning the beam in place. 'It will most likely hold,' he decided.

'Most likely?'

Charlie was thinking of Maria, captive somewhere. 'Stay here if you like,' he said. 'I need to hear what's being said.'

Lily muttered one of her strange gypsy curses. Then the beam shuddered, and she began working her way towards him, her silk dress rustling as she moved.

A door opened. Charlie saw an incredibly beautiful woman enter, dressed in a dizzying display of wealth, flanked by a pack of five guards. He recognised her instantly. It was Lady Castlemaine, the King's infamous mistress. She approached the foreman, who seemed to be expecting her.

'What's she doing here?' asked Lily. 'If she sees me, we're both dead.'

'You've made an enemy of Lady Castlemaine?'

'Something like that.'

'I have a bad feeling,' said Charlie, 'that the foreman must have sought out Lady Castlemaine and told her we were here asking questions. Which suggests this missing lord and lady are important.'

The coin pressing stopped, and the workers stood out of respect to their visitor. But their faces barely disguised their contempt. Charlie could imagine what the coin-pressers would say to their plain-dressed wives, eating their supper of watered oatmeal. The King's whore wore a dress expensive enough to pay the Mint's annual wages several times over.

'Where are these spies now?' Lady Castlemaine's cut-glass vowels rang around the now-silent room.

'I sent them to the old pressing house.'

Lady Castlemaine nodded. 'I have guards at the exits. The girl is called Lily Boswell. She's dangerous. We'll arrest her along with whoever she is with and throw them in the Tower.'

Fear coiled through Charlie's stomach as the guards hurried off to search for them.

The foreman said something that Charlie didn't hear. He moved closer.

'We have no hope of finding the green-and-gold dress,' said Lady Castlemaine to the unheard question. 'The talk of the brothels is it's been stolen by a Wapping whore. She vanished into the stews near Temple.' Lady Castlemaine sighed. 'It's only fortunate the thief doesn't know what she has stolen. Whoever gets hold of the dress can find the Lord and Lady. What of the seals?' she demanded.

'Safe. No one uses the shaft anymore. And men won't go near the old forge. Not after the horrors done there,' the foreman said, crossing himself. 'The Lord and Lady escaped the flames. But the others were burned there.'

Lady Castlemaine's small jaw tightened. 'You *burned* them?' Her eyes narrowed in disgust.

The foreman shook his grizzled head. 'Not I, Your Ladyship. Nor any men I knew. They had to bring in a special man. One of Cromwell's lackeys. He was the only one who would do such a dreadful deed and even he baulked at it, I reckon.'

Lady Castlemaine's face darkened. 'How?' she demanded. 'How could the Lord and Lady have left the Tower unseen?'

The foreman rubbed his jaw. 'Old magic?' he suggested. 'The fairy folk can disappear and reappear at will.'

Lady Castlemaine gave an unladylike snort of disbelief. 'More likely someone thought to make his fortune by protecting them.' She thought for a moment. 'You're certain they won't go near the old forge?' she demanded. 'If Lily Boswell finds the key to Avalon it will be all your necks. She might piece something together.'

Charlie heard a strange noise behind him. He turned to see Lily had turned a waxy pale, her face slick with sweat. She was fainting from the heat.

Charlie inched back as fast as he dared. Lily's eyes were rolling upwards as he made it back level with where she lay. She began to slip sideways and he threw a desperate arm out, pinning her to the wooden rafter.

She blinked, shook her head and looked at him in confusion.

'You were fainting,' he explained. 'The heat.'

Lady Castlemaine was turning to go now.

'Come on,' said Charlie. 'Let's get out of here.'

Lily nodded and, as she did so, a large droplet of sweat shook free from her forehead and splashed down. It hit Lady Castlemaine's ringed fingers and there was a long moment whilst she looked at her wet hand in puzzlement.

Charlie and Lily stayed completely still on the rafter above, not daring to breathe.

Then, very slowly, the King's mistress lifted her beautiful face and looked up.

Her large violet eyes landed square on Lily and Charlie, clinging monkey-like to the beam.

'Get them,' she commanded. 'Find out what they heard.'

Chapter 43

Maria awoke with a start. Someone in the dark room was screaming. She sat up, alert, heart beating fast. It was a man's voice, so thick with fear it filled her with panic. He was pleading with someone. Then she realised: it was Tom's voice. He must have fallen asleep on the floor near her.

'Tom?' she called into the dark. 'Tom?'

The shouting was close, and she managed to feel for his hand. It was cold, the skin flaking away. She gripped it hard and squeezed. Her eyes had adjusted now, and she could see a sliver of moonlight barely illuminating the attic. She made out the shape of her captor, rolling around in his sleep, face wracked with terror.

'Stop!' he shouted. 'No more! He will die of it!'

It occurred to Maria that Tom must have inadvertently rolled nearer to her in his sleep. She might be able to search his prone body for a key or a weapon. Her first reaction had been pity, but now sense took over.

Her gaze dropped to his hip where a short sword was sheathed. She took a gentle hold and tried to pull it free. But the blade was stuck, rusted and old. She slipped a hand under his coat. There was something inside. A leather vial of liquid. Poison? She remembered the dead girl. Could she steal it, use it?

The sudden possibilities overwhelmed her. She was manacled, she didn't need to remind herself. He would likely realise she had robbed him. Perhaps his sleeping was another trick. Could he be acting to entice her to try to escape?

He quietened, and she drew her fingers back fearfully, contemplating her options. Perhaps she could pour the liquid directly into his sleeping mouth.

Suddenly Tom's eyes were open, pale pools in the half-light. Maria felt bitter disappointment fill her stomach. The chance to escape had slid away. She'd missed it.

He was staring at her.

'You're frightened of ghosts?' asked Maria. She didn't know why she said it.

He sat up and she felt his fingers flex. She realised she was still holding his hand.

'You tried to comfort me?' he asked. 'In my sleep?'

She nodded, not daring to speak in case her voice gave away the lie.

'You didn't try to escape,' he said. 'Why?'

'I . . . I pitied you,' said Maria, feeling guilty. 'You sounded so frightened.'

There was a pause. He slipped his hand free and moved away from her.

'What did you dream of?' she asked.

His face clouded. 'Fairies do not dream. We have . . . thoughts, is all. Thoughts that come back at night.'

She waited, and he lifted his eyes to hers. In the dark it was difficult to see his expression.

'Burning,' he said, fingering his arm. 'It's always burning.' He chewed his lip. 'When I meet with the Lord and Lady,' he said, 'the terrors will stop. They will send me back to my own kind.'

Maria hesitated, sensing Tom was more vulnerable than usual. 'I know we're in a theatre,' she said. 'You worked in one, didn't you? You must have.'

'My family thought theatre a great sin,' he said.

'So did mine,' said Maria.

Tom's eyes widened. It was a curious gesture that made him appear suddenly childlike.

Maria took a chance. 'Play it for me,' said Maria. 'Show me what happened to the Lord and Lady. It's no sin to tell a story,' she added.

He breathed out and she saw he was tempted. She'd judged it right. His compulsion to show his skill was getting the better of him.

There was a silence and Maria thought she'd over-baited the hook. But then a light flared in Tom's eyes. He stood, stepped lightly back and straightened his shoulders.

'The scene opens in the dread Tower of London,' he said dramatically. 'London's most impenetrable prison. Deep in the depths are the cells where the most important prisoners are kept and tightly guarded.' Tom took a step to the side, hunched his shoulders slightly, and his entire demeanour changed. He was a hulking man, with penetrating eyes. 'Cromwell wants 'em burned,' said Tom, affecting a gravelly voice. 'No one is to know how they met their end. Throw the ashes in the Thames.'

'You play a Tower guard?' guessed Maria.

'A great soldier named Barebones,' said Tom, reverting to his usual voice. 'But Cromwell didn't trust him to guard the Lord and Lady.'

Maria noticed pride flare in his face. Tom played on.

'I've never known Cromwell fear anyone,' continued Tom in the deep voice of Barebones, 'but he's afraid a' them. He came down here clad in his iron armour, and I heard him talking to them. Shaking his finger, calling them fairies and false gods, swearing to protect Christian men from their evil.' Tom fingered his sword, continuing the acted part. 'Cromwell said they weave their spell on men, whisper to them their greatest desire. Only Tom Black cannot be seduced by them.' He rubbed his chin, and once again Maria noticed his scarred knuckles.

'You were the only man Cromwell trusted?' she asked, playing to his pride and trying not to stare at the ugly knotted wounds.

'I was set to guard them,' said Tom, pleased. 'And when the time was right, burn them.' He had a sudden uncomfortable memory of the last time he spoke with Cromwell.

'They are what we truly fought against, are they not, Tom?' Cromwell had said. 'Love for these wicked creatures is the reason why so many good men died.' But the Lord Commander hadn't been able to tear his eyes away from the Lady's beauty. 'We must not forget what horrors they are responsible for,' he said finally. 'No matter how lovely they look to us.'

'But the Lord and Lady were smuggled free.' Tom hesitated. A troubling memory drifted back. Something he was too ashamed to play aloud. The Lady had spoken to him, her voice soft and musical.

'We know what is in your heart, Tom Black. Free us and you shall be returned to your fairy kingdom.'

Tom's eyes flicked to Maria. She was watching him. Did she know he'd wanted to disobey his orders? He'd told the Lady he couldn't save her. But temptation had coiled around his soul and she'd known it.

The Lady's tinkling musical laugh had echoed around like fairy bells.

'You don't need to save us, Tom Black, you need only make us disappear.'

Chapter 44

Charlie and Lily were hurtling through the rickety corridors of the Mint with Lady Castlemaine's guard hot on their heels.

The labyrinthine warren spilled into a dizzying chaos of tiny rooms, meandering wooden corridors and ladders leading to unexpected mezzanines.

'The foreman talked of an old forge,' Charlie gasped as they fled. 'I remember seeing a chimney on the outside. I think the room of seals must be this way.' He caught Lily's expression. 'Lady Castlemaine's guards are at all the exits,' said Charlie. 'The foreman mentioned a shaft in the room of broken presses. That sounds like a way out, doesn't it?'

'And if you're wrong?'

'Then we're dead in any case.'

'Lady Castlemaine doesn't want me to get the key to Avalon,' said Lily, breathing hard as they ran. 'Which makes me think it's worth finding.'

Her dark eyes had a determined quality Charlie had seen before. He felt sorry for Lady Castlemaine.

Charlie was desperately trying to apply his memory of the exterior, with its hundred tiny windows, to the crazed building inside. His eyes dropped to the floor ahead. Deep track grooves had been worn in the floor. As though something heavy had been dragged. He made a quick assessment. The marks led away from where the other new coin presses were being worked and wound off to a room ahead.

'This way,' said Charlie. 'Follow those marks on the floor. I think they show where a coin press has been retired.'

The grooves led through a doorway into a larger room filled with bales of metal ready for working. Huge rolls of sheet bronze were arranged in rows, wedged in place with wooden blocks. Charlie ducked behind the nearest, kicked out the block and rolled the metal bale against the doorway. Then he replaced the wood-wedge at the base and gave it a solid kick.

He heard the guards stack up on the other side, slamming their hands against the outsized roll of metal.

'We have a few minutes before they manage to move that roll of bronze,' said Charlie. 'The tracks from the coin press lead over there.'

They followed the tracks across the room, weaving in between the rolls of metal. A door at the back led to yet another room, smaller than the last.

'There!' said Lily, pointing. 'An old forge.'

The large brick construction was like an outsized bread oven, with a thick waist-height slab where the fire was lit and an arching brick top. They both stopped, looking over the abandoned fire. A broad chimney stack led up through the ceiling.

'They burned people here,' said Lily, swallowing. 'That's what the foreman said.' She was taking in the vast forge. 'No wonder it's been abandoned,' she concluded. 'It's likely haunted.'

'A hidden cupboard would have been built with newer wood,' said Charlie, taking in the small room. 'Even if they used old timbers, the new nails would stand out. Nothing here has been changed in decades.'

He sat on his haunches for a moment, absorbing the structure of the room. They could hear Lady Castlemaine's guards hammering on the heavy roll of metal blocking their entrance.

'You work in the Mint,' he said, thinking aloud. 'You need to put something out of view, for political reasons.' He was acutely aware that Lady Castlemaine's guards would soon get to where they were. 'Not stored in wood,' he muttered, thinking aloud. 'But the brick . . .' Charlie's eyes settled on the chimney. It was vast.

He stood, walking towards the huge chimney breast. It spanned almost the entire width of the room, with an enormous hearth and several other brick openings for coin forging. Charlie stepped closer to the forge and held a hand up inside the chimney.

'No draught,' he said. 'It's not clearing properly. And if it's been used for horrors, it's the kind of thing people keep away from.' Charlie stood back. 'If it were me,' he decided, 'I might just knock a hole in the side, where no one could see it. And put the bricks back quickly with whatever I had to hand.' His eyes tracked to the side of the chimney, where a cluster of bricks were held by a lighter-coloured mortar than the rest. 'Not real mortar at all,' he observed, testing the bricks with his fingers. 'Just a paste of bone-glue and sawdust.' He slid a brick free.

They heard a shriek of metal on wood from the far room, shouts of effort.

'I think the guards have found some way to move that roll of bronze,' said Charlie. 'We don't have much time.'

Lily came to help him. The bricks came away easily, revealing a sizeable hole in the side of the vast chimney. It was stacked with old crates filled with seals.

Chapter 45

Tom stared at the mirror. A heavy curtain had been laid over the glass. He reached forward with long pale fingers and tugged it away.

Arching black brows, pale-green eyes and pointed chin. His own face.

Tom watched.

Then from deep within the mirror the changeling boy stepped forward. His face was youthful, with pixie features, his mouth contorted in a cruel smile. His clothes were from a different time, and the world behind the mirror was strange, upside down.

Tom felt himself bristle with fear.

'Praise-God Barebones,' said the boy. 'Your old comrade does your bidding? His apprentices search the brothels as we planned?'

Tom's fingers were tapping a dance on his hands. Of course the boy knew. He was baiting him. The boy's eyes opened comically wide.

'He betrayed you?' he demanded, his voice frighteningly calm. 'That is why you turned to the thief taker for help?'

'I . . .'

'Humans always do,' said the boy. 'You were a fool to trust him. I am the only one who cares for you. Remember it.' Something else flashed in the boy's face. Tom felt dread fill his stomach. 'Does Barebones know of the dress?' the boy whispered. 'The dress that speaks of where the Lord and Lady are hiding?'

Tom closed his eyes and nodded.

'You grow weak,' said the boy. His eyes were dead, like a doll's. 'Barebones will find them and our chance will be gone.'

'No.' Tom shook his head. 'I need more time . . .'

'You ugly broken thing,' said the boy, balling his fists. 'I watch you, from behind the glass. In *my* place. *My* world. Yet you refuse to do the smallest thing to make amends.'

Deep in the mirror, a bell had begun to ring.

'The thief taker,' said Tom, wincing at the sound. 'He searches.'

More bells rang now.

'I had forgotten the girl,' said the boy softly. 'You think she will be enough persuasion?'

'The thief taker will find them,' promised Tom.

'He must do it faster,' said the boy. 'It will soon be too late for me.'

Tom knew instantly what he was thinking and felt sick. 'Better to kill her cleanly,' said Tom.

'You dull fool. Haven't you understood it yet? We took the girl to force Charlie Tuesday to find them.' The boy smiled coldly. 'Their powers will restore us. I will finally be returned to my rightful place. You will go back to your own kind. It's what we always talked of.' He eyed Tom. 'You think I don't see you, acting a part with her? She is changing you.'

'Perhaps she is,' said Tom. 'And perhaps your time in the fairy kingdom has changed you. You have fallen in love with their charm and cruelty. Their love of trickery and chaos.'

The boy's cold, cruel smile grew. 'Maundy Thursday is tomorrow. I have a feeling your thief taker won't deliver in time. And your girl, Maria, will die very badly.'

Chapter 46

Charlie and Lily began pulling out crates of seals and coin-making equipment from the abandoned forge.

'Where's the escape route?' asked Lily, peering inside the hole. 'I thought you said they'd be a tunnel for us to get out.'

'Maybe behind the crates,' said Charlie.

He reached in and pulled one free with effort. It jangled with metal contents as he drew it clear of the chimney. The top of the crate hadn't been sealed and the contents were covered in a thick layer of fine ash and dust.

'Old press plates,' said Lily, plunging a fist into the box and lifting a square of metal embossed with a plain set of shields. 'These made hammered coins for the Republic.'

'I remember these,' said Charlie, turning the plain coins. 'Money with no king's head.'

He reached in and pulled out the furthest crate. There was nothing behind it. No escape hatch, no wink of daylight.

Lily opened the crate. 'This is it!' she said excitedly. 'Royalist seals.'

They both began lifting them out of the crate. The top held older seals, from the beginning of the old king's rule. But as they dove deeper there were newer seals, from when the war started.

'There's nothing that stands out,' said Charlie, glancing over his shoulder. 'No heraldic suns.' He let a few seals fall through his fingers. 'Avalon,' he said. 'The key to Avalon. It was a paradise island. Apple trees.'

'I think there's an apple,' said Lily. She rifled through and seized on a small seal. It had a curving handle and the face showed a simple apple shape.

'I've seen that apple before,' said Charlie.

'Look at the handle,' said Lily. 'It has writing on it, the same script as the ring.'

She read.

The key to Avalon.

'The key to Avalon. Charlie!' she said excitedly. 'This is it!' She turned the seal. 'But where does it get us?'

Charlie sat back, trying to remember where he'd seen the sign before. 'Avalon,' he said suddenly. 'Apple trees. But apples have another meaning in London. Apples of Venus. Brothels.'

'Boys playing at spying,' said Lily disdainfully. 'I suppose they must have their little jokes. So the paradise island is a brothel?' She tapped the seal. 'But surely even a fine bawdy house wouldn't have their own seal?'

'When I was a boy,' said Charlie, 'some of the finer brothels held masques. Expensive parties for very fine people. Even royalty. Guests were disguised, but entry was ticketed. The best tickets were stamped with a seal.'

'The key to Avalon,' said Lily.

'The Golden Apple in Covent Garden,' said Charlie. 'That's where I've seen it before.'

Loud shouts came from behind them.

'The guards are in,' said Charlie. He looked at Lily. 'I made a mistake,' he admitted. 'The shaft the foreman spoke of.' He looked up at the forge. 'Shaft is another word for chimney. I have a bad feeling that's what he meant.'

'There must be another way out,' breathed Lily. 'Lady Castlemaine won't show us any mercy if her guards catch us here. She's the very devil for spite,' she added, scouring the room. 'Took my privateer's licence for nothing. Can I help the way the King looks at me?'

Charlie nodded in a way he hoped seemed sympathetic.

'Can we climb up the chimney?' suggested Lily, desperately, glancing back at the approaching guards.

Charlie shook his head. 'It's blocked,' he said. 'We're trapped.'

Chapter 47

Barebones was eyeing the decorated front of the Golden Apple. The apprentices gathered behind him.

'Where are the women?' muttered one boy nervously. Unlike the Wapping brothels, there were no half-naked girls hanging out of the windows. No sign at all that it was anything other than a grand house.

'They think themselves a theatre,' said Barebones. But he had an uneasy look on his face, taking in the large windows, the solid brick. 'We did not falter before,' he decided, 'when men in fine clothes told us they were our betters. Will we fail now, when painted jades try the same?'

The boys cheered, but it lacked the bloodthirsty edge of their Wapping cries. Most had never been west of Fleet Street in their lives. They were looking wide-eyed at the carved front of the house, the grand windows.

Barebones turned to Repent and nodded. A shudder of excitement passed through the boys. Repent drew his hand back and hefted the stone. It sailed high in the air, then smashed through a glass window. There was a moment of silence. The apprentices could hardly believe their own audacity. Then Barebones raised his sword and gave a barking military cry.

'Charge!' he bellowed, the force of his voice echoing off the close-set buildings. 'Breach the door!'

The apprentices moved towards the house in a half charge, hefting iron bars, poleaxes and staves. A mason's apprentice threw a hammer at the thick black door, splintering the wood.

'Whores!' he shouted. 'Be afeared of your sins!'

Behind him the other boys attacked the door as a pack. The heavy entrance was smashed apart, and the boys poured through. The first room was filled with beautiful furniture, long silk curtains and a table laid out with a crystal decanter of red wine.

The apprentices fell on it, smashing, tearing. One picked up the decanter and threw it against the tastefully decorated wall. It exploded in a blood-red spray.

Barebones came in behind them and paused in the doorway. Repent moved to go past, but Barebones held his hand up.

'Something's not right,' he muttered. 'Where are the whores and punters? The Golden Apple is a den of sin, day and night.'

A bugle sounded from outside. Barebones strode quickly to the window. Moving towards the house was a pack of expensively uniformed guards. Barebones stepped back, incredulous.

'It's a false flag,' he said. 'That prick-sucking jade told us the wrong street. This isn't the Golden Apple. It's an ambush house.' He allowed himself a slight smile, watching the private guard surround the house. 'She has us in a pincer.'

Tramping footsteps resounded.

'Why lure us into a house?' asked Repent, his pockmarked face taking in the expensive interior.

'She waited until we broke the law,' said Barebones. 'Burglary. A hanging crime.' Barebones moved into the hallway, placing himself between the front door and the boys. 'Get out, those who can!' he shouted as the first men crashed through the open door. 'Windows, cellars! Any port in a storm!'

He hefted his short iron sword and swung it in a wide circle. The first guards came at him as the boys ran in every direction. The uniformed guard struck boys to the floor, grabbed others by their collars.

Barebones fought, ducking and swinging. He'd brought down three guards when a high cry made him turn. A guard held Repent by his greasy hair. Barebones ran at them, bringing a punch under the captor's ribcage. Repent fell free, gasping.

'Go!' shouted Barebones, placing himself between his son and the guard. 'Give this to Bolly!' He hurled his iron sword at his son.

Repent caught the weapon, then ran.

Barebones drew a second sword.

'Liberty of conscience!' he bellowed, the old soldier's cry coming easily to him. He charged, weapon forward.

Seven guards fell on Barebones, beating and punching. He swayed for a moment, then went down.

A guard sat on his back and began lashing Barebones's wrists together with tough rope.

'It's Lent,' growled Barebones. 'The law turns a blind eye.'

'You silly bastard,' said the guard, not without sympathy. 'You think the doxy queen doesn't have a few traps for those who mean her harm? You've fallen for the serpent's trick, my friend. Mrs Jenks will see you hang.'

Chapter 48

Lily and Charlie watched as the guards closed in, passing between the large rolls of sheet metal.

'What now?' said Lily, eyes scouring the room. 'There's no way out.'

Charlie's gaze settled on a patch of floorboards riddled with the tell-tale fungal circles of damp. Then he looked to the large abandoned coin press. It had a heavy base of thick metal, atop which was a wooden frame holding a weighty screw mechanism and a broad turning bar at the top, like the yoke of a plough.

Charlie raced towards the rotting floorboards and laid hold of the bar.

'Help me,' he shouted. 'We need to tip over this press.' He leaned back and pulled. The press was far heavier than he had anticipated.

Lily's dark eyes darted from the press to the floor. She ran to his side.

'Pull!' shouted Charlie. 'Help me! There's water under here,' he added, seeing her expression. 'This part is built over the river. That's why the planks are rotting.'

Lily understood immediately and moved to the other side of the press.

Gunfire exploded through the Mint. Shot sprayed against the metal press, ricocheting off.

They ducked instinctively. Charlie glanced up to see one of the guards pointing at the ancient ceiling, explaining something. They didn't want to shoot again in case they brought the building down on their heads. One signalled that they should fan out and move in as a pincer.

'These things are counterweighted at the base,' said Lily. 'We need a lever.' Her eyes settled on a discarded hammer. She picked it up and fitted the flatter end under the base. 'It's going!' she shouted, as their combined efforts tilted the press.

The guards were surrounding them.

Charlie dug in his feet and heaved. The press teetered, then overbalanced, falling fast towards the old floorboards. Charlie grabbed Lily's arm and pulled her aside. The press crashed downwards, tearing a jagged hole in the rotting floor and sending up a font of fetid water from the moat below.

The guards leapt back.

'Jump!' said Charlie, taking Lily's hand.

She pulled back, eyes wide. 'I can't. I can't swim.'

It came back to Charlie suddenly: the drowning penalty for gypsies; Lily's mother. He took her face with both hands.

'I won't let anything happen to you,' he promised. Then he wrapped his arms full around her waist and sent them both plummeting into the water.

Chapter 49

'Taken? The dress has been taken?' Amesbury was striding around the large room. He reminded Mrs Jenks of a caged bear. 'We gave you the theatres,' he said. 'That was your reward for loyalty. Every whore who cavorts in a Covent Garden playhouse is owned by you.'

'It was kept for six years,' Mrs Jenks said defensively. 'It was never expected to be so long.' Her belladonna-wide black eyes rested on him. 'Tell me true now, Amesbury,' she said. 'No more fairy tales. We knew powerful people went missing. Who are they? Why can they not return?'

'They will return when the time is right!' interrupted Amesbury angrily. 'When the King is strong. God's blood, woman, can you imagine what any upheaval would do to him? Plague, fire, the Dutch snapping at our heels and now apprentices tearing the city apart. Those boys need only the slightest provocation and all hell will break loose.'

'This is your doing,' said Mrs Jenks. 'One of your plots.' She moved a little closer. 'I know you, Amesbury. I think you wish Cromwell had killed those people.'

'We didn't know what kind of king he would be.' Amesbury sat heavily. 'You've done well from how things are, Emily. Why should you complain?'

'Have I?' She looked at him. 'Have you any idea the things I've had to do?'

'You were bred to ruthlessness,' said Amesbury. 'Same as I. Middle-gentry confers such necessities on its children, does it not?'

Mrs Jenks opened her mouth to reply, then seemed to reconsider. 'Barebones,' she said. 'He knows something. He is looking for them.'

'Barebones thinks them fairies,' said Amesbury. 'But a fool with a zeal for righteousness is a dangerous combination. He thinks them evil. Wants them killed.'

Mrs Jenks nodded. 'He riled up a pack of apprentices to sufficient courage to storm my house.' There was a slight admiration to her tone.

Amesbury nodded. 'I heard. You had him arrested. I'm not sure it will bring the outcome you want.'

'Without their ringleader, they're just a pack of motley boys,' said Mrs Jenks.

'The rioting captures public feeling,' said Amesbury. 'The people are tired of paying for a party they're not invited to. They might attack the whores, but make no mistake, it's the King they truly despise. The apprentices could storm Whitehall.'

Chapter 50

Charlie's arms were tight around Lily as they fell through the broken floor of the Mint. She flailed as they plunged into the dark waters and he almost lost his grip on her. Then he kicked them both upwards and they surfaced, gasping. Above them, the floor of the Mint showed a jagged hole where they'd fallen from. A guard appeared holding a gun.

'I see them,' he shouted, angling his weapon.

Charlie pumped his feet madly to take them downstream. A spray of shot threw up deep splashes in the water. He manoeuvred them to the edge of the waterway and they floated out into the wider moat that surrounded the Tower.

A few surprised Beefeaters looked down on them. Behind them, Lady Castlemaine's men had burst free of the Mint and were scouring the waters. Keeping hold of Lily's dress, Charlie aimed for a narrow sewage sluice leading out to the River Thames. As they entered the arch of the tunnel, blackness encircled them. Lily went strangely limp as they were propelled fast along and out into the Thames with a heavy splash. Behind them was St Katherine Dock, with its thick consignment of merchant and navy ships.

'We're safe,' gasped Charlie, keeping a tight grip on Lily and kicking towards the dock. 'We can vanish amongst the sailors and merchants.'

Lily said nothing as Charlie towed them to a jetty and they climbed up a seaweed-covered ladder. She shrugged him free when they made it to the top, then punched him in the stomach.

'Never push me in water again,' she said.

'Ow!' said Charlie, doubling over. 'I saved your life.'

'I'm grateful for that part,' said Lily, adjusting her wet hair. 'Come on,' she added, 'I'll buy you a cup of ale whilst we dry off.'

If the landlady at the Hoop and Grapes tavern thought two dripping-wet customers strange, she didn't remark on it. After logging their request for ale, she took their tankards without comment and shrieked a command down to the cellar.

A boy who seemed to be made entirely of limbs clambered up the steep ladder, took the drinking vessels and vanished back down again.

Lily sat near the small fire, where a pot of puddings boiled away for hungry drinkers, and fanned out her sodden skirts. A few groups of drunk sailors leaned over to look at her.

Charlie took the mourning ring off his finger and handed it to her. 'Your payment,' he said, 'for getting me into the Mint.'

She slowly took the ring. Her clothing steamed gently. 'You realise I'll be helping you find the Lord and Lady?' she said.

Charlie's brown eyes widened slightly.

'I owe it to Lady Castlemaine,' said Lily with a slight smile, push-ing the ring on her finger. 'I swore I'd pay her in kind for taking my privateer's licence. And if she's trying to get to the Lord and Lady, it seems to me they must be worth something.'

'You're concerned for Maria too, aren't you?' said Charlie, seeing something in her expression. 'You liked her.'

'The foreman was talking of a group of people burned alive, in secret,' said Lily, ignoring the suggestion. 'You could choose many better places than the Mint to commit such an atrocity. More private places with fewer witnesses. And why choose burning as a method of execution?'

'The Mint has a large forge,' said Charlie. 'Witches have been burned there. Perhaps something about those people was magical. Cromwell certainly wanted to be sure they were dead. Did you hear what Lady Castlemaine was saying?' asked Charlie as the boy returned with two foaming tankards. 'Someone stole a dress from the Golden Apple. Why should she be interested in that? What are the odds it's the same one Maria was looking for? The same dress that summons the Lady.'

He must have let his thoughts show on his face, because Lily unexpectedly took his hand.

'Maria's kidnapping was not your fault,' said Lily, with uncharacteristic gentleness. 'And if anyone can find her, you can.'

'I can't help but imagine how she must be feeling,' said Charlie. 'She must be so frightened, Lily. What if he's hurting her . . . ?'

'You can't think like that,' interrupted Lily. 'If you want to help her, solve the riddle.'

Charlie swallowed, turning the apple seal in his hand. 'Lady Castlemaine thought you might learn something from this,' he said, weighing the seal in his hand. 'The Golden Apple is important. Most likely it was a safe house during the war,' he added. 'Royalists used this seal as an invitation to get inside.'

'A clever trick,' said Lily approvingly. 'Possessing a whorehouse invitation is no evidence of treason. Finally these Royalists have realised how to cover their tracks.'

'What if the lost dress was put deliberately in the Golden Apple?' suggested Charlie. 'A Royalist clue in a Royalist safe house.'

'Hardly matters if it was,' Lily pointed out. 'Lady Castlemaine said the dress was stolen. The thief escaped into the Temple Bar stews. And a whore in the stews,' she concluded, taking a sip of deeply tannic beer and wincing, 'is a needle in a haystack.'

'I'm a thief taker,' said Charlie. 'I make my living finding people.'

'You think you can find her?' Lily was torn between disbelief and admiration.

Charlie nodded. 'Lady Castlemaine said the girl was from Wapping. So for my money, she fled the destruction there.'

'And went to the safety of Covent Garden,' said Lily. 'The apprentices don't attack the theatre district. Mrs Jenks operates under Royal sanction.'

'So she's no fool,' said Charlie. 'But she immediately stole a dress. Which makes her short-sighted.'

Lily nodded. 'Mrs Jenks will hunt her from Covent Garden. She loses the only safe part of the city.'

'And why flee to Temple Bar?' continued Charlie. 'If she wanted to escape the law, she might have gone to Alsatia. It's right next to Temple and offers criminals sanctuary.'

'She might have gone to sell the dress,' suggested Lily.

'Cheapside, London Bridge, all would give a better price,' said Charlie. 'But what they don't have is a gin shop.'

'You think she was a drunk?'

'It would best explain why she turned to thieving at exactly the time she needed to earn a good reputation and fled to a place serving the strongest drink in London. And,' he added, 'the Temple Gin House buys clothes at knock-down prices from desperate drunks.'

'Those stews are ugly places,' said Lily. 'You go to ground there you don't come out. She's just as likely dead as alive.' Lily helped herself to a pudding from the cauldron, lifting it free with a poker and peeling away the cheesecloth wrapping.

'True,' said Charlie. 'But there's a good chance she sold the stolen dress before someone stuck a knife in her.'

He pinched a piece of hot pudding from Lily's hand, put it in his mouth and chewed. It was sweet, with a hint of spice. Contraband cinnamon, he guessed, since they were so near to the docks.

'Charlie,' said Lily suddenly, 'can you be sure Maria is not already dead? Tom Black sounds like a madman.'

'I just know it.'

'How? It would be far easier for him . . .'

'Lily,' said Charlie, his voice tight, 'I can't let myself think that way. If I imagine something has happened to her' – he pressed a hand to his head – 'it tightens up in here. Nothing works.' His brown eyes settled on hers. 'Trust me, she's alive.'

Lily had a peculiar expression on her face. 'It sounds like you should have married her,' she said lightly, 'before this Percy came along.'

Charlie shook his head.

'But you don't think Maria should marry Percy?' said Lily.

'I never said that.'

'Charlie,' said Lily, 'we're headed to Temple Bar, the lawyer's district. Percy works there. He could help us, but you've never once suggested we visit him. Are you certain you're thinking from your head? Or is it your heart making decisions?'

'Percy can't help us,' said Charlie with more force than was necessary. 'What good is a lawyer? Would he write some clever words asking Tom Black not to murder Maria? Wag his finger at the apprentices whilst they tear him to pieces?'

Lily hesitated. She looked as though she meant to say more, then thought better of it. 'So we're back to hunting a dress,' she said after a moment, turning the gold rings on her fingers thoughtfully. 'A dress to summon a lord and lady.'

Charlie nodded. 'Then to Temple Bar,' he said, downing the thick dregs of his beer. 'The cheapest place to buy a woman in London.'

Lily looked at the window. It was dark outside and the moon was up. The fire was warm against their dripping clothes. 'My skirts are nearly dry,' she said with a yawn. 'It's late. Tomorrow is Maundy Thursday.'

Chapter 51

Lynette was sitting on the dressing room table. The cream ribbons holding up her red stockings had unravelled and slipped down to below her knees.

'I must thank Lady Castlemaine,' said Lynette. 'I'm told she taught you everythin' you know.'

Charles's dark eyebrows raised. 'Perhaps not everything. There were one or two women before Barbara.'

'One or two?'

He smiled and stood to face her. 'We were at war. I lose count.'

'You rogue!' She looked at him, sliding her hands around his waist and pulling him close. 'I'm to be on stage in a few moments,' she said.

'Why do you think I cleared the dressing room?' asked the King. 'I'll have the pleasure of watching you act, knowing what I've just done.' He pulled her close. 'And what I'm about to do.'

Lynette kicked her stocking feet against the table. 'Charles,' she said, chewing on a fingernail, 'are you sure you should stay to watch the play? The riots . . . People will say you are weak if you ignore them.'

He toyed with a strand of her hair. 'My father did much showing of power,' said Charles. 'They took his head for it. I am not fool enough to do the same.'

Lynette put her hands on his shoulders. 'Listen to me, I know London. I've heard things. This ain't no ordinary riot. They've gone as far as Chiswell Street. Mrs Jenks has paid a guard to arrest the ringleaders.'

'The old madam who dresses like a young girl?' Charles was picturing the thickly made-up face and the low-cut dress.

'Mrs Jenks is the theatre bawd,' explained Lynette patiently. 'Every whore 'oo plies the Covent Garden playhouses is employed by her. Mrs Jenks is clever. She's ruthless. But she's fine bred. Don't understand common folk.'

'But you do.' Charles was gazing at her.

'Her clever trick arresting the leaders 'as only made 'em angrier. Shown 'em the whores hold the power in London. What d'yer think they'll do with that?'

'Tell me.'

'I hear someone's riling 'em up to break into Finsbury Gaol,' said Lynette.

Charles hesitated. 'Where all the dispossessed people are? The ones we couldn't rehome after the fire?'

'Don't look so sad.' She stroked his face. 'You tried. I know you did.'

'Everyone thinks I spent the rebuild money on the new theatre.'

'Stop feelin' sorry for yerself,' said Lynette. 'It's a ready-made mob. If they get a taste of blood, all hell breaks loose.'

There was a roar of applause from outside the dressing room. He leaned in closer and kissed her. 'But I am forgetting myself,' he said, putting a hand on her bare thigh and carefully moving her skirts aside. 'A great slight on my reputation has been made. I must amend it.'

'Oh?' She was smiling, despite herself.

'I need to show you some things that Lady Castlemaine didn't teach me.'

Chapter 52

'I've never seen the Temple Bar Gin House,' said Lily, as they entered the dark and malodorous buildings behind the lawyers' district, 'only heard of it.'

'You don't see the Gin House,' said Charlie. 'You smell it.' There was a roar from down the street. He took off his coat. 'Put this on,' he said to Lily, eyeing her low-cut red dress. 'You can't walk into the middle of a riot dressed like that.'

'We're walking into the middle of the riot?'

Bells rang a constant alarm. But louder was the roar of destruction, screams and jeers. Rioters were smashing their way into a glass-fronted shop. Inside, the owner and his two sons were brandishing cudgels, trying to fight them off, but it was a losing business.

The front of the King's Head tavern had been completely destroyed. Rioters were robbing patrons, whilst staff switched between fighting back and ferrying terrified drinkers into the wine cellars.

People were racing away, wide-eyed. Some carried their own possessions. Others were bearing ill-gotten gains from shops and warehouses.

In the middle of the road, a huge carriage lay on its side, giant wheels turning, flames rising from its gutted innards. Children were darting back and forth from the blaze, ripping away what remained of the silk curtains and gilded carvings.

Charlie took Lily's arm and steered her into a rank-smelling door-way. She recoiled, covering her mouth.

'What's that smell?' she managed.

'The worst of human nature,' said Charlie. 'Gin, filth and black despair.'

At first glance, the Gin House was little more than a boarded-up building with a black hole for a doorway. But as they stepped inside, the stomach-turning smell of alcohol fumes was almost enough to choke on. The shop's furniture was a wooden table, behind which bubbled a strangely shaped alcohol still. A woman was topping it up with a bucket of Thames water. She completed the task, then poked at the fire beneath. The still gave an ominous belch and a foul-smelling steam rose from the top.

The only other decoration besides the still was a large and compli-cated-looking tally of debts scrawled on the wall in chalk, with symbols taking the place of names.

'The morning after the night before,' murmured Charlie, taking in the slumbering inebriates.

Dawn was breaking, and the first chinks of light could be seen through the boarded-up window. A woman in a woollen dress was slumped for-ward, a widening patch of urine soaking into the earth floor. Elsewhere, ragged people sat silently or slept, gin pipes clutched in their hands. A pregnant woman was feeding sips of gin to a feral-looking toddler.

Lily froze. 'That's wild-eyed Jack,' she hissed, nodding towards a man in a tricorn hat snoring face down on the floor. 'He's a pirate. A bad one,' she added. Her eyes moved to another drinker with a sawn-off manacle still attached to his wrist. 'This isn't a good place, Charlie,' she said, swallowing.

'They probably won't wake up,' he reassured her. 'It's only first light.'

The owner of the shop turned to them, assessing them with slow eyes. Every red and purple vein on her ancient face was broken, and her grossly round belly and wasted limbs gave the appearance of an apple propped on toothpicks. She was roughly covered by a dress that had been cheaply risqué a long time ago but was now a filth-stiffened assortment of hanging rags. She wore her drunkenness in the same way as her clothing: long-established and layered, with a hint of monstrosity buried beneath.

'Gin.' It was a command rather than a question. She'd used a collection of black felt dots to hide the ulcers on her face, and they danced as she spoke.

Charlie slid her two pennies, trying not to follow the bouncing patches, and she filled two little cups.

'We drink to Ironsides in 'ere,' she added, filling her own significantly larger cup, raising it and fixing them with a challenging gaze. 'He wouldn't have let London rot in ruins after a fire.'

'To Cromwell,' said Charlie, raising and upending his cup.

The woman seemed to relax slightly. 'King promised to rebuild St Paul's,' she said. 'We ain't sin it. But I'm blowed if Lady Castlemaine doesn't 'ave a fine new house, grander than any cathedral, so I've heard.' She cast another suspicious assessment over them both. 'Not seen yers round 'ere before.'

'I grew up in the north of the city,' said Charlie.

'Orphan, eh?' opined the old woman. 'We get lots of 'em. Gotta drown yer sorrows, don't yer? Feels right sorry for yers. I'd rather me old dead mother, God rest 'er wicked cruel old soul, above them nuns.' She gave a dramatic shudder.

'Did a new girl come to you today?' asked Charlie. 'With money for gin?'

The facial patches jiggled alarmingly. 'What makes you think we trade in that kind of business?' she demanded.

But Charlie noticed her eyes made a slow-motion flicker towards the ceiling of the grimy shop.

'We're looking for an old dress,' said Charlie. 'Green and gold, with leaves sewn on.'

He saw an unmistakable mark of recognition flash in her deeply drunk eyes.

'Mebbes we sin it, mebbes we ain't,' said the landlady, leaning back and crossing her arms across her chest. 'Wha's it worth?' She slurred this last part, leaning forward and bathing him in gin fumes.

Charlie resisted the urge to recoil and knew better than to indicate the location of his purse in a place like this. 'A shilling,' he said carefully. 'For what you know.'

The landlady narrowed her piggy eyes. Charlie realised the shot of gin was hitting her hard.

''Oo d'ya think you are?' she said, lurching to a sudden nonsensical fury. 'We don't 'elp your lot in 'ere for money,' she added obscurely, waving her hand at some unseen posse. 'Fuck off, the lot of yers.'

'Whatcha doin' bringin' 'er kind in 'ere?' A gravelly voice rang up from the bodies at their feet. Then a bulky woman heaved herself upright and addressed Lily. 'Thought we burned all your lot during the war and good riddance.' She glared at Lily, taking in the toffee-coloured skin, dark eyes and thick swathe of gypsy charms dangling from her neck, then shoved her hard.

Lily jolted back, catching herself on the gin table. Her face clouded with rage and her stance shifted. Recognising the threat, her burly attacker balled her scarred fists.

A few closed eyes on the shop floor had blinked awake now, enjoying the prospect of some entertainment. The woman had the muscular arms of a laundry worker and the broken nose of a fighter.

'Peace.' Charlie tried to step between them.

'Oh ho!' jeered the landlady. 'She must fight fer 'erself in 'ere. Ain't that right, Joanie? No men-folk.' The landlady grinned. 'Looks like we got ourselves some sport,' she said, gleefully noting Lily's furious expression. 'Thas my price for this dress. Your gypsy to fight our Joan.'

Chapter 53

The parliament men exchanged glances. The King kept looking at the door.

'Your Majesty,' said one. 'Might we begin?'

'One moment.' The King held up a ringed finger and moved close to Amesbury. 'Where is she?' he whispered. 'I *commanded* her to be present.' Charles lowered his voice angrily. 'The last thing I need,' he decided, 'is another faithless, difficult woman.'

'Very good.' Amesbury nodded, drawing the King to the side. 'There's a new actress. Italian. I understand she will be whoever you wish for a thousand pounds a year. Loyal. Obedient. Beautiful.'

There was a strange shriek from outside. Amesbury looked up sharply, assessing. The parliament men followed his gaze.

Charles waved his hand. 'Do it then,' he decided. 'No more of this "I demand nothing of you". Let us pay a fair price for a fair service. I'm not a young man of fifteen any longer, Amesbury. I haven't the energy for these capricious ladies.'

The shrieking sound came again. Louder this time. Then a series of barks.

'What in God's name is that noise?' The King moved towards the window, frowning. It took him a moment to realise what he was seeing. Then his face opened in a wide smile.

Lynette was on the grass with two of the royal children. She knelt on all fours pretending to be a dog, chasing them about the green. They were running away, shrieking with delight. Lynette caught one of them by the leg and he went down, hysterical with laughter.

Amesbury moved to the King's side. 'Should I call the nursemaid?' he asked, watching the King's face.

On the grass, Lynette had opened the shirt of three-year-old George, Duke of Northumberland, and was gnawing on his bare pink belly.

'No.' Charles bowed to the men, as the boy's happy squeals drifted through the window. 'Gentlemen. Might you indulge me for one moment? I'm going to see my children.'

They nodded uncertainly.

The King walked alone from the room and onto the green. He stood for a moment, watching, a smile on his face.

A harassed-looking nursemaid burst from the palace, saw the King and stopped mid-run with an awkward curtsey. 'Your Majesty.' She faltered, glancing from him to the children.

The King looked up genially.

'They got out of their lessons,' she managed. 'I'll return them immediately.'

'Allow me,' he said. 'You go back to the nursery.'

The nursemaid retreated, curtseying.

Then Lynette saw him and paused in the act of chasing four-year-old Charlotte, Duchess of Lichfield. The little girl raced behind a hedge and ducked out of sight.

''Ow long you bin standin' there?' Lynette demanded, grinning. 'I should charge you for peeping.'

'You were supposed to be at my side,' he reminded her. 'I asked you. I commanded you.'

'Did you now?' She ran her hand through her red hair. 'Thought I told you I don't care much for being commanded.'

He moved towards her. 'They're in there,' he said. 'The men who killed my father.' He dropped his voice. 'I needed you.'

She shook her curled hair, moving closer. 'No, you didn't,' she said, looking up at him. 'You are king.'

He stood for a moment, taking in her flushed cheeks and bright eyes. 'Don't go back to the Birdcage,' he heard himself say. 'Join the King's Company. Act on the Drury Lane stage. Become a licensed player.'

Lynette took his hands. 'Charles,' she said, 'it isn't me.' She squeezed his fingers. 'I can't even read. Most 'a what I act is straight from my head. 'Ow would I learn me lines in time?'

'The Birdcage is dangerous,' tried Charles. 'The apprentices might attack.'

'All the more reason for the show to go on, I reckon.'

'You are so stubborn,' he sighed, shaking his head with a smile.

Charlotte's face popped up from behind the hedge. 'I'm here!' she shouted hopefully at Lynette. 'Come find me!'

Lynette smiled, gave his hands a final squeeze, then turned and ran towards the hedge. 'I have every faith in you,' she called over her shoulder as she fled. 'You've run this whole country with a hangover. Means you can do anythin', I reckon.'

Chapter 54

The Gin House landlady smiled in a way that sent her three wobbling chins vanishing into her fat neck and stood back delightedly.

Lily looked at Charlie.

'Looks like we gots some ent-ter-tain-ment,' said the landlady, raising her voice as she laboured with the long word. 'Gypsy fight.'

'No one is fighting anyone,' said Charlie, trying to quell the rising atmosphere of excitement in the Gin House. His eyes sought the board on the wall tallying debts. He matched the thick-set woman to her symbol – a closed fist. A few surreptitious bets were being chalked by it, all against Lily.

Lily pushed Charlie out of the way. 'I can defend myself against a gin-soaked old hag,' she muttered, flexing her knife hand.

The fat landlady glanced to the ladder leading upstairs in a way that convinced Charlie the dress was in her attic room.

'Tell me first of the dress . . .' Charlie began, directing his request to the landlady.

From nowhere, Joan swung a meaty punch with surprising accuracy for a drunk. Lily swerved, and the other woman fell full-force into the table, sending a great crack along its centre.

'The dress!' Lily hissed, as Joan collected herself.

A few people were getting to their feet now. Charlie could sense the atmosphere turning ugly. All eyes were on Lily.

Charlie hesitated, then ran and climbed the ladder. He glanced down to see Lily was circling the cracked table, evading the larger woman.

He emerged into an attic room with a low sloping roof and a strong smell of unwashed sheets. In the gloom he could make out two make-shift beds, partitioned by curtains.

To the sound of legs and skirts flurrying below, Charlie's eyes settled on a collection of dog-eared dresses strung over a thick piece of cord at the top of the stairs. He fell on them, searching. His heart sank. It wasn't here. He'd been so sure the thief was on her way to the Gin House. And the landlady's expression seemed to confirm she'd bought the dress.

A sudden movement stopped him. One of the mattresses he'd assumed empty was occupied.

'You gotta clear it with the landlady to lie up 'ere,' said a sleepy female voice. 'I pays 'er for the bed. Tell 'er Clancy gave a full penny, and she ain't woked up yet.'

In the dark, Charlie could make out that Clancy had a certain pret-tiness, but her long nose, lank brown hair and prominent teeth leant her a weasel-like quality.

Her eyes were young and wary. They settled on his hands, still hold-ing the dresses. 'Whatcha doin' with them dresses?' she asked, taking a sudden step forward. When she saw his face, she gave a start. 'You're the thief taker,' she said. 'I knows you.'

Like everyone else in the house, she was blind drunk, Charlie realised. The smell of gin rolled off her. Charlie glanced down and sud-denly saw it. She was wearing the dress he had been searching for. A gown of green-gold leaves, gossamer thin, old.

He moved slowly towards her. 'I can pay you . . .' he started to say.

There was a bolt of movement from the bed and suddenly the girl pushed past him.

'Wait!' shouted Charlie.

Charlie moved fast, but he'd misjudged her speed. Clancy was down the little ladder in moments. He jumped down just in time to see her joining the sodden drunks.

His eyes sought out Lily and found her. She had Joan pinned against the far wall, knife against her throat.

'You ain't allowed to use no knives,' managed the fat woman. 'It's not in the rules.'

'I'm a gypsy, remember?' hissed Lily. 'We don't have rules.'

The bigger woman swallowed, eyes tracking down to the cold metal.

The sleeping drunks were wide awake now, keen to join the affray. A card sharper was taking bets on the women, shuffling his pack to number the odds.

Clancy was elbowing her way out.

'Lily!' Charlie shouted. 'Stop her! The dress!'

Lily made a grab at Clancy. Her hand got a hold on the dress, but Clancy tore free, leaving Lily clutching a handful of silk leaves.

Lily's sparring partner took advantage of her distraction and landed a punch in her kidneys. Lily gasped, the wind knocked out of her.

'He's a thief taker!' shouted Clancy, as she raced for the door.

'I knew you was trouble!' The landlady was pointing at Charlie, roaring in outrage. 'A curse on thief takers!'

Every unfriendly eye now turned to Charlie. A few men began moving towards him. He twisted to see Lily had slipped free of Joan. Two knives were pinning the larger woman against the bar by her skirts.

'I've four knives left,' said Lily, eyeing the crowd near the door. 'It's not enough,' she added as the motley drinkers began closing in.

Charlie grabbed the pack of cards from the card sharp and flipped them arcing in the air. Whilst heads automatically followed the display, Charlie drove his fist into the stomach of the man closest to him.

'Throw your knives towards the door!' he shouted to Lily, as the man doubled over.

Lily flung a volley of blades. They stuck into the wooden door frame in a perfect square.

The crowd parted, and Lily and Charlie raced for the door.

Chapter 55

Repent looked up at Finsbury Gaol. Barebones's arrest had scattered the apprentices. But Bolly had managed to regroup many of the frightened boys. He'd even recruited some of the wealthier apprentices on their way to Finsbury, Repent noted jealously. Farriers and leatherworkers, with their fancy tools.

Repent twirled his father's short iron sword inexpertly, strutting in front of the prison. The apprentices looked at him differently, he thought, now he carried a weapon.

'They're in there,' said Repent, nodding. 'My father. Our boys.'

Bordering the prison was a wide patch of scrubland.

'Look at all the people without homes,' said Bolly, eyeing the mass of refugees from the Great Fire. 'The King said he would rebuild.'

'Aye,' said Repent. 'We all know where the money went. Look at the fine new theatre.'

The dispossessed Londoners were starving, ragged and pitiful. A few empty flour sacks were all that remained of a food delivery from months ago.

'He forgot about them,' said Bolly.

Repent frowned. 'We are not women, Bolly,' he said. 'Save your soft heart for the whores. We must be men if we are to break my father free from prison.'

The apprentices were still swelling in number. They bore pitchforks, sticks and pikes.

'You're certain Barebones was taken to Finsbury?' asked Bolly, looking doubtfully at the prison. 'The guards don't look as though they've arrested any men recently.'

'My father meant me to lead you,' said Repent self-importantly. 'I carry his sword. A soldier does not question his commander.' Repent pointed the sword, enjoying himself. 'New offenders are taken to the Meet House,' he said, trying to affect Barebones's gravelly authority. 'The guards won't have had time to allocate them to a different building yet. We strike now,' he added, pounding a fist into the palm of his hand in what he hoped was a warlike gesture.

He was looking at the entrance of the prison. It was a thick wall bearing two large wooden doors, one of which stood slightly ajar.

'The guards are not prepared for attack,' said Bolly. 'If everyone charged, we could make it in. Likely boys would be killed. But Barebones would give his life for us. He's been like a father to me. So long as you're truly certain he's inside . . .'

'Imagine my father's face,' interrupted Repent, gloating, 'when I break him free. He'll never be able to scold me again.' He held up the little sword. 'Charge!' he bellowed. 'Take the gaol! We'll tear it down with our bare hands!'

The apprentices began to mill uncertainly. None took up the command. 'A prison break is treason,' muttered one, eyeing the guards. They were looking at the mass of boys now, curious. One pointed and began to unhitch his sword.

Repent reddened. He cupped his hands and bellowed into the crowd. 'When Adam delved and Eve span, who was then a gentleman?'

C.S. Quinn

A deathly silence settled on the apprentices. It was an old Republican cry, from the civil war. Repent had just shouted treason. Bolly watched a few boys from the wealthier apprenticeships exchange glances and shoulder their tools to leave.

Then, from the scrubland of homeless Londoners, an old man took up the chant. A few more of the dispossessed were taking notice now, standing up, joining in. From nowhere, a full-bloodied battle song rose up. People began cheering the apprentices.

The richer-placed apprentices had changed their minds about leaving now and were grinning at the approbation.

'Them high-ups don't care about us!' called a scrawny woman. 'A pox on the King and his whores! They lock us up for speaking our minds!' She spat on the ground.

The gesture had an electric effect on the encampment. Half-starved people began hurling stones at the prison.

Sensing his moment, Repent raised his sword. 'Charge!' he bellowed.

The prison guards were uncertain now. It seemed like a baying pack of devils was headed for them. A thick-limbed guard with ox-like shoulders raised his sword.

One small apprentice broke clear of his fellows and ran directly towards him. The guard's expression recalibrated to battle ready. He swung his sword with the deadly intent of a soldier. As the apprentice closed, the guard swung, his sword sinking deep into the other man's skull. The apprentice fell.

There was a deathly hush. Then the people charged again. On and on they came, ragged, starving, furious. With nothing to lose.

In moments the unfortunate guard was besieged by apprentices, striking, gouging and bringing down cudgels. Despite his size, he was no match for the numbers and as his mighty frame was felled other guards came racing to his aid.

But now the mob had tasted blood. They attacked as one wild feral thing. Like rats pouring from a burning building, they threw themselves against the half-open door and pounded into the prison.

Behind the walls was an open yard, spotted with prison buildings.

The attackers began smashing at doors and looting sacks of food. Prisoners surged free, overwhelming the guards.

'He's not here,' said Bolly, watching as the last prisoner escaped the day lockup. 'Barebones wasn't taken to Finsbury.'

But Repent wasn't listening. He was watching the chaos, a wide grin on his pockmarked face. 'Look what I did, Bolly,' he grinned. 'Wait until Barebones hears. We're going to be the boys who took down the King.'

'We should try the Clink,' said Bolly.

Repent looked at the marauding boys, assessing. 'We can do it without Praise-God Barebones,' he said. ''E's like a big dark cloud, always bringin' me down. I see the way 'e looks at me. I know what 'e's thinkin'. Why didn't you die instead of her?' He glanced at Bolly. 'No more rules, Bolly. No more preaching. The Merry Monarch, isn't that what they say? I think it's time we joined his party.'

'You don't mean Covent Garden?' Bolly's expression was caught between horror and excitement. 'Those are the King's whores. They'll hang us for traitors.'

'They'll 'ave to catch us first,' grinned Repent, nodding to the mass of people behind him. 'I say we go to Covent Garden,' he said, 'and find ourselves some actresses.'

Chapter 56

Charlie and Lily burst out of the Gin House without pausing for breath. They ran from the mouldering streets of the stews and into the smarter lawyer's district of Temple Bar. The grand wooden arch of the famous city approach was thick with lawyers in their colourful coats and messengers racing back and forth bearing papers. A cluster of alehouses, where younger and less well-off lawyers could rent rooms, buzzed with life. An elderly lawyer shuffled past them, swaying slightly from the effects of a liquid lunch.

Clancy was nowhere to be seen.

'She knows we're looking for her,' said Charlie, 'and she's fast.' He sensed the opportunity had slipped away. 'It would take days to find her,' he said. 'We don't have time.'

He looked at the sun. It was morning on Maundy Thursday. He tried not to let hopelessness overwhelm him.

'Maybe this will help,' said Lily. She opened her curled fist to reveal the handful of silken leaves, torn free from Clancy's dress.

Charlie looked at them.

'Cheaply made,' Lily observed, letting the clutch of leaves and ribbons flutter in her hands. 'Woven to look like silk from a distance.'

Charlie took the leaves, thinking. 'A dress to summon the Lord and Lady,' he said. 'That's what was in the confession Maria found.'

'So it calls to them?' suggested Lily. 'There are spells to summon fairy folk using clothing. Perhaps a piece could serve as well as the whole,' she added, nodding to the torn fabric.

'We're missing something,' said Charlie. 'A Royalist arrived at Damaris Page's house, wearing this dress.'

'Safe-passage networks often use disguises,' said Lily with a shrug. 'Damaris said so herself.'

'So what's the link?' pressed Charlie. 'How does this dress lead to a lord and lady?'

Lily returned her attention to the torn fabric leaves, with their green-and-gold stitching. 'Single stitch,' said Lily, nodding. She peeled one open to show Charlie. 'See here? Running stitch. No dressmaker would do that. You'd stitch a backstitch double, even triple. A good dress is made to last. This wasn't,' she said. 'English ribbons, not French.' She held up the ribbon ends. 'And only a little melted pewter to finish. The ribbon ends of a quality dress are usually sealed in silver and stamped with a crest.'

'Which means?' asked Charlie.

'Perhaps made for a cheap whorehouse . . .' began Lily slowly. She gasped suddenly. 'Charlie, that's it! This is a costume. It's a theatre costume!'

'But there were no theatres during the Republic,' said Charlie. 'Only illicit performances held in brothels.'

And then it struck him in a rush. 'Lily!' exclaimed Charlie. 'What if the Lord and Lady weren't hiding walled up somewhere or alone or on the run? What if they were hiding in plain sight? Unnoticed amongst a group of people?'

'A theatre company!' breathed Lily. 'It would be a perfect place to hide. But I thought the companies were all disbanded.'

'Most were,' said Charlie, 'but one kept playing. The King's Company went underground. Their actors performed in places like the Gilded Lock and the Golden Apple.'

'They were risking their lives,' said Lily. 'Acting in the name of the King.'

'The royals have always protected the theatres,' said Charlie. 'What's the betting the King's Company were a vital component of the Royalist safe-passage networks?'

Lily was nodding slowly. 'Ready access to all kinds of disguises,' she said. 'Actors change their voices, their appearances.'

'And wouldn't that be a good way to hide two recognisable nobles?' said Charlie. 'Acting in different costumes, in a theatre troupe. Always on the move. Anyone who acted as part of the King's Company during the war might be able to give us vital information.'

'But we have no way of finding those actors,' Lily pointed out. 'The city is in turmoil. The riots are clearing out the official theatres and the actors are going to be in hiding.'

'Maybe we can't get to the actors,' said Charlie, 'but I know a scenery painter. And he's painted for theatres since anyone can remember. Man named Dawson. Well, that's one of the names he goes by.'

'Are you talking about Strange Ol' George?' asked Lily. 'The mad Royalist?'

'Everyone who works for the theatre is a Royalist,' said Charlie evasively.

'How do you even know a man like that?' asked Lily.

'I helped him once,' said Charlie. 'Recovered his paints.'

'I thought he was a kind of vagabond.'

Charlie hesitated. 'Dawson made a home for himself in the ashes. The rubble around Lud Gate. He is a strange man,' Charlie conceded with a shrug. 'He's built a kind of stronghold.'

'Charlie, you're not suggesting we go into the ruins?' demanded Lily. 'It's dangerous around there. Like . . . another world. Robbers and thieves prowl around the rubble.'

'We must be a little careful, is all,' acknowledged Charlie. 'But if we find Dawson, he could tell us where the Lord and Lady hid all those years ago.'

Chapter 57

Clancy was weaving a little, fresh from a breakfast of gin, feet striking the filthy mud track uncertainly. She leaned against a urine-soaked wall, eyes drooping. The street was strangely empty, but there was a background noise nearby. Like a crowd roaring. But that wasn't possible. They were too close to Covent Garden and everyone knew the apprentices never attacked the King's whores.

She closed her eyes. Perhaps she'd slept a little; she wasn't certain. Then a man in merchant's dress was walking past. She lurched towards him and took his arm.

'What business?' she asked, voice high and false. 'A penny for the best fuck in Temple.' She accidentally slurred her words.

The man looked at her with an expression of pity and disgust and shrugged off her arm. 'Get off the streets, you foolish girl,' he snapped. 'The apprentices are near.'

Clancy watched him go, considering her dress. The men who raided Damaris Page's house had been looking for a dress. And now a thief taker had come for her. She knew it was valuable. She just had to find the right buyer.

Clancy brushed the green-and-gold leaves. She just wanted to rest, in a nice warm tavern, with a big mug of ale. But for that she needed money.

She began walking towards the hum of the crowd. All she had to do was find Praise-God Barebones and sell him her stolen dress.

But as Clancy turned the corner, the swell of people took her by surprise. It was a great surging hulk of a crowd, rolling along the street. They marched under a Republican banner, waving flags and makeshift weapons.

'Blow me,' muttered Clancy. 'It's an army.'

She hesitated, some buried instinct suggesting she run. Then she identified a familiar weapon. A stubby iron sword waving towards the front.

Praise-God Barebones's sword. She commended herself on recognising it and made for him, a plan formulating. A few blue-aproned boys pushed and spat at her as she shouldered her way through, but she hardly noticed.

When she reached the short iron sword, her brain took a long time to connect what she saw. The dark blade was tied with fluttering ribbons. Women's garters, she realised.

By the time she realised it wasn't Praise-God Barebones holding the weapon, someone was pointing at her. A tall skinny boy with scabbed legs and pockmarks shaped like a beard. He wore a suit that looked to have been looted.

Clancy turned to run. The boy gave chase. She made it into a side alley, but he was fast. Or perhaps she had got slower. All she knew was he caught her easily in a few strides, tripping her so she fell in a tangle of skirts.

'Where are you going?' he taunted, pinning her to the ground.

She struggled, twisting under his grip, but he was too strong.

'My name is Repent,' he said. 'I'm delivering justice hereabouts. Some of my boys noticed you wore a very special dress. You bin hiding the evil ones.'

Clancy had stopped struggling now. Her head turned helplessly, looking for anyone who might come to her aid. But the street was empty.

'No one is coming to your aid,' he said. 'Tell me where they are.'

'I don't know nothing about no evil ones,' said Clancy, terrified. 'Let me go.'

'First,' he said, 'you must tell me where you got this dress.'

'I din' steal it,' she said. 'I only found it.'

'Where?'

Clancy thought of Viola, working at Mrs Jenks's house, and closed her mouth tight shut. Repent took out a rusty knife, the blade laced with dried blood. A guttural shriek came from Clancy. She bucked and twisted, but Repent held her firm.

'I mean to complete my father's mission,' he said. 'I'll be sending the fairy king and queen back to hell. And any whore who stands in my way will be marked for what she is.'

Clancy plumbed her mind for something to save herself. 'There's someone else looking for this dress,' she whispered. 'A thief taker.'

'Who?'

Clancy was breathing hard. 'His name is Charlie Tuesday. He's with a girl. She's dressed a bit whorish, but I think she's something else. Actress, maybe. I watched them for a bit, when they thought I'd fled. They said somethin' about the King's Company.'

Repent drew back. Of course fairies would choose a theatre to hide in. Why hadn't his father thought of it already?

Even better, Repent considered, the mob hated the theatres. The King had spent money glorifying his royal playhouse whilst commoners lived in ash. It would be easy to lead his army to the King's Theatre. The idea of presenting his father with two bloodied fairy corpses swelled in his imagination. Barebones would have to acknowledge his son wasn't feeble and inept, but brave and strong.

Repent decided his cleverness deserved a celebration. He looked down at Clancy, lying helpless. He lifted his father's iron sword. 'See these?' he said. 'These are garters. Want to know how I got them?'

Clancy glared at him. 'You think you can take something from me?' she slurred. 'Remember, I am a whore. All you gain is a debt.'

Chapter 58

At the edge of London's black rubble, Lily had begun sliding off her many rings and putting them in her pocket. The ashy heart of the fire stood before them, the deepest ruins, where black walls and tunnels made a strange new world.

'At least you're not at risk of a robbery,' said Lily, taking in Charlie's bare feet and battered coat.

'Don't believe it,' he said. 'Anyone who struck up residence here would sell your skin to a tanner for a groat. This whole place is filled with robbers and footpads.'

'Footpads?'

'It's slum-speak,' said Charlie. 'Highwaymen without horses. Rougher, more barbarous and no one lives to write poetry about them.'

'Sounds like pirates,' said Lily, lifting her tangle of charms and necklaces over her head, letting her shining dark hair fall back.

'People inside have lost everything,' said Charlie. 'They're desperate. The King hasn't any money to rebuild.'

'There's always money in London,' said Lily, dropping her charms into her hanging pocket and drawing it shut. 'So long as you're not too wedded to principle.' She pushed the pocket down the front of her dress. 'It's why I'm getting out, just as soon as I get another ship.'

She was staring uneasily into the gloom. Deep in the depths of half walls and collapsed roofs, someone moved.

Charlie was trying to track a path to Lud Gate, where Dawson had made his home. But his usual mental map was failing him. This wasn't like any London he knew. It was a dark place. An underworld. A city twisted and strange.

'Come on,' he said, moving forward into the dark. 'I think it's this way.'

As soon as they stepped inside, the spongy earth threw up puffs of fine ash. Lily coughed and covered her mouth. Another movement flickered in the depths. Then a scratching sound.

'I think this way,' said Charlie, trying to lead them straight. The tangle of devastation made it impossible. They climbed crumbling walls and crawled through low tunnels, hands over their mouths, coughing through soot.

The first signs of human dwelling stopped Charlie in his tracks. There was a battered square of hessian fabric nailed over one of the fallen roofs to make a kind of tent. A few smouldering sticks, a dirty pan and a waft of sewage.

They moved on uneasily as the sad signs of habitation grew more numerous. Broken things, wet clothing, rudimentary attempts to make fences and roofs.

'Where are all the people?' said Lily.

'I don't know,' said Charlie. 'I don't like it.'

They heard a sudden noise behind them again. Then a stone pinged off a metal pan. Another struck the ashy floor ahead of them and then a third rebounded off a wicker roof.

'Footpads,' said Charlie. 'Run.'

They plunged through the rubble, stones ringing around them now, striking the ground like hailstones. Ahead was a ring of tall spindly brick fronds; skinny remnants of what had once been a large building. They twisted up into the sky like strange fairy turrets, warped metal grids of what had once been windows hanging askew.

'We're at Bridewell,' said Charlie, suddenly recognising the distorted remains, the buckled cell bars. 'This used to be the old prison.'

Between the spindle towers was a low opening, an old brick doorway, arched at the top.

'In there,' said Charlie, pointing. 'It will protect us from the stones.'

'Wait,' said Lily. 'I know pirates, Charlie. This feels like a flush-attack.'

'A what?' A stone struck Charlie's arm and he flinched.

'They want to flush us into somewhere with no way out, so they butcher us,' she said, sweeping her eyes around their immediate locale. 'Charlie, trust me, this isn't your city anymore. It's far more like the wild seas I know.'

Her gaze settled on another route through. Stones flew down.

Charlie flung off his leather coat and threw it over both their heads. Stones ricocheted off the leather and struck their feet and legs.

'The stones are mainly coming from that way,' said Lily, looking towards a narrow pathway through the rubble. 'That's the way they don't want us to go. Come on.'

She grabbed him, and they ran towards the main onslaught. Charlie saw a rock coming straight for his face and swerved. Lily gasped in pain as she was pelted.

'They're going to kill us,' said Charlie. 'We need to turn back.'

'Just a little further.' Lily had a tight grip on his hand. A sharp rock smashed painfully into Charlie's shoulder, sending him reeling sideways. Then, suddenly, the spray of missiles eased and stopped.

They'd emerged in a wider, less densely packed area of devastation.

'The footpads will keep to the walls and the hidey-holes,' she said. 'It's too open here, too risky.' She eyed where the charred timbers closed in again. 'Maybe they'll come from that way,' she decided.

'Why do you say that?' Charlie was looking up ahead, trying to understand how Lily was predicting the route of attack from nothing more than a pile of rubble.

'It's what I'd do,' she said with a shrug. 'Do you know where we are now?' she added.

Charlie was trying to take in the shape of the old prison. The site had been a large rectangle with a yard inside, the Fleet River to the south. He tracked round the edge, then north to a broad-shouldered hump on the horizon.

It was unrecognisable from its former self. An uneven clump of fortress, with black-eyed holes for windows. The proud English flag had long burned away, the sentinel gatemen fled. Only the charred skeleton of a parapet and a familiar portcullis convinced Charlie he'd found what he was looking for.

'There it is,' he said, pointing. 'Lud Gate.'

'Then let's go,' said Lily, as a shout sounded close by. 'Those foot-pads will be regrouping as we speak.'

Chapter 59

Barebones was sitting wide awake in the locked cell. Since he had prior connections with the prison service, the arresting guards had thought it more sensible to hold him in New Bedlam. The asylum had been hastily flung up after the war and boasted a small lockup into which Barebones had been temporarily confined.

Three other inmates were asleep in the room, but a man with a tick who remembered Barebones from the Battle of Naseby was listening to Barebones's rant.

'The Lord and Lady give the King fairy powers from the under-world,' he insisted. 'See how royals wear fine clothes and dance and drink sweet wine? Fairy ways. They held this country in their magical sway for five hundred years. We were asleep. Then we woke. Now we must fight them again.'

'Fairy lords and ladies?' his comrade said, his facial tick jerking. 'In London? Come on, Barebones. You know the fey folk don't like cities. They've not been here for one hundred years or more.'

'They're the power behind the throne,' said Barebones. 'Kill the Lord and Lady and all the evil goes out of England. The light is bright and the way is hard, but by God's grace we will endure.'

'How's your son?' asked his fellow soldier, tiring of the sermon.

Barebones shook his head. 'Brought him up best I could without his mother. Apprenticed him as a brickmaker; I couldn't find the fees for a grocer or a goldsmith. I fear he's of an evil disposition.'

'Sons,' said his old comrade sympathetically. 'You pray for 'em. Then they bring all manner of shit down on your head.'

The door opened and a battered face peered in. 'Praise-God Barebones?' the guard called.

Barebones stood.

'The Lady wants to see you,' said the guard.

'Who?' Barebones's face clouded in confusion.

'You'll see,' said the man, beckoning to indicate that he should follow. 'Says she knows you.' He was looking Barebones up and down. 'You should count yourself blessed,' he added. 'She's been here these five years last and you're the first prisoner I've ever taken to her.'

Barebones said nothing, following the guard through the maze of corridors. They reached the large cell reserved for aristocrats. The guard opened the door.

Barebones's eyes grew wide. 'You,' he managed. 'I thought you were dead.'

Bridey Black had the same unusual blue-green eyes as her son. Barebones had a memory of her in the Shambles, Tom Black trudging dour-faced at her heel. She smiled seductively and gestured that the guard should leave them.

'Praise-God Barebones.' Bridey stood as the door shut and sashayed towards him. She was acting as though Barebones had arranged some emotional reunion. 'After all these years.'

'You asked to see me,' he said, trying to dispel her dramatics. 'You knew I was coming.'

Her face was still attractive. He remembered it as being hypnotically beautiful.

'I am a prophetess now,' she said. 'I have powers.'

'Oh, aye? The power to drag a man from his prison cell? I've heard of the London Prophetess,' he added contemptuously. 'You spin a great many predictions for our new king. Anyone would think you were courting a visit from His Majesty. Hoping your faded beauty might lure him still?' There was a pause. 'Your boy came to me,' said Barebones.

Bridey looked frightened.

'He said something had been found,' continued Barebones. 'A confession buried all these years. Something that could uncover the Lord and Lady. Tom wanted me to use my influence. Guide the apprentices to particular brothels. Find a particular dress. I thought you dead. Now I discover you are alive, I think it was you who sent Tom to find them.'

'Do you?' She leant her chin on her hand coquettishly. It was a strange gesture to see in an older woman.

'I know what you want, Bridey. You want every man to fall at your feet. And now you are old and your beauty holds less sway, what now? You think the Lord and Lady will give you back what you've lost?'

Bridey moved closer. 'Do you remember all those years ago,' she whispered, 'that you had me in that back room? I whispered to you of the fey folk and how they danced.'

'I was a young boy, sowing wild oats,' said Barebones, embarrassed. He'd thought her young and peculiar and it had been an effort to finish, with her babbling her fairy nonsense. She made him play a lord and declare their union sacred. He couldn't call the memory to mind without blushing.

'I saw how you looked at me on my wedding day.' Bridey put a hand on his chest. 'I think,' she whispered, 'there is something between us.' She tilted her head and looked up at him, her strange round eyes wide.

'You were nothing to me but a fresh-faced girl on Honey Lane,' said Barebones. 'I have no feeling of that kind for you. I have a wife . . .'

'Your wife is long dead,' said Bridey. 'I know you would not sully yourself with whores. Fine, upstanding Praise-God.' She was staring into his eyes with uncomfortable intensity.

Barebones didn't answer.

Bridey let her robe fall to her hips. Barebones's eyes instinctively dropped to her naked chest. She was older and thinner than he remembered, but not unattractive.

'Men have needs,' she said. 'You must burn with them. So long with no woman to comfort you.'

Barebones felt himself casting a glance over his shoulder, just as he'd done all those years ago. An old, forgotten lust thickened. 'Come on then,' he said gruffly, moving towards her.

Bridey began to get down on the floor. She'd done that the first time, arranging her naked limbs in a star shape.

Barebones took hold of her. 'Not this time,' he said. 'I'm not a young boy. I will have you as I want.' He pinned her upright to the wall of her cell, hiking her robe over her hips. He'd never had his wife like this. Only in a proper married way. The thought brought a surge of desire.

Bridey kept moving as he was doing it, writhing around in some acted pleasure that didn't seem real. When she began whispering of lakes of blue fire and fairy dancing, he put a hand over her mouth. He turned her head away, so she couldn't look into his eyes. When he'd finished, he took his hand away and began buttoning his clothing.

Her eyes watched him with admiration.

'I will not come again if you summon me,' said Barebones shortly. 'Tell your boy I mean to kill the Lord and Lady. I will set him free.' He touched his hip, where his iron sword had once hung.

'You don't know,' Bridey realised. She shook her head. 'They cannot be killed the way you think. Not by cold-forged iron.'

He said nothing, rearranging his clothes.

'You'll come back,' she taunted. 'You always do. You are weak, Praise-God Barebones. Why do you think your son is how he is? It is your bad seed. Your wife had no love for you. It was the talk of the Shambles.'

He struck her across the face. Bridey fell, hitting her head on the hard wall. She lay still.

Barebones moved nearer, holding his breath.

Bridey sat up, smiling at him and pulling her robe into place. 'You can't resist me,' she said.

Barebones looked at her and was filled with sudden revulsion. The spell was broken. He saw nothing now but an ageing woman, twisted with bitter regrets. 'You always were too young for the Shambles,' he said. 'Our girls grow up fast and fierce.' He was remembering his wife, Sarah: strong, dependable, quick with a joke. He missed her with a pain almost physical.

'You pretend you're godly,' spat Bridey angrily. 'You're the worst sinner of them all.'

'I feel sorry for your husband,' said Barebones, banging on the door to summon the guard. 'He loved you and never deserved what you dealt him.'

Chapter 60

Charlie could still make out the squat shape of Lud Gate with its portcullis. But nothing more of the old fortification was recognisable. The brickwork was thickly coated in deep-black soot, making it appear as a devilish castle in a land laid to waste. On the broken crenellations at the top waved a single plucky flag bearing the King's coat of arms.

'Dawson is up there,' said Charlie, pointing. 'It's good for painting. All the light.'

It was soon to be midday, Charlie realised, taking in the sun over the gatehouse. Less than half a day left. But if Dawson could direct them to the Lord and Lady, they'd still have time to find wherever Maria was being held. The possibility of coming to her rescue seemed tantalisingly close.

There was an ear-splitting grinding noise, and the blackened portcullis shuddered, then rose a few feet upwards, above the scorched earth.

A small boy in a scuffed page's outfit ducked beneath it. 'You come for the Master?' he asked, eyeballing them.

'I'm Charlie Tuesday,' said Charlie. 'He knows me.'

This seemed enough for the child, who ducked back beneath the portcullis, gesturing that they should follow. Charlie and Lily crawled under it, old ash drifting up. They followed the boy up a stone spiral staircase, with crumbling fire-torched plaster and newly painted royal crests on the wall.

'Dawson believes the King should rule without Parliament,' explained Charlie as they passed. 'He's styled his home on an old Royalist stronghold.'

'Tell me again how you know this man?'

'He owes me money.'

'I thought remembering pauper debts wasn't one of your strengths,' observed Lily as they climbed. She was looking at his face with a new keenness.

'I've . . . some new obligations,' admitted Charlie. 'In Covent Garden.'

'You've a mistress?' The disbelief in her voice was tinged with something deeper.

'Not exactly.' His mouth twisted. 'There's a child. Rowan's.'

'You send money for your dead brother's child?' Lily's face softened. She opened her mouth to say more, but then she saw Dawson's strange living quarters.

In the black ashy devastation, Dawson's penthouse, high atop the old Lud Gate, was a world of colour. Each surface was layered with a speckled mix of old paints. Thousands of dried flecks and splatters formed a rough circle around where the painter stood, giving him a backdrop explosion of colour.

As Lily and Charlie approached, Dawson was sitting with his back to them, an elaborate leather strap covering the back of his head. The midday light was casting a warm glow on several huge canvas scenes arranged along the top of the gatehouse. With every degree the sun crossed the sky, Charlie thought, Maria's life ebbed with it. He balled his fists, willing Dawson to give them the answers they needed.

Dawson turned as they entered and his brown eyes were hugely magnified behind a pair of glass goggles. In his hand was a paintbrush, which he held up quizzically as they moved towards him.

'Why does he dress like a ghost?' whispered Lily, taking in the frilled white ruff and forked beard. Atop his long grey hair, Dawson wore a black chimney-hat with two white goose feathers pointing straight up.

'He's a painter,' said Charlie. 'They like to be different.'

'Charlie Tuesday,' said Dawson, standing with an apologetic smile. 'I haven't any money for you yet, I'm afraid.' Dawson nodded to the small boy in the page's outfit, who was hovering uncertainly. The boy scampered away.

'I'm willing to give you as much time as you need,' said Charlie, 'in return for a little help.'

Dawson slid off his stool with impressive agility for a man of his advancing years. His eyes had settled on Lily. 'You've brought me a muse,' said Dawson admiringly. 'We're always looking for exotic stock in the theatre.' He took her hand and kissed it. 'Would you consider sitting for me, my dear? You could be a background Italian.' He had a clutch of missing teeth on one side, from an old jaw injury, which gave him a slight lisp.

'How much money do you owe Charlie?' asked Lily.

His charming expression faltered. 'A few shillings,' he said vaguely. 'But as soon as these sell, I'll easily pay all my debts.' He gestured to the canvases. 'Now my paints have been returned, I can make three of these a week. They sell to the best theatres for ten shillings a piece. Standard scenes,' he added, 'temples, tombs, city gates and chambers. I sent out a palace last week.'

Lily's eyes lifted to the current canvas. It was a large image of poplar trees. 'Italy?' she asked, nodding to it.

'It could serve as any rural scene,' said Dawson proudly. 'That's the skill of the scenery painter. I'll turn my hand to anything. Except prisons,' he added, his face falling darkly.

'What's this one?' asked Lily, looking at a fantastical scene of castle turrets and green rolling hills. A few mythical-looking people were dotted in the far distance. Maidens, knights and a frightening old crone.

'Ah,' said Dawson proudly, moving to her side. 'What a good eye you have. This is one of my best pieces. It's Avalon. The place where King Arthur went to die.' He eyed it proudly. 'I have hopes of selling it to the palace.' He cupped his hand over his mouth in a conspiratorial gesture. 'All kings are desperate to claim some ancient lineage running back to Arthur and swords in stones,' he divulged. 'Henry had his face painted on a round table.' Dawson took a last admiring look at his own work, then turned back to Charlie. 'You talked of extending my debt,' he added hopefully. 'What would you want in return?'

'Information,' said Charlie. 'About a lost lord and lady who we think might have been kept hidden in London since the war.'

Dawson blinked for a moment. 'You don't mean . . . You cannot mean *the* Lord and Lady?'

'We thought they might have been sheltered by the King's Company during the war.'

'Well, yes they were,' agreed Dawson, nodding slowly. 'Certainly I was told so. They took part in every performance.'

Chapter 61

Up in Dawson's strange paint-splattered tower, time seemed to have slowed.

'The Lord and Lady performed with our theatre group after they were smuggled free from the Tower,' explained Dawson. 'That's what I was told.'

'The Lord and Lady performed with the King's Company?' confirmed Charlie.

Dawson nodded patiently. 'One of the leading actors let it slip to me after too much wine. Cromwell knew it too,' he added philosophically. 'His men came searching.'

'Were you told anything else about what happened to them?' asked Charlie, his heart pounding.

'Cromwell searched all the theatres. He was desperate,' said Dawson. 'I understood the Lord and Lady to be most important people.'

'Heirs to the throne?' suggested Lily.

'No.' Dawson shook his head. 'More important than that. They are gods. The last of the old gods. From when we had many. King Arthur was a Christian who ruled by forging an alliance with the old ones. The Green Man and his lady.'

'But our kings are Christian,' said Charlie. 'They don't worship old gods and fairies.'

'They did,' said Dawson. 'But no more. Cromwell and his men were known as the Ironsides, were they not? They went to war against the fairies, and the old gods. The Puritans in their iron armour weakened the Old Ones so they were barely more than mortals.' Dawson shook his head sadly. 'As I say, Cromwell's man came, years ago. Praise-God Barebones. He came first to my workshop, smashed up many of my paintings. Then he went to the theatre. I couldn't warn the players in time.' He paused. 'The players put up a good fight. Barebones took the whole company to the justices.'

'So they were whipped?' asked Charlie. 'Imprisoned?'

'I was whipped and put in the stocks,' said Dawson, gesturing to his broken jaw. 'I was fortunate. But as for the actors, feelings at the time ran high.' Dawson's eyes met Charlie's. 'Praise-God Barebones had them all executed,' he said. 'I always assumed the Lord and Lady died with them.'

Chapter 62

In the dirty streets of Covent Garden, Tom knew immediately she was the one. A little orange seller skirting around the edges of the theatre. The height and build were right, and her long dark hair could be easily rearranged. The eyes were blue rather than brown, but that never mattered. The eyes changed.

It was mid-morning, which usually made no difference here. Drunks staggered, beer and wine barrels were rolled in and out. Players acted in the streets and gaudily dressed whores were everywhere.

Today Tom had noticed something was different. The women were less sure of themselves, and a few illegal theatres had been boarded up. Was it possible the riots would come to Covent Garden?

A shudder ran through him at the thought. *Chaos. Like before. No rules. No king.*

Tom rearranged his handsome face in an expression he knew to be charming and approached the girl. She was a nobody; he could easily see it. Scraping a living selling fruit in the theatre and whoring herself for pennies when the chance came.

She flinched as he tapped her shoulder – some innate intuition he'd never quite understood how to overcome. When she turned, her face was slightly fearful. Tom gave her the smile he'd practised to perfection.

Charming, apologetic. Teamed with his handsome face her trepidation dropped away, but not completely.

'Might you help me?' Tom gestured with a wince to his arm held in a sling around his body. 'Sprained it,' he explained, 'when my master's horse reared. He wanted me to go for oranges in Covent Garden, but I've missed the early market and the cook must have them. Might I buy your oranges? I'll pay theatre prices.'

He could see her taking him in. The temptation to sell her entire stock overcame the girl's lingering doubts. She nodded, reaching to take the basket from her head.

'Only might you carry them to Brewer Street?' he asked, stretching his charming smile and nodding apologetically to his arm. 'I will pay an extra penny.'

She hesitated, casting a final glance at his handsome smiling face, then followed him down the alley.

As soon as they were out of sight, Tom pulled out his knife.

The girl's features rapidly rearranged themselves into what Tom understood as fear. He would have liked to study her face further, but he risked people disturbing them, even in this dark alley.

Then she began raising her skirts, glaring. 'Be quick then,' she said, setting the basket of oranges down. 'And a curse on you.'

Tom lowered the knife, confused. He was trying to put the pieces together. The raised skirts meant . . . Fornication. She thought he was trying to force himself on her. The unexpected response was so unsettling he had to steady himself.

'No,' he said, keeping the knife high. 'I am one of those from the King, come to find out spies and those who plot against him.'

The girl hesitated, confused now. 'I know nothing of the dissenters,' she said slowly. 'I cheered with every other Londoner when His Majesty made his triumphant return.'

Quick as a flash, Tom removed a flask from inside his coat. 'Then prove it,' he said. 'Drink a toast to the King's health.'

The girl was staring at the flask.

Tom uncorked it, removed a tankard from his belt and filled it. 'To the King.' He put the vessel to his lips and took a deep drink. The girl watched him.

She reached out and took it with work-callused fingers. Then she raised it, her hand shaking slightly. 'This is all I need do?' she said. 'Drink a toast? Then I might get back to the theatre?'

Tom nodded. 'And I'll buy your stock of oranges to make amends for the affront,' he added, opening a purse filled with little coins.

She moved it to her lips. 'To the King,' she said, upending the cup. 'It's sweet,' she added, wiping her mouth.

As the girl handed back the tankard, the world seemed to be shifting as though she were looking through water. There was a distant ringing in her ears.

Her attacker was looking at her keenly. 'Do you hear them chiming?' he whispered. 'The fairy bells?'

She frowned, swallowed and tried to turn her head. The ringing was louder now, and her heart was beating faster. Too fast. She tried to take a step and somehow there wasn't enough blood in her limbs.

As she fell, the girl noticed the alley had turned yellow. A happy colour.

'They're coming for you,' he said, kneeling beside her. 'Can you see them? The fairies are coming.'

Prone on the floor, the girl's heart was hammering, but her mind felt soft and comfortably far away. The yellow haze was growing thicker. But she thought she could see . . . flashes . . . lights, like flying creatures at the edge of her vision.

'You drank it too,' she managed.

'I was given it throughout my childhood,' explained the man. 'The effect on me is no longer so strong. But I see them too,' he assured her, 'the fey folk. It's their chimes you hear. They're coming to take you away.'

Tom watched her dying face, imagining the girl she would replace. The boy would kill Maria, horribly, of that he was certain. Nothing he could do to change that. But he could make sure she wouldn't die alone. He would give Maria a companion to hear her last desperate shrieks. But this required another changeling offering to the fairy folk.

He had already chosen the next girl to be vanished. Maria would die along with someone dear to Charlie Tuesday.

Chapter 63

Charlie felt as though the world were closing in on him. 'You're certain?' he heard himself saying. 'The whole troupe?'

'Many good men,' said Dawson sadly. 'They went into the prison and never came out. Stories were told of gaol fever and such, but we all knew the truth. They'd been vanished. By Cromwell's dark man.'

Charlie and Lily looked at one another.

'I've heard of Praise-God Barebones,' said Lily. 'He's one of the riot leaders.'

'Doesn't surprise me,' said Dawson. 'He was the deepest-dyed Puritan you'd ever meet. Black-and-white thinking, you know, like their clothes.'

'So this Barebones,' said Charlie. 'He executed the players at the King's Company?'

Dawson nodded. 'We heard that Tom Black refused. So I suppose he had some loyalty to us.'

'Tom Black?' Charlie snapped to attention.

'Cromwell's assassin,' said Dawson. 'He was known as the foxglove killer. Poisoned his victims. He worked alongside Barebones. The soldier and the assassin. But long before that he used to work for our theatre company.'

'You knew him?'

'He was a peculiar boy,' said Dawson. 'He never told a lie, worked hard. Belonged to some unusual sect of Puritanism and was frighteningly clever. But some of the actors thought him strange, the way he watched. Tom worked on effects. He had a talent for illusions and tricks of the eye, and a vivid imagination. I used to plunder him for ideas for scenery. A funny thought now,' concluded Dawson, glancing to the picture of Avalon. 'Tom became the most dangerous man alive during Cromwell's reign. Capable of unspeakable horrors. He was famed for burning men to death.'

Charlie was trying to get a grip on what he knew. 'If we could find Praise-God Barebones,' decided Charlie. 'He could tell us something of Tom Black. They worked together. For Cromwell.'

'So what do we do?' asked Lily. 'Walk into the brothel riot and ask for him?'

'Barebones is being held secretly,' said Dawson helpfully. 'I hear all sorts from my little spies,' he added happily. 'The apprentices tried to break him out. But they went to the wrong prison.'

'There are twenty prisons in London,' said Charlie, feeling the opportunity slip away. 'There's no time to search them all.'

A little bell rang from below and Dawson moved to the side of the tower. 'One moment,' he said. 'A message for me.' He disappeared out of sight.

'They're dead then,' said Charlie as Dawson left. He rubbed his scarred lip. 'I think I knew it all along, deep down,' he admitted. 'This hunt never felt right. Hidden people always give something away,' he said. 'They can't help it. There's food, possessions, things that leave a trail. A human haze of thoughts and feelings that bobs about anyone they associate with.'

'If the Lord and Lady died,' said Lily, 'they can't be found.'

Charlie nodded. 'We have less than half a day until Good Friday,' he said, feeling the ground shift beneath his feet. 'We cannot bring Tom

Black the Lord and Lady. All we can do is try to find him before he hurts Maria. We've lost so much time. I should have been hunting him from the beginning.' Charlie tried to order his thoughts. It wasn't possible to track a man in only a few hours. 'It can't be done,' he said, feeling a powerless panic rise up. 'We're looking for a man who can look like anyone. An actor. Who could be anywhere in London.'

Lily was twisting the black-and-gold ring on her finger. 'Do you remember before,' she said, 'when you said I was helping you out of concern for Maria?'

He nodded.

'I don't care about Maria,' said Lily. 'I care about you. And I know you care for her.'

'What are you saying?' asked Charlie.

Lily sat down suddenly and took both his hands in hers. 'I'm saying don't you give up, Charlie Tuesday,' she said. 'I'll help you. You are my friend. Albeit a friend who leads me into the worst peril. But,' she added with a small smile, 'I always did like danger. Listen, I think there could be a clue to finding Tom Black's identity in Dawson's picture of Avalon. He said Tom's strange stories inspired some of his more fantastical scenes. Dawson's your friend, he might . . .'

She stopped. Dawson had returned and was walking quickly towards them. His expression was furious. 'Charlie Tuesday.' Dawson's voice rang with affront. 'Why didn't you tell me you were wanted for treason?'

Charlie opened his mouth to reply, but Dawson kept talking. 'You lied to me!' he accused angrily, pointing at them both. 'You're wanted criminals. There's a guard here to make your arrest.'

Chapter 64

Lily and Charlie were staring at Dawson.

'You brought Lady Castlemaine's guards to my door!' Dawson accused. 'The worst of Jezebels has reason to seek me out. Her men say you broke into His Majesty's coin house,' he continued. 'Stole a quantity of silver coin!'

Charlie held up his hands. 'Wait . . .' he began.

'And this . . . person,' continued Dawson, looking at Lily, 'is a pirate!' His voice had risen an octave.

Lily turned to Charlie. 'It isn't true,' she said, speaking quickly. 'Not all of it . . .'

Dawson's long finger stabbed the air. 'Lady Castlemaine is offering a reward of thirty pounds from her own ill-gotten purse,' he said, his voice shaking slightly with anger. 'For information leading to the capture of two villainous thieves and pirates. Lily Boswell, who has been wanted this year past for piracy. My boy told me all. You were followed here.'

'You're a pirate?' demanded Charlie.

'It was a mistake,' said Lily, 'a misunderstanding. We took a ship after my privateer's licence was revoked.'

'And the bounty you took?'

'Sank,' said Lily. 'I need to repay it to earn the King's forgiveness. Only Lady Castlemaine . . . She doesn't like women who look like me,' she concluded bitterly.

'So that's why you're risking your life to help me,' accused Charlie. 'There's a price on your head.'

'It wasn't only that,' said Lily angrily. 'You always think me out for my own gain. Just because I'm a gypsy . . .'

'I care *nothing* that you're a gypsy,' shouted Charlie. 'I only care that you lie. Had you ever considered telling me the truth? Did you not think I might help you? That I'm your friend? I would never . . .'

'Neither of you told me the truth,' interrupted Dawson, 'and now you've put me in a terrible situation.' He shook his head. 'Theft I can forgive. But treason? I am sorry for it, Charlie, but I mean to let those guards take you. My loyalty is to our God-appointed king.' He was frowning deeply. 'My pageboy has bid the guards wait,' concluded Dawson. 'You may have a few moments to collect yourselves. But I will not harbour traitors.'

'Dawson, wait,' said Charlie, forcing aside his sudden anger at Lily. 'Think. Why would Lady Castlemaine be involving herself in the apprehension of a pirate?'

Dawson hesitated.

'It's a strange use of her money, is it not?' pressed Charlie. 'Why should she be putting her own funds to finding us? Could it be that she is seeking the Lord and Lady herself?'

Dawson's eyes flicked to the painting of Avalon.

'Lady Castlemaine is losing her power over the King,' said Charlie. 'You said had the Lord and Lady lived, they'd discredit the King's rule. Couldn't Lady Castlemaine benefit from that?'

Dawson pulled at his forked beard. 'Lady Castlemaine is the worst of harlots,' he said, nodding sharply. 'Her intentions are never to the benefit of our great king. I am at your service,' he concluded.

'Thank you,' said Charlie. 'Can you tell us anything more of Tom Black? You mentioned he inspired the fairies in your scenes.'

'All that scenery is long gone, I'm afraid,' said Dawson apologetically. 'The only one from those times is Avalon.' Dawson moved towards it. 'That old woman,' he said, tapping the balding crone. 'Tom described her vividly. She sounded terrifying.'

'Tom's mother?' suggested Lily, looking closer. 'She looks too old.' There was a shout from below.

Dawson moved to the edge of the crumbling black crenellations. 'It seems those guards are not waiting as patiently as I expected,' he said. 'They mean to enter by force.'

Charlie was staring at the picture. Ideas were forging together. 'Lily,' he said. 'Tom Black was the foxglove killer. Foxglove is a poison. It yellows the eyes, stops the heart. It's also known as fairycaps.' He tapped the balding crone in the picture. 'And fairycaps,' he continued, 'is widely used by cunning women to send back changelings.'

'But there's hundreds of evil hags who sell poison in London,' said Lily.

'Not as many as you might imagine,' said Charlie. 'But there is one cunning woman famed for such tricks. She's the most wicked old crone you'll find in London. And she lives just outside the Shambles. Perhaps she's the woman in the painting.' He gestured to the scene of Avalon.

Lily's lips were moving soundlessly, putting the facts together. 'Tom Black grew up in the Shambles.'

'With his mother, Bridey Black,' said Charlie. 'What if it was Bridey who first visited the cunning woman who later supplied her son with poison?'

'Women confide in cunning women,' said Lily. 'They tell them everything.'

Charlie was nodding, feeling possibilities flood in. Maria. There was still time. If they were right, and the cunning woman told them

239

what she knew, they might be able to rapidly deduce where Tom had hidden Maria.

There was another shout from below.

'We just need to get off this gate,' said Charlie. He turned to Dawson. 'Can you help us?'

'I always wished I'd been more gallant during the war,' said Dawson. 'Perhaps God gives me another chance for glory, to defend the Royalist cause. Come,' he added. 'I do have a means of escape. Of sorts.'

'Of sorts?' Lily was looking around the top of the turret.

'Fear not, fair maiden.' Dawson grinned, his lopsided jaw jerking. 'I have a flying machine.'

Chapter 65

Lady Castlemaine stood in her private chamber, arms outstretched as the little tailor fluttered around her, sewing her into her dress at lightning speed. He hesitated at the waist, drawing silk between his fingers.

'Perhaps more space here,' he said. 'Your shape has changed a little . . .'

She looked at him. The tailor ducked his head and continued to sew, drawing the stitches tight. She grimaced, then regarded herself in the mirror.

'Better,' she decided, turning this way and that to admire her curving body.

There was a knock at the door.

'Enter,' she called.

To the tailor's surprise the man who entered was not the King. But he was nevertheless familiar. The handsome man was an actor from the Birdcage where Lynette acted. He was young and Italian, with curling brown hair falling to his shoulders and the upright posture of a seasoned performer. Lorenzo, the tailor thought his name was.

'Leave us,' commanded Lady Castlemaine.

The tailor bowed and left.

As the door closed she moved fast towards the man. 'We are quite alone,' said Lady Castlemaine. 'Tell me all.'

His plucked eyebrows drew together in affront and she realised she'd offended him by treating him like an informant.

'I've missed you,' she said, lifting one hand to touch his cheek and sliding the other between his legs. She could smell his perfume, an Italian affectation she despised.

'*Mio amore*,' he murmured, resting his smooth cheek on hers.

Lady Castlemaine was seized with a memory of the King, when they were young, in Holland. For a moment nostalgia gripped her so tightly she felt the air squeezed out of her.

'You said you'd get me place,' said Lorenzo, labouring his words. 'In the King's Company.'

'How can you doubt it? I would die for you.' She knew how he enjoyed dramatics. She was pulling him from his clothing, wondering how his halting English was understood on stage. 'Soon, my love. Soon. Only tell me what have you discovered in the Birdcage, so I might make better plans.'

'I find what I can,' he said, closing his eyes as her hands moved. 'Lynette's old husband was seen with a girl. A very pre-etty girl,' he added pointedly. 'Called Leely Boswell. She is so be-yu-tiful. Dark hair, mouth like . . .' He glanced at Lady Castlemaine and stopped talking abruptly.

'Lynette's old husband has been seen with Lily Boswell?' she said. 'You're certain?' She felt Lorenzo tense. 'You are so clever to have discovered it,' she soothed, backtracking.

'You know Leely Boswell?' he asked.

'She's a spy,' said Lady Castlemaine. 'Who recently broke into the Mint. With a man I didn't recognise. Now I discover that man is Lynette's old husband, well' – she gave a little laugh – 'I think they commit treason.'

'What were they looking for in the Mint?' Lorenzo's brow furrowed.

'It doesn't matter,' said Lady Castlemaine.

'You treat me like leetle boy, Barbara,' snapped Lorenzo tetchily, pulling away from her. 'I am nothing. Mean nothing. I leave London,' he added. 'I owe money . . .'

He let the sentence hang.

Lady Castlemaine reached into her hanging pocket and withdrew a little bag of money.

'My love,' she said contritely, 'I only wish I had more to give you.'

Lorenzo's eyes flashed briefly as he fingered the small purse. 'People at theatre, they laugh at me,' he said, 'call me fool. They talk about you. They say you bad.'

'There's always talk.' She tried to keep her tone light. 'What do they say?'

'They say you pay men to break playhouses,' said Lorenzo.

'Surely you don't believe such lies?'

He looked to his feet, hand tightening on the purse of money.

She took his shoulders. 'I swear to you,' she said, looking deep into his eyes and blinking with sincerity, 'I mean no harm to the theatres. It's you I love. Why should I care if the King dallies with actresses and whores?'

'You don't look for this . . . Laird and Leddy? Try kill them?'

She laughed bright, high and false. 'Of course not.' She smiled. 'I have far more important people in mind.'

Chapter 66

'A few people are hunting me for debts,' explained Dawson, leading Charlie and Lily to the high side of Lud Gate tower. 'So I had some theatre friends rig something up for me.' He pointed to a strange kind of pulley system. 'It's the latest thing,' he said proudly. 'Allows an actor to fly through the air.'

Lily was staring at what seemed to be nothing more than a tangle of knots and hempen rope.

'You've tried it?' she asked.

'We shall be the first mortal men to fly as angels.' Dawson grinned.

'You mean,' said Lily, 'it's never been tested before.'

'Rigorously tested,' said Dawson proudly. 'Three of the goats survived. It's safe. I give you my word as a man of the King. Wait there,' he added. Dawson raced to the edge of Lud Gate and peered over. 'I have the criminals here,' he bellowed to the guards below. 'They cannot escape!' He ran back to where Lily and Charlie stood, face flushed with excitement. 'The enemy approach,' he said, 'but we will elude them.'

He pushed down his strange leather magnifying goggles and winched his narrow body into the assortment of ropes and a bagging harness. Then he tucked his feet into two stirrups and sat on the edge of the gatehouse.

'What are you waiting for?' he called. 'Fix your feet and hands there.' He threw over some lengths of rope with stirrups attached and a second harness.

They could hear shouting on the stairs now. Guards were approaching. Charlie stepped towards the rope-and-pulley system.

'The lady will have to share the harness with me, I'm afraid,' said Dawson cheerily. 'I've not yet the facility for more. But it's strong leather. It will hold.' He patted his skinny thigh. 'Come sit.'

Lily's expression was unreadable as she seated herself on the old man's lap and suffered him to secure her with a number of large buckles. Charlie watched them and approximated the same with the second harness.

The guard broke through the top of the stair. Charlie recognised them to be the same men who'd given chase at the Tower of London. They were staring in confusion at the assortment of ropes and winches.

'Witchcraft,' said one uncertainly, pointing a gun.

'What fun.' Dawson beamed. 'I knew I was wasted in theatre. Ready, my dear?'

Without waiting for Lily's reply, he pushed with his feet and launched them free of Lud Gate. They dropped over the edge and Dawson shot out a hand, pulling Charlie with them.

They all three plummeted down, Dawson whooping with delight. A counterweight of sandbags jolted their ropes, slowing the ascent.

'It's not slowing us enough,' said Lily, panicking as the rope roared through the metal pulley. 'The rope is burning.'

An ominous curl of smoke was snaking from the metal pulley. The cord holding Dawson and Lily had begun to break apart, sending them into a spin. They rotated downwards at speed, then landed in a heap. Charlie arrived with slightly more grace beside them. Goose feathers floated up.

'Lucky I softened the landing,' said Dawson, unbuckling the harness and smacking a hand on a sack of feathers. 'That fall would have killed us both.'

Lily moved away from him wordlessly, eyes radiating unsaid trauma.

A shot went off. The guards were taking aim from the top of Lud Gate.

'Flee!' said Dawson dramatically. 'Go find what you seek.'

'What about you?' asked Charlie, glancing up at Lud Gate. When he looked down again, Dawson was already running back into the ruins.

'Don't fear for me!' he called. 'The footpads know I have no money!'

'We've got a head start,' said Charlie. 'But I think Lady Castlemaine's guard will give chase.'

'Then what are we waiting for?' said Lily grimly. 'Let's go find out about Tom Black.'

Chapter 67

In the narrow blood-soaked streets of the Shambles, packs of butchers were working in teams, defending their alleys. As Charlie and Lily approached, ragged people flew past them, clutching stolen meat. Women fled, holding aprons full of steaks and chops. Two bone-thin men were staggering determinedly under the weight of a whole pig.

'There.' Charlie pointed at a tumbledown building, the front half-burned from the fire.

Someone had tried to rebuild with mud bricks, but had given up after a few rows.

'The cunning woman has been in this old mansion since anyone can remember,' said Charlie. 'Fire won't have pushed her out.'

'Who pays for repairs?' asked Lily, looking at the devastated building.

'It's a tenement,' said Charlie, as the floor beneath turned to scalded Tudor-rose tiles and ash. 'A noble house that has become unfashionable and is rented to the poor. Tenants are liable for upkeep, but in reality it just crumbles.'

They ducked beneath charred beams and reached what had once been a stable block at the back of the building.

'What's that? A warning?' Lily was looking at the blackened wood of the stable doorway where a dead rabbit hung, suspended by its ears from a length of string.

'That's the sign of the cunning woman,' said Charlie. 'Any old woman who thinks herself able to cure ailments, speak with demons or worse goes by that sign.'

'In the country we just call them witches,' said Lily.

They moved through the doorway and were immediately greeted by the strong stench of urine. Lily recoiled, then put her hand over her nose.

The room beyond was jumbled with found objects. In the middle was an old crib made of thick dark wood. It was crammed full of grubby linen, odd little poppets and tiny old shoes.

The acrid stench of urine deepened as they drew further inside. There was a wide chimney breast and a sad little fire. Next to the smoking sticks was a wooden cup, filled with what might once have been milk. A poker lay at the side, threaded with the remains of spit-roasted rodent. It was a rat or stoat, half-eaten, tiny teeth bared.

A dark bundle of rags had been amassed in the centre of the room. The terrible sour smell poured from it in waves. Then it shifted.

Lily started back in alarm and took Charlie's hand. He closed his fingers around hers and she yanked her hand free.

'I was a little startled, is all,' she said, turning her rings to hide her embarrassment. She took a few steps forward. 'Why did it move?' she asked. 'What is it?'

'That,' said Charlie, 'is the cunning woman.'

Chapter 68

The huge bundle of stinking rags rose. Two skinny arms dangled from a rounded hunchback, the bare skin liver-spotted and ancient. The little head that emerged from underneath the bent spine was squat and so filthy that only the pale eyes could be easily discerned. There was the suggestion of a stubby nose and a lopsided mouth, framed by knotted tendrils of grey hair. She reminded Charlie of a snail emerging from its shell. Then the mouth opened, revealing three long bottom teeth.

'What truth do you seek?' Her voice rumbled with catarrh. She'd been sitting on a little stool and risen as they approached. But the height difference with her bent back was so slight it was barely noticeable.

She had something in her hand. Some filthy piece of fabric, which she stroked as she spoke. It was a child's bonnet, Charlie realised. Old and falling to pieces.

'Do you sell distilled foxglove?' asked Charlie. 'Fairycaps?'

'My changeling potion,' agreed the cunning woman. 'I make it here. If a changeling won't return by himself, you can manage him in this world. Keep his spirits low. Confused. Stop him making evil tricks.'

Charlie was absorbing this. 'It's deadly in large doses?' he said. 'This changeling brew?'

The old woman nodded. 'If you give too much. Yellows the eyes and stops the heart. I only sell it to women with changed babes,' said the cunning woman, 'and fairies.' Her eyes glinted.

Charlie put the pieces together. 'You sold it to Bridey Black's changeling?' he said. 'Tom Black?'

The old eyes settled on his face, considering. The cunning woman was likely half-blind, Charlie realised. The milky eyes were thick with cataracts.

'Are you fairy?' she asked after a moment.

Charlie hesitated, wondering how best to reply. 'No,' he said.

'Tricky,' she muttered. 'He is a trickster. We must be careful.'

There was a pause. Her little fire spat a feeble ember. Then she reached out a raddled hand towards him.

It took all Charlie's resolve not to back away as she felt across his features. The knotty fingers moving across his broad eyebrows, feeling the kink in his nose and the scarred upper lip.

'Horse?' she said suddenly. 'Horse did that?'

Charlie nodded, wondering how she knew. He usually told people it was a knife fight.

'Nasty beasts.' She coughed, honking loudly. Charlie tried not to breath in. 'Perhaps not fairy.' The horse injury seemed to satisfy her.

Her old fingers dropped down suddenly to his key, feeling the shape. His hand shot up to protect it.

The old woman gave a cackling laugh. Her fingers withdrew. 'You are an orphan-foundling perhaps?' she suggested. 'Your mother left you a trinket, so she might find you again?'

'Perhaps,' said Charlie. The key had been his only possession when he and his brother were committed to the terrible Foundling Home.

'But she never returned,' decided the cunning woman. 'Foundlings always have something of the fey folk about them. You are stuck creatures, caught between this world and the next. And now the poor foundling seeks the truth.' She cocked her head, lopsided mouth turned into what might have been a smile. 'I will tell you,' she said. 'But your key is my price.' Her fingers extended towards it greedily.

Charlie stepped back. He looked at Lily.

'Why do you want that?' tried Lily. 'We can give you money . . .'

'No, no, no,' said the woman, shaking her head slowly. 'I have named my price. And you, little gypsy, must give me your medallion.'

Lily bit her lip. 'What good can my spy medallion do her?' she muttered.

'You come to the cunning woman, you pay what is most dear,' said the old woman, sinking back onto her little stool.

'Let's go, Charlie,' hissed Lily. 'She's not in her right mind. I'll bet she doesn't even remember who Bridey Black is, if she came to her at all.'

'I remember Bridey well,' said the cunning woman. 'Her babe had been changed. The fairies took him.'

Charlie and Lily exchanged glances.

'I can tell you everything you need to know,' she continued tantalisingly, 'about Tom Black. His true mother and father. The Lord and Lady. Their powers . . .' Her eyelids fluttered closed, then opened sharply. 'Tom Black believes they will grant him his greatest desire.'

'What is that?' asked Charlie.

'The same as all fey folk. He craves mortality. Yearns for it.' She looked at them. 'Unless the Lord and Lady send him home, Tom means to kill the girl he has taken when the sun sets today.'

'No,' said Charlie. 'We have until Good Friday to free her. It's still Maundy Thursday.'

The cunning woman tilted her head. 'Shambles folk follow the Puritan faith. Lent ends when the sun sets on Maundy Thursday,' she said. 'Good Friday starts this evening.'

Charlie felt his stomach turn. 'That only leaves us a few hours,' he whispered. 'We didn't have enough time when there was half a day.'

'Perhaps you have even less time than you think,' said the cunning woman. 'The world Tom Black knows has started to unravel. The fairies in him rise. Your girl won't last long.'

Charlie looked at Lily, one hand clutched defensively around her precious medallion.

'How about a game?' he suggested carefully.

'Fairy!' the cunning woman hissed, drawing back. 'I dealt with your kind before. I know what it is to play your games.' Her raddled old hands were stroking the ragged bonnet fast.

Charlie looped the key off his neck. He rested it on the broken table amongst the little jars of tinctures.

'You're a card sharp,' he said, 'after a fashion. You read people. Pick up on cues. Your skill against ours. If I read you right, you tell us what we want to know. If I'm wrong,' he nodded to the key and the medallion around Lily's neck, 'you keep our most treasured possessions and we walk away with nothing.'

'Charlie!' hissed Lily.

A smile lit the lopsided mouth. 'What is to know?' she said. 'There is nothing of me to tell. I am only an old woman.'

'But what if I could tell you,' said Charlie, 'about the fairies?'

The cunning woman uttered a strange hiss. 'Very well,' she decided. The cunning woman was looking at Lily now.

'Lily,' whispered Charlie. 'Put the medallion down.'

She hesitated, then drew it off slowly and put it on the table. Lily slipped a sideways glance to Charlie. 'If you lose it,' she muttered darkly, 'I'll never forgive you.'

'I'll try not to.'

He was taking in the cunning woman. Her home. Her dirty things. 'You weren't born here,' he started. 'You're from the country. The way you tie your skirts and ribbons is country. But you've no country possessions.' He glanced around the room. 'Which makes me think you came to London because something bad happened.' His eyes flicked to the crib. 'Something you wanted to forget.'

The cunning woman gave the slightest of nods.

'The fairies,' continued Charlie, 'came to you. Spoke to you.'

There was something in her face, then, that he couldn't quite seize hold of.

His eyes settled on the child's bonnet in her hand. 'You had a baby,' he said, 'out of wedlock. The fairies took it.'

The cunning woman's face twisted. 'No,' she said, shuffling a curled hand towards the key and the medallion. 'You have it wrong. You are no truth-sayer.'

The twisted fingers moved to take his key.

Chapter 69

Maria was working on her manacles in the dark, rubbing furiously. The old rusted metal had taken on a patina, something approaching a shine. She thought, in the right light, it might offer a muddy kind of reflection. Alone in the dark, Maria had realised something. Tom's dull metal sword. His strange refusal to leave her a pail of water to wash with. The narrow scars criss-crossing his knuckles, as though he'd repeatedly driven his fists into glass.

She wasn't certain, but she thought he might be afraid of mirrors. So she'd started work on making a reflective surface.

A mirror to frighten a fairy. It was such a strange thing to be doing she almost laughed at herself. But what could be stranger than the place she was currently in?

Maria froze suddenly. Something was moving in the dark. Her stomach lurched. Had he heard her polishing the manacles?

'Tom?' she ventured, trying to keep her voice normal.

There was no reply. Fear rippled through her. Then she heard laughter. Faint and mocking.

A tinderbox struck, and a candle flame floated in the dark.

'I've been waiting to meet you,' said Tom's voice.

Maria tried to stay calm. He was only playacting. 'You try another part?' she asked. 'You wish I should act with you?'

But something was wrong. And when he lifted his eyes to look at her, she shrank back at the cold cruelty there.

He lifted a bony finger to his lips. 'Shhhhhh.' He smiled. 'I have got out.'

Maria hesitated, taking in the altered expression, the mad eyes. 'You're not Tom?' she said.

Tom shook his head slowly. 'No,' he giggled. 'Tom is behind the mirror.' His eyes rolled around the dark room. 'The riots,' he added, 'set me free, for a little while. Chaos.' He smiled. It was Tom, but it wasn't. Even in his acted parts, Maria felt sure she had never met this person before.

Facts were rushing together in her mind. 'You're the boy,' she said, realising, 'the changeling boy. The one who was taken, and Tom left in his place.'

The boy nodded, then tilted his head, birdlike, towards Maria. 'He keeps me locked away behind the mirror. He talks about you. He is different when he speaks of you. It is a problem I have been thinking over.' He leaned forward, his face taut with excitement. 'Let me tell you a secret,' he whispered. 'I am growing stronger. Tom will not be able to keep me trapped much longer.' He breathed deeply. 'He won't be able to defend you.'

'What does he need defend me against?' asked Maria, trying to keep her voice from shaking.

The boy smiled. 'Why, me, of course. Tom restrains himself, but I have no such compunction.' He laughed coldly. 'Perhaps he is the Puritan and I the indulgent Royalist.'

Maria swallowed, saying nothing.

'Do you know the best of it?' gloated the boy. 'You're the one who will set me free. You gave me the answer.' He made a horrible smile. 'My sainted mother. You made me see her differently. It's all so clear

255

now. When I put her behind the mirror, the glass will break.' He leaned forward and lit a candle. 'Tom has starved me of the things I like best,' he told her. 'I mean to sate myself utterly.' The boy lifted the candle and the flame bloomed. He waved the flame as he moved in. 'I have dreamed of it, how I will burn you, the way your face will twist and contort.'

Maria acted on sudden impulse. She took a fast step forward, and as the candle moved towards her, she held up the polished part of her manacles.

The boy opened his mouth to laugh at her, stepping out of her reach. And then his gaze settled on his outline in the manacles and the laugh dropped away.

'No!' he mouthed, catching sight of his blurry reflection. 'Don't put me back!'

Then the boy's crazed face receded and Tom was blinking back at her.

'What did you do?' He sounded drugged and groggy.

'You were dreaming again,' said Maria. She patted his chest comfortingly and in so doing, located the glass vial, hidden inside his coat.

'You have angered him,' said Tom. 'You shouldn't have done that.'

Maria swallowed.

'It will go worse for you, I'm afraid,' said Tom. 'He is furious for the trick you played on him. He means for you to suffer unspeakably.'

Tom was watching the growing terror in Maria's face with interest. And he didn't notice her slip free the glass vial.

Chapter 70

Charlie watched as the cunning woman's hand closed triumphantly over his key. His heart sank. He'd set the terms of the wager and now he'd lost.

'You sold your baby,' said Lily suddenly. 'You sold your baby to the fairies. In exchange for your powers.'

The cunning woman stopped. Her gnarled hand opened.

'A girl child,' said Lily. 'You were on the road to London. Near King's Cross where the gypsies camp.'

The milky eyes filled with tears. 'I never spoke of it,' she whispered. 'Not to a living soul. I tried to go back, but it was too late.' The cunning woman's anguish was strangely juvenile. As though this particular memory had conjured a younger self.

Lily hesitated, glancing at Charlie. 'Tell us what we need to know. A promise is a promise.'

The cunning woman's mouth tightened in annoyance. 'How did you know about my babe?' she demanded. 'Tell me.'

'First tell us about Bridey Black,' said Lily sternly. 'No tricks.'

The old woman rocked on her stool. 'Ah, but there were tricks,' she said. 'To make Bridey's changeling return. We burned him,' she said, 'cut him, put him close to the fire. We left him out in the snow with no clothes on.'

Charlie felt his stomach tighten. Facts were rushing together.

'How could you?' Lily's voice caught in her throat.

The old woman's strange smile remained. 'A mother knows,' she said. 'A mother knows when her babe is changed. I hurt no innocents. Only force the fairies to come and take back their own.'

Beside him, Charlie felt Lily move. He took her hand and squeezed it. This time she didn't pull away.

'Where is Tom Black now?' asked Charlie.

'You have met Tom Black already,' said the cunning woman. 'His face is one you recognise. You do not know him by his true name. But the Lord and Lady can lead you to him.'

'They are dead,' said Charlie. 'We tracked them to the King's Company. They were executed by Praise-God Barebones.'

To their surprise, the cunning woman laughed, a strange, loud sound. 'The Lord and Lady have lived for five hundred years, from the time of the first king of England,' she crowed. 'They cannot be killed, only vanished.'

'You know who they are?' said Charlie, confused.

'They are much talked about by those who know the fairy folk,' she replied. 'They are born of fey folk, but not of them. Half our world and half theirs. Tom Black is of their blood.'

'They are related to Tom Black because he is a fairy changeling?' said Charlie, trying to weigh the information. 'That is their connection to him?'

'All fairies are kin to the Lord and Lady,' agreed the cunning woman.

'How can you be so certain Barebones didn't kill them?' said Lily.

'They can only be destroyed by burning,' said the cunning woman. 'And that in the strongest forge in the land.' Her eyes slid to Charlie. 'Tom and Barebones were the prison guard. Tasked with their destruction.'

'They worked together!' said Lily. 'So Barebones might know something about Tom. He may even know where he's keeping Maria.'

'If Barebones was a prison guard,' said Charlie slowly, 'that explains why he wasn't in Finsbury Gaol. It would have been too dangerous. He'd likely know the other guards, perhaps talk his way free. If I were to imprison such a man,' continued Charlie, 'I wouldn't choose a prison. I'd choose an asylum. Bedlam was rebuilt after the fire and is secret and secure.'

'Then how are we to get inside?' asked Lily. 'If they've locked up a criminal there will be guards. Lady Castlemaine has likely given our descriptions to every mercenary in the city. And you are known to all the city watch,' she added.

Charlie nodded at the truth of this. 'We need a distraction. We'll get in the same way Barebones has been combing the city. With the apprentices. All we need do is let it slip, where Barebones is locked up.'

'And if it doesn't work?'

'It will,' said Charlie. 'Maria's life depends on it.'

Chapter 71

Bridey was looking keenly at Tom. He stood twitching, his eyes roving around her large cell.

'You've changed,' she said finally. 'What happened?'

In answer, Tom raised his arm, letting his sleeve fall back. He frowned, looking at his burned skin, the criss-cross of knotted tissue.

'Why did you continue with the changeling tricks?' he asked quietly.

Bridey's face clouded. 'You are a wicked creature,' she said. 'You always were.'

Tom nodded at this, still staring at his arm. 'And yet' – his blue-green eyes lifted to hers – 'and yet what if, all this time, I was not what you said?' He began tapping his fingers on his chin distractedly.

'You've been talking to women,' said Bridey. 'Whores, all of them. Didn't I warn you Tom, they are not to be trusted?' She backed away from him and picked up a large jar. 'You must make a penance,' she decided, shaking out a circle of salt from the heavy vessel. 'My circle,' said Bridey, moving inside it. 'No fairy kind may cross.'

Tom looked at his mother. 'The boy thinks you should be put behind the mirror,' he said calmly.

Bridey looked up, fear flashing in her blue-green eyes. 'You may not step within.' She stooped and lit a cheap taper with shaking hands.

Tom took a stride forward, then another. He stepped straight-backed across the thick line of salt.

Bridey's mouth dropped open in horror. 'You cannot . . .' she stammered. 'It is not possible for a fairy to cross.'

Tom looked around, taking in Bridey's face. Then he smiled, a horrible doll-like expression.

Bridey was backing away.

'Perhaps I am your boy returned,' said Tom, his voice clipped. 'Perhaps I stepped through the glass.' He held up his hands and looked at them.

Bridey shook her head vigorously. 'You think I would not see my own boy?' She crossed herself, then scrabbled back, picking up a discarded eating knife from the corner of the cell.

Tom advanced. 'You have no notion of how I suffered,' he said. 'Trapped behind the glass whilst he lived out my life. I stayed a boy whilst he grew old.'

'Stay back!' Bridey swiped at him with the blade. In an easy gesture, Tom grabbed her throat with one hand and her wrist with the other.

Bridey made strange choking sounds as he sent the knife spinning free. Tom picked it up and examined it with interest, his other hand still holding his mother by the neck. Bridey was turning blue, gasping as he choked her. Tom frowned at the noise. He looked at her face for a while, regarding the bulging eyes. Then, slowly, he opened his fingers one by one. Bridey stepped away coughing and retching.

'You are a monster,' whispered Bridey, her lower lip wobbling. 'It was right you suffered. You took my life from me.'

Tom picked up one of the candles.

'You never wanted me back,' he said quietly. 'You wanted to use the fairy powers for yourself. To make your prophecies. So all the men might look on you. You only pretended you cared for your lost son, stranded in the fairy place.'

'I was a devoted wife,' she whispered, 'the best of mothers.'

'You chose my father because he was soft-minded enough to overlook your cruelty,' said Tom mildly. 'You lied to all the Shambles folk so they might overlook what you did to me.' Tom stepped closer. 'Every hurt you have done will be revisited threefold,' he decided.

'I am your mother,' whispered Bridey, her eyes following the candle. 'Please, Tom.'

'I am not Tom,' he said, watching the flame. 'You said it yourself. I am a monster.'

Chapter 72

Lily and Charlie were sitting on the top of the wall of New Bedlam. Charlie had procured them both blue apprentice aprons, and a rudimentary disguise for Lily.

'This is never going to work,' said Lily, regarding her threadbare breeches and ragged shirt. 'Even if the apprentices come, people will never believe me a boy.'

'You were at sea,' said Charlie. 'How many stories are there of girls who passed themselves off as sailors?'

'Those girls didn't look like me.'

'Pull the hat down lower,' advised Charlie. 'It's a riot. People won't look too hard. Only keep your head down.'

They heard a roar in the distance.

'Apprentices,' said Charlie. 'I told you they'd come.'

'I never knew it was so easy to lead a London mob,' said Lily, looking with trepidation towards the direction of the sound. 'How many people did you bribe to shout out Barebones's location?'

'Only three.'

A few front runners had rounded the corner towards them now. They wore blue aprons and waved pikestaffs and broom handles. Charlie watched as they beckoned to an unseen mob behind, pointing to the asylum.

Charlie eyed the approaching crowd as it began surging towards them. It was a great deal larger than he'd anticipated.

'Holy hell,' said Lily. 'How many are there?'

'Come on.' Charlie slipped from the wall as the thronging mass neared New Bedlam.

'Down with the King!' screamed a ragged boy. 'Free Praise-God Barebones!'

'This way,' said Charlie, pulling Lily with him.

The surge of apprentices had taken the asylum guard completely by surprise. The few milling at the front were in no way prepared for attack. They hesitated, eyeing the multitude, and in their hesitation the boys seized their advantage.

They pelted forward, on and on, overwhelming the guards and pouring through the large open gate. Charlie and Lily raced in behind them. Beyond Bedlam's thick wall were several enclosed vegetable gardens, and a sturdy central building.

There was a shout from the apprentices. 'Barebones! Free Praise-God Barebones!'

On the far side of the asylum, boys began smashing in doors. Doctors were running for their lives.

Charlie took in the scene. 'I think Barebones is over there,' he said, pointing to a small lockup. 'It's where they keep inmates waiting to be assessed. Very secure,' he added, nodding towards a thick wooden bar laid over the door, 'and they don't usually post a guard.'

Lily nodded in agreement, looking at the out-of-place guard, who was now taking in the mass of apprentices in disbelief.

People were surging in behind them, filling Bedlam's enclosed yard.

'There's too many,' said Charlie. 'There's going to be a crush.'

He began pulling Lily to the side, but the rioters were piling in too fast. In a matter of moments, thousands of people had surged in, and more still were pushing behind them.

Suddenly an explosion came from high behind. Then a huge chunk of stone wall fell. The largest piece smashed an apprentice to the floor, breaking his head open like an egg and splashing bloody gore in a wide arc.

'Someone's using gunpowder,' said Charlie, as people began hemming them in on all sides.

'Guards?' asked Lily. 'Or apprentices?'

'It doesn't matter,' said Charlie, looking for a way out as the crush intensified. 'People are having the breath squeezed from their bodies. Now they're panicking.'

They heard screams and the patter of stones thudding down as more of the wall gave way. Blood was everywhere. Near the destroyed wall, an apprentice toppled, grabbing onto his fellow. The next apprentice fell and in moments there was a surge as the thick crowd lost their footing.

'Move,' said Charlie, as the surge of falling people made for them like a tidal wave.

'I can't,' said Lily, as she was squeezed tight by the crowd.

She slipped down out of view, and Charlie dived after her. Then boy after flailing boy fell on top of them. Under the tumult of writhing bodies, Charlie twisted to see Lily's terrified face. He felt the great weight of people push him down, felt the terror of complete powerlessness.

'I can't breathe,' whispered Lily.

Charlie saw black spots. He tried reaching out with his hands, but all he could feel was clothing and limbs. Then suddenly his hands touched something hard. A metal grate, set into a wall. Charlie reached out and grasped it. He dug deep and pulled, inching himself out from the pinioning crush of the fallen boys. Above him, apprentices were dragging themselves up. He saw Lily, lying limply, and took hold of both her arms, drawing her from the crush.

She stood shakily, her clothes ripped and bloodied, brick dust lying thick on her hair.

'Are you hurt?' asked Charlie, looking her over.

She shook her head. 'Someone else's blood,' she said.

A gunshot sounded. From the wall, doctors had gathered arms and were raising guns to fire into the crowd.

Charlie sought out the lockup, now unguarded. 'This way,' he said. 'If Barebones is inside, we don't have long.'

Chapter 73

'Mrs Mitchell.' Mrs Jenks dropped an elaborate curtsey. 'You don't answer your door yourself?'

'I learned it all from you,' said Mother Mitchell with a laboured smile. She stood. 'Wine?'

Mrs Jenks gave the slightest of nods, taking in the fine room, the furnishings. Next to Mother Mitchell, Mrs Jenks seemed very small. Whilst Mother Mitchell had physically expanded into her status, Mrs Jenks retained the slighter figure of her girlhood, wearing the latest fashions tight against her bony frame.

'You honour me,' said Mrs Jenks, watching as Mother Mitchell picked up a crystal decanter of her best wine.

Mother Mitchell nodded in reply. Then she selected a crystal goblet for herself and a plain chalice for her guest.

'What do you want?' Mother Mitchell handed Mrs Jenks the wine. 'Come to poach more girls? Spread more lies? Brought me some black pudding, have you?'

'I don't come to fight over old affronts,' said Mrs Jenks carefully, seating herself on a long sofa.

Mother Mitchell's mouth pressed very thin. She nodded to the false blonde curls arranged around Mrs Jenks's painted face.

'I noticed you admiring my fine new clock,' she said. 'You have until the minute hand reaches twelve before I break this glass over your sugar-pasted head.'

Mrs Jenks stood a little too quickly. 'I have a proposition for you,' she said, speaking quickly. 'The apprentices are coming. Throw your house in with mine. Our girls can protect each other.' She offered Mother Mitchell her best brothel-keeper's smile.

Mrs Jenks's expensive lead face paint had hairline cracks running across it, Mother Mitchell noticed. Any exaggerated expression sent a new network of tiny fissures running through it, like an eggshell breaking.

'You divided us, Mrs Jenks. You live with it,' said Mother Mitchell. 'You took Covent Garden for yourself and the leavings were for me and Damaris to fight over.'

Mrs Jenks's scarlet mouth tightened. 'Do you not see? These riots. It's an attack on all of us. On the King's ways.'

'How convenient you want us to all throw in now,' said Mother Mitchell, 'but not when there's money to be shared.'

'Help me,' said Mrs Jenks. 'They'll come for you next.'

'Then we'll be ready for them,' said Mother Mitchell. 'My girls are bred on the streets, every one. They're born survivors and there's no apprentice alive could best 'em.' She took a long sip from her goblet. 'Find some other fool to help you,' she decided.

Mrs Jenks stood, shaking slightly. 'Everything you are is down to me,' she said. 'When you arrived in London, you thought a goose feather in a straw hat was high fashion.'

'From my understanding,' said Mother Mitchell, 'there won't be much fashion left in Covent Garden by the time the apprentices are done with you.'

Chapter 74

Praise-God Barebones was sitting on a plain bench. On the other side of his prison door he heard the heavy wooden barricade lifted. Barebones stood with the instinct of a soldier. He frowned as Charlie and Lily were revealed.

'You're not guards,' he said after a moment.

'Praise-God Barebones?' said Charlie.

'It's what men call me. My real name is overlong.' Barebones had even features, blond hair cut in the Roundhead style and the smell of a man who scrubbed vigorously in homemade soap.

'Longer than Praise-God Barebones?' asked Lily.

Praise-God coughed. 'My father was a travelling preacher,' he said. 'My given name is Were It Not For Jesus Christ Thou Wouldst Be Damned.' A sideways smile slid onto Barebones's face. 'But don't let the name fool you. I wasn't a Puritan during the war. We had the pick of new religions, didn't we? I'm no fool. I was a Ranter. Drinking and singing. Naked frolics in fields. Women dressed as Eve.' He smiled fondly. 'I miss those times. What can I do for you?' he added.

'I'm Charlie Tuesday.'

'I've heard of you,' said Barebones. His eyes were unsmiling, assessing. 'The thief taker.'

He retreated to his prison bench and picked up a knife and a stick. Barebones tilted his head, looking up, then began to whittle rapidly.

'Thought you'd be taller,' he observed, as wood shavings began settling in drifts on his square-cut boots. 'So, Mr Thief Taker. I assume you're here to catch a thief. But I don't see how I can help you. On account of folks I associate with being on the wrong side of the King's law. If you want to know of my comrades, you've come to the wrong man. I'll tell you nothing.'

'After the war,' said Charlie, 'two people went missing. A lord and lady.' He was watching Barebones carefully. 'You've heard of them?' he pushed.

Barebones looked down at his stick and began cutting a deep curl of wood. 'We all have,' he said, without looking up. 'The fairy king and queen. England's last magic. Hidden away, or lost, or killed or something. Depending on who you believe, and I believe no one.' He glanced up to give a surprisingly warm smile, revealing well-kept teeth.

'Do you know a man named Tom Black?' asked Charlie.

Barebones's smile dropped away. He stood a little upright, and tapped his knife against the skinned stick. 'Tom was . . . a necessity of the Republic,' he said. 'Did what he was told. Honest. He'd never tell you a lie. Not even to save his own skin.'

'What if I were to tell you he'd murdered a girl?' said Charlie. 'An actress.'

'I'd tell you there's many who think all actresses are whores,' replied Barebones, chipping forcefully at the blunt end of the stick. 'And you cannot murder a whore. Only send 'em back to the devil.' Barebones straightened, clicking his neck. 'Men like Tom and I made England a better place. We were no criminals and broke no laws. Only fought for the Cause and won. Parliament makes the rules now, do they not?'

He glared at them, daring them to disagree, and Charlie saw a glimmer of the determination behind the men who'd smashed England's tyrannical monarchy.

'And what if Tom were threatening to kill a good Christian girl?' demanded Charlie, feeling anger rise up. 'What if he'd taken her and was holding her captive? Would you stand by him then?'

Barebones seemed to retreat in on himself slightly. 'Tom has taken a friend of yours?' he asked quietly.

Charlie nodded, not trusting himself to speak.

'Something happened to Tom,' said Barebones after a long moment. 'I've seen it with men of his stamp before. They can swallow death and horrors easy as blinking. But he felt he'd failed Cromwell when the Lord and Lady escaped.' Barebones frowned, searching for the right words. 'Soon after, Tom was found in a stable block where the old court mirrors were housed. All the glass was shattered, and some men were in a bad way. It was put about Tom burned them. Cromwell turned a blind eye,' he continued. 'We needed people like Tom. Men to do things others couldn't do.'

'What are you saying?' asked Charlie.

Barebones paused. 'Tom's mother was murdered today,' he said carefully. 'I spoke to the poor guard who found her body. I don't think he'll ever recover from what he saw. Bridey Black was burned to death, piece by piece. I think a part of Tom became twisted. Now his darkness rises worse than before.'

Charlie felt his stomach tighten. Maria was in the clutches of a torturer and a murderer. And time was running out.

'Was Tom tasked with burning the Lord and Lady?' asked Charlie.

The stick in Barebones's hand jerked and went clattering to the floor. He bent and picked it up. 'The time for talking is over,' said Barebones. 'I'll say no more.' He studied the stick in his hands, then looked to the door. Beyond, the roar of rioters could be heard.

'Your apprentices will fail without you,' said Charlie. 'They need a leader and without one they run wild. They'll hang, if the rioting continues. The King will make an example.'

Barebones looked up at Charlie, an expression of deep pain in his blue eyes.

'I can get you out,' said Charlie. 'Or you can stay here and leave them to be executed as traitors.'

Lily looked at Charlie in horror.

Barebones raised a blond eyebrow. 'If you free me,' he said, 'I will kill the Lord and Lady. Your girl who Tom Black has taken,' he added, watching Charlie's face and snapping his fingers, 'dead.'

Charlie felt a shiver of fear at the mention of Maria. Could Barebones know where she was being held?

'You'll have to find the Lord and Lady before me,' said Charlie, his heart beating faster. 'And I know you'll tell me true. Men like you don't lie.'

'Reckless, like the Royalists,' said Barebones thoughtfully. 'But are you as lucky, I wonder?' The old soldier considered for a moment. 'Very well,' he said. 'We'll strike a bargain. You're right to think you can trust my word. I'm no liar. I'll tell you what I know. But you're not going to like it.'

Chapter 75

The mob had reached the top of Drury Lane. A giant maypole marked the start of London's most notorious party district.

Repent brandished his sword of garters. They slowed as one and then Repent took up the charge. 'To the theatres!' he bellowed.

A young apprentice began shinning up the maypole. 'Make a rope!' he called down. 'We'll pull it down, the King's big pole!'

There was a moment of industry as a huddle of boys joined belts in earnest. Then the result was thrown up to the apprentice atop the maypole. He slipped it around the top and tightened the nearest buckle. The climber jumped free, the leather rope dropped into the waiting hands below and the boys pulled.

A great cheer went up as the maypole began to lean. For a moment it held, the heavy ballast at the bottom keeping it in place.

'Heave!' cried Repent.

A great crack sounded. The thick maypole was splitting. It fell slowly at first, then faster. A drunk apprentice dodged as the maypole headed towards him at full force. He tripped, and it felled him in a single blow.

Repent stood over him as he lay unconscious and twitching. 'Broken back,' he said without remorse. 'No help for him.' He knelt and made a quick slash across the dying boy's neck.

A river of blood poured from near the stump of the maypole, now little more than a broken-toothed mess of splinters.

Repent mounted the broken shaft. 'We stand before the harlot's heartland!' he announced. 'Covent Garden. A thousand little chickies are within. Actors. Link boys. Shall we show them the price of their sin?'

'Aye!' the mob bellowed as one.

'The King promised to rebuild and has he?'

'No!' screamed the mob.

'And where does he spend his money?'

'The theatres!' bellowed a boy.

The cry was taken up. Repent beckoned with his sword and the mob poured past into the dark streets of Covent Garden and towards Drury Lane.

Chapter 76

In the Bedlam lockup, Barebones had stopped whittling his stick.

'To my mind,' he was saying, 'everything began to unravel after the Lord and Lady were captured. Cromwell went peculiar. Wasn't sure he'd done God's will. Old Ironsides was a man to win battles. But once it was won, well' – he spread his hands – 'keeping a country is more difficult than winning it, isn't it? Paranoia was rife. Our most loyal followers began to desert.' Barebones regarded his whittled stick. 'Tom was in charge of disappearances,' he said. 'People who needed to vanish, for the stability of the country. I should have been put on guard, to watch the Lord and Lady. But in the end, Cromwell only trusted Tom.' Barebones made a little wince of betrayal. 'It was thought they could seduce any normal man into saving them. Then even Tom couldn't keep 'em locked away and I've never seen old Ironsides look so afraid.'

'You never saw them for yourself?' asked Charlie.

Barebones shook his head. 'I knew enough. They are the last of the power of kings. I followed the trail to the King's Company, but there was not hide nor hair of them. We put it about that we'd executed the

Lord and Lady with the others. But it wasn't the truth. We found only mortal men in that company, no fairies. They got away somehow and their powers grew. I still feel it. See it in the King's court. Then not so long ago Tom Black comes to me. Tells me there is a dress hidden in a brothel. And with it, perhaps a way to find the Lord and Lady.' Barebones touched the sword at his side. 'I mean to save this country. To drive cold iron through their hearts.'

'Then why not help Tom Black to find them?'

Barebones gritted his teeth. 'Because he has no plans to kill them,' he said, settling his gaze on Charlie. 'He means to use their powers.' He twirled his stick. 'But now you and I have a problem. You don't live as long as I have without reading people. I saw the look your woman gave you, when you suggested setting me free. And I think I know the way she leans.' Barebones smiled, nodding at Lily's clothes. 'Let's just say I have a nose for Royalist women.'

He took a step towards Lily. Charlie moved a little in front of her.

Barebones raised his blond eyebrows. 'You'd let her take you to hell?' he said. 'I have a feeling you are not for tyranny.'

Charlie held his ground.

'I cannot let her free,' said Barebones. 'Knowing what she knows. It would do none of us any good. But you could join me. We'd find them together.' He waited, eyeing Charlie. 'Very well,' said Barebones. 'Both of you then.'

He stood, his knife in one hand and the sharpened stick in the other. Charlie spread his feet slightly, waiting for the attack. Behind him, he heard Lily slip a knife into each hand.

Barebones moved fast, and Charlie dodged and punched upwards. But the blow never connected. Barebones had dodged. Instead of going on the offensive, he stepped neatly out of the cell and threw the door shut behind him.

Charlie ran at the door in time to hear the heavy wooden bar being heaved back into place. Lily threw herself at the door as well, but the thick closure repelled her back.

'I mean to find the Lord and Lady and kill them,' called Barebones from the other side of the door. 'Anyone trying to deliver them to Tom Black is my sworn enemy and, believe me, my enemies don't fair too well.'

Chapter 77

Mrs Jenks was inside the King's Theatre, her silken dress swishing back and forth as she paced. 'They're coming,' she muttered, her red mouth drawn tight. 'Forty thousand. People are saying there are forty thousand. It's not just apprentices now. It's a mob. People from all over the city are joining. We've no guard. The only soldiers left to be got are the King's. And they won't fall to my employ. Not for any sum.'

'What of Mother Mitchell?' asked Millicent hopefully. 'Will she come defend us?'

Mrs Jenks shook her head, her eyes a studied blank. Several faces fell.

Viola stepped forward, moving a strand of glossy dark hair from her eyes. 'If I may,' she said, her Italian accent causing her to falter slightly. 'I've met with them, Mrs Jenks. I think I can help.' Viola was thinking of the men who'd chased her and Clancy from Damaris's Wapping brothel.

'Then out with it, girl,' snapped Mrs Jenks. 'It's all of us will suffer at their hands.'

Viola stood a little taller. She was thinking what Clancy would do. 'With respect, Mrs Jenks,' she began, 'it is you who stands to lose most.' She waved a hand. 'Your stock of dresses, furnishings. It's my understanding wealth of that kind makes the boys angry.'

'You'll be first in line when they come,' said Mrs Jenks. 'Pretty girl like you. Best tell me what you know.'

'No,' said Viola carefully. 'I 'ave enough of threats, of being frightened. We all have.' She took in a few of the assembled girls and drew courage from their expressions. 'If they catch me, then what?' She shrugged. 'Bruises heal. They won't do nothing twenty men a day don't already do. Why should I care?'

'What do you want?' Mrs Jenks's shark eyes were trained hard on Viola. 'Money?'

'A new silk dress,' said Viola, 'and a part on the stage. A lead part,' she added.

Mrs Jenks eyed her with something approaching respect. 'Very well,' she agreed.

'If Barebones is gone,' said Viola, 'I think his son will assume leadership. His name is Repent. He's young. Vicious.' Something passed over Viola's face. 'He is searching for some fairy thing,' she said. 'Magic. And do we not have the means to make magic? Our theatre things are the very latest. And we can act. I think we should stand up to him.'

'Are you suggesting we fight them? You girls?' Mrs Jenks scoffed.

'I saw a play in Italy,' said Viola, 'about a war. We have the advantage. The territory is ours. We know it. We have access to the buildings. The high places. I have a plan. I think it could work.'

Viola told them. Mrs Jenks's small red mouth drew up into a smile.

Chapter 78

Inside the prison, Lily hammered on the door.

'No lock to pick,' said Charlie, eyeing the thick entrance. 'That's the problem with old prisons. The simplest methods are often the most effective.'

'Barebones can go wherever he wants with his apprentices,' said Lily, frustrated. 'We're stuck in here . . .' She stopped herself, but Charlie knew what she was thinking. Somewhere in the city was Maria. Time was slipping away.

'Barebones is so certain they're alive,' Charlie said. 'A fairy king and queen. How can that be?' He paced the cell, examining the walls and the barred window.

'What could Tom Black want with the Lord and Lady?' asked Lily. 'If they aren't relations of his.' She turned to Charlie. 'Perhaps he thinks you have some personal connection to the Lord and Lady. What if they are your relations? Or relations of your brother's child?' suggested Lily. 'The nephew you keep.'

Charlie hesitated. Lily's face widened in understanding.

'You haven't seen your nephew?' said Lily incredulously. 'Have you? You've only sent money.'

Charlie toyed with his key uncomfortably. 'My brother did some dark things, in the end,' he said. 'I didn't know if the mother would want me to come.'

'That isn't true,' said Lily. 'What are you really afraid of?' She was staring at him now. 'Charlie,' she said, 'I've nearly gotten myself killed for this lord and lady. If you think them relatives of yours, if there's something you know, you must tell me.'

'I . . .' Charlie hesitated. 'I'm afraid of where I might have come from,' he admitted.

Lily considered this. 'There's dark in everyone,' she said finally. 'You needn't fear it. If you don't choose to use it then it needn't come to define you.'

Charlie closed his eyes and tried to think. 'I find people,' he said, 'it's what I do. This doesn't feel right. But this lord and lady . . . It's like there's nothing to them at all. It's too clean.'

'Perhaps they really did die,' suggested Lily. 'Someone covered it up. Barebones has become obsessed after years of searching. Cannot accept they're gone.'

Charlie was shaking his head, trying to unthread the confusing tangle of information surrounding the Lord and Lady. 'There's no . . . feeling for them. For all the talk, no one is angry or sad or even indifferent. There's an emptiness, do you not think? A coldness.'

'Fairies then,' said Lily. 'Fairies are drawn to theatres.'

'Everything has led to a theatre,' agreed Charlie, 'and everything about Tom Black is theatrical. He worked in theatre. He went there for his victim. The girl we found hanging.' Charlie thought of Maria and her enjoyment of acting. Something she'd once said to him drifted to mind. 'The monarchy is all theatre,' said Charlie slowly. 'That is what Maria used to say. The King must be the most accomplished actor of all, to hold his crown. Because royalty is made by performance, ceremonies and public spectacles.' Charlie had an image of King Charles, his triumphant return to London after the long exile. Something occurred to him. 'The Lord and Lady,' said Charlie, thinking aloud, 'what if they aren't people? Or fairies. What if they're objects?'

'What kind of objects?' asked Lily.

'Priceless objects,' said Charlie, ideas coming together now. 'Magical, holy things from a time before kings. But objects nonetheless.' And then it all came together at once. 'I know how they did it,' said Charlie, speaking fast. 'I know how the King's Company hid the Lord and Lady and I know why they've stayed lost all these years.'

'You're not making any sense,' said Lily.

'The Lord and Lady *were* hidden amongst the King's Company,' said Charlie. 'We had that part right. But we didn't know what they were. Neither does Barebones.' He was shaking his head at how simple it all now seemed. 'They have been hiding in plain sight,' said Charlie, 'and in the last place Tom Black would look. His own theatre company. A thousand people have seen them and not known them for what they are.'

'What are they?' asked Lily.

Charlie told her.

Lily's eyes bulged wide. 'No wonder Cromwell wanted them destroyed,' she said. 'Charlie, the apprentices are attacking the theatres. What if Barebones finds them?'

'If he stumbles upon them, he's clever enough to make the connection,' said Charlie. 'And both the Crown and Maria will be lost.'

'And we're trapped.' Lily slammed a fist on the door in annoyance.

Charlie eyed the window. Apprentices were still shouting outside.

'Perhaps not,' he said, moving to the small grate. He cupped his hands and shouted through. 'Barebones is in here!' Charlie watched as a few apprentices turned to listen, then shouted it again. He moved away from the window and sat back on the bench. 'They're coming,' he said. 'We'll soon be free.'

'Wait,' said Lily. 'If the Lord and Lady are what you think, they'll be in the King's Theatre?'

Charlie nodded.

Lily was shaking her head. 'Surely you don't expect us to walk into the heart of the riot?'

'I must save Maria.'

'Must you?' Her dark eyes searched his. 'Or do you want to rescue a mother who died a long time ago?'

Charlie found he couldn't answer.

Lily looked away. Charlie caught her hand and she turned back, an unreadable expression on her face.

They heard apprentices approach the door outside and hands fall on the heavy wooden bolt.

'What of your privateer's licence?' said Charlie. 'The Lord and Lady will buy back your favour with the King.'

'It's not enough, Charlie.'

'Then what? What would buy you?'

Her little chin was tilted up. 'Hasn't London's best thief taker figured it out?' she said. 'I don't want money.' Lily walked towards the door.

'I need you, Lily. I can't do it without you.'

Lily stopped and turned. She stood for a long moment, assessing him, then stepped closer. 'I want what you should have offered me,' she said, 'when you left.'

Charlie felt blood rush to his head. 'Which was?' he asked quietly.

'A partnership,' she said. 'You're London's best thief taker, Charlie. Everyone knows it. But you can't turn down a lost cause or a lame dog. You need someone to manage your work and chase your debts. Or you'll still be living hand-to-mouth above a butcher's shop on your dying day.'

She was right, Charlie knew it. But for some reason he felt disappointed. He tried to catch hold of his swirling thoughts, but something about Lily's proximity made them skitter away. He forced himself to focus, remembering Maria.

'Very well,' he heard himself saying. 'If that's what it will take. When this is over, we'll be partners.'

Lily nodded firmly. 'Good.' But there was a shade of disappointment in her tone.

She took his hand and shook it. He found his fingers lingering on hers a little too long.

The door began to open.

'Now,' said Lily, her usual determined expression resolving itself, 'let's go get ourselves killed.'

Chapter 79

The apprentices were lined up at the entrance of Covent Garden, their blue aprons bloody, young faces flush with drink and excitement.

'The King's Theatre,' said Repent, pointing. 'Through Drury Lane. Let's tear down the King's sin shop.'

The apprentices were taking in the length of Drury Lane, with its cobbled streets and brick buildings.

'You're sure there's enough of us?' Bolly glanced behind him. 'Others come this way, there's strength in numbers.'

'There's nothin' in Covent Garden but drunks and whores,' said Repent scornfully. 'We're soldiers, fightin' against the throne. We don't want our glory to go to a ragged mob.'

A figure emerged, alone on the street. A woman in a fine dress, walking slowly towards them. She held a dark mask to her face and wore curling goat horns on her head.

'Look at this,' said one of the apprentices, grabbing at his groin. 'Someone wants to have some fun with us.' But he sounded uneasy.

The woman stepped closer, then drew away the mask. Beneath was a strikingly pale face, with disconcertingly large pupils and false blonde hair. Her expression was vacant, far removed.

'Is she possessed?' whispered one boy.

'I know you,' crowed Repent. 'It's the famous Mrs Jenks. Think you to threaten us?'

Mrs Jenks's haunted expression didn't change. But her eyes settled on Repent's face. 'This is our place,' she said, throwing her voice wide and high. 'We mean to hold it.'

'Repent,' said Bolly, tugging his arm. 'We should be careful. Mrs Jenks is the doxy queen. Trickier than a serpent she is.'

Repent started laughing. 'Is that so?' Repent hefted his sword of garters. 'What think you, lads? Shall we let a whore bandy words with us? Mrs Jenks's whores work the playhouses, isn't that right? Shall we break up her theatre of sin?'

There was a roar of assent from the crowd. The apprentices were drunk with violence now, fuelled by stolen wine and the heady thrill of power.

'An attack on the King's Theatre is an attack on the King,' said Mrs Jenks. 'We have every right to defend ourselves.'

'You and whose army?' Repent grinned. 'You'll need more than a few whores to stop us, and the last I heard you were all fighting amongst yourselves.'

'I don't need an army.' Mrs Jenks smiled.

Several apprentices dropped back uneasily.

'Didn't you know?' whispered Mrs Jenks, eyes widening dramatically. 'Us whores are in league with the devil.' She gazed at them, her strangely dilated eyes, doll-white face and smiling vermillion lips. 'We heard there was an army of you,' she said. 'We prepared for such. But I see no army here. I see no soldiers. Nothing but half-starved boys, addled with drink and far from home.'

Suddenly an explosion sounded. Then a ball of stinking yellow smoke rolled out from both sides of the street. The apprentices started, coughing and covering their mouths.

When the mist cleared, Mrs Jenks had vanished. A few apprentices gasped.

'Where did the fine whore go?' demanded one, peering into the thick smoke.

'She makes witchcraft,' muttered another.

'Hold firm,' said Repent. 'She's an actress. She only plays a part. Uses theatre things to frighten us. Advance.'

They began to move further into the lane. It was eerily quiet.

'See how she runs,' crowed Repent. 'Let's show her what bravery is, lads!'

'Where are all the women?' asked an apprentice, staring at the empty street.

'Run, fled,' said Repent with satisfaction. 'Let's start tearing down buildings.'

There was a sudden yodelling shriek, high-pitched and distinctly female. It seemed to come from high up. A few apprentices started in confusion. It came again. From somewhere in the rooftops. Now everyone was looking, shouldering weapons, faces to the sky.

The missiles came from every upper window. First a deluge of stinking liquid sprayed the crowd. Then the first unmistakable spatter of excrement hit the upturned faces.

'The chamber pots!' cried a shocked apprentice. 'The whores are emptying their pots.'

When the second wave of urine and faeces flew from the upper windows, the apprentices were in disarray. They flung up their arms and ran to the sides of the street to gain shelter.

'Piss off!' bellowed a woman's voice from one of the nearer windows. 'Covent Garden's ours!'

The first chamber pot smashed onto the cobbles, narrowly missing the apprentices. It exploded into ceramic shrapnel, sharp pieces flying into the mob. The second knocked an apprentice to the ground, breaking his nose in a spray of blood.

A girlish cheer went up along the street. More chamber pots began to smash against the cobbles. Then came a sudden deafening boom like thunder. A flash of lightening. More yellow smoke poured down the street.

Cries of alarm went up from the apprentices. Several ducked.

A great grinning devil's head appeared before them, floating in the smoke. Another thunder crack echoed around, and a spurt of flames appeared from the red mouth of the fiend, jetting out towards the mob.

The apprentices fled in all directions, the ceramic chamber pots spattering them as they retreated.

'Hold!' shouted Repent, but the onslaught was too acute. His eyes surveyed the winding streets. 'The marketplace!' he commanded. 'To Covent Garden market!'

Chapter 80

'I'm telling you,' said Lily, 'there's no way into Covent Garden. The mob mean to take the King's Theatre. They'll have broken in and sacked it by now.'

'Perhaps not.' Charlie was eyeing the smoky sky. 'No fires have been started west of Covent Garden market. I think the whores might be defending their own.'

Lily shook her head. 'Even so, there's no way in.'

'There have always been tunnels between the Strand and Covent Garden,' said Charlie. 'They transport wine and beer barrels to the taverns and theatres. More recently King Charles used an old tunnel to visit an actress in The Swan. That's in the heart of Covent Garden.'

'He hasn't been seen with that actress for years,' said Lily.

'But the King does often arrive at the King's Theatre unexpectedly,' said Charlie. 'The Swan is very near. What if he had his old tunnel rerouted? The original tunnel starts in a grocer's shop on Catherine Street,' Charlie added. 'All we need do is get inside their cellar and discover where the hidden door is.'

'Simple,' said Lily, taking in Charlie's patched breeches and worn leather coat. 'They'll call the watch on us as thieves before we take two steps inside.'

'All have packed up to protect themselves from looters,' Charlie pointed out. 'We need only break into an empty premises and get down into the cellar.'

'It's a plan with no flaw,' said Lily. 'To save time later, shall we get some hemp rope and hang nooses around our necks as we carry it out?'

Chapter 81

The apprentices poured through Long Acre and into the wide muddy expanse of Covent Garden fruit market. They were met by the confused stares of fruit sellers, peddling the last of the day's wares.

'We will regroup!' said Repent. But the apprentices were tired, injured and sewage-streaked. They were drifting away, vanishing between the fruit and vegetable stalls.

'Courage!' tried Repent. But no one was listening.

An apprentice tendered a pat on Repent's arm. 'We've had our fun,' he said. 'We're going home before they hang us. Best you do the same.'

Repent's pale face was set in rage. He stood for a long moment, watching his forces disappear. Then, from around the corner, emerged a blue-aproned army. Repent watched, surprised, pride flooding through him.

They were older apprentices, muscular from hard work and tough from London life. The men wore sashes of green, the Republic colour, and brandished poles, staves and house-pulling hooks.

One saw the battered gaggle of apprentices amongst the mouldering fruit and vegetables. 'You're covered in shit, boys,' he observed.

'The whores,' said Repent. 'They threw chamber pots.'

The older apprentice laughed. 'We heard you little ones were having a party,' he said. 'Thought you'd take Covent Garden without us? A little starving rabble of the poorest trades.' He assessed the boys. 'What you got? A few plasterers and wheelwrights and painter-stainers.'

''E's a locksmith,' said Repent, nodding to Bolly nervously.

'Well, you got the mercers and the goldsmiths now.' The older boy smiled. 'They sell it like a dream, the high-ups. Work hard, you'll get your rewards. But every day that passes, every day you wear the skin from your fingers, you realise. You'll always be dirt poor. Nose pressed up against the glass, looking in.' He slapped Repent hard on the back. 'And you little boys had the balls to do it,' he said. 'Our fathers had their glory, didn't they? Soldiering, winning wars. What have we got? Work hard till you die. And watch all the girls get ahead of you by lifting their skirts.' His eyes drifted to Covent Garden, the hedonistic loins of London. 'Might as well have some fun along the way.'

'We mean to take the King's Theatre,' said Repent. 'Actresses. Wine. Come with us.'

Chapter 82

'You never told me you were such a good burglar,' said Lily, as Charlie slid an expert hand around the back window of Bourne Brothers Grocers. They'd got into the merchant house's little garden through a stable block behind. Medicinal herbs grew in neat quadrants, releasing a gentle mix of fragrances.

'Hunger was a powerful teacher,' said Charlie. He slid his hand inside and pressed where he knew the catch to be weak. 'Lucky it's an old style of casement,' he added. 'I haven't done this in a long time.'

Charlie slipped through and landed lightly on bare wooden floorboards. The room was a wrapping area for food and wares purchased in the front shop. A number of hanging hooks held wads of thick blue paper ready to package sweets and confections. Cloths to wrap cheese were soaking in lemon water.

A large serving hatch divided the back room from the front grocer. Charlie could see a wide wooden countertop, polished to a high shine with lavender oil and displaying an ostentatious set of brass weighing scales on top.

Behind him, Charlie heard Lily slide in through the window.

'Now where?' she asked.

'Shhh.' Charlie raised a finger to his lips and pointed to the ceiling. 'The merchant and his family live above the shop. They might be holed up there, waiting for the riots to pass.'

Lily nodded. 'Where's the cellar door?' she asked, dropping her voice to a whisper.

'Outside on the street, at the front of the shop,' said Charlie.

'Then why aren't we there?' asked Lily.

'Because the opening is sealed with a thick bolt and in plain view,' said Charlie. 'But the merchants most likely keep an extra hatch,' he added, 'for sending up smaller consignments of stock.'

He moved into the front shop. Shadowy shelving was lined with decorative ceramic jars and canisters. A pungent aroma of cardamom, nutmeg, rose oil and pig fat hung in the air. Charlie crept towards a large rug that lay on the floor and lifted it. Beneath was a trapdoor with a circular brass pull sunk into the wood.

'Here,' he said, hooking his finger through it and lifting. 'This way.'

The trapdoor opened smoothly to reveal a set of steps leading into the dark. They heard the patter of mice scattering below. Charlie peered into the gloom. He could make out a few bulging sacks.

There was a sudden sound of rapid footsteps from above. A door crashed open.

'Someone heard us,' said Charlie, lifting his eyes to the ceiling. 'We need to go.'

They raced fast down the wooden cellar steps and closed the trapdoor above them. It was almost entirely dark, with only the barest chink of shadowy light showing from between the gaps in the floorboards.

'What now?' hissed Lily. 'We're trapped down here.'

'We'll find the tunnel,' said Charlie, feeling in the dark. He stumbled over a sack of coffee beans. 'If the King used it, it won't be well hidden.'

'Who's there?' demanded a voice above them. 'I know you're here, you villains! You'll not rob us under the cover of riots!'

'They think we're apprentices,' said Lily.

'So they'll shoot first and ask questions later,' said Charlie. 'An apprentice's life isn't worth a single sack of this stock.'

The trapdoor above them raised a few inches and the muzzle of a gun poked through.

'Take cover!' hissed Charlie, pulling Lily behind a row of tea crates.

The explosion blew apart a box of sweet oranges, spraying them with juice.

'This way,' said Charlie, grabbing Lily's hand. 'I think I saw an archway that could be a door.'

They negotiated the stock, feeling in the dark until they reached a brick wall. Charlie ranged his hands over it.

A fine powder drifted down between the cracks in the floor. Lily swabbed at her shoulder where some had landed and licked her finger.

'Gunpowder,' she said, looking up. 'Someone is reloading, badly.'

Charlie's hands found wood and a royal crest. 'I think it's here!' he said. 'A door.' But in the dark, he couldn't find a catch. Behind them, the cellar door levered open a few inches once more.

'Rogues!' shouted a tremulous voice. 'I've called the Watch!'

Charlie heard the click of the gun being cocked and realised they'd never make it through in time.

Then a female voice rang out from above. 'You'll destroy our stock, you dolt! Give me the gun!'

Charlie's hand found the catch. He pushed, and the door swung open. And as the merchant's wife admonished her husband in the shop above, Charlie and Lily disappeared into the dark.

Chapter 83

Lynette felt the carriage wheels turn beneath her and grinned excitedly. It was the first time she'd ever been alone in a carriage. Now there was no one to see, she let her fingers travel across the padded silk lining the interior walls.

Her carriage. She reminded herself. *Her* liveried driver. Were they her horses too? She supposed they must be. It was overwhelming. She had to stop herself bouncing with glee.

It was noisy outside on the street and Lynette's instinct for London flared. She knocked on the roof of the carriage.

'Why do we come this way?' she demanded. ''S rioting near.'

But instead of obeying her orders, to Lynette's surprise, the carriage stopped. She heard the driver hop down.

'What is it?' she asked.

'Lady Castlemaine ordered your carriage stop here,' he said apologetically.

'And you followed her orders?' demanded Lynette, realising the driver had been threatened or bribed. 'You realise the 'prentices are on the move? It's not just my neck,' she added. 'How d'ya think they'll treat a man driving a whore around?'

The driver was shaking, his face white. He was very young, Lynette realised, her anger at him melting away.

'She said I must stop,' said the driver, casting a terrified glance up and down the street. 'She said I must.'

They were outside a private house and Lynette watched as Lady Castlemaine appeared at the door and made her way down the steps.

There was a roar from the bottom of the street.

'They've seen the carriage,' said Lynette, fear mounting. 'Get back to the horses. Quick.'

Lady Castlemaine approached the coach. She looked up the street. A group of loud boys was shouting and pointing. She frowned and stepped up and into the carriage.

'Drive!' shouted Lynette, knocking on the roof as hard as she could. 'God's fish, drive!'

The carriage began to move, jolting slowly over the cobbles as Lady Castlemaine sat, closing the door behind her.

Lynette was shaking.

'Look at you,' said Lady Castlemaine contemptuously, settling herself on the plump seats. 'You put up a good performance on stage, but when confronted with your betters you're terrified.'

Lynette shook her head. 'They saw you get in the carriage,' she said. 'The 'prentices. Do yer not hear them?'

Lady Castlemaine frowned. The crowd noise outside had risen in volume. Then a sharp patter of stones sounded on the thin wall of the carriage. Shouts came from ahead. The mob was blocking off the carriage's escape.

'You fool.' Lynette was shaking her head. 'They hate you. Do you not understand? They riot because of *you*. Because of your greed. You've just driven us both straight into the middle of them.'

The carriage lurched suddenly. Lady Castlemaine clutched the seat to stop herself falling. The haughty arrogance had vanished now. A thud sounded out. Then another.

'They throw clods of mud,' said Lynette, 'and God knows what else.' She sat back on her hands and breathed out.

'Drive!' shouted Lady Castlemaine in panic. 'Why do you not drive? Ride over them if you must.'

'You've not seen a London mob before,' said Lynette. 'Once they get started there's no stopping 'em.'

The horses were twitching and slowing now. Men laid hands on their reins. A taunting shout had now risen up outside the carriage. It was a baying rhythmic chant. 'The Catholic whore! The Catholic whore!'

Lady Castlemaine clutched her crucifix. The glass carriage window smashed, and a dead cat landed unceremoniously at their feet. Lady Castlemaine drew back her feet in horror. Hands began appearing through the window now, grabbing, punching.

'What will they do?' screamed Lady Castlemaine, trying unsuccessfully to pull the curtain as a barrier.

'If we're lucky,' said Lynette, 'they'll only kill us.' She thought for a moment, then she stood and began drawing back the curtain at the window.

'What are you *doing*?' Lady Castlemaine grabbed at her dress.

'My old mother always told me don't sit around and wait for the Reaper,' said Lynette. 'If I'm going, I'll go doin' what I do best, playing to the crowd.' She adjusted her dress, tucked her hair behind her ears and grabbed the nearest pair of clutching hands. Then she kissed them. The rough fingers drew back in surprise. 'Lend us a hand, will you?' she shouted. 'I'm coming out.' Lynette pushed her head and upper body full out of the window and bellowed at the top of her voice, 'Good people! Be civil! It is the Protestant whore!'

There was a murmur and a few laughs. Lynette shouted the same words a second time. Now the laugh had rippled through the crowd.

'If you tear me to pieces, I can't learn me words for next week,' she boomed. 'And I've a special jig for the King I need both legs for.'

'It's Lynette!' Male cries were sounding from the mob.

The tone had changed now. Bloody threats had become whistles.

'Sing us a song!' cried a man loudly.

Lynette took a breath and began singing. 'Lady Castlemaine's got a hole, a hole a holey hole hole! A whole lot 'a jew-els from Charlie the King . . . !'

There were whoops of delight from the crowd now. The carriage jerked as people cleared and the driver began urging the horses through the clearing crowd.

'Not too fast, John,' hissed Lynette. 'Don't stir 'em up again. I'll keep singing and you keep it steady.'

They began moving at a slow trot, with Lynette bellowing ever more colourful lyrics as they went.

They rounded into the familiar cobbles of Whitehall as Lynette sang about Lady Castlemaine stroking the King's cocky-cock cocker spaniels. As they cleared the crowd, Lynette sunk back inside the carriage with a sigh of relief.

Lady Castlemaine was wearing a strange expression. 'You could have got out of the carriage and left me to be torn apart,' she said.

Lynette turned to her. 'We are sisters, no matter what you think. And those are your sisters in the bawdy houses. You have a lot of faults, but you are no coward. If you have the money to help them, you should.'

Lady Castlemaine's expression was a peculiar mixture of confusion and hatred. She stood, shaking. 'I am *nothing* like you,' she said, her voice quavering strangely. 'Do you know how many actresses he's bedded? You are nothing. One of many. Nobody will remember your name. My children have titles, they are royalty.'

'Not all of them,' said Lynette mildly. 'Your last little girl is as common as me.'

Lady Castlemaine's face contorted to dark rage. 'Let me out,' she demanded, knocking on the roof. 'I'll not stay another minute with this harlot.'

Chapter 84

In the tunnel below Covent Garden, Charlie and Lily could see a row of torches flaming.

'It's been used recently,' said Charlie.

'All kinds of madness happens after dark in Covent Garden,' said Lily. 'The King isn't a man to miss out.'

They passed beneath a set of exposed floorboards with a square section of a trapdoor cut into it. Charlie scratched at the soft wood and licked his finger.

'Tavern floor,' he confirmed, tasting the tang of a century of spilled beer. 'I'll wager The Swan is right above us. But the tunnel goes on.'

He noticed something else. The sign of the Sun in Splendour had been scratched deep into the dirt floor at their feet.

'An old safe-passage sign,' said Lily. 'This must have been one of the tunnels the Royalists used during the civil war.'

Charlie looked forward. A newer section of tunnel had a bright brick floor and smelled of freshly dug earth. Thick oak struts kept the city above from crashing on their heads.

Charlie mapped the route above, north away from the Strand, and east towards Drury Lane.

They ran forward over the new bricks, following the ground curving up and around a corner. The tunnel joined a few wooden steps and came to an end at a red velvet curtain.

'The King's own private entrance,' breathed Lily, climbing the steps and lifting the fabric to reveal a smart wooden door.

Charlie turned the handle and a familiar odour of beer and bitter oranges greeted them.

It was the King's Theatre.

Charlie and Lily's feet met thick carpet. The tunnel door had taken them through to a small box, right next to the stage. There was a crashing sound from the front of the theatre. Then splintering of wood.

'We're too late,' said Charlie. 'The apprentices are already here.'

Chapter 85

'We need to get backstage,' said Charlie. 'If the apprentices find the Lord and Lady all is lost.'

They ran along a narrow corridor and threw open the dressing room door. It had been abandoned in haste. Clothes were strewn around, and on a wide table holding a large wood-framed mirror there were half-pint pots of white-lead face paint, a tray of disordered mouse-hair eyebrows and patches and some jagged mounds of red lip paint.

'The actresses and actors weren't expecting an attack,' said Lily, taking in a wall hung with wigs. 'These are expensive things to leave unguarded in London.'

Charlie's eyes tracked to a little cupboard in the corner, unlocked, with 'Company Property' scrawled on the door.

'What's in the cupboard?' asked Lily, moving forward.

'Props,' said Charlie. 'Every theatre troupe has property they carry with them. Wands, crowns, wooden swords. The host theatre is supposed to lock them in this cupboard. But it's bad luck to use real jewels or anything of value on stage. So they don't usually bother. Ironic,' he added, 'because inside are the most valuable things in all of London.'

He twisted the catch and the cupboard opened easily. Inside were an array of motley props. A skull, an hourglass, a few bent swords and a moth-eaten velvet cloak. And there, resting towards the gloomy back, were the two things Charlie had been searching for.

The Lord and Lady.

Chapter 86

'Tom, what happened?' whispered Maria.

'Don't call me that.' Tom was sitting on the ground, hands clamped over his ears. He was rocking in a strange juddering motion, thudding his back against the wall. 'It isn't my name.'

Maria's mind went to the vial of poison stolen from his coat. She'd hidden it in the corner of the room, near the wine and food he'd left her.

'You went to her, didn't you?' guessed Maria. 'Your mother?'

Tom was shaking his head. 'I'm not her son,' he said. 'I am a changeling.'

Maria stepped towards him.

'No!' Tom shouted. 'Don't you see? It's dangerous? You lure him.' Tom looked at Maria. 'You,' he said. 'You have changed me. He knows. You haven't long, Maria. I have seen how he kills. He has horrors planned for you. Good Friday approaches. I cannot contain him.'

Maria's gaze slipped to the wine he had left her. 'Take a drink,' she said. 'Calm your nerves.'

She picked up the vial of poison and tipped it into the bottle with a shaking hand. Tom was in the corner, looking at the floor. She went to him and passed him the bottle. He took it unthinkingly and raised it.

'Cromwell thought me sent by God to help his cause,' he said, hesitating, the bottle at his lips. 'He thought wine a sin.' He shot her a look of deep longing. 'Fairies in the old tales are fallen angels,' he murmured. 'Magical beings fallen foul of God's grace and stranded in the human world.' Tom smiled. He drank deeply. Then he moved the bottle away from his mouth and looked at it quizzically, as though it contained a flavour he recognised. 'You didn't?' began Tom. His fingers moved to search his coat.

'I'm sorry,' whispered Maria. 'Truly.'

'You fool!' said Tom. 'He comes! You've summoned him.'

Maria brought both hands together and clubbed at his head with all her might. Her manacled wrists struck the side of his face hard and Tom went down, stunned. Maria dropped to the same height, searching in his coat for a key.

Suddenly Tom was screaming, rolling back and forth, holding his hands over his ears. Maria grabbed at him, trying to get hold, but he rolled out of reach.

'You broke the mirrors!' His voice was a screech, high-pitched and accusing. 'You trapped me in the glass again!'

Maria inched towards him. She thought she could perhaps get a grip on his foot, pull him back into her circle of movement.

He twisted suddenly towards her. His eyes had a terrible expression. Maria drew back.

Tom's lips parted, and his voice came as a slow, drugged drawl. 'You didn't give me enough,' he managed. 'He is coming for you.'

Chapter 87

In the backstage of the theatre, Charlie realised he'd been holding his breath. In front of him were the two most priceless objects in all of London. Enough to start a war. To depose a king, or bring a man wealth for life.

He reached to take them when the door behind him flew open. Charlie stepped back quickly, letting the cupboard door swing shut.

Repent stood in the entrance, grinning. 'Charlie Tuesday,' he said. 'A little whore told us about you. You're looking for the Lord and Lady.'

Charlie felt his heartbeat quicken. Lily touched his hand with her fingers. 'Don't let him bait you,' she whispered. 'It will do you no good.'

Repent was drunk. He nodded at the key at Charlie's neck. 'That key unlocks them, I reckon.'

Charlie unlooped the key from his neck and held it out. 'This is nothing but a foundling token. Something so my mother might find me one day.'

They could hear boyish shouts now. And the crashing of serial destruction.

'Your mother never found you?' sneered Repent. 'I reckon she made her coins raising her skirts for nobles.' His eyes glittered.

'Charlie . . .' began Lily. She was looking at the door behind them.

Charlie's hand shot forward so fast that Repent had no time to react. The sharp end of the key plunged into his face. Repent howled in pain and then Charlie punched low, driving left and right into Repent's abdomen. Charlie straightened up and hammered the full weight of his head forward into Repent's face. The apprentice's nose exploded in blood and he staggered back. Then Charlie heard Lily cry out in pain behind him.

He looked around to see she was struggling against a tall apprentice who had grabbed her. He had a cherubic appearance. Blond hair and angelic features. But his eyes were hard and thick with drink.

'Charlie!' said Lily, writhing. 'Run!'

As she spoke, more apprentices poured in behind. They were cornered. Repent straightened up, holding his nose.

'Take hold of the thief taker,' he growled. 'We're going to slice him up worse than the whores.'

Apprentices grabbed at Charlie's arms, pinning them to his sides. Repent moved forward and punched him in the stomach. Charlie doubled over, gasping.

'Bolly, bring the girl over here,' Repent called over his shoulder. 'Let the thief taker watch.'

'Wait,' gasped Charlie, catching his breath. 'Wait. Let her go and I'll tell you where they are.'

'What?' Repent bent forward and Charlie could smell body odour and beer.

'The Lord and Lady,' managed Charlie. 'I know where they are.'

'Charlie, no,' said Lily.

'They're in this theatre,' continued Charlie.

'We've already searched it,' said Repent. 'There's no one else hiding in here. We would have found them.'

'The actors hid them from Tom Black,' continued Charlie, 'in the last place he'd look. His old theatre company. They've been acting with them ever since. Disguised in plain view.'

'Nah.' Repent rubbed at his smallpox-scarred chin. 'That whole company was put to death, back in Cromwell's time.'

'There's a secret tunnel in this theatre,' said Charlie. 'The Lord and Lady have been hiding there.'

'It isn't possible,' said Bolly. 'No one could have hidden underground for that long.'

'They're fairy folk,' countered Repent. 'Their powers grow underground.' He eyed Charlie thoughtfully, his scarred face twitching strangely. Blood ran down his cheek. 'Take us to the tunnel,' he said.

Chapter 88

'What are you doing?' hissed Lily, as Charlie led Repent and his gang of apprentices to the tunnel.

'I've an idea,' whispered Charlie. 'It could work.'

'No talking amongst yourselves!' shouted Repent, giving Charlie a prod with his gartered sword. 'Just take us to them.'

They reached the secret side box at the side of the stage, with the hidden door at the back.

'This is it,' said Charlie, holding his breath. 'They're through there.'

Repent glanced over his shoulder. 'You boys wait here,' he said, moving towards the door.

Bolly made to follow him.

'Best I go alone,' said Repent self-importantly. 'Keep the gypsy here in case Tuesday tries anything.' He eyed Charlie. 'Try to cross me and your girl will have a bad time up here with all these boys.'

Charlie met his gaze but said nothing.

Repent nodded to the door. 'Lead on.'

They went through and down underground.

'This way,' said Charlie, 'where the older part of the tunnel is.'

They reached the part where the trapdoor leading to The Swan had been sealed over.

'Your father,' said Charlie. 'Does he approve of what you do? With those women?'

'A boy must become a man.' Repent shrugged. 'Jesus himself had a whore. How can a man teach his wife if he knows nothing himself?'

'You hurt those women,' said Charlie. 'Mark them.'

'You cannot rape a whore,' said Repent. 'I only make certain others know them for what they are.' But he sounded uncomfortable.

'I think your father is frightened of what you have become,' said Charlie. 'Is that why you seek the Lord and Lady? Their powers turn you to sin?'

'Show me where they hide,' growled Repent. 'I don't need a sermon from you.'

They were standing under the old boarded-up trapdoor now. The rotting roof beams cut into the old dirt ceiling.

'Up there,' said Charlie. 'See how the fairy lights flicker?'

Repent licked his lips, breathing heavily. He was staring up at the lights.

'Up there you say?' He rotated his sword nervously in his hand. 'I see nothing.'

'You saw them in the dressing room,' said Charlie. 'The Lord and Lady. Hiding where everyone can see.' He was trying to figure out where the ceiling was least secure.

Repent shook his head in confusion. 'You're saying they used magic to hide down here?'

'The Lord and Lady is the name given to the Crown Jewels,' said Charlie, eyeing one of the rotten supporting beams. 'The orb and sceptre. There are no fairies.'

'It cannot be,' said Repent, shaking his head in confusion. 'All my life we have hunted . . .'

Taking advantage of Repent's confusion, Charlie sent out a well-aimed kick. The beam split, but didn't break as Charlie hoped. Repent turned around, face black with fury.

310

'You fucking sneak thief,' he said. 'I'll cut out your fucking eyes.'

Charlie kicked again, and this time the beam creaked and then gave way. He saw the ceiling above buckle and dived away. Repent lunged towards him, just as a tonne of London clay collapsed downwards, knocking him to the ground, burying him chest-deep in heavy earth.

Chapter 89

'They call them the Lord and Lady,' explained the King, 'because of what they represent.'

'Oh?' Lynette was trying on a new dress, arranging it around her pale shoulders.

'The straight sceptre is the man,' continued the King, 'the curving orb is the woman. It shows that a ruler must be balanced. Hold both powers equally.'

Lynette turned to face him, a pair of pearl earrings dangling from her hand. 'But what has that to do with fairies?' she asked.

'England once had many gods,' he said. 'The Green Man in the fields, goddesses of the ash and elm, hearth and home. King Arthur, so the legend goes, won Pagans and Christians by honouring both in his rule. The old gods became fairies, a jewelled man and woman, held in a king's hands at every coronation. His promise never to forget the old ways. The crown symbolises Jesus, the King of Kings.'

'So your kingly power comes from some old leaf gods?' laughed Lynette. She thought. 'Is that where the alchemic symbols come from?' she asked. 'The circle and cross for a woman, stick with a cross for a man.'

Charles nodded. 'Those symbols must be at every coronation for a king to be legitimate,' he explained.

Lynette fitted the earrings into her ears. 'Sounds like the sort of poppycock you nobles come up with,' she agreed. 'What d'yer think?' she added, swinging around so her skirt twirled.

He stepped back to take her in: the green dress, simply cut to reveal her elegant figure and shining hair; the pearl earrings and necklace, luminous against her lovely skin.

'You look good enough to be queen,' he said admiringly.

She grinned. 'And I am whore enough to be a duchess.' Lynette moved forward and took his face in her hands. 'You're troubled?' she asked. 'About the Crown Jewels? You think they might show up in the hands of some dissenter and cause problems?'

'There is some legal issue if they are found,' admitted Charles. 'We had new ones made, but we might have to consider a second coronation, which would problematise the first. Certainly, it would be embarrassing,' he added, lifting his eyes to hers, dark and soulful. 'As if my cursed reign need any more embarrassment.'

She kissed him on the mouth. 'I always thought the King's sceptre meant something different,' she said, winking. 'And I've some orbs of my own if you'd like to hold them.'

Chapter 90

Charlie broke through the secret door, into the King's Theatre, eyes wide with terror.

'They have him!' he gasped, grasping Bolly's skinny arm. 'The fairies took him.'

Bolly released his grip on Lily. The apprentices were now uncertain. Without their leader they were in complete disarray.

Charlie turned to them, capitalising his advantage. 'Repent is gone,' he said. 'You've broken inside the King's Theatre. That's treason.'

The boys looked at one another.

'Already the King sends men,' lied Charlie. 'If you run now, no one will know you were here.'

The apprentices were inching back.

'You'll not tattle?' confirmed a small red-haired boy nervously.

'We never saw you,' said Charlie. That convinced them. They fled as one, exiting through the main door and back out into Covent Garden.

Charlie moved towards Lily, then stopped himself. They looked at one another awkwardly.

'Is your neck badly hurt?' he asked.

She shook her head. 'I've had worse. What happened down there?'

'I distracted Repent with the truth,' said Charlie. 'Floored him with a few tonnes of loose soil. But he'll be on his feet before long and now he knows what the Lord and Lady really are he'll be after them. And if Barebones finds him . . .'

'Let's hope this Lord and Lady really can tell you how to find Maria,' said Lily. 'Let's go.'

They raced to the chaotic backstage room and Charlie flung open the cupboard. He moved forward and pulled the Lord and Lady free from the other bedraggled props.

Lily was at his side. 'This is them,' she said in an awed whisper. 'Hidden all these years. They must have appeared in a hundred or more plays.'

'Every play with a coronation,' agreed Charlie. 'Disguised with cheap paint so everyone thought them painted lead.'

'And no one noticed the treasure hiding with all the worthless things,' said Lily.

In one hand Charlie held a curving orb, in the other a long sceptre. They'd been daubed with imitation gold, copper leaf ground down and faded over the years. But as Charlie rubbed away the old paint, a gleam of real gold flashed through.

'So this was what Cromwell tried so hard to destroy,' said Lily. 'The Crown Jewels.'

Chapter 91

Tom felt the old sickness in his stomach. The fairy potion.

To dull the senses and keep him confused.

Thoughts had become slippery. He could see a familiar gilded mirror, but that wasn't possible.

'You're not here,' he told the mirror. 'You broke.'

Then an icy winter world appeared in the mirror and the boy stepped forward, wrapped in furs. He stood in a dark theatre with twisted trees growing from the stage and ragged gossamer for curtains. A bell sounded, far away.

'They're coming,' whispered Tom. 'The Lord and Lady. I can feel it. We're going home.'

'I?' The boy gave a hard laugh. 'You imagine I could return, after all these years? Look at me. Look at what you have done to me.'

Tom looked. For the first time he realised that the boy was as small and pale as when he'd first appeared, all those years ago, by the hot fire.

'You didn't grow older,' said Tom.

'You imagine I could simply come back?' demanded the boy. 'A grown man in a child's body? I would be the stuff of the circus.' He struck suddenly forward, and a deep crack appeared.

Tom drew back, mouth dropping open in horror. 'You tricked me,' said Tom.

The boy stared at the crack in the mirror. Slowly he brought his pale fingers to touch it. 'Charlie Tuesday will learn your true name,' he said. 'He searches even now. Soon he will match your face to the one he knows from before.'

More bells sounded, jangling from the fairy place.

Tom clamped both hands over his ears. 'Stop,' gasped Tom. 'Stop.' He pressed so tight he felt his skull would burst, but the ringing only grew louder. In the mirror he saw a trickle of blood escaping his nose. He fell to his knees, head pounding.

The boy stepped forward. His palm rested on the splintered glass and began to glow.

'You grow weaker,' said the boy. 'And you can no longer contain me here. Did you see what I did to Bridey?'

The cracked glass feathered in a hundred directions like a spider's web.

'No!' said Tom, making to cover the mirror. But it was too late. The glass fell away and the boy stepped forward and grasped his hands.

Tom felt them grow burning hot. The boy brought his small face very close to Tom's.

'You were right,' he said softly. 'I tricked you. I never meant to change places. My body is small and weak from the fairy world. To survive here I need a human form. You've stolen my life all these years. I think I'll take yours.' And he stepped forward into Tom's body.

The boy blinked, turning his head experimentally left and right. He appeared to be in some kind of attic. The theatre. He remembered now. Then he saw the girl, Maria, chained in the corner. His mouth lifted cruelly, eyes considering the burning candle.

'How good to see you here,' he said, his voice brittle, the words over-nuanced. 'I have great plans for you.'

'Where is Tom?' Maria chose her words carefully.

'There is no Tom now,' he said. 'He is gone. Only Robin Goodfellow remains.'

Chapter 92

Charlie was holding the lost Crown Jewels. They were heavy.

'We must find Maria,' he said. 'Tom Black said the Lady would tell us how.'

'Have you run mad?' demanded Lily. 'Charlie, don't you see? London is in chaos. These jewels could pay for troops to put down the riots. The pearls alone . . .'

'So what do you suggest?' asked Charlie. 'We give up on Maria? Deliver these jewels to the King? I won't do it.'

Lily grabbed his arm. 'Charlie, wait. Think. What could a Cromwellian do with England's lost Crown Jewels, in the midst of the biggest riot London has ever seen?'

Charlie felt his throat tighten. 'I suppose they could incite a mob to march on Whitehall. Claiming the King was never truly crowned.'

'The King would have no choice but to attack his own people,' said Lily. 'All-out war. Charlie, I could take the Crown Jewels to the Earl of Amesbury. He's not sentimental. He'd clip off the gems and have men mobilised within a few hours.'

'I won't risk Maria's life. She was taken because she was trying to help me.'

'Take them to Maria's betrothed then,' bartered Lily. 'The lawyer.'

'Percy?'

'He is the only one with the right to make this decision,' said Lily. She was watching his face carefully. 'Or do you think otherwise?'

'You think I'll leave Maria to be tortured to death?'

'Charlie, if it's her or England, she'd want you to choose England,' said Lily softly.

'Enough,' snapped Charlie. 'All you care about is earning the King's regard. You want to return the jewels so he might give you gold and lands. Or is it something else?' He glared back.

Lily's expression twisted in affront. 'That's what you think of me?' she said quietly. 'I want to play royal courtesan?'

'I should have known what to expect from a gypsy.' As soon as the words were out of his mouth he regretted it.

Lily stood for a moment, her mouth open. Then she shut it tight and turned away. 'I'm going to find Percy,' she said. 'He should know what you plan on doing in the name of his wife-to-be. You're on your own,' she threw back over her shoulder as she stalked away. 'You always were.'

Chapter 93

In the tunnels beneath King's Theatre, Barebones was digging Repent free. He'd been buried to his waist by the fallen ceiling.

'You're fortunate young Bolly was good enough to find me,' said Barebones. 'You could have been here for days.'

Repent coughed, trying to pull his legs out of the heavy earth.

'You've been drinking wine, boy,' said Barebones. 'I can smell it on you. Think yourself a lord now, do you? Thought you could take the city with a pack of drunken boys?' The old soldier shook his head disdainfully.

'We got into Covent Garden, Father,' said Repent, freeing one leg, then another. 'Further than any apprentice ever dared.'

'Your only thoughts were to indulge your lusts and bodily pleasures,' said Barebones in disgust. 'You lost all hope of finding the Lord and Lady. How are we to discover the dress in this chaos?'

'I found the dress.' Repent couldn't keep the pride from his voice. 'I found the Lord and Lady.'

'What?' Barebones barked.

'You were wrong,' said Repent, relishing the words. 'All these years you've been chasing something that doesn't exist.' He rubbed his legs.

Barebones's expression was stony. 'Out with it boy. What do you suppose to have found?'

'The Lord and Lady are the Crown Jewels,' said Repent. 'The thief taker told me. Cromwell hid away the orb and sceptre. Tried to burn 'em. All that time,' concluded Repent nastily, 'you thought yourself Cromwell's chosen one. 'E 'ad you thinkin' you guarded fairy folk. Old Ironsides must 'a bin laughing at you behind your back.'

Barebones's expression was tight with rage. 'The orb and sceptre,' he asked quietly. 'Does the thief taker have them?'

'He tricked me,' whined Repent childishly. 'Lured me down here.'

'He'll take them to Tom Black,' said Barebones. He rubbed his face, thinking, then began hauling Repent free from the earth. 'The people rise,' said Barebones, considering. 'The King has no guard.' He turned to Bolly. 'How many riot?'

'They fill the roads from Threadneedle to St Paul's,' said Bolly. 'Covent Garden is thick with apprentices. I'd say forty thousand have taken to the streets.'

'At least a quarter will be starving ragged folk,' calculated Barebones. 'Good cannon fodder, easily led. Half will be lusty young boys' – he cast a sad look at Repent – 'looking only for wine and frivolity. But that leaves perhaps ten thousand good men, who mean to fight for a real cause.'

'The whores were organised,' offered Repent, keen to be part of the discussion. 'They threw chamber pots, made theatre tricks.'

'Mrs Jenks?' said Barebones.

Repent nodded.

'She thinks herself clever as the devil himself,' said Barebones, his voice tight with contempt. 'Women like her are the festering canker at the heart of London's sin.' He thought some more. 'Where is she now?'

'They all fled to the Golden Apple,' said Bolly. 'It's the only safe place in Covent Garden. Thick doors, and even the rioters don't dare attack. It's the King's place. His women inside.'

'There will be gunpowder inside the Golden Apple,' said Barebones. 'For theatre tricks.'

'If we have ten thousand troops we have no need for gunpowder,' said Bolly. 'Most on the streets are armed. Pikes and staves. Attacking the Golden Apple lays us open to a treason charge.'

'Do we let old whores laugh at us now?' demanded Barebones. 'Gunpowder would make a statement. We take the Golden Apple.'

Chapter 94

Charlie watched Lily go, resisting the urge to follow.

She's not in any danger, he reminded himself. *Don't fail Maria now.*

But first he had to find her. He called to mind Tom Black's words: '*The Lady will tell you where to find me.*' But how was that possible? 'The Lady' was nothing but a ball of gold.

Charlie rested the sceptre down and concentrated on the orb. Then he took the edge of his coat and scuffed away the old paint. More gleaming gold was revealed, along with a row of tiny pearls and some large red rubies and emeralds.

Charlie held it to the light.

This was ancient treasure. Could it really have fairy magic? Charlie ran through what he knew about fairies. Should he run widdershins around a church, perhaps?

The heavy orb rested in his hand. Charlie closed his eyes, trying to feel for some magical power. But there was nothing. He remembered what the cunning woman had told him: '*You know Tom Black very well . . . You need only discover his true name.*'

Was Tom Black's identity a clue? Charlie looked back to the orb.

'You're just a lump of gold and jewels,' he decided.

Charlie let his hand run along the jewels. They formed a belt around the middle of the orb.

'The girdled lady,' he muttered. It reminded him of something. He fished inside his coat for the poem Tom Black had left him and read it from memory, staring at the paper for clues.

Deep and dark the old ones sleep,
Crowned Lord and girdled Lady of the Keep,
Around the first and last, they will come,
And false earthly Kings will be undone.

'What does it mean?' whispered Charlie. The image of Maria in danger loomed suddenly, so clear and real it was overwhelming.

What if Lily was right? said a voice in his head. *Tom Black is playing you, leading you to a dead end. Maria will die whilst you try to solve an impossible puzzle.*

Either way, Charlie decided, he needed to leave before the apprentices returned and found him standing with the Crown Jewels. But just as he moved away from the mirror, he noticed something.

One of the letters of the poem was a strange shape. A 't' was much shorter and broader than its fellows. It matched the cross on the top of the orb.

Slowly Charlie moved the drawn cross to the one on the top of the orb, lining up the two. The paper fitted perfectly around the orb, Charlie realised, wrapping it.

Beneath the paper the red of the rubies could just be seen. Their soft light aligned with three words from the poem. Charlie read them aloud slowly and painstakingly. 'Girdle. Around. Earth.'

Where had he heard that before?

The answer came to him almost immediately. He saw Lynette's smiling face, back when they were young and recently married, reading from *A Midsummer Night's Dream*. '*I'll put a girdle round about the earth.*'

A fairy had said it, he thought. Puck. Did that mean something? He let his mind roam larger, scanning London, searching for a fit.

It was theatrical, of course. The clue could be that Maria was held in a theatre. But those numbered in the hundreds, if you included the illegals.

Charlie tapped the paper against his hand. Then he remembered. There was one theatre, famed for Shakespeare plays, that would make the perfect place to hold a kidnapped girl. It had been partly destroyed and abandoned since the war.

The Globe Theatre.

Charlie called it to mind. Cromwell's soldiers had torn apart the famous theatre and it had been fenced off to be sold for tenements. But money to build had not been forthcoming. Many believed it haunted. The more Charlie considered it, the more certain he became.

'An old abandoned stage,' murmured Charlie. 'What better place for a man like Tom Black to keep a prisoner?'

Charlie cast his eyes around the room, grabbed up a discarded turban, unravelled the long colourful fabric and wrapped it around the jewels.

The Globe was south of the river. The sun was setting. He judged there to be less than an hour until Lent was over.

He heard Lily's voice, as if speaking from another place. '*The country will be at war,*' she was saying. '*And this time there's no Cromwell, no defender of the people. Only a madman with a talent for acting.*'

He tried to think what Maria would suggest. He saw her coming out from the dark, her blonde hair and even features.

'*Tom Black is a performer,*' she said. '*Go see his play.*'

Chapter 95

The Birdcage dressing room was empty. Lynette sighed. The apprentices had them running scared. No one wanted to hang around. Not to mention the barrel of punch had been finished. Of course they would have all gone to the alehouse. She'd given up drinking a long time ago. Shortly after they'd dragged her gin-soaked mother out of Vauxhall pond.

Lynette's costume sat heavily on her shoulders. Titania from *A Midsummer Night's Dream*. The fairy Queen. There was no one to help her undress, but she had had years of practice unfastening her own clothing.

Slowly she began unlacing and unbuttoning, careful not to pull any threads. Actresses paid for costume damage. As she let the front of the dress fall, she realised there was something tucked into the seam. A piece of paper she hadn't seen before. Some love letter, she assumed, but its presence made her suddenly uneasy. How had someone got into her dressing room unseen and put something inside her costume?

All was quiet. Now that she thought about it, that was strange. Even with the cast gone there were always seamstresses and servant-boys, orange girls and beggars milling about after a performance.

Her eyes settled back on the note, regretting her illiteracy. There were symbols though. Things she recognised. Male and female. Him and her. The Lord and Lady.

Something told her she should leave.

Take off the costume, she reminded herself. *You can't risk damaging it.*

Lynette's fingers worked fast now, picking up the skirts and tugging them over her head.

For a moment she was blind. And it was then that she heard a movement behind her. Like soft footsteps. In a panic she snagged the fabric on a hair pin as she pulled the dress free.

That's this week's wages. Lynette was annoyed with herself now, looking about her for the mysterious sound. Nothing. Then she saw him. Tall, dark and not-quite-handsome, sitting easily on one of the prop tables.

'Hello, Lynette.' He smiled.

Her face flashed recognition. 'You,' she managed.

He smiled. 'I've come to take you away.'

Chapter 96

Southwark felt eerily quiet as Charlie made his way towards the Globe Theatre. The orb and sceptre clanked uncomfortably at his side, wrapped in their makeshift covering. He made out a long wicker fence that surrounded where the Globe had once stood.

Charlie stood looking at the fence. It was old and had sprouted in places. His mind drifted to Lily, somewhere else in the city. Perhaps informing the King that his precious Crown Jewels had been recovered. Charlie had never felt so alone.

Charlie secured the Crown Jewels to his belt, then took a few steps back, ran at the fence and leapt high, grasping the top with his fingertips and hauling himself up. He dropped down behind the fence, the long sceptre making his landing ungainly.

Inside was the remains of the Globe Theatre. Without any people, it seemed far bigger than Charlie remembered. The enormous stage jutted forth, its square shape large enough to fit a London house, the planks smashed in several places by heavy axe blows.

Charlie's heart beat faster. Someone had set the stage for his arrival. He moved nearer.

Two candles flickered at the edge and an old canvas scene had been roughly arranged. The painted display showed the inside of a tomb.

A heavy 'thunk' rang out and a noose dropped down from the overhang above the stage, swinging with the motion of its fall. He recognised the sound with a sick feeling in his stomach. It was the same mechanical reverberation that had preceded the hanging corpse in the Birdcage.

Charlie looked on and, as he watched, the noose began retracting upwards, with a loud ratcheting. He was sure Tom Black's skill in theatre effects had allowed him to set up this drop from a distance. Which meant Maria's kidnapper could be anywhere in the Globe.

Keep calm, Charlie warned himself. *He's watching you. Don't let him read what you're thinking.*

He forced himself to steady his breathing, to take in the wider theatre. There was a sound behind him. Very faint, but to Charlie's trained ear it was the unmistakable click of a latch sliding into place. Then a dead woman rolled towards him from underneath the stage.

Charlie froze as the pale face of the corpse slumped to a halt at his feet. The eyes were yellow, a stranger's eyes. A street seller or some other low trade, he thought, by the gaunt fatigue of her dead face.

But the clothes she wore made his breath catch in his throat. Charlie knew what it meant. Another changeling. Tom Black had taken her.

It's a trick, Charlie told himself, the terribly familiar clothes making his heart beat faster. *He doesn't have her. How could he?*

But a terrible fear was coiling around his heart.

His eyes ranged the theatre. He couldn't see or hear Maria. The only place she could be was up above, he decided. There was a vast overhang held up by mock Grecian pillars.

An explosion sounded from the direction of the stage and smoke filled the air. A stench of sulphurous burning reached Charlie's nostrils. He looked to see a man had appeared on stage. Charlie had seen those pale eyes before.

The actor took a low bow. Charlie swallowed hard. He recognised him all too well. His appearance was completely different now, as if an entirely different man inhabited his body. But there was no mistaking it. Standing before him on the stage was the man Charlie had thought was Percy.

Chapter 97

The apprentices had amassed outside the Golden Apple. They were armed for destruction.

The thick wooden doors of the illegal theatre were bolted shut. Its brick walls seemed to offer an impenetrable fortress.

'We come for the gunpowder!' bellowed Barebones. 'Give it up and perhaps we'll be easier on your girls.'

They were met with silence.

'Pull it down!' boomed Barebones. 'We'll see how brave the little duckies are when we pluck them from their nests.'

Men hefted their staves. Then a window opened on the first floor. A familiar figure stepped onto the balcony.

'Barebones,' said Mrs Jenks. 'Do not drag these poor boys to the noose with you. If you attack the theatre, there's no going back. This is no brothel.'

'His Majesty has deserted you,' said Barebones. 'Left you to your fate. Like all old whores. Your theatre trickery won't work a second time. We'll take your gunpowder and storm Whitehall.'

A shape appeared behind Mrs Jenks. A second woman. Mother Mitchell stepped onto the balcony. She took Mrs Jenks's hand. 'We stand for the King,' she said. 'He has been good to us, and we do not forget our debts.'

'We'll burn you out,' said Barebones. 'And pull down your houses. Destroy your fine clothes and jewels.'

Mother Mitchell narrowed her small eyes. 'Then do your worst. But know this. We whored these streets whilst you silly men had your wars. Your fellows are long dead and we remain. There have been whores in Covent Garden since London began and when you are long gone here we shall be.'

Barebones laughed. 'I fought for Cromwell, you stupid hag.' He spat in the dust. 'I've gutted fat old hens like you for sport. You're about to find out what war really is.' He eyed the door. 'Break it down,' he said. 'Get to the gunpowder. If anyone stands in your way, kill them.'

Chapter 98

Charlie closed his eyes and opened them again. But the likeness was unmistakable. Tom had masqueraded as Percy. And Charlie had never questioned that the man at the Birdcage wasn't Maria's betrothed.

Charlie wondered vaguely what had happened to the real Percy. Was he somewhere in London, uncertain where Maria was? Or had Tom killed him?

If Tom had acted a part to perfection, there was nothing of that man left now. Where Percy had been uncertain and stuffy, this man burned with a fanatical intensity. The transformation was incredible.

'Charlie Tuesday, did you enjoy my performance?' said Tom, smiling. He narrowed his eyes slightly, letting his body assume a more nervous, twitching air and adding a haughty superiority to his voice. '*My* wife would never do *acting*,' he said, morphing into the part of Percy with such skill that he seemed to be a different man entirely.

Charlie said nothing. He was madly trying to work out Maria's whereabouts.

'And yet Maria will act,' said Tom, his eyes flicking upwards. 'I have a very special part for her.' Tom straightened, his fingertips tapping a dance on one another. 'Fairy folk know about circles of power,' he said. 'Take a man away from his and you remove his strength. And yours is the old city. The wandering alleys and grimy streets. But here you are quite exposed.'

'Not everyone does as you expect,' said Charlie.

'I hoped for many years that that was the case,' said Tom. 'I searched for a worthy opponent for a long time. I had high hopes for you.' His eyes dropped to the orb and sceptre, wrapped in their turban. 'Did you bring me the Lord and Lady?'

Charlie nodded, unwrapping the turban to reveal the jewels. A strange feral expression flared in Tom's face and he instinctively took a step towards them.

Charlie drew back. 'First deliver me Maria safe,' he said.

Tom smiled as if this childish request was to be expected. 'It wouldn't be a play,' he said, 'without our leading ladies.'

He moved to the side of the stage and manoeuvred a large lever. There was a clanking sound and then a whirring. A wooden platform lowered slowly down. Charlie felt time stand still. On it were two women.

They had ropes around their necks, hands bound behind their backs. Their mouths were gagged.

It was Maria and Lily.

Chapter 99

The King was inspecting ceremonial robes. An array of jewelled garments and shoes had been laid out before him. He tried not to think he might never get to wear them.

'The Lord and Lady,' Amesbury was saying. 'We put it about they were fairies. Magical beings. If it is discovered that they survived Cromwell, people will say you were never legally crowned.' He waved a thick hand. 'In this climate,' he said, 'can you imagine the effect it would have? Londoners need only the slightest reason to march on Whitehall.'

'The Crown Jewels were destroyed by Cromwell,' said Charles, with certainty. 'Burned in the Mint forge. Talk that the orb and sceptre survived is nothing but a story.'

Amesbury looked at the King, wondering what he truly believed.

'You must send troops,' Amesbury said. 'These riots have become something else. Remember the civil war? This was how it started.'

'I remember,' said Charles. 'But there is nothing, Amesbury. There are no funds. My guards can barely be coaxed to remain at the palace.'

'There was a reserve,' said Amesbury. 'The tax on coal.'

The King shook his head, smiling slightly. 'It's gone. I gave it to her.'

'The actress?'

'No.' The King frowned at the idea. 'She wants nothing of that kind.' His eyebrows lifted at this thought. 'She isn't like that. No titles. No gold.'

'Then who?' Amesbury was trying to think who else the King might be sleeping with.

'My little Betsy,' said Charles. 'It's signed in trust.'

'She is not even your child! You give another man's daughter an annual income for life?'

'It doesn't matter, Amesbury,' said Charles. 'None of that matters. Barbara and I . . . We loved each other. For a long time. She was loyal to me when I had no one. Now I repay her debt.'

Amesbury was deep in calculation, mentally ransacking the empty treasury. 'Parliament,' he decided. 'They might be called upon . . .'

Charles lifted his hands. 'It is over, Amesbury,' he said. 'Parliament won't put down a cause they support.' He patted the old general. 'You'll survive, you always do,' he said. 'As for me, I'm spending the last night in my palace in the arms of a woman I love.'

'You're going to Lady Castlemaine?'

'To the actress,' said Charles. 'I collected her from her dressing room earlier,' he added. 'Gave her safe escort back to Whitehall. I think she understands,' he added, his eyes far away. 'I'm too tired for another fight. This is the end.'

Chapter 100

Inside the Golden Apple, the great doors were shuddering, splintering. The girls waited, hand in hand, as the thick wood smashed apart.

Barebones appeared in the broken doorway, sword held high, face battle-ready. He walked forward into the theatre. Apprentices began pouring through behind him, Repent and Bolly leading the charge.

On the small stage stood Mother Mitchell and her girls.

'Look at this,' whispered Repent, nudging Bolly and licking his lips. 'Mother Mitchell's kept the best ones for herself.'

Bolly's eyes were fixed on the pit. Huddled inside was a small body of men, holding swords and pistols.

Barebones took them in. 'You haven't enough troops,' he told Mother Mitchell, assessing the assembled men. 'We will tear through them like butter.'

'You haven't counted the women,' replied Mother Mitchell. 'Do you think my girls will run from a pack of apprentices? They were raised in worse streets than your boys. Have you ever seen a slum girl in a fight?'

Barebones regarded the girls on stage, arranged in their expensive dresses, hair curled and faces made, and shook his head in derision. 'Repent,' he said. 'Time for you to put some whores in their place. The guard is mine.' He eyed the armed men coolly, then raised his sword. 'Charge!'

Barebones ran at the guard, a bloodcurdling battle cry echoing around the theatre. The older apprentices fell in behind, makeshift weapons drawn.

As the pit fight raged, Repent stepped sideways, towards the stage, his gaggle of scrawny boys moving with him. Beneath their lipstick and paint, the girls' pretty faces hardened. Their dainty manners had vanished. They stood like hunters.

Bolly made it onto the stage first. One of the girls stepped forward and kicked him so hard in the groin his skinny frame was lifted in the air. He staggered back, and she grabbed a handful of bagging shirt, dragging him to the floor. As he tried to stand a second girl moved in, kicking him mercilessly in the head.

She turned to the approaching boys, a smudge of fresh blood on her shoe. ''Oo's next, then?' she screeched.

More boys poured onto the stage, grabbing and punching. Repent watched as a girl in a pink dress landed on an apprentice's back in a flying leap. The boy howled as she sank her teeth deep into his ear.

Then Repent noticed a few whores who weren't fighting like the rest. Five breathtakingly beautiful girls had taken flight, running towards the back of the theatre, silk dresses flying.

Repent nudged the boy nearest to him. 'Look a' that,' he breathed excitedly.

The other boy stared.

'Let's get 'em,' said Repent, 'before the older ones see 'em.' He raised his voice, addressing his own ragged apprentices. 'Come on, boys! This way!'

Repent gave chase, beckoning the younger boys to follow. They poured behind him, following the fleeing girls towards the back of the theatre. Repent recognised one of the whores as they ran. It was the Italian girl who'd got away from him at Damaris Page's house. He grinned, singling her out.

Viola looked back over her shoulder, and to her horror saw the look on Repent's pockmarked face. She and the other girls ran into an empty dressing room.

Repent and his boys crowded into the doorway.

'No way out.' Repent smiled. 'You boys guard the door,' he decided, pointing to five of his troop. 'You'll have your turn.'

He advanced into the dressing room, the rest of the apprentices behind him. The five girls were watching them warily, backing away.

'The purple dress is mine,' said Repent, making for Viola.

The girls broke apart as the boys flew at them, scattering around the dressing room.

Repent got hold of Viola's long dark hair and pulled her to the ground. She floundered, trying to kick. He was on her before she could defend herself. Viola spat in his face and he grabbed her throat tightly, bearing his weight down on her. She felt her breath squeezed, fought for air.

'See these?' Repent grinned, waving his sword. 'Tributes. Shall we see what colour you wear?'

Viola noticed something familiar, dancing in the air. Clancy's garter was tied to his stick.

She couldn't breathe and panic set in. Her vision was swimming. Repent had an expression of concentration. His hand was busy with something. His clothing.

Black spots appeared. Clancy's red ribbon garter blurred.

Then suddenly the pressure lifted. Viola gulped in a breath. Repent made a strange strangled sound and his eyes shot wide open.

Viola pushed him and Repent rolled easily away. She saw the little needle blade sticking from his back.

Clancy stood over them, watching Repent with satisfaction. She leaned down and pulled out the blade. A trickle of blood ran from the wound. Repent was making oddly gulping shallow breaths, eyes flicking back and forth in panic.

Clancy leant low. 'That's yer lungs filling with blood,' she told him. 'Yer's drowning from the inside.' She spun the knife in her hand, then slashed the garters free.

'Like I told you,' she said, 'you owe me a debt. This is mine and I'll take a few more for interest.'

Her eyes landed on Viola, who'd lifted herself to her elbows. The dressing room was filling with unfamiliar women now. Harlots of every shape and size were surging in droves from a hidden doorway at the back.

'Mother Mitchell was right,' Clancy observed. 'The apprentices didn't know about the dressing room door.' She nodded to the entrance. 'Only harlots and theatre-folk know the high-ups have their own entrance, so's they can peep at the actresses undressing.'

'How did you bring so many?' managed Viola hoarsely, rubbing her neck.

'Damaris rounded us up,' said Clancy. 'Said somethin' was happenin' in Covent Garden. We come back to defend the King, dint we?' She nodded her head to outside. ''S a few more girls arrived than ol' Barebones expected,' she added with relish, waving the bloody knife and shoving the garters inside her bodice. 'Us harlots 'av 'ad enough of smashed windows now. Time we fought back.'

'You can come back to Mrs Jenks,' said Viola. 'When this is over. She's given me work as an actress. I can help you.'

'Nah.' Clancy shook her head. 'I'm not like you. I belong in Wapping. Always did.' She nodded to Viola. 'Think of me, wontcha, when you're playin' to the crowd? You never did fit with us Wapping whores. But girls like you give hope, fer the little ones growing up.'

Viola nodded dumbly as Clancy fled the scene, bloody knife still in her hand.

Chapter 101

Charlie pulled himself up onto the huge stage. In front of the tomb backdrop Maria and Lily had each been dressed in a theatre costume. Maria in a flowing white toga, with large wings at her back and a crown of summer flowers. Lily wore a court dress with wide skirts and a high wig. Her generous lips were stained deep red and red rouge circles decorated each cheek.

Each woman had a noose drawn close around her neck.

'Stop,' said Tom coolly, as Charlie mounted the stage. 'Come no closer, or I will kill them both.'

They were on opposite ends of the stage now, Tom towards the back.

Charlie closed his eyes, trying to understand the mechanism, how the ropes were supported. Tom was standing close to a lever that seemed to connect.

He delights in tricks and traps. Don't let him play you.

Maria's blue eyes searched Charlie's face, frightened, questioning. Lily looked straight ahead.

'You're wondering how I got to your friend Lily?' said Tom. 'The truth is, she came to me.' He shook his head. 'She thought to help you, poor girl, going to where Percy was. Instead she walked into my trap.'

Charlie could feel the world come crashing around his ears. His plan was to save Maria. But he'd underestimated Tom at every turn. If rescuing one girl was unlikely, two was impossible.

'You've been an enjoyable interlude,' said Tom, absorbing Charlie's mounting despair. 'You're a piece of theatre in yourself. Far more complicated and intriguing than I initially gave you credit for. I thought it was time you made a choice.' He waved an explanatory hand towards the lever. 'An angel and a harlot. Once I pull it they drop. There's time enough for you to save one, but not both.'

Charlie felt his mouth turn dry. He was a few feet from the stage, but not close enough.

'Now,' said Tom, his eyes shining, 'deliver me my prize.'

'No!' Maria had managed to work the gag from her mouth.

Charlie turned towards her, relief at the sound of her voice washing through him.

'Charlie!' she shouted. 'Don't give him the orb and sceptre.'

'Maria,' said Charlie. 'You're not hurt?'

She shook her head. 'Listen to me,' she said. 'We're dead no matter what you do. He means to start a war.'

Charlie hesitated.

'He'll lead a mob to the King's door,' said Maria. 'And claim he was never truly crowned.'

'Be silent!' Tom threw out an arm and caught Maria in the stomach. Charlie made for her, but Tom held up a hand.

'First the Lord and Lady,' he said. 'Give them to me. I will keep my word. One will live.'

'He won't,' said Maria. 'We are both already dead, Charlie.'

Charlie looked at Lily. She was still staring furiously ahead. He closed his eyes and saw his mother's face, the hands at her neck. He opened them again.

'I feel sorry for mortals,' said Tom. 'So enslaved to your feelings. If you were not so weak, you would leave them all to their fate and prevent me escaping. But you will run to their aid, and London will fall. How sad to be so powerless.'

Charlie's eyes darted back and forth over Lily and Maria's faces. Both looked resigned. He could see Lily flicking her gaze to Maria. Her eyes were saying, *choose her.*

Charlie gave the tiniest shake of his head.

'Charlie Tuesday,' taunted Tom. 'So easy to send him where you want him. All you need do is present him someone who needs rescuing and he'll come running.' Tom tapped his head. 'Reason flies away. You cannot help yourself. It's a compulsion for you. A mortal weakness I can't claim to understand.'

'You have a weakness of your own,' said Charlie. 'A blind spot. You underestimate what people will do for love.' He found his eyes had moved to where Lily stood.

'On the contrary,' said Tom. 'I depend on it. How else could I have forced the great Charlie Tuesday to arrive without a plan, hoping his good fortune would hold?'

'I was married to an actress,' said Charlie. 'Before we wed, she acted here in the Globe. So I was able to plan a little, despite my haste to get here. I know something of stagecraft. And I think you underestimate my ruthlessness.'

'Indeed,' said Tom Black. 'Shall we find out?' And he reached forward and pulled the lever. There was a horrible screech of rope and pulley and then Lily and Maria were hoisted high by the ropes around their necks.

Charlie dropped the Crown Jewels and ran towards Tom Black.

Chapter 102

Barebones and his apprentices were fighting hard with Mother Mitchell's guard.

'We need reinforcements,' he said, as a pistol shot took down a grocer's apprentice. 'Pull Repent and his boys back.'

But as he said the words he realised his son and the troop of boys were no longer in the theatre. Barebones ducked free of the fighting and followed a trail of blood and debris across the stage to a dressing room at the back.

As he stepped inside his mouth opened, but no sound came out.

The younger apprentices lay about, moaning and bleeding. All around were girls Barebones recognised. They'd been in Damaris Page's brothel, fleeing in terror. But they weren't running now.

In the corner, one girl had removed her beautifully embroidered shoes and was battering a helpless apprentice with the hard heels. Another was throttling a red-faced boy with a garter.

Damaris's girls had been joined by ragged whores, who were fighting as though their lives depended on it. The whole of Covent Garden's back alleys seemed to have emptied into the room.

Mother Mitchell was watching on. She saw Barebones, took in his stricken face.

'We know a little of warcraft,' she observed, 'though we are nought but silly women.' Mother Mitchell nodded to the injured boys. 'I believe it's called a pincer movement? Lure your enemy into a dead end and attack them from all sides with forces they didn't know you had? We know this terrain better than you and us whores are not so divided as you imagine.'

Barebones saw a familiar boy on the floor, blood gushing from his mouth. He ran to him. 'Repent!' Barebones knelt. 'Repent!

The bloodied mouth moved slowly. 'I am sorry, Father,' said Repent. 'I didn't listen to you. I didn't resist temptation. We are lost.'

Barebones looked around, his face set with fury. 'We will not lose, boy. You may not live to see it, but we will root out the poison at the heart of it all. These whores might have bested a few scrawny younger boys, but we have an army of stronger apprentices who will prevail.' His eyes settled on Mother Mitchell. Barebones took out his iron sword. 'Fairies come in many forms,' he said, standing. 'They have tricked us, with their glamour, their illusions. But now I see.'

He advanced on Mother Mitchell.

Chapter 103

As Charlie raced towards him, Tom tilted his head, a slow smile spreading.

'Very good,' he whispered, 'the mortal learns fairy ways.'

Tom shifted slightly on the stage, watching where the jewels had fallen.

Then, as Charlie mounted the stage, there was another explosion and Tom vanished in a ball of reeking smoke.

Charlie leapt at the side of the stage, where the scenery ropes hung. He let his fingers trail through the ropes, then drew out his knife and slashed quickly through one that held taut. A sandbag crashed to the ground and he heard the two nooses go whipping over the scenery joist and drop to the stage.

Charlie saw Lily and Maria fall heavily, gasping and rubbing at their necks. His eyes flicked to the wider theatre. Tom Black was racing towards the Crown Jewels.

Charlie ran to the fallen women. He cut their bonds. Lily grabbed off the noose at her neck, but Maria turned her attention to Charlie.

'You fool!' she exploded, as he raised her to standing. 'You let Tom get to the jewels.'

'Nice to see you too,' said Charlie, smiling.

She threw her arms around him and buried her face in his neck. 'Thank you,' she breathed. 'I knew you'd come.'

Lily stood behind them, looking awkward.

'But you should have sacrificed us,' scolded Maria. 'Tom will be headed to rile up the mob to storm Whitehall.'

'Tom Black isn't going anywhere,' said Charlie. 'I know this theatre. Lynette acted here before we wed. I memorised every hidden place, just to catch a glimpse of her.' He was moving towards where he'd dropped the Crown Jewels.

Now there was a dark hole in their place. Down inside, caught in the narrow space, was Tom Black.

'It's an old trapdoor hardly no one knows about,' explained Charlie. 'At least' – he corrected himself – 'no one but a lovesick boy intent on seeing his sweetheart.' He smiled down at Tom. 'I know every inch of this theatre,' said Charlie. 'Learned all there was to know of theatres and stage-trickery. Love is a powerful thing. And if you hadn't been so transfixed by the prospect of the Crown Jewels, I think you might have noticed where I dropped them.'

'What now?' asked Maria, looking down sadly at Tom.

There was a commotion behind them. A guard had arrived, escorting a silken-skirted lady into the Globe.

'That's Lady Castlemaine,' said Maria, taking her in with awe.

'I sent her a message,' said Lily. 'I thought it best.'

Lady Castlemaine and her guard surrounded them. She looked Charlie carefully up and down. 'So you are the old husband,' she murmured. 'Now I see you closer, I suppose I can understand the appeal.' She turned to Lily. 'Where are they?'

Lily pointed to the trapdoor. Lady Castlemaine moved towards it, peering over the edge. She motioned to her guards and they vanished below stage.

'You came to save us?' asked Maria, looking at Lady Castlemaine in confusion.

'With no thought to my own safety or reputation?' Lady Castlemaine laughed. 'Of course not.' Her violet eyes surveyed the Globe. 'Perhaps we had best not run away with the idea I came here at all,' she added. 'We'll keep it to ourselves.'

Three guards burst back above stage. Two were restraining Tom, his eerily cold eyes flicking about the theatre. One held the orb and sceptre.

'What should we do with him?' asked the guard, nodding to Tom.

Lady Castlemaine strode towards them, her little silk shoes clicking on the wooden boards, wafting expensive perfume as she passed. Her white ringed fingers rested on the orb and sceptre.

'I think these belong to me.' She lifted the Crown Jewels and held them lightly, the staff gripped in one hand, the orb resting gently in the palm of the other. 'Nothing but some worthless theatre props,' she said, eyeing her guards carefully. 'Nevertheless, these old things have great sentimental value to me. As you know, I love theatre. I even act in private, from time to time, for the King's pleasure.' Her lovely eyes glittered. 'He wanted me for his queen,' she said, more to herself than anyone present. 'A long, long time ago. I chose freedom. Perhaps I chose wrong.' She seemed to recollect where she was. 'I'll take these as a token of your appreciation,' she said, looking at Lily and Charlie. 'You'll find a new privateer's licence is waiting for you at Whitehall,' she continued, addressing Lily. 'And as for you.' Her gaze drifted to Charlie. 'Perhaps you'll find some royal mysteries to solve in future. In any case,' she concluded grandly, 'you're no longer wanted citizens, at least by me.'

Without waiting for an answer, she turned in a rustle of scented silk and made for the door. Her guards crowded around her, and she was gone.

As Lady Castlemaine vanished from view, Maria moved to Lily's side.

'The real Crown Jewels,' said Maria wonderingly. 'The only question is whether she'll return them to buy Charles's favour, or melt them down for her own spending.'

'She'll melt them down,' said Lily with certainty. 'They'll be lost forever.'

'Those are sacred jewels,' said Maria. 'They've existed for half a century. They give the King his power, his legal authority.'

'Maybe Cromwell had some things right,' said Charlie, smiling. 'It's not jewels and fur coats that give our kings their rule, is it? It's us. The people.'

'I don't know what you're so happy about,' grumbled Lily, watching where Lady Castlemaine had exited.

'Didn't you hear what Lady Castlemaine said?' beamed Charlie. 'She could see my appeal. They'll never believe it down the Bucket of Blood when I tell them.'

Chapter 104

Barebones closed in on Mother Mitchell, dragging her struggling to the ground.

'You'll be begging on the streets when this is over,' he said. 'There'll be nothing left.'

'No matter what you do we shall rebuild,' gasped Mother Mitchell. 'Aye, and fuck our way back to the top.'

Barebones drew out a knife. 'You'll only be fit for soldiers after I've finished with you,' he said, resting the blade against her nose.

'Unhand that woman,' said a loud voice. 'She is under the King's protection.'

Barebones hesitated, then turned to see the direction the announcement had come from. Arranged behind him were a pack of uniformed King's Guards.

Their leader pointed. 'Seize that man in the name of the King,' he said. 'He is the ringleader of a treasonous group.'

Guards laid rough hands on Barebones, hauling him to his feet. Behind him a large body of armed soldiers were taking command of the theatre, breaking up the riot.

'You'll be executed as a traitor at Tyburn,' said the guard. 'They'll cut off your testicles and show them to you. I imagine a few familiar women will come to watch your end.' The guard turned to Mother Mitchell, lying prone on the floor. He extended a hand. 'Allow me to help you,' he said. 'You're not the kind of woman to lie on your back for free.'

Mother Mitchell pulled herself to standing. 'The King paid for a guard?' she managed, taking in the uniformed men pouring into the theatre.

'The money came from Lady Castlemaine,' said the guard, shaking his head. 'Who would have thought the biggest whore in London would come to defend her own?'

Chapter 105

'I've brought you something.' Lynette was holding a writhing sack.

'A gift? For me? You really are a very unusual mistress for a king.'

'A man with wooden teeth was selling them off cheap near Piccadilly.' Lynette began opening the bag. 'Got a whole basketful for a shilling.'

'Now you really do spoil me.'

A little yap sounded from the bag, followed by a succession of others.

Charles smiled delightedly as four puppies bounded free. 'Dogs?'

'Puppies.' Lynette grinned. 'Little spaniels. Red and white. England colours.'

Charles picked one up. It was tiny in his large hands. 'Hello, little puppy.' He smiled.

The dog wriggled and licked his face.

Charles laughed. 'Another impudent subject,' he said. 'I imagine you chose spirited dogs on purpose.'

'Course I did,' agreed Lynette. 'They'll keep you company whilst I'm gone.'

'You're going?'

'Only for a few months,' said Lynette, sliding a hand across her stomach. 'But you've a little time with me yet.'

He looked at her. 'You're pregnant?'

'I think it's yours.' She pretended to look uncertain.

He beamed. 'Don't tease me.'

'I bin thinkin',' she said slowly. 'All this fuss with the 'prentices. Maybe you're right. Maybe we should show London the playhouses are not brothels, that theatre is not sin.'

A great smile began to form on the King's face. 'You don't mean . . . ?'

'I might give actin' in your licensed company a try,' she said, pretending to examine her fingers. 'Just for a bit. See what it's like.' She looked up at him fiercely. 'But if I'm not good enough, you're to tell me straight. I don't want people sayin' I only got the part cause I'm beddin' the King.'

'Of course.' He tried to look serious.

'And I'm changin' me name,' she added. 'No more Lynette. Tryin' to be what I'm not. I'm just plain Nell from now on. Nelly if you want to get familiar.'

'Nelly Stuart?' he teased.

'Ha! Not for the wide world. Mrs Nell Gwyn, if you please, and I'll thank you to remember the Mrs.'

'And what shall you call me?'

'I've had a few Charlies before you,' she said. 'So you'll have to be my Charles the Third.'

Chapter 106

Maria walked slowly into the dank prison. She held her hand over her mouth as a waft of stinking sewage enveloped her.

'He's in there,' said the guard. 'Only sits, looks straight ahead. Won't take no food, though we did offer him some fine things. Parliament takes pity on him, yer see. One o' our old heroes.'

Maria went to the cell door and the guard stopped her. 'He's dangerous,' he warned. 'Killed a lot of men. Cromwell's assassin he was.'

Maria looked carefully at Tom's face through the bars. 'I'm not afraid of him,' she said. 'Open the door.'

The guard pushed it back. Tom looked up at Maria as she stepped inside.

'Why do you come?' Tom asked, standing.

'I wanted to tell you I forgive you,' she said. 'I thought that might matter.'

There was a tiny smile on Tom's face. 'You are good,' he said. 'But I am an evil creature. Fairies may not be redeemed.'

Maria stepped forward and took his hands. He gave a little start of shock but didn't pull them away.

'I want to tell you a story,' said Maria. 'A fairy story.'

'I've heard all the fairy stories.'

'Not this one.'

Tom hesitated. 'Then tell it,' he said.

'Once,' said Maria, 'there was a beautiful baby boy, with a wicked mother. One night whilst he slept in his crib, his mother pretended he'd been stolen away by fairies. She raised him to think it, and did terrible cruelties to him. But, after all, this little boy was just a boy and not a fairy.'

There was a far-away look in Tom's eyes. 'How does the story end?' he whispered.

'I don't know,' admitted Maria. 'It's up to you.' She held on to his hands. 'Perhaps he repented, forgave those who'd wronged him, and God welcomed him home.'

Tom was looking at his white hands, the flaking fingernails. 'I cannot do as you suggest,' he said quietly. 'I have not the capacity.' He gave her a small smile.

Maria nodded.

'You made me see things differently,' he said. 'I am thankful.'

'You don't fear to die?' she asked.

He tilted his head. 'Why should I? Fairies are lives suspended. We crave mortality. Ultimately a fairy longs for death, but it cheats us.'

'They mean to make an example of the rioters,' she said, her eyes searching his. 'They'll execute you as a traitor.'

'You must not fear for me,' he said. 'Fairies cannot die.'

She nodded and stood to leave. As she touched the door she heard his voice.

'Wait,' said Tom. He hesitated, an expression on his face she'd never seen before. 'I never did understand love,' he said. 'I always tried to. It seems to me a fleeting uncertain thing.'

She waited for him to go on.

'I know you are due to wed,' he concluded. 'But I think you love the thief taker.'

Chapter 107

In the aftermath of the riot, people had come out to clean up Covent Garden. Ordinary men and women took to the streets with brooms. Builders and carpenters gave their time to rebuild.

Charlie watched them as he approached the unremarkable little house and knocked on the door.

A remarkably pretty woman with glossy dark hair opened it.

'Bess?' asked Charlie.

Her eyes flickered over his face, lips moving slightly. 'Charlie?' she decided finally. 'Rowan's brother. You've been sending money.'

He nodded.

She reached out a hand and touched his cheek. 'You look like him.'

She was about to say more when a sturdy little child toddled to the door. Bess scooped him up and the tiny boy reached for Charlie.

'This is little Rowan,' she said.

'Yes.' Charlie felt himself smiling. There was something so familiar in the small features. He felt as though he were looking into another time.

The little boy reached out chubby arms.

'He likes you.' Bess smiled proudly.

She passed Rowan across and Charlie took the warm weight. The child grasped a hank of his blond hair and tugged it hard.

'Don't pull at your uncle,' scolded Bess.

'His father did the same at his age.' Charlie said, disentangling the determined hand.

Bess smiled. 'I've been hoping you'd come,' she said. 'I wanted to thank you for the money. A lot of men wouldn't have felt the need to provide for . . . for someone like me.'

The little boy wriggled to be free and Charlie set him down. He saw the strong resemblance to Rowan was tempered with something else. Something softer, from Bess's face. It was a good combination, he thought.

Rowan toddled off and began occupying himself with a wooden spoon, rapping it against a wall and turning to be sure he had an audience.

'He's a little dramatist,' said Bess. 'I take him to all the plays. He's already been on stage. Played Titania's pretty stolen babe,' she said proudly. 'Of course,' she added hurriedly, 'I'll be sure to look to a respectable position for him, as he gets older. I'll look for a good apprenticeship. Theatre is so unreliable.'

Charlie smiled at the little boy. 'I think things are changing,' he said.

Chapter 108

Lily and Charlie were sharing a barrel of beer and a pile of pig knuckles at the Birdcage. The illegal theatre was looking smarter. The players had found the money for a large arched stage.

'Will you go back to Maria now?' Lily asked, glancing up at Charlie. 'Don't look at me that way,' she added. 'It's clear she's never stopped loving you. Perhaps it's time you got a house and home.'

'She'll go back to Percy,' said Charlie with certainty. 'It's the right thing to do.'

'Percy is alive then?' asked Lily curiously. 'Tom didn't murder his mark?'

'He was working away in Temple Bar the entire time,' said Charlie. 'He thought Maria had jilted him and was waiting for her to come around. Never even knew Maria was missing.'

'Surely that's reason enough to forgo the wedding?'

'Not for Maria,' said Charlie. 'She'll honour her promise.'

'You sound bitter.'

'Do I? Maybe I do,' admitted Charlie. 'Perhaps I made a mistake to let her go.' There was a silence as he frowned down into his beer. 'You were right,' said Charlie suddenly, 'when you said I left you to go out to sea alone. I should have come.'

Lily was staring straight ahead. 'Why didn't you?'

Charlie let out a breath. 'I was afraid to leave London. It's everything I know.'

'You know what I learned at sea?' said Lily. 'You can't do it all on your own. You need to trust your crew. If I'd have learned it sooner, I wouldn't have lost my ship.'

'Is this your way of saying you still want to be partners?'

She smiled. 'We haven't talked terms. But I'd be open to it.' She leaned forward, her eyes gleaming. 'What say you, Charlie? I could manage things, be sure you collect your debts. We wouldn't be rich, but we'd have money enough.'

'Don't you want to get back out to sea?'

Lily gazed out across the theatre. 'I'm liking London more,' she said. 'It's a good place for a woman.'

Charlie nodded.

Lily's eyes slid to his. 'Who would you have saved from the noose?' she asked, and he detected the strain of her trying to sound casual. 'If you'd have had to choose?'

'You,' said Charlie.

Lily looked shocked. Then her eyes narrowed. 'You'd say the self-same to Maria,' she accused.

'Of course I would. You think I know nothing about women?'

Lily smiled into her beer.

Charlie looked at her, and for a moment Lily thought she saw a glimmer in his eyes. Something that made her think perhaps he would have saved her.

About the Author

C.S. Quinn is the bestselling author of *The Thief Taker*, *Fire Catcher* and *Dark Stars*. Prior to writing fiction she was a travel and lifestyle journalist for *The Times*, the *Guardian* and the *Mirror*, alongside many magazines.

In her early academic career, Quinn's background in historical research won prestigious postgraduate funding from the British Arts Council. Quinn pooled these resources, combining historical research with first-hand experiences in far-flung places to create Charlie Tuesday's London.

30530008R00216

Printed in Great Britain
by Amazon